BLOOD RELATIONS

The Fifth in the
Cycle of the Aphotic World

BLOOD RELATIONS

Tobin Elliott

This one is about realizing that those who share your DNA — your blood relations — are not always your family. So, this one is about finding your real family.

This one is for those who became my family. Ryan. Lisa. Dale. You are my brothers from other mothers and my sister from another mister.

And yes, this also goes out to those who showed me that mothers and fathers and daughters and sons can get along, can love each other, and can be a real family. Karen, Madison, Hunter, you are my heart and my blood. And seeing my kids as they begin to create their own families is a joy to behold.

Thank all of you for showing me what family truly can be.

ACKNOWLEDGEMENTS

Once again, I'm thanking all the people I usually do. This time, I got it out of the way in that dedication on the previous page. But it doesn't lessen their impact on me.

Aside from my family, I must once again tip my hat to Jennifer Dinsmore, editor extraordinaire. Without her carefully sharpened eyeballs and shocking skills with those twenty-six letters in all their various combinations, and the punctuation that makes them less confusing, I'd be spitting out unreadable messes. Word gumbos. Still horrifying, I'm sure, but for all the wrong reasons.

A special call-out to Pat Flewwelling, one of my first creative writing students, and eventually, friend and co-worker, and the one who poked the hell out of me when I stopped writing. She's also the one who said, "Try something different! Try writing a mystery novel!" Yeah, well, that mystery novel stank, but the bones of it got me to this novel…which hopefully stinks far less.

Thank you to the Muskoka Novel Marathon for getting me to the first aborted draft of this non-mystery version. And also to my tablemate, who graciously allowed me to use her in the opening scene.

And a final thank you to the COVID-19 lockdowns, which got me off my ass and gave me the time to finish these damn stories that were living rent-free in my head for so long.

"The fool doth think he is wise, but the wise man knows himself to be a fool."

— William Shakespeare

PROLOGUE

"A RE YOU HERE for the birthday party?"

"Yes ma'am." The girl stood under the awning, her raincoat shedding the moisture from the hissing rain. It was so dark out for mid-afternoon.

The first thing that caught Cheryl's attention was the girl's voice. It was remarkably deep for one so young. She seemed a little old for her son, Will, but then again girls matured so much faster than boys. She was so polite. And her eyes were so big and blue.

Will was only turning seven, but still, Cheryl could see him falling for such a pretty little thing. She had brought a lovely wrapped gift for him. Obviously she'd have to ask Will about…then she realized she had no idea what to call her.

"I'm sorry," she said. "I didn't get your name?"

"Glory, Mrs. Koechlin." Then after an awkward pause. "Your first name's Cheryl, isn't it?" Cheryl was shocked enough that she nodded before thinking. "It means *beloved*," Glory said. "You are beloved."

Well, she knows my name. Yes, I'm definitely going to have to ask Will about this one.

"Well, thank you, I didn't know that." Smiling, she stepped to the side and held her hand toward the interior. "Come in out of the rain, honey," she said. "We're just about to serve some cake, then open the presents."

"Great," Glory said.

"Hope you like devil's food cake?"

"My favourite," she said, her lips curling into a small smile. *Oh yes*, Cheryl thought, *you're going to be dangerous in a few years.*

Cheryl led her into the room with the other guests. Will had invited a small group of friends. One, that really nice kid, Stanley Holt, couldn't make it. Only three others sat around the table. Will's father, as per usual, had chosen to find something else to do rather than attend his own son's party.

"Jesus, Cher," he had said. "He's only turning seven. Really? These are the pin-the-tail-on-the-donkey years. Call me when he's shaving."

She knew he thought her superstition about this whole seventh birthday thing was, as he so elegantly put it, bullshit.

Cheryl chose to tell Will his father was working late. She hoped he was, but figured he likely wasn't. Things had changed radically in the past eight years. He'd been the triumphant WWII veteran coming home to his war bride, seeming to live only to be with her.

Then along came Will, her little boy. And it was as though his presence seemed to somehow irk the man. *Maybe he feels he's been replaced or something,* she'd thought many times over the years. Cheryl didn't know if that was the answer or not. She only knew that, as the world seemed to enter into this new prosperity of the fifties, her husband seemed more and more distant.

Anyway, she would deal with that in due time. For now, it was time to put on a brave face. *Let's just get through this party first.* She looked around the table at Will and his three friends. Will, with his shocking blond hair, almost white. He seemed a little sensitive about it. She thought it gave him character, but each time she stated this, he only snorted.

Seven years old and already gaining an attitude. The next seven would be much more trying than the last, that was something she could take to the bank. Probably just as trying for him as for his father. Still, she needed to get Will through this day. Through this meal.

"Will," she said, and all four boys turned to look at Mrs. Koechlin. Then they all stared at the girl.

"Who's that?" Billy said. Billy, friend of Will. Willy and Billy.

"Glory," Glory said and again, Cheryl became aware of the deepness of her voice. "You *know* me, Billy Mathers."

"Oh," was all he said, nodding slowly. "Yeah, of course."

Cheryl noticed the unusual expression on Will's face, but put it down to being a little flummoxed by the appearance of an actual girl at his party. She thought, *Maybe he didn't invite her. Or maybe she invited herself. Maybe she's the one with the crush?*

Cheryl got Glory seated. As she bustled off to the kitchen, she wondered a bit at how the room got so quiet. It was unusual, but she was more concerned with the cake.

The cake.

Seven years in the making.

God, I hope he doesn't taste it.

She'd chosen his favourite, mainly for the extra chocolate taste, and loaded the icing on it, maybe a bit heavy. She hoped it would hide the one bitter, but vital, ingredient.

She pulled the cake from the fridge and placed it on the counter. As she grabbed the candles and matches from the drawer, she wondered if her husband was right. Maybe this was bullshit.

Seriously, she thought. *What mother does this? Feeds this to her own son, part of his own birthing?* She imagined she could see that addition swirled into the batter. Of course, she couldn't. She'd ground it fine, almost to dust. There's no way it would be seen. No way.

Still.

She placed both hands on the cake plate, briefly considered dropping it on the floor and taking them all for ice cream. But no. What's the worst that could happen? A bellyache? What kid doesn't get a bellyache from a birthday cake?

She hoped there was enough baked into the entire cake. She needed the slice she would feed him to be potent enough to...

To what, Cheryl? she wondered. *To make sure your boy doesn't turn into a vampire? Are you seriously going to do this? Feed his caul to not only him but his friends, too?*

She paused for a moment longer. Then made up her mind. She'd try and get him to eat two, just to be sure.

Are there rules to this? She didn't know the answer to that. She was running on information from her grandmother, the one who, on hearing that Will had been born with a caul over his face, had demanded that it be preserved. Everyone thought she'd been crazy, but she'd been insistent, and Cheryl had complied.

After Will's birth, her grandmother, her Babcia, had pulled her aside and told her the stories. Terrible stories. She told her she could save Will. Then she told her how.

When her Babcia had died, five years ago, she made Cheryl make a death-bed promise to her that she would fulfill her role on the boy's seventh birthday. Cheryl had promised.

Five years later, here she stood, in her own kitchen, with this horrible cake. Her death-bed promise. She *would* feed it to her son.

As her husband said, it was probably all bullshit anyway.

If it worked, she'd never know. But if it didn't...

Well, she'd likely know then, wouldn't she?

She sank six of the seven candles into the frosting around the perimeter of the cake, careful to not smear the *Happy Birthday Will!* message in the icing. She pulled the box of matches open, selected one, then closed the box and scraped the tip against the rough surface and the match flared to life.

She stood, transfixed for a moment by the flicker of the flame. Then she touched it to the remaining candle, watched it catch, then shook out the flame on the match, dropping it in the sink to be dealt with later.

She touched the lit candle to the six others in turn, then pushed the candle into the frosting, dotting the "i" in *Will*. It was ready. There was no more reason to delay.

She took a steadying breath, placed a hand on each side of the plate, lifted it, and went back out to the dining room.

"Happy birthday," she sang in her shy, too-quiet voice, counting on the boys—and the girl—to pick up the song. Seven-year-old boys? Yes, they'd start quiet, and get silly by the end of it.

They didn't disappoint.

Yet, as they sang, a single voice rang high and sweet over the others. *It's a cliché*, Cheryl thought, *but Glory's voice is like an angel's*. Beautiful, confident, like the voice of a seasoned stage performer. Strange for a girl with such a low speaking voice.

It was enough to stop Cheryl for a moment. For a brief slice of time, likely less than a second, but feeling like minutes, Cheryl simply couldn't pull her eyes away from Glory. The girl sat to one side of the table, her sweet cherub mouth releasing the sweetest sounds. Cheryl felt the prick of tears in her eyes, but caught herself, blinked rapidly, then kept on, approaching the table and setting the cake down in front of Will, who looked equal parts impressed and embarrassed.

They finished up the song, with the boys riding over Glory with the obligatory, "You look like a monkeeeeeeeey and you smell like one, toooooooooo."

She waited until the last, drawn-out note fell away. "Make a wish," Cheryl said.

Will took his time, really thinking it over. Long enough for Cheryl to glance around the table. The other three boys eyed the cake with hunger. But Glory? She only had eyes for Will.

She watched him intently.

Strange.

Will blew out the flame, leaving seven curls of smoke rising in an odorous twist.

Then the world turned on its head.

Glory cleared her throat. Cheryl turned her attention back to the strange little girl once again. She followed the girl's gaze.

A red-haired boy about the same age as Glory, dripping rain water, entered the dining room. Someone late to the party? How many did Will invite?

"Oh," Cheryl said. "Hello. And you are...?"

"You can call me Red."

Red? What kind of name is that? Okay, the hair, but still...he seems a little young for a nickname. "You're a friend of Will's?"

"I am now," he said. His voice held the confident air of someone with a lot more years under their belt. He walked into the room like he owned it. He almost had a swagger to his walk, and an easy smile. The kid was Frank Sinatra in a boy's body.

Glory stood up. The two of them paced the room, circling slowly, one at each side. It reminded Cheryl of sharks in a tank.

"I'm sorry," Cheryl said. "I don't understand."

"Let me ask you all a question," Red said, ignoring Cheryl's comment.

Cheryl could only stare at him. She was stunned that this little brat would simply dismiss her. She'd be having a talk with Mr. Red's parents, and that was a fact.

"How many of you heard the Vilni church bell ring last night?" he said.

"I did," Billy said.

"Yeah, me too," Jonathon said. "It woke me up."

"I did too," Derek said, his brows furrowing. "Weird."

Cheryl didn't say anything. Red looked at her, obviously waiting for her to answer.

"Yes," she said, shocked that she was responding to this…this impudent little boy's question. "I did as well." It had surprised her, the church bells ringing so late at night.

"Excellent," he said, but his voice wasn't the same. It had become a thunderingly low thing, the three syllables leaving his mouth as though they had travelled through caverns all the way from hell itself.

He smiled.

Oh God, Cheryl thought. *Oh my dear Lord in His heaven.* And she knew then and there that her husband was wrong. *It's not bullshit.*

In that smile, she knew.

When Red smiled, she saw his teeth. His horrible, terribly sharp teeth.

"Will?" Cheryl said.

Will seemed too stunned to look at her, only stared at Red's smile. She tried to keep the urgency and panic out of her voice. "Will, I need you to eat some cake honey."

"But…"

"Will, honey, don't argue with me, don't worry about a fork, just eat some cake." She didn't like how her voice was so high and thin, as though her windpipe had been constricted.

"Why?"

That was enough to pull off all the controls and filters. She found her voice. *"Just eat some of the goddamn cake, Will!"*

Will lifted a tentative hand.

Red didn't say a word. He just stared into Will's eyes and shook his head no.

Will's hand retreated, and Cheryl let out a sob.

Then Glory, who'd somehow managed to get around behind Cheryl, leapt onto Cheryl's back and before she could react, the girl had plunged her teeth into her neck. *Deep* into her neck. Cheryl felt the puncturing of her skin, felt muscles twist and tear under the pressure.

Cheryl bucked and spun, but the girl had a firm grip, her arms and legs wrapped around Cheryl like a lover, her teeth locked on her neck. Then she felt warmth down her back, down her left breast, warm through her blouse and bra, right to the skin. But she couldn't look down. Glory first shook her head as though she was a dog with a stick, then, her teeth firmly planted, held Cheryl's neck tight with the pressure…and was she… Was she *sucking* at her neck?

Then the screams started around the room. Jonathon, Derek, Billy. But not Will.

Cheryl slid to the floor, unable to stand upright, unable to fight back. The blood in her body surged toward her neck. The children's screams silenced, one by one.

"Glory?" Cheryl heard. It was the boy, Red. "A little help?"

Glory detached herself from Cheryl's neck. Everything felt wrong, as though her head couldn't be supported by her neck anymore. But she could still crawl to the phone in the front hall.

Then she felt Glory's hands on either side of her head. "Sorry, Mrs. Koechlin." And she seemed to be sincere. "But you shouldn't have tried to feed him that goddamn cake." That deep, deep voice.

Will had been the only one not to say he'd heard the church bells. The only one not to scream when Red and Glory attacked.

Oh my dear Lord in heaven. It's true. It's all true.

Cheryl wondered what would become of him. *My little boy.*

"Don't worry, Cheryl," Glory said. "We'll be Will's new beloved."

PART ONE
COMING HOME

"No new horror can be more terrible than
the daily torture of the commonplace."

Ex Oblivione
H. P. Lovecraft

First Interlude

THE BEAST COMES aware as it finishes chewing its way out from its mother's belly. It has no words yet, but sounds are in its hindbrain. Three distinct noises.

Mar. See. Ah.

Then, not a word, but a knowledge: *Mother*.

It's mostly blind, but it knows it's enclosed in an artificial structure and knows it shouldn't be. It needs the open, not the confined.

It escapes into a more natural area, full of mostly living things and strange, upright structures with rough skins and outstretched arms with soft appendages that spread out and provide shelter.

There is knowledge buried inside the beast, but its brain needs to develop more fully before that knowledge can be processed, sorted, understood.

Utilized.

For the first dark-light-dark revolution of this strange, foreign world, the only goal of this newly born entity is survival. It is not wholly conscious, but it carries certain instincts, a certain awareness. The first had been to seek the open, to escape any possible danger. The next was the realization that it was small, weak, lacking knowledge. The third was to change all aspects of the second. The last instinct is set aside for now, until it is ready.

Until it is ready for that last instinct, the beast seeks out the living things, quick, skittish things, but not quick enough to escape. Not skittish enough to evade capture.

The beast feeds well and its growth is exponential.

Chapter One

"So, you're fucking him now?"

"Lex, we didn't plan for it to happen."

"That's a good one, Kelly," I said. "You didn't plan for it to happen." Fuck. Did she think I didn't have eyes? Every damn show for the past month, instead of playing rhythm guitar up to my left on stage as my stage sister, she'd been moving toward the back of the stage, up to where Kevin played drums.

I had to admit, for a guy, all tight pants bulging suggestively and lion-maned hair and perfect teeth, he was a good-looking man, if you were into that kind of thing. I wasn't. Kelly could be, depending on her mood. Or urges, I guess.

Whether it was mood, urge, the perfect teeth, or the suggestive bulge, I didn't know, but Kelly had made the conscious decision to dump me, the woman who played the role of Ann Wilson, and take up with Kevin.

Yeah, I'd watched her as she pulsed with the sounds coming from her guitar — really, she was far too talented to act as my stage sister and play rhythm in a crappy little Heart cover band. She could blow out those riffs, but she was equally talented as a lead guitarist. And it didn't matter if it was acoustic or electric, six-string or twelve, she could work her sorcery and bend that guitar to her will.

And for the past two years, she'd been mine.

Not anymore. She was Kevin's.

Really, what else was there to say?

Apparently, a lot. I was pissed enough to say something I knew damn well I'd regret in the morning. Actually got to the point where I opened my mouth.

Then my cell phone rang. *Saved by the bell*, I thought.

I didn't want to look at it. I really didn't. I hated when I talked to someone and they paid more attention to their phone than they did to who was right in front of their face.

But I was looking for a distraction—was actually in need of one. Because I knew I was going to say something really shitty. I *knew* I was.

So instead, I dug into my pocket and pulled out my cell phone. Saw the name. *Fuck no.* Considered. *Not this asshole.* Should I pick it up? *I really shouldn't.*

Kelly made a frustrated noise. My choices…*Kelly? Or the waste of flesh?* I saw the frustration on her face. That settled it.

I chose the waste of flesh calling me.

I didn't say hello. No, that was too good for Ray. Instead, I opened with a solid proof of attitude "The fuck do you want?" then didn't say much else for a while.

Because the fucker actually had something to tell me.

Then I disconnected.

"Really?" Kelly said. "That was *that* important?"

"Yeah, Kelly. It was."

"Really." She was good at letting her voice drip with sarcasm. I used to love that about her when she'd been directing it at others. Coming at me? Not as much fun.

"More important than talking to me."

Apparently Kevin was.

"Didn't think so, but turns out it was." Still, I managed to hold back, knowing that, as horrible as it was, what I was going to say would shut her up.

"So you're actually admitting that you—"

"Kelly," I said, cutting her off. "I just found out my mother was murdered," I said.

Yeah, that shut her up. Like using a nuke to kill a fly. Way too much overkill.

Still, I wouldn't need to regret it in the morning.

Jesus, I'm such an asshole, I thought. *Mom was just murdered, and I'm using her as punctuation in an argument. What the hell's the matter with me?*

♦ ♦ ♦

ANY NORMAL PERSON with a normal job would have needed a day or two to extricate themselves from their duties, but the truth was, since it was mid-June, the band was in a bit of a dry spell right now, so it was easy to bail. Things wouldn't pick up again until September, once summer vacations were out of the way.

My other gig was freelancing for an online news site and I had just finished up my last article. I had a couple more I was working on, but there was no real deadline for them, so they could hang for a few days.

Twenty-seven years old and no steady job. A girlfriend who played Nancy to my Ann, now fucking my drummer. My fake sister. My ex-girlfriend. In my fake Heart band.

Fake hearts, all around.

And, despite what I'd thought, I now regretted how I'd told Kelly about my mom. The way I'd used it to shut her down.

Jesus, I really need to get my shit together.

The next morning, after sending a terse, succinct email to the band and our manager, and a slightly less terse but equally succinct email to my editor at the news site, I paid a couple of bills, packed a small bag, locked the door of my apartment, grabbed some road coffee, and took the next four hours to drive to the closest thing to hell my mind could conceive. The town of New Hope.

My hometown.

The place I'd left to get my shit together ten years ago.

And…I'd failed to do that one thing so far.

I really need to get my shit together.

Chapter Two

OVER THE NEXT four hours, I talked myself into an attitude adjustment. No interviewing insipid Hollywood stars or musicians who thought pearls of wisdom dropped from their collagened lips. No blue hairs swaying their arthritic hips to thirty- to forty-year-old hits from a band poorly masquerading as a far more talented one.

No watching Kelly angling her guitar and her affections to a guy, instead of me, the one she had supposedly loved.

Yes, my mother was dead, but I hadn't dealt with that yet. How the hell could I? I hadn't seen the woman or talked to her in almost a decade. It felt like something happening in another country. Intellectually, I understood it, but my gut wasn't buying in. It wasn't real for me yet.

I knew it would get real, and soon, but not just yet. It was what the keyboardist in my band referred to as a *SONY* moment. *Soon, Only Not Yet.*

I prided myself on pushing off the shit I didn't need to deal with right away. Like Kelly.

SONY.

Like my mother.

SONY.

Like getting my shit together.

SONY.

And then there was the small matter of the nightmares. The ones I had when I grew up here. Terrible ones. They'd gone away and I hadn't even thought of them in years, but last night, I had another one.

Something else to push off if possible.

Yeah, right, girl. How you do push off a nightmare?

I told myself to shut up and, at least for a couple of days, until shit got real, treat this like a vacation. One long overdue. Even if it was to a town I hated.

Fuck it, I thought. *Let's make some fucking lemonade.*

I smiled, goosed the pedal a bit, and gained another few miles per hour.

◆ ◆ ◆

ONCE I'D ARRIVED, despite my misgivings, I'd wanted to take a tour of the town, see what had stayed and what had been sacrificed to the gods of profit, but my bladder and stomach sang a pretty convincing duet to the joys of elimination and rejuvenation. Too much coffee and not enough solid food.

Instead of entering the town proper, I turned into the motel just a couple of hundred yards past the town sign. It was nice to see that the Howard Johnsons and the Holiday Inns of the world hadn't gobbled up the local places, but the motel — once the notorious Pine Lodge, now the Cozy Pine Inn — was a big unknown. Though I'd never stayed in the old Pine Lodge, I'd heard the stories. Beds with unsavoury stains and major dips in their centres. Carpets that were more cigarette and roach ash than actual fibres. And towels so stiff they threatened to break in half if pulled with too much force off the racks. And the Black Russian-drinking barmaid/owner had been legendary. For all the wrong reasons.

Ray had assured me the place was definitely better now. But this was Ray, who was as reliable as a politician's promise, so I had to see it for myself.

I parked in front and entered, avoiding the spiky wrought-iron fencing on the way.

The front office was a lot nicer than back in the old days, lots of windows to let in the westering sun and suffuse it with a warm glow. The large woman behind the desk greeted me with a smile that was just as warm.

"You're here for the funeral?"

"I am so!" I said, deciding to play it cool. Her smile widened a fraction more. "Under the name Hedges. I made reservations—"

"Ms. Alexandra Hedges," she said, cutting me off, but more like old friends did, as though she knew me from long ago and couldn't quite remember my name.

"Call me Lex."

"Oh my goodness. You're her daughter. Mrs. Hedges."

"Yes I am," I admitted. I set my keys on the high desk surface between us, leaned my forearms on it. "Look, can I ask a big favour?"

The woman looked at me, an eyebrow arched.

"It's my mom, yes, but I don't want people moping around me, okay?" I stopped for a moment, searching for the right words. "The circumstances suck, but still, I'm back in my hometown after many, many years away. By choice, I might add. As stupid as this sounds, I want to enjoy it a bit, if at all possible."

"You going to be able to do that?" she asked.

"I certainly hope so. My mother would have wanted me to." *Probably. Maybe. Okay, I'm not sure, but it sounds good.*

"Okay then."

"Deal?"

She nodded. "You'll get no argument from me." She nodded again, just once, as though to seal it in her memory. "Okay, Lex Hedges." She scanned the computer screen, her head tilted slightly up, and looked down through her reading classes. "Ah, yes, I have you right here."

I smiled and, to lighten the mood, made a show of looking down at myself, then back to her. "Well, yes you do." That got a laugh and I decided I really liked this lady. Anyone who laughed at my lame jokes got my vote. And if they didn't act stupid around me because I'd just lost a so-called loved one, even better. All things considered, it was pretty easy to get into the Lex Hedges fan club, but still, the membership was low.

She leaned forward conspiratorially and said, "That really is a stupid expression, isn't it?" She winked, smiled, and thrust out a hand. "Ann McDonald. Call me Annie. I own the joint. Well, me and Ambrose, but if you got any issues, you come to me first. I'll treat you right."

I took her hand in mine, gave it a firm shake.

"Lex, but you know that. And you can call me whatever you want. I'll treat you right too, lady." I wasn't one to advertise my sexual preferences, but I didn't mind a little flirtatious banter in small doses with the right audience. It was always a risk, especially in a small town like New Hope, but what the hell, I'd hidden it all the time I lived here. Maybe it was time to loosen the reins a bit. I was only here for a couple of days.

Then Annie surprised and delighted me.

As she retracted her hand, her other was already fluttering above her large bosom. She affected a southern drawl and said, "Oh mah kand lady, theah is no need to be puttin' on aihs. You got mah heart all a' fluttah! What would Fathah McKenzie say?"

We both giggled like school kids and I pulled out my credit card.

"Ooo!" she said, "And she pays promptly. You and I are gonna get along famously, Lex."

We finished up the paperwork, I got my key, she pointed out my room, and we made small talk for a few more minutes.

All the while, my admiration for Annie grew—personable, pleasant and efficient, what more could I ask for? For possibly the first time ever, brother Ray had given good advice. I sure as hell didn't get service like this in Toronto.

She told me there were a few others already arrived for the funeral and was pretty sure they were all in the dining room. If I hurried with my bags, I could probably catch them. Surprised that there were others here for my mother's funeral, I asked who was there.

"There's a Mr. and Mrs. McGregor…"

"Gerry and Ruthle…um, Ruth," I said.

She smiled. "A Mr. Funk."

"Crazy old Randy. You watch out for him, Annie. He's a scoundrel and a cad and he'll only break your heart."

"I believe you are well on your way to doing that to me already, Lex." She briefly fluttered her hand again and we both chuckled. "And finally, there's also a Mr. and Mrs. Burke and…"

"And their four hundred kids?"

"Something like that." She leaned over the counter, eyes wide. "Three rooms," she whispered, as though delivering the wisdom of the ages.

"Yeah. Bear always did have a problem keeping that nasty thing in his pants." I looked around as though checking for others, then leaned in to whisper, "Good Catholics. God forbid birth control."

"Fastest way to get a ball team," Annie said.

She offered to help me with my bags, which impressed me further, but I declined. I headed back out to the car, briefly blinded by the setting sun. As my eyes adjusted, I took a second to simply soak in the view of the sun-reddened hills over a calm-as-glass Lake Kwanashishing. Late afternoon, birds off in the distance were singing for their supper. From somewhere else, a dog barked. The air was sweet and heavy with summer heat.

It wasn't all bad when I was here. I closed my eyes and took in a big lungful. I wanted to just hold it all in and remember it just like this.

There was no denying it, I hated the place. But still, I had to admit, I didn't hate all of it.

"I missed you," I said, then started the car and drove down to my room.

♦ ♦ ♦

AS MUCH AS I wanted to hook up with some of my old friends, I still needed to do something else first.

This was the part I had been dreading. But I couldn't delay dealing with it.

Fuck.

♦ ♦ ♦

I DROVE DOWN the narrow laneway, a quarter-mile through trees now grown taller in the intervening years. The twists and turns were still in my muscle memory. When I reached the section where the trees widened out to a clearing that was the backyard of my old house, I slowed the car.

The house was a long single storey, with a detached garage separated only by a small opening my mother called the "breezeway" back when she still had a pulse. The yellow siding I remembered from my youth had now faded to more of a bland tapioca. The paint had peeled in areas and showed the grey of the wood slowly petrifying underneath.

I swung the car to the left, pulling in beside the Lumina van. *Jesus Christ.* That van had been parked in the same spot the day I'd left, all those years ago. They'd never replaced it.

The more things change, the more things stay the same, I thought. *Even the shitty van.*

I got out of my car, shut the door, keyed the alarm from my fob out of habit, then chided myself. All those years in Toronto had done their damage.

One more glance at the house, then, setting my mouth in a grim line, I crossed the gravel to the walkway and then to the door. And there I stopped.

Do I knock? I wondered. *Just walk in? Technically, I'm still family.* I didn't know the protocol here.

I chose a combination. I knocked, then entered the foyer. "Hello?"

"Hello, Lex."

That voice. Deep. Smooth. Dark, somehow.

My father's voice.

The voice of the man I swore I'd never even look at ever again. Every nerve, tendon, and bone in my body screamed that this was a big, steaming mistake.

I wasn't good at being sensible. The last time I'd managed it had likely been ten years ago when I ran away from the person now standing in front of me.

"Father," I said. There was no embrace, no kiss on the cheek. We simply stood, facing each other. Time had not been kind to him.

He had once been a—handsome likely wasn't the right term—strangely attractive man. Slim, lightly muscled, with piercing almond eyes.

Now, though…now he looked, as my keyboardist would say, "ridden hard and put away wet." He was in a shapeless bathrobe that didn't quite cover the shocking weight gain. He'd probably been a lean hundred-sixty pounds the last time I'd seen him. He was easily double that now, his face jowly and blotched. His hair was far too long and a tangled mess. He hadn't showered or bathed in a while, judging from the funk of body odour wafting off him. His face, his body, his hair, his nails, his teeth, his breath...all of it told a horrific story of neglect.

He was bad enough, but as I looked around the house I hadn't seen in so long, what pissed me off even more was the equally horrific neglect I saw. It had obviously gone on a decade-long downhill slide. Familiar furniture, just a lot more beaten up and grey with layers of dust, the sofa and chairs offering up their foam guts through frayed and torn material and insufficient duct tape. There were several ashtrays sprayed strategically throughout the living room and dining room, each one mounded with butts and ashes. Where there hadn't been an ashtray within easy reach, there were glasses, bowls, saucers, and discarded meal trays to take up the job of preserving the dead cigarettes. Their smell, and the smell of dirty clothes and two unwashed male bodies permeated the air. The carpet, once a tan colour, now had dark, greasy paths worn into it from dirty feet, and spots and splotches from things dropped and never cleaned up.

How the hell had Mom put up with this?

As bad as this all was, I thought I could smell the other, more perverse odour running heavy underneath the others. The smell of something I'd run away from once, long ago. The stink of something gone rotten and perverse.

The memory was still as clear, as bright, as painful as it was back then, when I had run through this room—less a full decade of dust and decay—to escape out the front door.

Every nerve in my body told me to run, to get the hell away from this shithole. Again.

Then my brother Ray came out from the bathroom. "Hey, bra," he said.

"Really Ray? 'Bra'?"

"Yeah, bra."

"I'm your sister. *Sisss-ter.* The proper term's not good enough for you? Or 'Lex'? Or hell, even 'bro'?"

"Naw," he said, smiling. "You're a dyke. So, you're basically a dude. Bra's more brotherly."

Ignore him, I thought. *Ignore the ignorant redneck asshole.* I didn't though. "And why's that?"

"Bra," he said, saying it slowly, drawing it out. "More…supportive."

Goddamn, I'd fallen right into that one. I dismissed him with a look.

"What? You're a chick. You wear them, amirite? Bras? Or did you turn into one'a them bra-burnin' dykes?"

Fucksake.

Turning back to my so-called father, I said, "So. My mom. Tell me what happened."

"Murdered, dude."

I shot up a palm. "Shut up, Ray. Let the adults speak now."

"You ain't been around in a while, bra. Dads ain't always coherent now."

"I'm right here, Raymond," my father said. "I can speak for myself."

"Sure," Ray said. "You can right *now*." He made a disgusted noise and walked over to the couch and plopped himself petulantly onto it, a small cloud of dust puffing up around him.

"Marcus?" I prompted. There's no way I could refer to him as my father anymore. "You wanna fill me in?"

"Like Raymond said, Alexandra. She was murdered."

He filled in the details dispassionately, as though relating a recipe. My mother had been travelling between New Hope and Carry's Cove. Somewhere along the way, she had come to a remote three-way stop, and someone had pulled her from the car.

From there, she'd been pulled a solid mile into the surrounding forest and tortured, most of her major bones broken. "But that wasn't the worst," he said.

"Ah no, Dads," Ray said. "Really, I don't wanna hear it again."

"Then either go outside or to your room, Raymond." *Jesus. Guy's almost thirty and they're still stuck talking to each other like he's a child.*

Ray rose amid a smaller cloud of dust and passed through the kitchen and sunroom to the front yard. He pulled out a pack of cigarettes and lit one. I watched him trying to smoke it with style. Mostly he looked like a dick.

Okay, so he is still a child.

"So," I said. "What's worse than having all your bones broken by a fucking psychopath?"

"Watch your mouth, Alexandra."

"I'm not a kid anymore, Marcus. Unlike your son. *You* watch my mouth."

He made a face. "After the bone-breaking, the…killer…flensed the skin from your mother's breasts. The aureole and nipples."

"Jesus."

"There's more," he said flatly. "They also flayed your mother's genitals."

"What?" I was sure I hadn't heard that right.

"The killer. Flayed. Your mother's. Vagina." He gave me a moment to take that in again. "From what I understand, it looked as though it had been run through a paper shredder."

I ran a hand through my hair, scrubbing at the spikes. "Jesus Christ."

"This was all when she was still alive." Still in that calm, dispassionate voice. "It wasn't until the killer cut off her head that she died."

And I thought *I* was the cold one. Then again, my father had never really met the conventions of normalcy, so I should not have been shocked by this.

"Apparently, the first officer on the scene was so distraught that he's now on desk duty while he recovers. It's what I've heard, anyway."

"What's wrong with you?" I said.

"In what way?" he said.

"You not only deliver this information like you're explaining the rules of a fucking card game, but you're telling this to your daughter." I swallowed the bile rising in my throat. "And this is your wife of what…three decades?"

"I can't do anything to change the facts, Alexandra. I'm not sure what you want of me here."

"How about you act more like a husband and a father and less like a fucking lizard?"

"We each react to a loved one's death in our own way, Alexandra." He sighed. "Apparently, I'm not emotive enough, and you are profanely so."

I couldn't answer that. Instead, I walked to the kitchen, pulled the coffee pot from its base, rinsed it out, poured fresh water in it. Lifting the lid, I saw the previous filter in there, coffee grounds nestled under a surprisingly massive lump of greenish mold, made a face. "You ever clean anything here?"

"As little as possible." He still stood in the middle of the living room, watching me.

I started filling the sink with hot water, looked in vain for dish soap, gave up, dumped the filter in the overflowing garbage, then plunged the parts into the hot water and scrubbed at them with some napkins I found sitting on the counter that didn't look too sketchy. Before they disintegrated completely, I pulled the pot back out, scrubbed it as well, and refilled it with water. I counted on the heat to kill off anything I might have missed.

"Coffee? Filters?"

"Refrigerator. Cupboard to your right."

I gathered both and dropped some generous scoops into the filter and started it brewing. Maybe a change of topic was in order. "What's shithead"—I pointed outside to Ray trying out his best Clint Eastwood squint through the cigarette smoke—"talking about, saying you aren't always coherent?"

My father looked down and swiped a finger through the dust frosting an end table. He made it quite clear he was not going to answer me. *Yeah, well, fuck you. I don't give a shit anyway.*

Let's move back to the topic he seemed to have no problem talking about. "You said 'killer,' singular."

"Don't read much into it, Alexandra. I just said killer. It could have been killers."

"Okay. Why Mom?"

"Why not?"

"Jesus Christ."

"I'm sorry, Alexandra. That's how it works. Ev—"

"Don't you fucking dare, Marcus."

"Don't what?"

"Don't give me that 'everybody dies sometime' line."

"It's true."

"Don't care. It's Mom."

"What's Moms?" It was Ray, fresh from his stylish smoke, stinking of nicotine and cancer.

"Why can't I have a normal fucking conversation with my…family?" I said, almost choking on that last word.

"You can, bra. You can."

Yet again, I ignored him. I couldn't take someone seriously who tried to act so much younger than they actually were.

Then I thought, *Shit, I hope it's an act.* I couldn't be sure, and had no plans to stick around long enough to find out. Which reminded me. "What's going on with the funeral?"

"They'll release her body in a couple of days, then we'll bury her. Your brother and I went and picked out a casket for her, and we have the plot. Most of it is already arranged, so there's not much to do. I guess you should just think about what you want to say at the funeral."

"That's easy enough. I didn't really know her anymore. Hadn't talked to her in a ridiculously long time. She didn't think to even try calling or emailing me, even though I'm all over the Internet. And she was the only family member I kind of liked." I looked in the fridge for milk or cream. Found none. "So, what I'm gonna say is a big, fat nothing. Just like she said to me for a bunch of years." I spread my hands out to either side. "Silence."

"Profound, bra."

"Shut the fuck up, Ray."

"I'm not going to tell you again, Alexandra. Watch your mouth."

Something in me, something that had been pushed to its limit, finally broke. "You know what, *Dad*? Fuck your idiot son there, and fuck you too."

Ray bristled. "Not cool, Lex, not cool."

"See you at the funeral," I said. "*Bra.*" Then, with the sound of the coffee maker burbling, I pushed past both family members and out the front door and to my car.

I managed to make it back to the main road before pounding on the steering wheel and yelling.

♦ ♦ ♦

I GOT BACK to the hotel as the reds of sunset were streaking the sky. I really needed a drink. Coffee wasn't going to do it anymore. I needed alcohol, and I needed a lot of it.

I parked the car out front and didn't even bother heading to my room. Instead, I ran the long hall back to the front desk. Again, it struck me how much of a good vibe I got from this place. *Score one for Ray.* On the heels of that, came, *Then again, even a stopped clock is right twice a day.* It didn't matter about Ray right now. *This place…*

It was the wood, the faint smell of pine in the air, but more than that, Annie's cheer seemed to have soaked into the very foundation of the place.

Whatever it was, I liked it. After the stupid meeting at my old family home, I found myself smiling in anticipation of meeting some of my old high school buddies. My step was light. *I'm damn near Ginger Rogers here*, I thought.

I reached the lobby and saw Annie cradling the phone on one shoulder while writing something, but she still managed to shoot me a wink as she cocked a thumb at the dining room to let me know my friends were still in there. I nodded and headed in.

Straight into a *Monty Python* sketch.

"Oh, an' look 'oo it is, then!"

"'Ow'er, she's not the Saviour, she's just a naughty little guuuuhrl!"

Life of Brian was never my movie, so I thought, *screw it*, and changed it up on them.

Pointing at Randy, I busted out my worst French-accent-done-by-an-English-man-done-by-a-Canadian-woman and laid it on thick as I said, "Your muth-hair was a hamster, an' your fahth-hair stank of eld-ah-berries!" Better than a decade on, I impressed myself with how fast the words came back. Pointing at Gerry, I said, "Ah point hatcher privates an' fahart in your general di-hrection, you dirty English pigdog kiniggit!"

Twenty minutes ago, I'd wanted to kill something. Now, I took the ensuing ovation with all the humility it deserved. Then I flipped all and sundry off as I bowed. "Fuck you! Fuck you, very much!"

Robert had a beer waiting for me already. Back in the day, there must have been a sale on the name because there were far too many Roberts, Bobs, Bobbys, whatever. So instead, Robert was always—

"Bear, you dumbass!" Randy said. "You were supposed to do the whole Black Knight thing!"

"Robert can never remember that stuff like you guys," Grace said, and placed a protective hand on his arm. Grace always did stick up for him, even before they were married. I often wondered why. Grace had been my gateway into this ridiculous group. I'd had a bit of a thing for her, but I knew damn well it would never ever be reciprocated. So, instead, I accepted my friend-zone lot in life and I'd hung out with her. She, in turn, had been dating Bear, who had been friends with Gerry and Randy.

"More like he doesn't wanna look like a goof"—pronouncing it *gewf*—"around his kids," Randy said. Turning, he put a hand on my shoulder. "Lex friggin' Hedges! How you been keepin'? Should I be insulted you ignored all my get-together requests over the years?"

Randy had been the glue that had tried to keep the group together. About six or seven years back, he'd started sending out social media and email requests, set up groups, and tried to organize events to get us all back together. Bar crawls. Murder mysteries. Camping. Even one very misguided skydiving thing that was quickly shut down. I'd politely but firmly declined them all.

It only took a parent getting tortured and murdered to finally bring me back into the fold.

I took a grateful swig of beer and gave him a smile. "I been keepin', Randy. It's all good. And no, don't be insulted. I've been a bitch to everyone, not just you." I went around the table. "Gerry! Good to see you! How long's it been?"

Gerry grimaced, shook my hand, and pushed his glasses up his nose. Same old Gerry, just more grey, and the creeping baldness was taking root. "Geez, what? A century? A millennia? Something like that?" At one point, Gerry and I had been tight. I'd been his token Gay Best Friend. I think we eventually migrated to BFFs. Only, in this case, that last F fell off a long time back.

And sitting beside Gerry was the reason why.

"And Ruth!" I said, holding my arms out for a hug neither of us wanted to participate in. "You look good," I lied as I felt her stiffen in my arms. In actuality, she'd ballooned up and looked even meaner than she did the last time I saw her. But once again I told myself, *What the hell, it's only a couple of days, right?* I could suck it up for a couple of days.

"Lex," was all she could manage. Now I knew how my father felt.

Oh hell, who was I kidding? I didn't have a fucking clue how that alien life form thought.

Or Ruthless, for that matter. Wouldn't even look me in the eye. Couldn't stand the thought of Gerry having a female friend. *Bitch. Okay, maybe I'll have to rethink that whole sucking-it-up-for-a-few-days thing.* Then I dismissed her from my mind. I was quite good at that. I had better things to think about, better people to hug. I turned from her.

"Grace, how's the baseball team?" She came in for a much more heartfelt and genuine hug. Grace and I had been inseparable at one point. It felt good to hug her again. We'd tried to connect a few times over the years, but life and kids got in the way. But I always thought she was way too good for the guy she married, but hell, like I was any expert on marriage? Not bloody likely.

She was so tiny, I had to bend way over for the hug, but she squeezed tight. "It's so good to see you again, Lex. It's been too long."

We broke and I held her at arm's length, taking her in. "You too, girl. Jesus, all those kids and you still look like your grad photo." Okay, maybe there was a bit more weariness around the eyes, but I wouldn't mention that.

"I'm so sorry about your mother. Don't let these idiots make you feel we forgot about that. We all came to support you."

"Thanks, Grace." I looked down. "Holy Christ! You pregnant again?" She gave me a tired smile.

"And Bear, you wild man," I said, tipping the beer in thanks, then quickly setting it down as the big man roughly shook my hand with his own calloused paw. Bear wasn't a hugger. "You never learned how to cage the beast? Or do you still not know what makes babies?"

Bear ran his other hand through his thinning—but still blond—hair. "Jeez, Lexi, you never change, do you?" He was blushing. I had always known how to push his anti-gay and no-sex-talk buttons and it looked like they're still as sensitive as they always were. *Excellent,* I thought. *Maybe I can have some fun this week after all.*

I came back around and parked my ass in the chair and grabbed another mouthful of beer. It was going down too smooth. I figured I better get some food into my gullet soon.

As though reading my mind, a large man in spotless whites came by the table. He had the ruddy complexion of someone who enjoyed cranking their blood pressure up through the liberal application of cholesterol.

But it was the stunningly bad hairpiece that captured my attention. I figured the man likely had to go out and special order something as bad as that rug. It looked like three-week-old badger roadkill perched on his melon. *My god. Mind-blowing.*

"How you doing, young lady? Ambrose is the name. What can I getcha?"

This is Ambrose? Annie's other half? I figured I'd better dial back on the flirtations. She might be serious.

I barely choked out a request for a burger and fries and, after looking around the table, eyebrows raised in the universal *anything for the rest of you?* sign, he headed off back into the kitchen. I was obviously late to the party. Everyone else had already eaten.

I did my best not to giggle at Ambrose. Then I saw Randy slide five dollars across to Gerry. He glared at me with a sour look on his puss. "I was sure you wouldn't be able to keep it together."

I lifted my beer in toast to Gerry's obviously superior knowledge.

"So," I said. "Who else showed up for my mother's funeral party?"

"A couple. Y'know my cousin Norman's living back here again, right?" Randy said.

"Norman? Gutty?"

"Yeah, try and keep the Gutty thing on the down-low." Randy said. "Ol' Constable Gustafsen has his reputation to uphold."

Randy filled the group in on how Gutty—Norman—left Carry's Cove and got into the police force out on the west coast, got married, and settled down. Eventually, he found his way back here. And now he was a cop in the New Hope police detachment of the OPP. Pretty funny, considering how many times he came face-to-face with Chief Flewwelling back in high school. Puked on Sarge's standard-issue boots at least once.

"That's great," I said. "And he's married? Anyone I'd know?"

Gerry and Bear obviously caught this part earlier and quickly found something fascinating on the floor. But staring at the floor didn't hide their smiles.

"I keep forgetting you left before graduation." He paused, took a mouthful of beer. "Yeah. You might remember her," Randy said. "Kayla."

"Kayla...Kayla..." I said, digging through years of mental muck. This only made the two idiots across the table smile wider.

"Kayla Young?"

Oh. My. God. Kayla.

"KY Kayla? Kayla the KY Queen?" Gerry said, trying to prompt my memory. It didn't need prompting. I always thought she'd gotten a raw deal in this town.

"Ye-eah…" The word was drawn out for a couple of beats. "Norm doesn't go much for those nicknames much anymore either."

"I can see why," Grace said. "Show some respect, guys. She's a respectable mother and wife now. Can we just drop this topic please?" She wasn't necessarily pissed, more disgustedly amused. But disgust wasn't far behind.

It was one mom giving some backup to another one. I raised my beer. "I'm with you, Grace."

The guys had the sense to look somewhat chagrined. Gerry would likely catch hell from Ruthless behind closed doors later.

We cast around for different topics of discussion, then Randy smirked. "Ran into Monica Holt." He widened his eyes. "She's…kinda wow."

I kept my face impassive. It took effort.

"Still…?" Bear cupped his hands in front of his chest. This earned him a punch on the shoulder from Grace.

"Robert!" she said. "God! Hello? I am sitting right here!" She pointed to her stomach. "Pregnant with your sixth child, I might add."

Bear looked properly chastened until Grace looked away, then he smirked and waggled his eyebrows at Randy.

Randy mimicked the same cupping motion, completely ignoring her. "Still defying gravity."

I glanced over to Gerry's postal code and saw he was enjoying the hell out of this, but was biting his tongue and keeping a tight lid on it. Ruthless looked like she'd been sucking lemons, her mouth squeezed to a tight sphincter.

That's the Ruthless I remember, I thought. *Humourless bitch.*

Looking at Grace, she wordlessly appealed to me to change the topic. Despite my passing interest in Mrs. Holt's boobs, I was self-aware enough to find it really sad that I was the only one other than Grace to be the mature one in the room. I searched desperately for an acceptable subject, but, being me, only unacceptable ones came to mind.

As I came up dry, Ambrose and the badger that seemed to be fucking his head showed up with my burger, which provided a good break and gave me an idea that was likely Grace-friendly. I hesitated for a second, but then thought, *Screw it, let's dive into the deep end.*

"So, my good man," I said, clapping Randy on the shoulder. "Did the Randy Fuck ever settle down with a fine, young, randy filly?" I reached for my burger as Randy, Gerry, and Bear angled in for my fries. Some things never changed, obviously.

"Nope. Still haven't met the right one yet," he said, chewing. Gerry and Bear rolled their eyes.

"Haven't met the one that'll put up with your bullshit, you mean?" Grace was all smiles.

"Well, yeah," he said. "That too."

"And Gerry?" I said. "No kids?"

Ruthless leaned in, putting her hand on Bob's knee as though to say, *I got this.* "We decided we didn't want children."

That was news to me. Gerry had always been the one taking heat from the guys in high school because he talked about what his kids would do. Then again, that may have been the defence mechanism he used to try and dispel those rumours of him being gay—rumours that likely started because he hung out with another rumoured gay…namely me—but I didn't think so. Okay, well, maybe he did, but still, I thought the "we" was actually "she" in this case. Knowing Ruthless, she was the decision-maker of the two.

"So you're the proverbial DINKs?"

Ruthless, ever ready to take offence at something I said, looked offended. She leaned forward even more and I, with some satisfaction, saw her cheeks redden. Gerry repeated her earlier motion, placing a hand on her knee. Obviously this was the McGregor family code.

"Yeah," he said. "Double Income, No Kids. That's us." He looked at Ruthless, who was busy dropping at least two DEFCON levels. "Gives us more time and money to travel."

"That's always good," I said, showing my teeth to Ruthless. I figured she was smart enough to clue in that I wasn't smiling.

"You got married, didn't you?" Gerry said.

"You a dink, too?" Ruthless said, mirroring my smile. It was obvious from her tone that it was the word, not the acronym, she lobbed. She was probably chomping at the bit to call me a dyke, too. *Whatever*, I thought. *It's not on yet, bitch, but watch your ass.*

"Came close once, but never managed to land the right one." I didn't think it was worth it to get into the whole Kelly thing.

"There you go!" Randy said. "And now you know why I haven't found the right woman yet! If you can't, being a woman and all—"

"Thanks for noticing," I said drily.

"—how can I ever hope to find one?"

"Obviously, you haven't been looking in the right places, Randy." The voice was smooth, musical. "Hey, Gerry, Ruth, Robert. Grace, how's the family?" Grace nodded as I turned.

"Lex."

"Monica," I said. And then I didn't know what else to say…except, possibly, "Oh my god."

♦ ♦ ♦

MY RELATIONSHIP WITH Monica in high school had always, upon reflection, struck me as one of those weird circumstances. We had both been painfully aware of what was going on, but, beyond Monica's longing, unrequited looks and my quick, avoiding glances away, it was never really acknowledged. It became so much more than just an elephant in the room. It became a circus tent full of elephants.

She'd been pathetic and I'd been a kid too scared to acknowledge the truth.

Monica had always been a pretty girl, but throughout high school, she had some issues. Almost six feet tall, she already stood out from the crowd. Being overweight—not necessarily fat, more what would be charitably called "Rubenesque"— hadn't helped in the cruel fish tank of high school. The one thing that likely spared her—though it was definitely a double-edged sword—was her spectacular breasts. It slowed down some of the cruel high school shenanigans, but it was obvious that attention to her chest mortified her.

And to make matters worse, she was easily the nicest person anyone, myself included, would ever want to meet. But who the hell looked for nice during high school? Not me. I was still too busy trying to fake an interest in guys, while having zero interest. And trying to fake a friends-only interest in Grace.

The icing on this tragic cake was, back in high school, it was obvious—nakedly, unabashedly, ridiculously obvious—that she had been head over heels for me. God knows why. All those years ago, I was sixteen, too tall, scrawny, zitty, with too-small boobs and no butt to speak of, and all wrapped up in an incredibly morose gift wrap. I hadn't really had a lot going on for myself back then, but she saw something in me. Something I couldn't see myself, apparently. And me, suffering from the brain infection of insecurity over my sexuality but deep down just wanting to find a hot girl with no morals to screw my brains out. A KY Kayla or Grace, or any one of a dozen others, none of which were anything more than straight.

Monica was the treasure that hung out on my periphery, bravely out and patiently waiting for me to come to my senses. And I was the one busily not coming to my senses and avoiding her longing looks.

She'd been searching for love. I'd been searching for a compromise on normalcy.

Both of us, searching in vain.

It's incredible how stupid a person — okay, me — can feel about something that happened so long ago, I thought. Not stupid for not sleeping with her, just not being more of the friend — or the girlfriend? — that she always wanted me to be. But then, I thought ruefully, life has a way of coming around to kick my ass.

And right now, I was feeling the boot. Uncomfortably so. My father. My brother. Now, Monica.

Monica Holt had gone from the ugly duckling into the most beautiful swan I had ever seen. And here I was, ten years older, and still flailing around in the shallow end of the pool.

I really need to get my shit together.

♦ ♦ ♦

AS I STOOD, she waited. She wore a soft, oversized white cotton blouse, set off with a delicate gold cross hanging just above discreet cleavage, with tight blue jeans and low-heeled leather boots. A carefully tousled mane of blonde hair surrounded a face with very little makeup. All the curves where they were supposed to be. Dangerous curves.

Monica smiled. She knew she looked good. And that was the main thing that made her attractive. She'd always been brave, but with an undertone of insecurity because of her height and weight.

Gone was the insecurity, replaced by an obviously hard-won confidence. Not conceited, not cocky. Just confident. It had obviously taken her a while, but the hunched awkwardness had been replaced by a spine of steel.

Bear laughed at me, earning him another punch from Grace, and I finally shut my mouth just as Randy was reaching over to close it with two fingers to my chin.

"How are you, Lex?" Her voice was warm butter. She had always been a singer, but that warm, sultry contralto now crept into her everyday speech. By contrast, my own voice — despite being a singer as well — seemed gawky, as though I was going through puberty again.

Hell, I felt like I *was* going through puberty again.

"I've been doing okay," I said, and then, just because it needed saying, I added, "Monica, you look fantastic."

She smiled and gazed straight into my eyes. *Have her eyes always been this captivating?* I thought. *Was I really that ignorant of them back then?* "Thank you," she said. "You're not so bad yourself." She reached out and brushed a light hand over my short, carefully tousled hair. "Really like this," she said. My scalp tingled at her touch.

Shit. So did other parts of me.

She put a hand on the back of the chair next to mine. "May I?"

"Of course!"

My burger was barely half gone, but all thoughts of eating disappeared. Suddenly, I didn't want to do something that might make me look awkward or stupid around her. Like slopping ketchup on myself. And I would, I knew I would, with the state of mind I was in right now.

The badger and Ambrose sailed by and Monica waved at him. He raised an eyebrow and she held up a finger.

He brought her a beer and a glass. She ignored the glass

and, hooking two slender fingers around the neck, drank straight from the bottle. If it hadn't been obvious before now, I realized I was in love.

"No glass?" I said.

"It's in a glass," she said, her smile only disappearing as she kissed the bottle to get another mouthful. She seemed too graceful to be human. I enjoyed the simple pleasure of looking at the long curve of her neck.

Oh, I got it bad, I thought. *I have to stop gawking before I'm called on it. There's three guys here who will not hesitate.* I grabbed at my own beer and took a swig, scanning the others around the table that had, for a few moments, simply disappeared. *Bear already made an overture, can't give him any more ammo.* But they'd all gone quiet, watching the two of us.

Shit shit shit. Someone's gonna say something…

Without looking at any of them, knowing they'd see the look on my face and attack like sharks to chum, I carefully picked up my burger and, before biting, kind of hefted it and said, "You eaten yet?" I really didn't want to eat. I knew I would fuck up, but what else was I going to do? Before I got myself in trouble, I stuffed it in my mouth and chewed. A lot. Grinding it down quickly was the only thing holding me back from choking to death on a side of beef.

"Yes," she said. "I've eaten, done all my chores, done the three S's—"

Obviously spying her bewilderment, Gerry leaned over to Ruthless. "Shit, shower, shave," he explained. Her face sphincter tightened.

"—so I'm free for the evening." She looked around the table. "Is there anything planned?"

Bear squirmed a bit. Grace said, "We can't go far, it's the first night in the rooms for the kids, so we want them to get accustomed. After tonight, Cody and Connor should be fine for babysitting. Opening night jitters."

"Of course!" Monica said. "So, do we just want to hang out here and catch up?"

Gerry looked at Ruthless, who adjusted the shape of her sphincter mouth. Apparently he'd learned to read the nuances, because he turned back to Monica and said, "We're in!" I would never have read that from that look, but Gerry obviously had a lot more practice.

Randy piped in. "Don't care. Long as there's alcohol and tits, I'm good."

"Randy!" Grace said.

"What?" he said, all innocence. "I was totally talking about your funbags, Grace. Pregnant chicks always have the rockinest boobs."

"You're gross," she said.

"Can't say I disagree, Grace," I said. "They are pretty spectacular."

"You're both gross," she said.

Randy said, "It's true!"

Monica nodded, said, "Got mine beat, Grace," which got me laughing.

Grace was laughing now too, but she said, "Okay, you're *all* gross!"

"Yeah?" Randy said, as Bear tried to wave him off. "Then why'd your husband totally agree with me?"

Punched. Again.

I looked around at my friends. It was likely wrong that I was sitting in a hotel, laughing and cracking jokes only a couple of days since my mother had been the victim of a horrible murder, one day after I'd walked away from my cheating girlfriend, and only an hour after the disastrous family reunion, but if this—right here, right now, laughing with old friends—wasn't what the doctor ordered, I didn't know what was.

Laughing, Monica turned to me. "I'm assuming you're in?"

"Can't miss out on the grossness," I said. "Of course I'm in."

◆ ◆ ◆

WE WASTED LITTLE time in clearing the table and getting some pitchers set up. Not for the faint of heart, this lot. Livers to be tortured. Kidneys to be taxed. Memories to be dragged into the light and generally pummelled and abused. The badger and his pet Ambrose did their thing with efficiency and aplomb, and we got down to some serious boozing and reminiscing.

And, even better, through it all, there was still Monica to look at.

"Sorry about your mom, Lex," Monica said, taking advantage of the current of conversation swirling away from the two of us for a moment.

I thanked her.

"Any leads?" she said.

"Nope," I said, not wanting to talk about it.

Randy, maybe sensing my reluctance, maybe seeing the look on my face, changed gears slightly. "Your mom was all right, Lex."

The others all joined in. I looked around at them.

"Thanks, guys." I sipped at my beer, stared at the foam for a moment. "But I think you're all full of shit."

Grace opened her mouth to protest. I held a placating hand out. "No, no, don't worry about it. I'm not giving you shit or anything. It's just that..." I stared into the depths of my mug again, not lifting my eyes from it. "...It's just that, I think you all know I never had the best of families. I mean, hell, of the lot of them, Mom was the best, god knows, but still, that was likely because she tended to just opt out of most of the shit."

Monica laid a hand on mine. "Lex," she said, her tone sad. I didn't move my gaze.

"Hey, it's what I admire most about her. She could check out every so often. I couldn't. Well, I did, but it was a lot more permanent."

I ran a thumb along the sweating glass surface.

"Truth to tell," I said, "I'll never regret walking away from that madhouse, but I am sorry I walked away from all of you, too." I finally looked up, and felt my eyes pricking with tears. "I can't tell you how much I appreciate you guys giving enough of a shit to get in contact with me again over the years." My voice was getting a little high and shaky, so I finished quickly. "Means a lot."

"Ah, hell," Bear said. "If we hadn't tracked you down, who'd be paying for the next round of beers?"

That got a small smile out of me. "You're an asshole, Bear." Then, before I could even attempt to protest my innocence, I turned, waved an arm at Ambrose. "Another flagon of ale, barkeep! For myself and my fellow Kinnigits of the Round Table."

Ambrose and the badger leapt into action.

A couple of hours and untold pitchers in, our little group hadn't even scratched the surface of all the crap we had done, the cringe-worthy moments we had experienced or inflicted on others. Some apologies floated around the table and were graciously accepted. In the end, we had, at the very least, opened what promised to be a miserable couple of days with a lot of good laughs.

When I considered all the dumb shit we did, it was pretty staggering. On more than one occasion through the evening, someone questioned how any of us were able to actually graduate.

"Hey, Lex," Gerry said. He and Grace were likely the only two who weren't sporting a slur in their speech. Grace because she had kids to get back to and a bun in the oven. Gerry likely because he was married to Sphincter Lady and she'd kick his ass or something. Didn't seem to stop her from knocking back the odd one. And she was getting sauced because she was actually starting to smile occasionally. Then again, I wondered if it might not just be gas. "You remember Mary's Camel?" Gerry finished.

Monica and I both cracked up at this. Monica and Mary had been friends back then and apparently still were, though now from a distance of a couple of provinces.

"Hell yeah, I remember!" I said. "Haven't thought of that in years!"

Monica said, "I remember it, and I remember it was actually *you* who stuck her with it, Lex, but I don't remember *how* she got stuck with it."

So I told them the story. How I had been watching a *M*A*S*H* rerun one night, laughing at Klinger trying for a Section 8 by walking around acting like he was leading a camel everywhere. A camel no one else could see. I'd thought it was funny and, in a weird mood the next day, I did the camel at school. Just for a laugh.

"What the hell did you name it?" Randy asked.

"Same as Klinger. Habibi."

"That's right!" Monica said. "Now I remember!"

"Yeah," I said. "So, I'm walking around all day and it's 'Come here, Habibi,' and 'Stop spitting, Habibi,' and all that."

"Yes, I remember all that," Monica said. "You were hilarious, acting like you were getting dragged down the hall by this invisible camel." Her eyebrows knitted together enticingly. "But how did Mary inherit it again?"

"By the last class, calculus with Mr. Pepper—"

"Dr Pepper," Bear said.

"Sgt. Pepper," Gerry said.

"Salt 'n' Pepper," Randy said.

"—yeah, anyways, I'm just sitting down at my desk, and Mary starts coming down the aisle and I tell her she can't, I tell her she'll step on Habibi." Gerry was laughing and I saw he was remembering this as clearly as I was myself. He should, he sat in the desk right beside me. "So she gives me this 'ooookayyyy' kinda look and backs out of the aisle, hands up to ward off the crazy, and goes down the other side.

"Pepper comes in, talks a bit, then starts handing out our tests that he'd marked, and Mary pipes up and says, 'Oh, you can't come down here, Mr. Pepper,' and he's like, 'Why?' and she says, "Cuz Lex's pet camel Habibi is here.' And that's when I turn around and look at her and say, 'What camel, Mary? I don't know what you're talking about.'"

"And she was stuck with that silly invisible camel for the rest of the year," Monica said.

"And then Mary and her camel were voted the king and queen of the prom!" That all-too-familiar voice came from just behind me.

They all turned to look.

"Cool story, bra!"

Fucking Ray.

◆ ◆ ◆

"THE FUCK YOU doing here, Ray?"

"I was just—whoa, Monica Holt! Lookin' good, Chiquita!" He actually, honest-to-god pronounced it as "cha-*kweet*-ah."

Monica stared at her beer. "Thanks, Ray," she murmured.

"Yeah, thanks, Ray. Why are you here?"

"Came over to see if you were doin' a little karaoke. Throwing out some classic rock tunes. 'Stayin' Alive' or juh-juh-juh-'Jive Talkin'.'" He struck the iconic Travolta pose, leg cocked, finger pointing upward.

Idiot doesn't know the Bee Gees from Heart. Good lord, how does he get dressed in the mornings?

"Nope," I said, took a quick sip of my beer. "So you can leave."

Randy looked like he was going to puke.

"Need to figure out what's going on for the funeral, bra. Just got word after you left. It'll be in four days."

"Bra?" Gerry said.

"He's being supportive." Gerry gave me a quizzical look. "Don't ask. Ain't worth the breath." Turning to Ray, I said. "There's nothing to figure out, Ray. Whatever schemes or plans you and Dad cooked up are fine. As I said a few hours ago to you and your sperm donor, don't count on any participation from me."

"But—"

"None."

"Dads is gonna be pissed."

"*Dads* can be anything he wants, as long as he doesn't be it around me. I trust you can relay that message to him without fucking it up? *Bra?*"

"You can't talk like that to him, you know," he said. "He's not the person you remember, bra. He's gettin' fragiler."

I watched Grace mouth *fragiler*, then, eyes widening, *wow*.

I set down my beer. All eyes were on me. I could feel them. I placed both hands firmly on the table and rose, slowly and deliberately. Ray had almost a foot on me, but what I lacked in height, I made up in confidence.

"I truly couldn't give a shit how *fragiler* he is. I can talk to him any way I want, Ray. I can talk to *you* any way I want. I'm a big girl now, all grown up, unlike you. You and that thing that fathered me don't like how I talk to you? There's a simple solution, big brother."

Ray stepped forward. We were inches apart. Ray's hands clenched into fists, then the fingers splayed wide again. "And what's that?"

I leaned in until we were as close to nose to nose as we could be. He'd kicked my ass quite a bit when we were younger, but no more. I stared into my brother's eyes. I enunciated clearly. I said, "Fuck. Off."

Bear stood, bigger and taller than either of us. He slid a hand between us and pushed on me to step back. I placed a hand on Bear's arm. Gently, but firmly, he pushed it away.

"I got this," I said.

"Yeah, little lezzie sister's got this, Beary. Why'nt you go back to your bi—"

I placed a hand on his chest. "Gonna stop you right there, brother Ray. You finish that word, you'll be in a matching coffin beside Mom." Then I pushed. Hard.

Ray stumbled back, then came back, fast. Suddenly, two more chairs were kicked back and he faced a blockade of bodies. Gerry and Monica joined Bear. I did a bit of a double take at the sight of the tall blonde to my right, but she stood, tall and unafraid.

I'd noticed that Randy didn't get up. No surprise there, though. Randy was a lover, not a fighter.

Still, there was a wall of us. And Ray.

Ray stopped. Reconsidered.

Then he reached out a hand to pat me on the shoulder. I caught it midway between us and pushed it back.

"Leave, Ray," I said. "Leave now. Don't come again. Or I'll fucking kill you."

"Fine," he said. "Fuck ya's all." He turned, then tossed one last comment over his shoulder. "Nice rack, Mon."

I advanced one step, but Ray left. He scraped enough faux dignity together to not quite go with his tail between his legs, but we all knew it was a close thing.

CHAPTER THREE

T HE NEXT THREE days were a blur.

My first morning in New Hope, I woke up late, cotton-mouthed and fuzzy-headed, around ten.

I'd had the nightmare again last night. The same one I used to have.

It'd kept me up for an hour or so, and that's why I slept in so late, only getting up when I did because I would have pissed the bed otherwise. I unwrapped the plastic cup and downed four cups of water from the sink. Even with my fucked-up pumpkin, I still managed to string a single thought together. *Sure doesn't taste like city water.*

After a long shower, I dressed and went in search of grease in the form of eggs, bacon, and toast with lots of butter. I also sought that holy grail of motivation: coffee. I passed through the dining room, but couldn't find the badger, or the Ambrose who lived under it, and kept going to the front desk. Annie was leafing through a magazine. She looked up, adjusted her glasses, and smiled brightly at me.

"Aw, honey, someone rode you hard and put you away wet."

Huh, someone else that uses that expression, I thought. "I wish," I said, managing a smile.

"A wee touch of the hangover?"

I squinched my eyes as I held up two fingers, close together. "A wee touch." I could tell she was holding back. There was so much that could be said.

"Ambrose said your group seemed to be having a good time."

"Yeah, for the most part." I considered for a second. "Which reminds me. You get a tall, skinny wreck of a human being, face like a caved-in ashtray, goes by the name of Ray, showing up here asking for me? Says he's my brother? Send him packing. Better yet, if you have any sort of peacekeeper behind that desk, use it without prejudice."

"I'll remember that," she said, her smile dimming a few watts. "Ambrose might have said something about that too."

"We handled it," I said. "I just don't want to bring my shit to your place of business. It happened last night, but I'll try to make sure that that's the only time, okay?"

"Not a problem, Lex," she said. "Goes to show ya, doesn't it? You can pick your nose, and you can pick your friends—"

"But you can't pick your family," I finished.

"Exactly."

"Can't wipe them on the back of the couch, either," I said.

"Too far, Lex, too far." It was her time to squinch her eyes, but she was laughing just the same.

"Story of my life," I said, sighing. "Oh, and while we're talking family, same goes for anyone claiming to be my father."

"All right." The laughter, then the smile, fell away from her face.

"Sorry, not trying to rattle you. I think the possibility's low. I don't think either of them leave their lair too often these days." At least, not judging from what I saw of the place.

Annie said nothing.

"You're being too quiet, Annie. You've heard about Ray and Marcus Hedges, haven't you?"

"I'm not going to lie to you, Lex," she said, her eyes direct. "You live and work in a small town, you hear things."

"Yeah," I said. "Sadly, they're likely all true." I stepped forward. "But I'm not one of them. Not anymore. Not for a long time. Okay?"

"Oh, Lex," she said, and lowered a palm deliberately to the desk. "I knew that as soon as I met you. You're a good person."

No, I thought, *I'm really not. But I'm trying. I just need to get my shit together.*

"Anyway" — I stretched those three syllables — "I'm desperately in need of the embryos of chickens, the meat of swine, and the bitter blood of coffee beans. Any chance of getting that here?"

Annie's expression grew pained. "Ah, Lex, I'm sorry hon. We close the grill around ten and don't get going again until around four, for dinner."

I did my best to placate. "No, hey, it's okay. I'm the one who slept in so darn late."

She glanced at her watch. "There's a McDonalds just on the far side of town —"

"No Hope has a Mickey Dee's now?"

"Yes, it does. Came in about three years back, just after the Tim's."

"This is truly a sign of the coming apocalypse, Annie."

"Indeed it is, young lady. But if you hurry, you can get an Egg McMuffin and a large double double before the four horsemen arrive."

"Annie, you're a doll. Don't ever let anyone tell you different."

"Just doing what I do best, Lex. Keeping my customers happy."

I backed out the lobby, pointing a finger at her. "You're trouble. My momma warned me about women like you."

She laughed and waved me away.

♦ ♦ ♦

TWELVE MINUTES LATER, I was biting into my breakfast sandwich. Say what you will about fast food, but after a night of drinking, this shit's manna from heaven.

◆ ◆ ◆

I'D JUST TOSSED my garbage in the can when my phone rang. I considered ignoring it, but the caller ID informed me it was the local detachment of the police.

I picked up the call.

"Ms. Alexandra Hedges? Daughter of Marcus and Sandra Hedges?"

"Yes, that's me. Call me Lex."

"Thank you, ma'am. My name is Constable Roberts, and I'm one of the officers assigned to your father's case."

Something Marcus said came back to me then. *Apparently the first officer on the scene was so distraught that he's now on desk duty while he recovers.* Wondered if Constable Roberts was the guy.

"Okay." I didn't have the distrust of police that many of my friends had. Sure, I always freaked a bit when I was driving and a cruiser tucked in behind me, but everyone felt that. Other than that, however, I didn't experience a low-level dread if I was dealing with them. I figured it was because I'd never been on the wrong side of the law, and never really did anything that would put me under their scrutiny.

"I know this is a difficult time for you, and you're likely very busy, but if you have a few moments to spare in the next couple of days, I'd appreciate it if you could come in and we could discuss your mother's case. Any assistance you could provide would be appreciated."

I'd been leaning against the trunk of my car. Now, I stood. "I'm actually free for a little bit right now. If it works for you, I could be there in"—I checked my watch, calculated the distance from here to there—"fifteen, maybe twenty minutes?"

"That would be perfect. Ask for Constable Roberts."

I ended the call. I'd have to drive two towns over, through Vilni to Opeongo Station, mostly just known as Opeongo, or

"Opie." I was filled to the brim with the food I'd just consumed and I still needed a coffee. I checked myself in the side-view mirror. Puffy, bloodshot eyes. Furry tongue. *Yup*, I thought, *I look like warmed over shit.*

I bought a couple of coffees—one for me and one for Constable Roberts—and went in search of a place that sold gum and eyedrops.

♦ ♦ ♦

JUST ABOUT HALFWAY to Opeongo, I passed through Vilni, which I always thought of as a deceptive little town. Most drivers simply passed by on the main road—it was called a highway, but it was still only a single lane in either direction. Gerry, back in our high school days, had once exclaimed, "This is no fucking highway. It's a goddamn *road*. It's a three dressed up as a nine."

Maybe he was right. More than a decade after Gerry's declaration, the road was still just a single lane in either direction.

It always struck me that there were really only three businesses a driver could access from that highway: a gas station, a hotel that was also the town's only watering hole, and, a little ways past the town, the massive church on the hill. Everything else had to be accessed through side roads.

But get on one of those side roads, and the town was bigger than it looked. It stretched away from the highway, and there were houses and farms for miles.

I'd always thought main roads went through the main part of a town, hence the name. But Vilni had no main road. Just this one poor excuse for a highway, barely grazing the northernmost tip of the town.

It was like most of the town preferred to be hidden away from world.

A deceptive little town.

◆ ◆ ◆

By the time I reached the Opeongo police station, which looked more like a house that had been repurposed than anything else, I was wishing I'd bought three coffees. Mine was gone and PC Roberts's was looking mighty tempting.

Still, I dutifully grabbed it and the little bag of sugars and creamers and headed into the station.

Inside, the office was like most of the television police stations I'd seen over the years. It was small, with eight or ten desks shoehorned into a space that was likely meant for four. A too-small air conditioner sat in a window, chugging away forlornly, pushing the air around more than actually cooling it. To the side, along a counter, a microwave and two coffee makers fought for space with boxes and paper. The walls were papered with notices, photos, service awards, and anything else related to the operation of the station, the prevention of crime, or the apprehension of criminals. More paper took up any space not already taken by phones and old computers, with the old-style non-flat-screen monitors, that squatted precariously on the edges of the desks. Phones rang, radios squawked, and people talked.

Organized chaos.

When I entered, a large officer who had been pecking away at a keyboard with two fingers—impressively quickly, from what I could see—glanced over, made eye contact, and carefully extricated himself from his chair and somehow found a narrow path over to me. "Miz Hedges?"

"Lex," I reminded him. "You must be Constable Roberts?"

"I am." He was even bigger standing in front of me, but it was his eyes that caught my attention. Haunted. Looking at me quickly, then averting to somewhere else.

I held out the coffee and bag. "Got this for you. Figured you could use one."

Roberts looked at the cup. "You didn't get one for yourself?"

"Drank it on the way over."

"You want another one?"

I didn't know what to say. Where would I get another one? "Well…I'd take one if…"

"All right. You take that one. I'll grab one from here." He turned and worked his way over to one of the two coffee machines, pulling an oversized mug from his desk on the way. He poured himself a cup and turned back. "Let's head out back. There's a picnic table there and it's a lot quieter and more private than in here."

On his way back to me, he grabbed a file from his desk and tucked it under his arm. Then he led the way back out the front doors and around the neatly trimmed grass to the back of the station. As promised, there were a couple of picnic tables positioned under a large tree.

Roberts lowered his mug to the table and set the file down, then put the mug on top to keep it from blowing away in any errant breeze. I sat, pried the lid off my coffee, and added some sugars and creamers. Roberts sat opposite me, grabbed his mug, and raised it in a mock toast, meeting my eyes for only a second before looking out across the neighbouring field and taking a sip.

"Hope you don't think I'm not grateful," Roberts said, raising his head slightly to point his chin at my coffee, "but I've been on office duty for the past few days. I must be getting used to this swill, because it's starting to taste good. It's been known to put the uninitiated in the hospital."

Marcus's voice in my head again. *Apparently the first officer on the scene was so distraught that he's now on desk duty while he recovers.* I was right. *Shit.*

"No problem," I said.

"So, I understand that you don't live around here anymore?"

"No," I said. "I left about ten years ago. Eventually ended up in Toronto."

"And what do you do for a living?"

"Couple of things. I write for an online news agency, mostly articles, nothing big or dramatic. And I also play in a band."

"Oh yeah?" Roberts said. Another flick of the eyes. To me. Away. "Would I have heard of you?"

"Doubt it."

"What kind of music?"

"I could beat around the bush here," I said, "but over the years, I've found it easier to just get it out there. I play in a Heart cover band." I paused, then, before Roberts could ask, I said, "Yes. The Heart you still hear on the radio. No, it's not what I'd exactly planned when I got into music. Yes, it pays well. No, I've never actually met any of the real Heart band. Okay, well, the original guitarist, Roger Fisher, but that's it. Not the sisters. And yes, I play Ann, the dark-haired one who sings."

Roberts smiled, watching the field. He took another sip. "You've been asked some of these questions before, I gather."

"Once or twice." We both chuckled. I actually got a longer, less fraught look.

"And your family. Your father and brother. You've had little contact with them over the years? Or your mother?"

"No contact. None whatsoever."

"I gather your leaving back then was a little…strained? You would have been what? Eighteen? Nineteen?"

"It was 2001. Before the towers fell. So, sixteen. Almost seventeen," I said. "And yeah. Strained. That's one way to describe it, yes."

Roberts paused, took another sip of his coffee, set the mug back down, twisted it in a circle with his fingers. "The reason I'm asking all this is because, quite frankly, we don't have a lot of leads."

"From what I understand—from what my father has told me in the roughly three hundred strained seconds I could bear to be in his company—is that she was pulled from her car, dragged through the forest, then tortured and killed? Somewhere between New Hope and Carry's Cove?"

"That's about right." Roberts looked to me, head slightly cocked to the side. "So you've talked to your father and brother?"

They've talked at me, yes, I thought, but figured it was wiser to keep to myself.

I made a face. "I have. My brother called me to let me know that Mom had…to let me know about Mom. Then I went over to the house yesterday, not long after I got into town, and had a very brief conversation with both of them. Which was a mistake. It didn't go well. Then Ray showed up at the hotel last night, caused a bit of a scene. Words were thrown around."

"Just words?"

"Just words. I like Annie and Ambrose too much to get into a fist fight in their place of business."

"The Cozy Pine Inn." Roberts smiled. "They're good people. I've known their family for years."

"They are." I wanted to ask Roberts about Annie and Ambrose. Were they husband and wife? Brother and sister? Cousins? And what was with the badger? But that haunted look on Roberts's face kept me quiet. We both sipped our coffee and looked back over the bordering, open rocky field that his eyes seemed to find so fascinating.

"My intention, bringing you out here, was to ask if you were aware of anyone who might have done this to your mother."

"No idea. I didn't really know her these last few years, but of the three people in that house, she was the quietest and most likeable. Frankly, I don't understand how this hasn't happened to Ray. I'd pick him as probable murder victim over my mother any day."

"Why do you say that?"

"This likely isn't news to anyone in this station, or this town, but…I say that because Raymond Hedges is a waste of flesh."

Roberts remained silent, encouraging me to fill it in. I've interviewed enough to know the trick.

"He's two years older than me. Pushing thirty. He still lives at home. If he even earns money, I guarantee it's not through lawful means, and likely not through lawful product." I took a sip of coffee. "Then again, I'm guessing you're well aware of that."

Roberts had a good poker face.

"And overall, he's just a fucking asshole."

Roberts remained silent.

"Pardon my French."

"So, it's safe to say you don't like your brother much."

"It's safe to say if he'd been the one murdered, I'd still be in Toronto, not wasting a moment's thought on him."

"Ouch," Roberts said.

"Hey, you want honesty, I'll give it to you."

"And your father? What's the issue there?"

For the first time in years, it came back to me. The vision that had haunted me since my teens. A vision I'd learn to first control and tamp down, and finally, I had thought, to banish.

Fingers. Madly working fingers.

"We…" I took another sip, though the coffee was lukewarm at best now. "We've had some pretty extreme differences of opinion."

"Sounds like it's a bit more than that."

"Let's just say he was the reason I left and haven't come back. Til now." *Why did I come back?* It felt like a mistake right then. "I will say it's an issue between him and me. It had no bearing on my mother."

"Okay." The look on his face told me he was willing to let it go for now.

It was my turn to remain silent.

"One last question."

"Shoot."

"Your brother." Roberts paused a moment, spun his cup a few degrees, then, with an effort, looked up and met my eyes. "Think there's any chance he could have done this?"

I think he finally locked eyes because, if I pointed a finger at him as the person who did what had been done to my mother, he wanted to know. To be sure. He'd seen a terrible thing that no one should ever have to see, and I could tell, in that look, that he wanted to find who did it, and take away any chance that they might do it again.

I couldn't blame him.

With all that in mind, I considered the question for a long time. Really thought it through. Finally, I said, "Do I think he's a scumbag? Yes. Do I think he'd sell my mother out for a bag of weed? Also yes." I rubbed a thumb along the ridge of the lid of the paper cup. "But do I think he could have dragged my mother out into the woods to torture and mutilate and behead her? No, much as I can't stand the asshole, I really don't think so."

"What about maybe getting someone else to do it for him?"

"Maybe, but I still don't think so." I put both palms on the table, leaned toward the officer to make my point. "This is gonna sound like me being a bitch or cracking a joke, but it's not. I mean this in all seriousness. What you're describing would take planning and forethought. Neither are really my brother's strong suit, you know?"

"What about someone doing this *because* of your brother's…inclinations?"

I considered. "Again, a possibility…" I thought some more. "And it's likely worth a bit of a follow-up, but to be honest?"

He nodded for me to continue.

"To be perfectly honest, Ray's such a heinous bastard, I'm still guessing he'd be the target, not my mother. If he's half the asshole to everyone else as he is to me, then even if he owes money or product, anyone's going to look at the debt and look at the benefit of not having to deal with the assoholic, and decide on the second course of action."

"'Assoholic'?" He smirked.

"Yes." I smirked as well. "One who is hopelessly addicted to being an asshole. The very definition of Raymond Hedges."

"I'm gonna have to remember that one," Roberts said. He shook his head, took another sip. Setting the cup back down on the file, he said, "What about your father?"

That one set me back. I took an even longer time to run it through. "Like I said, I haven't been around in a long time. I haven't been in contact in a long time. Hell, I don't even know how Ray got my phone number to let me know about Mom." I stared down at my hands pressed flat on the table. "So, I can't speak with certainty about the kind of person my father — or, for that matter, my brother — has become in all these years. And I won't say my father is *not* capable of it." An image was forming in my head — *fingers madly working, clenching and unclenching* — and I shook it to get rid of the memory.

"I won't say I'm as confident with this statement, but I don't think Dad would hire someone to do this." *The killer flensed the skin from your mother's breasts…flayed your mother's genitals.* "And I'm pretty sure he didn't do it himself."

"You really don't like your father too much, do you?"

My voice was barely a whisper when I answered. "No."

We both sat quietly for a few moments, letting the sounds of nature clean the air around us.

Roberts sighed, brought his hand down on the table with a soft tap. "I guess that's all I needed. Like I said, I was hoping you might have some ideas of anyone who wasn't happy with your mother, or had any reason to do this. But I understand. You've really had no contact with any of your family in a long time. You really don't know them that well anymore. Accurate?"

"That's a pretty good summary of it, yes. Sad, but true."

"Is there anyone in town who may have known the family? Anyone you know of who was close to them?"

"The only one in the area who likely may have had contact with any of them is Norman Gustafsen. But he'd likely know my brother more than anyone."

Roberts smiled again. "As you said, Ray Hedges is a known quantity to us."

"Figured as much."

"And Constable Gustafsen is partnering with me on this."

"That I didn't know."

"He's the one out in the field," he said. "I'm sure he'll be in touch as well."

We stood then, shook hands. Walking back around to the front of the station, Roberts watered the garden with the dregs of his coffee. I tossed my paper cup in the trash.

"If you get any leads, or have any more questions, you know where to find me," I said.

"I appreciate that. Thanks for stopping by."

When I was back in the car and heading back to the motel, I thought, *Well that was reasonably bloodless.*

♦ ♦ ♦

I'D TRIED TO call Monica, to see if she wanted to get together, but she begged off, citing work. I figured it was true, but I also figured she was likely feeding me back some of the mountain of shit I'd fed her in high school.

Yeah, well, I deserve that. Then I smiled. *But hey, if I'm getting fed more shit, this is a good time to gather it all together.*

Instead, I spent the next couple of days getting reintroduced to my high school buddies. I even watched Bear and Grace's kids the next afternoon so they could go shopping for a few hours and catch an afternoon movie.

Through the hours of downtime, I avoided opening my computer, avoided checking for texts on my phone, avoided my family. Instead, I walked into town, grabbed coffee, and did some thinking.

Trying to get my shit together.

It was all initial efforts, no real plan. More like a kid pulling all their toys into a pile before trying to sort them out. I was making quite a pile, too. Kelly. The band. My father. Ray. My friends. Monica. My mother. The nightmares. This town. My life. My past. My present. And whatever the fuck my future held.

I had a lot of questions, and no answers.

But hey, at least I'd made a bit of progress. The shit was getting more togethery, but now I needed a plan to deal with it.

Chapter Four

THEN IT WAS the day of the funeral.

My mother's funeral did nothing to dispel the idea that New Hope was still — despite some great friends — hell. During the entire ride back here, for the entire four hours in the car when I'd listened to a bunch of music that consisted of anything that had nothing to do with Heart, I had almost convinced myself to come back home with an open mind.

It's been so damn long, I'd told myself.

A lot of the people would have moved on and moved out, I'd told myself.

I had tried to ignore the fact that two of the people — the two I *really* didn't ever want to deal with again — would not only be there, but were part of my family.

Still, after trying to avoid them, mostly successfully, I tried not to wonder why I preferred the company of Monica and my friends to my grieving family. Hell, I would have taken Annie, Ambrose, and the badger over my family. I knew the reasons why, I just didn't want to scratch at that particular wound too much.

I also wondered why I wasn't asking more questions about the death of my mother. I called myself a journalist, for chrissakes. *Who, what, where, when, why,* and *how* had always been my mantra. But it was like the events had happened in another room, behind thick glass. I could take it in, but I couldn't push through.

Still, the morning of the funeral had come. I rose early, grabbed an early breakfast courtesy of Ambrose, the badger looking a little worse for wear first thing in the morning. I showered, got my hair in the perfect bed-head coif, and was just laying out my dress when the hotel room phone rang.

"Hey, Lex." Monica. A smile immediately lit across my face.

"Hey, Monica, how are you?"

"Oh, to hell with me," she said. "How are *you*?"

"Well, I'm about to bury my mom, who I last saw alive when I was still a teenager. Other than that, not too bad."

"Lex, quit messing around. I'm serious."

I took a breath. When was the last time I'd been real with anyone? Months. Maybe years. "I'm okay. Honestly. Not the best day of my life, but absolutely not the worst."

"Okay. Just checking."

Then there was a bit of a pause, where I listened to her take a breath, as though to say something, but nothing came.

"You want to say something," I said. "It's me. Just say it."

"You say that like that's the most natural thing in the world for the two of us. Saying whatever's on our minds."

"*Touché.*"

"Just saying."

"Yeah, yeah," I said. "I smell what you're cooking." That got a throaty laugh that sent a bit of a chill down my spine. I smiled wider. "Anyway, new rule: we say exactly what we want—or what we need—to say to each other going forward. Deal?"

"Deal."

"See how easy that was? So," I said. "Spill."

"Okay," she said. I heard her release a soft breath. "I've been kind of avoiding you the past couple of days."

"Oh, really? Hadn't noticed."

"Please, Lex," she said. "No jokes."

There was something in her voice. I said, "Okay, no jokes."

"Anyway, I've been avoiding you because, well, I like you a lot, Lex. I always have, and I think you know that…"

"Yeah," I said, my voice quiet. "I do."

"But you weren't always really nice to me."

"No," I said, in the same quiet voice. "I wasn't."

And even though she was at the other end of a phone call, I felt myself blushing with embarrassment. Probably a healthy measure of self-loathing, too.

"And I don't want to set myself up for that again."

"Can't blame you," I said. "I was a bitch."

"So, I guess, what I'm asking is, are you still a bitch?"

"Total honesty? Yeah, a bit. But I'm working really hard on it."

"Working on it?"

"Yeah, working on it. It's the best I've got right now," I said truthfully. "I'm being as honest as I can be."

"Okay." Was that some hesitancy I heard there?

"Sorry. But, Monica, I'm serious. I was a messed up teenager. I'm not that person now. I'm still not a *great* person, but I'm not *that* person."

A long pause. I held my breath.

"I believe you, Lex Hedges."

I said nothing.

"Say something."

"Okay. Um. Thank you, Monica Holt?"

"Yes, I can definitely see that great person thing still hasn't fully found you as yet."

"I'm a work in progress."

That got a laugh.

"All right," she said. "Don't think this too forward, but I was wondering if I could maybe attend the funeral with you. To support you?"

"I would be honoured."

"Cuz you don't have to."

"Monica, I put up a pretty good front, but if I'm honest, I'm a bit of a mess right now. My mom's dead, and I'm dealing with my asshole brother and even bigger asshole father. Did I mention my mother was murdered?"

"Lex…"

"So, what I'm trying to say is, I might sound like I've got most of my shit together, but I really don't, and if I had my way, I'd climb into bed and not come out for a long time. You're kind of the reason I don't. So the fact that you're offering companionship when I need any help I can get?" I blew out a breath. "Yeah, I'd be honoured. I'm out of my depth here."

"Okay." I heard her smile though the phone.

"Okay." I said. "Meet here? Maybe an hour?"

"Done."

That allowed me some time to put a little more effort into my preparation.

◆ ◆ ◆

MONICA ENDED THE call. *I think we're both out of our depth here, Hedges.*

It was time to ask for help.

◆ ◆ ◆

THE FUNERAL STARTED out reasonably well, considering it was a funeral. The Anglican Church was barely a third full, and most of that was my friends. Some of the others who warmed the pews were there only due to the violent nature of Sandra Hedges's death. Prurient interest, I figured, not legitimate grief.

The minister, who obviously didn't know my mother from a hole in the ground, got up and did his generic lecture that was one part this-is-not-the-end-only-the-beginning spiel, two parts come-to-Jesus-or-at-least-my-church sell-job. I hadn't been to a lot of funerals, but this one seemed to be the standard, basic, fill-in-the-blanks, cookie-cutter bullshit. Even going from the old information I had about my mother, I knew she would have hated it.

Then, seemingly running out of religious gas, the minister wound his own speech down and said, to my horror, "And now, we'll hear from Sandra Hedges's eldest son, Raymond."

Oh hell, I thought. *He's really gonna speak? This'll be a goddamn freakshow.*

Ray didn't disappoint.

He ambled up to the podium. All six feet of him, hunched down to more like five feet and change, almost as if he was a damn hunchback. *Would have been nice if you'd taken a couple of minutes to shave, you disrespectful bastard*, I thought. *Or at least put on a clean shirt. Or even iron the one that looks like wadded and unfolded toilet paper under that hideous suit.* As he approached the podium, I saw the glint from the pins that hemmed up the cuffs of his wrinkled, shiny dress pants. Peeking out underneath them were white sweat socks.

I thought, *Jesus H. Mom probably pinned that up for him years ago.*

Still, I had to give it to Ray. He was at least up there. More than I, the long-lost only daughter, was willing to do.

Ray leaned on the podium. He said something that was lost. Someone at the back, probably Randy, said, "Sorry, can't hear you," and then Ray, in reaction, sprawled across the podium, his arms hanging far out over the front of the stand, suit and shirt sleeves pushed way up his skinny forearms, his face a whisker's length from the mike.

"CAN YOU HEAR ME NOW?" His voice boomed, distorted, through the mostly empty room. The minister, seeing Ray wasn't going to change position anytime soon, quickly jumped up and adjusted the mike to a better position.

I felt Monica shift uncomfortably beside me. Then she took my hand in her own. I squeezed hers lightly in acknowledgement.

"How's that?" Ray said. The crowd murmured that it was fine. He nodded, then reached a hand behind him. "Gonna read you..." More digging. "...a poem I wrote for Moms last night."

Moms. The sound grated each time Ray called her that. Just as bad as the *Dads* tag. It had started out as mom-mom, and when Mom had once jokingly asked, "What, are you calling both your moms?" the name had stuck.

Ray finally scavenged a crumpled ball of paper from his pocket then swung his arm back over the podium, holding the paper at arm's length while he slowly unfolded it.

It took him what seemed like two full, excruciating minutes to get it reasonably flat. Monica's hand squeezed mine each time I sighed in frustration. She squeezed a quite a few times. Finally, he got the paper the way he wanted it. *At least it matches his shirt for wrinkles.* "Okay, so..." He paused, his eyes narrowing on the paper. "...so I wrote this for...for Moms. Last night."

He dropped the paper with a mumbled "shit" and it fluttered to the ground. A couple of people rose to retrieve it for him, but he waved them off. "S'okay," he said. "I got it."

He pushed himself up from the podium, ambled around the front, bent to grab the paper, lost his balance and stumbled forward, course corrected, reached again for the paper, snagged it, and ambled back to the podium.

I checked my watch. Four solid minutes and nothing yet. Another squeeze.

Ray assumed the same position, arms stretched out in front of him, paper clutched in his grubby fingers. "Okay, so, yeah." He squinted, opened and closed his mouth twice, then started.

"The wind…the wind blows across the…the…uh…"

He faded off, staring at the page. Then he crumpled it and tossed it to the side of the room with a disdainful flick of his wrist. "Can't read that. Probably just start fuckin' crying."

There was a muffled murmur of displeasure at the f-bomb, but still, the man had just lost his mother, so I figured the crowd was willing to give him some leeway.

"Look, I'm just gonna talk, okay?" He scanned the audience, as though daring someone to disagree.

He's so stoned, I thought. I snuck a quick glance at Monica. She gave me a supportive smile, but her eyes told me she knew it wasn't enough to make me feel better.

"So, my old lady. Moms." Ray took a deep breath. "She was…shit, she was just a cool motherfuh—" And I had to give him credit again, he stopped himself. He'd held his tongue twice in the past couple of days. *Not bad for a moron.*

"She was cool, y'know? Just a cool mom." He shook as head as though he couldn't believe how cool a mom his old lady really had been.

"Don't get me wrong," he said. "She kept us in line, me and Lexi. I remember having welts all over my ass one time when she caught me…what?" He stopped at the increased sound from the audience. One f-bomb could be forgiven, but now he was just riding roughshod over convention.

"What?" he said again. "She did! I was a stupid little bastard and she whupped my ass good for it."

And that was enough for me. I released Monica's hand and stood. Very quietly, I heard Monica say, "Be nice, Lex. It's your mother's funeral."

"And he's still a stupid little bastard, Monica. I've had enough."

I strode to the podium. Quietly, facing Ray, I said, "That's enough."

Ray straightened. "Whoa. Ladies and gents, my little sister, the world-famous Rita Wilson. Guess that makes me…ah, I don't know. Owen?" I didn't bother correcting him.

Angling closer to my so-called brother, I reached up to put an arm around his shoulders, and pulled him back from the podium. *God, you stink,* I thought. *You could have showered, at least.* Placing my hand over the mike, I said, very quietly, "I'm gonna bail you out of this train wreck, you fucking prick. Have the good fucking grace to walk away." Then I pulled my hand from the mike.

I turned to face everyone, but of course, the only one I really saw was Marcus. Eyes flat. Staring at me.

Fingers. His fingers.

I closed my eyes and forcibly pushed the thought from my head.

With no idea what I was going to say, I said, "Ladies and gentlemen, I think what Ray was trying to say, in his own unique way, is that—"

Ray made a move to lean forward into the microphone, but he'd telegraphed the move, so I tightened my grip on his shoulders and hauled him back. I dug my fingers into the meat of my brother's scrawny shoulder.

"—is that, in her own way, our mom loved her family very much. And of course, Ray, myself, and our…uh…our father did her, as well." I cursed myself for tripping over that last bit, but shit, I knew I couldn't, in a house of God, lie and say that Ray, our father, and I all *loved* the woman. I didn't even know her anymore, let alone know if I loved her. All I knew was I didn't like her that much, and had even less respect for her.

But love? Yeah, love was off the list.

Then there was the other hard word to say. *Father.* How long had it been since I'd even made that sound before a few days ago? *Father. Dad.* A long goddamn time. Most of my friends in Toronto thought my father long dead.

I realized I'd gone quiet. I became aware of expectant faces, patiently watching me. I couldn't look at Marcus again, so instead, I looked across the faces to Monica. Who gave me a small smile, and a small nod.

You've got this, that nod said. *Okay, Lex*, I thought. *You can do this.*

"I'll leave you with this." I thought for a second, settled on a Heart lyric, then immediately jettisoned it. Then I thought about getting my shit together, and said, "Our lives are a journey to become not what we could be, but what we should be. We're here not because Sandra Hedges died. We're here because she lived. Hopefully, she became what she should be." Then, gripping the bag of wasted flesh that was my brother, I said, "Thank you for coming today."

Holding my brother back from the stand, I stared pointedly at the minister, cueing him to get his ass back up for some more Jesus talk. The minister took the hint and hauled ass.

As I led my brother — *my big brother*, I thought. *What a fucking joke* — back to his seat, Ray smiled and waved at the audience and said, "Thanks, folks, I'll be here all week. Try the veal."

I pushed him down to the pew with a few nudges, each carrying far more force than was absolutely necessary. I leaned in, nose to nose, and said, "Now stay there and shut the fuck up." When he opened his mouth to talk, the sardonic glint in his bloodshot eyes, I squeezed at the loose flesh of his cheeks, really digging my nails in, pooching his mouth out. If it wasn't so damn tragic, it would have been funny. With his swampy breath in my face, I said, "Not. A fucking. Word." I threw all the menace I could into it, and I felt him nod slightly in my hand.

I knew, right at that moment, that my family was gone. Physically, they'd been gone for half my life, but that small, lingering hint of affection I'd carried for my mother had acted as a tenuous, gossamer strand of connection up to now.

But now, she was gone. And I realized, in my mind, so were the other two members of that family. I would never again think of Ray as my brother, nor Marcus as my father.

I have no family anymore, I realized.

I didn't meet Marcus's eyes as I got Ray situated. I couldn't even acknowledge his presence.

Fucking asshole.

The minister was prattling on about something again, which was good. I did my best to set a stony, noncommittal expression on my face and stalked back to my spot, Monica's eyes my beacon. When I sat again, she took my hand immediately.

I glanced over, more to silently ask if I'd made an ass of myself up there. Instead, she looked at me, love and concern in equal measure, and mouthed one word.

"Breathe."

I let out the breath I hadn't known I'd been holding for too long. And then I felt better. Not a lot, but better.

♦ ♦ ♦

THE ACTUAL BURIAL ceremony went smoothly. Ray seemed subdued after the earlier fiasco. His father stuck close by his side.

At no point did Marcus lose composure or drop a single tear for his brutally murdered wife. Not that I expected him to.

Unlike his son, he'd at least washed his hair and pulled it back into a neat ponytail, and had shaved for the occasion.

We got through the ashes to ashes and dust to dust stuff, Ray and Marcus — and really, why not call him by his name for the rest of my life, because he was not a father to me — laid a flower on the casket.

I will admit to being a touch surprised. Ray was awkward and looked like he had no idea how to act. He looked like he was going to toss the flower, then, at the top of the swing, he held on, looked embarrassed, then just dropped it. It landed on the lid and slid off, as though my mother had brushed it away.

But that wasn't the surprise. It was Marcus. As he stood, waiting his turn, it looked like he slipped into…what? Confusion? Up until now, there had been nothing but boredom and a decided lack of interest in the entire proceedings from him. But now, it was like he'd gone to sleep, then woken up and had no idea where he was. His mouth fell open, and there was a faint huffing noise coming from him. He looked at me, but his eyes travelled right past me, and I realized he had no idea who I was.

He looked at Ray with the same lack of recognition, but he followed his son's gesture and dropped the rose into the grave, then Ray led him away.

If the pair of them hadn't been such morally reprehensible people, it would have almost been touching. Instead, it was simply sad, the two of them grieving for someone they'd mostly ignored when I was still around, and likely ignored worse over the last two decades of her life. And obviously, from the state of the house, she'd likely checked out as well.

What apathy has that house witnessed, the three of them coexisting with no interaction, no affection, and only the slimmest of communication?

I thought it was hell when I was there. Perhaps I'd misjudged.

Either way, I was even more grateful I'd gotten out when I had.

A rose was offered to me. I declined, standing off to the side with Monica. She lobbed a *you sure?* look when I shook my head at the offer. I lobbed my best *damn right I'm sure* back at her.

The whole burial ceremony was completed in about fifteen minutes. Gerry, Ruthless, Grace, Bear, and Randy all gave me a hug and we agreed to meet up shortly.

As the few mourners gathered to offer condolences to Ray and Marcus, I scanned the crowd. I'd seen most of the people who'd entered the church, but as I looked around now, I saw one person I didn't recognize.

A woman around my age, maybe a few years younger. A friend of Ray's? Did Ray even have friends?

But she stared pointedly at me. The fingers of one hand made complicated motions that, to my eye, did not seem random. But I couldn't make out what she was doing. It almost looked like sign language, but she kept her hand low, down by her side.

The other hand was plunged deep into a pocket. I watched the bulges of her knuckles as her hand worked something there as well.

Who in the hell?

She stood far to the other side of the crowd, well to the back, but removed enough that I had a clear view of her. Her long black dress seemed to draw in any light around her, leaving more of a negative space, showing only her ankles, forearms, and face. Though I couldn't see fine details, just from the shape alone I saw the dress fitted her nicely around the waist and, while displaying no cleavage, accentuated her breasts. Her mousey brown hair was pulled back in a tight ponytail. She didn't seem to be wearing any makeup, or at least, so little that it was insignificant, however her eyes seemed to smoulder.

It was then that I realized. *She's too far away for me to even see her eyes. How can I think they're smouldering?* Yet, they were.

I was about to turn and ask Monica if she knew the woman when I found I couldn't look away from her, my eyes seemingly locked into her far-off gaze. I felt a tingling that engulfed my skull. It was not unpleasant, then sounds and colours and smells flitted through my mind. Small things, not even fully formed, but more like hints and suggestions of things.

The smell of wheat.

They coalesced, formed more substantial, yet still ephemeral, combinations. It felt as though I was being given a story, one random letter at a time. Seeing a picture fill in one pixel at a time. There was an order, a pattern, a storyline there, but it was chaotically inscrutable.

Blue sky. Heat.

But eventually it did begin to fill in. There was no voice in my head. No picture. It felt more like a memory being built, layer by layer, or piece by piece, including, as strange as it felt to me, the *memory* of that memory. As though the pathways for that memory were being laid so that, once this was all done, it would feel as though it had been in my head all along.

A blade of grass. Wind sounds across a field.

It was the most disconcerting thing I had ever felt.

It was a sense, a feeling, a memory being downloaded to my brain.

And though I knew it was there, knew the pathways, knew where and how to access it, I couldn't.

Maddeningly, it was right there, but locked down. Like a memory that's just out of reach, on the tip of my tongue.

I wondered if this was how Alzheimer's patients felt.

"…okay?"

The sound brought me back around. The attendees were heading back to the church. Only Ray and Marcus—his *Dads*—and Monica and I remained at the plot. I'd completely missed what she'd said.

I released the pressure on her hand. My hand hurt, so I must have really been squeezing. Ray and Marcus were heading over, the matter of a few carefully placed steps between us. Marcus looked like he was back in control of his faculties, grim determination replacing confusion on his face.

"Sorry," I said. "Come on." I tugged lightly on her hand and we turned toward the church, away from what used to be my family. Marcus's expression never changed, but I saw a flash of anger in his eyes, quickly snuffed. But from Ray I heard a mumbled epithet that I chose to ignore.

Flicking a quick glance to the spot where the woman had been, I saw only her retreating back, heading across the graveyard to the tree line.

What the hell just happened?

CHAPTER FIVE

WE SKIPPED ANY planned get-together after the funeral, billed as "a time of fellowship and remembrance for our loved one." *What a crock of shit.* I told myself I'd visit the grave later, once all the shit died down, to actually say my proper goodbyes. She was gone, and I'd mentally relinquished any hold my family might have on me, but I at least owed the woman a goodbye.

I knew everyone perceived me as cold, and to a certain degree, I likely was. I didn't care a whit for what Ray and Marcus were going through, because they deserved all they got. But my mother, while not blameless, hadn't really added to the shit.

She just hadn't done much to lessen it, either.

Still, of the bunch, Sandra was deserving of a proper send-off from her only daughter and I knew she'd never get it while those other two remained involved. I would say my goodbyes on my own terms, in my own time.

In the meantime, my friends had come back to town for me and stood by me. Hell, they'd stood by me more than my family ever had. They were the family that deserved my full attention.

We pressed Ambrose and his badger—rather stylishly coiffed this evening, I noticed—into service fetching several pitchers of his finest draft.

"So…" Randy said. "That was…"

"One crack-a-lackin' funeral," Bear finished.

"Robert!" Grace said.

"What?"

"You don't…" She sighed. "Do I really have to lecture you on what not to say about a funeral?"

"Apparently," Gerry said.

"Truth!" Randy said, raising his mug and, hell, it was good enough as a toast.

"Truth!" Bear seconded, raising his mug.

We brought up our mugs in a toast. "Truth!"

And so, the night progressed.

It was a couple of hours later when a random collision of two beer-saturated neurons collided in my brain and, before I could think about it or analyze it in any way, I said, "Hey, anyone see that strange woman off to the side today?"

"Off to what side?" Gerry said.

"She was kinda behind the group of you, but off to the side."

"A funeral crasher?"

"The fuck's a funeral crasher?" Bear said.

"Didn't you see that movie *Wedding Crashers*? Vince Owen and Vaughn…um…Wilson?" Randy said.

"You mean," Monica said, "Owen Wilson and Vince Vaughn?"

"Them too," Randy said.

"Them too," Bear seconded, raising his mug.

We brought up our own mugs. "Them too!"

The mugs came down.

"What were we talking about?" Randy said.

"That movie. Only different," Monica said.

"Oh," Bear said understandingly, but the look on his face said something different. "Owen? Lex's brother?"

"What?" Gerry said, totally lost.

Grace waved us off. "Don't worry about it," she said. "I'll explain it all out to him later. Carry on about your business."

Randy snapped his fingers. "I remember now," he said, "Woman at the funeral. In the church? Or at the grave?"

"Grave."

It was negative responses all around. Monica just gave a strange shake of her head. She must have seen her though. She'd been standing right beside me.

"Why?" Grace asked.

"It was just weird, is all," I said. "She just kinda stood there, off on her own. Didn't interact with anyone, didn't say anything to me. It wasn't someone I knew."

"Ooooo," Randy said. "Maybe it was Spooky Talia."

"Who's Spooky Talia?" Ruthless said.

"Who's Spooky Talia? Who's Spooky Talia?" Randy said. "Are you serious? Oh, wait, you ain't from 'round these parts." He raised his mug. "Okay, you're exceptioned."

"You're exceptioned!" Bear seconded, raising his mug.

"You're exceptioned!" we agreed in a toast.

"No, but seriously," I said, wiping my mouth. "Who's Spooky Talia?"

"Who's Spooky Talia? Who's Spooky Talia?" Randy said again. "Dude, you were born here." He threw out his hands. "No exception for you!"

"No exception for you!" Bear seconded, raising his mug.

"No exception for you!" we agreed in a toast.

"That's like..." Randy searched for something equivalent. "That's like not knowing about the boat wreck that happened out on the lake. The one where only the coffin made it ashore."

"I don't know anything about that either," I said.

"You don't..." The exasperation in Randy's voice was plain. "Jesus H., Lex, didn't you pay *attention*? The hotel in Vilni has a painting, and their placemats tell the story. Hundred years ago? The hell's the matter with you? How'd you miss all this shit?"

Bear slammed his mug down, slopping beer onto the table. He stabbed a finger in my direction and barked, "Who are you and what have you done with our Lexi?"

"Honest to god, guys, I have no idea about the lake, the coffins, or Spooky Talia."

Randy stared into his mug and shook his head. "So disappointed in you, woman."

I really gotta get my shit together, I thought. "Okay, lovely. Great. Fine. Can somebody fucking tell me who Spooky fucking Talia is?"

"I know a bit of the story," Gerry said. "My brother used to tell me stories to scare the shit out of me. But I don't know how true they were."

"I'm about the same," Bear said.

"I only really know what Robert knows," Grace said.

All eyes turned to Randy. "What?" he said.

"You seem to be the resident expert on all things Spooky Talia-related," I said.

"Yeah, well," he said. "About that. I just kinda know the name and that she's supposed to be all scary and shit."

"Nice." I sighed. "Real friggin' helpful."

Monica raised her mug. "Real friggin' helpful!" We toasted.

I wiped the foam from my lips and flicked it at Randy. "Dick," I said.

"What?" Randy said. "It's not like she's the one who was out in the graveyard. She'd be, like, what? Ninety years old? Maybe a hundred?"

Gerry hummed a song that I immediately recognized as Blue Öyster Cult's "Joan Crawford." "Spooky Talia has risen from the grave," he sang, changing up the name, then he grinned. He and I had always had this musical reference shorthand. It was good to see it was still functional.

"Talia Davis would be forty-four years old." We all turned to see who had spoken.

"Ambrose?"

"You know about her?"

"I did." He stood, a fresh pitcher of beer and clean, frosted mugs on a tray.

"How?"

"My father was Ellery McDonald." He stopped, as though waiting to see if anyone would catch the reference. No one did.

"Constable Ellery McDonald," he said. "My father arrested Talia's mother not long before…well, before they all disappeared."

"Disappeared?" I said. "Your dad ran off with Talia's mother?"

"Not quite," he said. He motioned toward the table. "You mind?" No one did. He set the tray on the table, pulled up a chair, grabbed a mug, then poured himself a beer and raised it. "On the house," he said.

"On the house," we said in a toast.

He continued to gulp beer long after the rest of us had finished, drawing stares and smiles. His head tilted farther and farther back, the coiffed badger defying gravity. Finally, he finished, dropped his empty mug to the table. He smacked his lips and said, "I do love beer."

Pulling his chair up a bit closer, he continued to handle the empty mug, absently playing with it as he related what he knew of Talia Davis.

"I'm a little fuzzy on some of the particulars," he said, "but here's what I know. Talia's parents were Glen and Diane Davis. Talia also had a sister, about five years younger, named" — and he cocked a finger gun at me — "Alexandra. Pretty sure she also went by Lex, or maybe Alex. But then, along the way, there was only Talia." He looked around the table. He had their attention.

"Talia's father…"

"Glen," said Ruthless, obviously trying to keep the names straight.

"Right. Her father had left a year or two earlier. Not sure what was going on there, but stuff happens, am I right?"

Bear looked like he was going to launch a *you are right* toast, but Grace placed a hand on his forearm and the mug stayed down.

We, however, all nodded in agreement that he was indeed correct. Stuff did happen.

"Anyway, while he was away, some bad shit happened. The younger daughter, Alex, came into the hospital." Grace brought a hand to her mouth, already in fear of what was to come. "If I remember right, both arms had been broken."

"Oh god," Grace said.

"Both of them broken here" — he pointed mid-bicep — "and here." He pointed mid-forearm.

"Good Lord," Monica said, bringing her own hands to her lips. "Honestly?"

"Honestly. I remember my mom telling me Pop teared up as he told her the story. And believe me when I tell you, Pop was a guy who never cried."

"So, what happened then?"

"Well, obviously both kids were pulled from the home." We all nodded that that made sense. "Lex stayed in the hospital and I believe Talia ended up living with the next-door neighbours. Couldn't tell you their names." He reached for the pitcher, paused. "Anyone mind?" No one objected, fluttered hands to get him to complete the task so he could continue the story.

Mug refilled, Ambrose continued. "Anyway, this is where my father comes into the picture. He and his partner, guy named Sydock, questioned Alex's mother, didn't buy what she was selling, and they contacted the proper people to get the kids pulled." He took a mouthful, swallowed, took a second. "Then the father came back from wherever the hell he'd been and took back the kids, moved back into the home."

"Sounds like problem solved," Bear said.

"Unless he kidnapped the kids or something?" Grace said.

"Maybe," Ambrose said, "but this is where it gets all weird." Another fortifying mouthful of beer. Then another for good luck. Or whatever. "This is all going down around the winter of 1976. I wasn't living in New Hope by then, I'd moved out west to figure out what I wanted. But I remember the call I got from my mother."

He stopped then. And he softly, gently placed a finger against the moisture beading the mug, stared at it intently. His voice grew soft.

He propped both elbows on the table. With each person he named, he popped a finger. "In a single night, my father, his partner Sydock, Diane Davis, the two neighbours who'd looked after Talia, Talia's father Glen, and her sister Lex, all...just...disappeared." Seven fingers.

"All of them." He clapped his hands together. "Poof."

There was no sound around the table. All of us sat, first staring at Ambrose, then slowly catching each other's eyes. Randy mouthed *what the fuck?* to no one in particular.

"Ambrose," Grace said. "What do you mean, disappeared?"

"My father was in a police cruiser with Sydock. They'd been in contact with dispatch a few minutes beforehand, but their cruiser was found slammed straight into a rock cut halfway between here and the Cove. Not a single drop of blood. And never a sign of either man ever again."

"Whaaaaaat?" Bear said, drawing the word out.

"Diane Davis was in a jail cell. Then she was gone." He drew his finger down the mug, leaving a wet trail. "The neighbours? It looked like they might have been in bed, but they were gone. From what my mother heard, the covers weren't pulled back, like either had climbed out of bed. It was more like there was sorta shape of them underneath the covers, but like they'd...well, I guess like they'd disappeared."

"I don't think I'm buying this," Gerry said, and Ruthless squeezed his leg in agreement.

"Don't have to. Just telling you what I heard. Oh, and apparently their dog was gone too."

"And what about the rest of the Davis family?"

"Yeah, that was the weirdest. Lex's bed apparently looked slept in. But she and her father Glen were gone. They found Talia in the home the next afternoon, after they'd figured out more than my pop, Sydock, and Diane Davis were gone."

"They found Talia?" Randy said. "Was she freaking?"

"No. Not from what I heard. The police knocked on the door, she answered, they asked where Glen was, she said she didn't know." He looked around at us. "When they went inside, from what Mom told me, she had the TV on and had made popcorn."

"She was watching TV?"

"Yeah. Not a care in the world."

"And this was in '76?" I asked.

"Yes."

"And she was how old?"

Ambrose dug a finger under the badger and scratched. "Around eight or nine, something like that."

"So she's what? You said forty-four?"

"Yeah, thereabouts. Born around '67. Maybe ten years younger 'n me."

"That's some fucked-up shit, right there," Randy said.

"Fucked-up shit," Bear said, raising a mug. Grace smacked him. No one toasted.

"Couldn't be her," I said.

"Why not?" Ambrose said.

"Because the woman I saw was young. Maybe more like our age. I figured she might have known Ray."

"Maybe you're right," Ambrose said. He finished his beer in one long swallow, bumped the mug on the table, and stood. "In fact, I know you're right."

"Why's that?"

"Cuz the last anyone saw of her was just around the time…sorry, Monica," he said, "but last time she was seen was just around 1984."

"That's when all the shit with the school went down, right?" Gerry said.

"No," Monica said, almost whispering. "That's when my dad's bookstore ended up a crater. Both my father and my grandfather were killed."

Shit.

The room was quiet for a long moment while everyone contemplated what they'd just learned.

Ambrose stood through the silence, looking awkward. Then he reached up, scratched the badger, and said, rather sheepishly, "Another round? On the house."

♦ ♦ ♦

OUR PARTY, SUCH as it was, broke up around midnight. Ambrose's story and Monica's revelation took the wind out of our sails faster than someone putting Pink Floyd on at a house party, and served to remind us that we were, in fact, there due to a woman being murdered.

As we rose, Monica touched me on the arm and I turned. She turned slightly away from the rest of the group, so I followed suit. "How you doing, hon? You okay?"

"Yeah, I mostly am." Then, looking closer at her, I said, "How are *you* doing? That was some heavy shit back there."

"I'm okay," she said. "I've mostly dealt with it."

"Mostly."

"Yeah," she said, then gave me a little smile. "I'm a work in progress."

"Good one," I said.

"What can I do for you?"

I knew I could have taken that lasciviously. Hell, a week ago, I likely would have. But not now. "Walk me back to my room?"

"I can do that."

"And, just so it's not awkward," I said, leaning in to keep my voice low, "let's agree here and now that I'm going to kiss you and it's going to be okay."

She smiled. "I'll agree that you can kiss me. I'll reserve judgment on whether it'll be okay or not. Though I'm more hoping for spectacular."

"Nothing like putting pressure on a woman."

We said our good nights to the group and everyone headed off to their rooms. We took a little extra time walking there, ensuring the others were firmly behind their own doors and not eavesdropping. At least, not obviously.

Monica held my hand all the way. We reached the door far too quickly for my taste, but there wasn't much to be done about that.

"So," I said.

"So," she said, smiling.

"This is it."

"It is."

"Spectacular, huh?"

"Nothing less will be acceptable."

I smiled and looked into her eyes. Reaching a hand up, I ran the back of my fingers against her hair, placed a gentle thumb on her cheek, then a palm. She closed her eyes and leaned into my touch. I took in the smoothness of her skin as I grazed my hand lower, my thumb lightly tracing the line of her lips.

I moved my hand to the back of her neck and with gentle, but insistent pressure, brought her down toward me. Much as I wanted to, I didn't rush it, took my time, and by the time our lips met, the air between us seemed charged.

It was the softest of pressure, skin on skin, light enough that I could feel the supple texture of her lips, feel the warm brush of her breath. I wanted to move faster, but faster wouldn't be spectacular.

I took my time.

And, by the end, I was pretty sure of the answer, but still, I pulled back and, with a tentative smile, asked, "So?"

"So," she responded, staring deeply into my eyes, "I've been wanting that to happen for about fifteen years, Ms. Hedges. I spent many, many evenings during my high school years, and, even quite a few post-secondary nights, thinking about that kiss, imagining it, wondering about it. Even after my situation changed, and I shouldn't have been thinking about it at all."

After my situation changed. Not sure what that meant, but I didn't ask. I waited, kept my mouth shut. She had a point and I would give her all the latitude she needed to get there.

"A few years ago, I decided to stop that because, by then, two things were becoming obvious. The first was, it was never going to happen and, the second was, even if it did, it would never live up to all those evenings I spent imagining how it would be."

Now I didn't know what to say. Instead, I held my breath.

"Obviously, I was wrong on both counts." She smiled down at me, then, very softly, said, "Breathe."

I let the breath out.

"Honestly, Lex, you have no idea."

"I think actually I might. But," I said, "as much as I was focused on making it spectacular for you, I will admit to two things."

A sarcastic smirk curled those beautiful lips. "Oh yeah?" she said. "And they are…?"

"First, it was quite spectacular from this side, too."

"Good," she said. "And the second?"

"Second…" I sighed. "I gotta wonder, why the hell did I wait so goddamn long?"

"Um…good things come to those who wait?"

"Yeah," I said, chuckling. Then I looked deeply into her eyes. "Monica, I have to say something to you."

She held my gaze, her eyebrows raised slightly.

"I have to tell you how sorry I am. I have to apologize for fourteen- to seventeen-year-old me. She was such a bitch."

"In some ways, yes, she was. But she was also grappling with a lot, and more than a little confused by some things."

"In some ways, Monica, she still is."

"But in many ways, Lex, like you said, you're a different person. And I'm a different person. I think we've both gone through enough that we now know what we want."

"You might be right."

"I know I'm right. So, shut up and kiss me one more time."

I did. This time, we took a little longer. It transcended spectacular.

When we broke for air, I said, "Okay, one last thing."

"Okay."

"As good as this is going right now, and it really is going good, I don't want to mess it up, okay?"

"I'm not sure what that means."

"Well, it means—and I may be messing it up simply by being so forward by saying what I'm going to say—but…ah shit, Monica." *Be honest.* I broke her gaze, leaned against my door, looked down. "Look, all I've been telling myself for the past few days is that I really need to get my shit together. You know?" I glanced up and saw her nod, but her brows were knitted together.

"Well, to be honest, I've needed to get my shit together for a hell of a long time. But I've never really had a reason to. My shit's not together, but it's not falling apart. Well, it wasn't falling apart until recently anyway."

"Sorry, Lex, not sure I'm following."

"Probably because I'm more talking to myself than I am to you. Sorry." I took a deep breath. "Okay, what I want to say is, I'm not sure, if I asked you, if you'd come into the room with me. But I'm not going to ask you. It's not because I don't *want* you to come in, it's just—"

"You want to take your time. Make sure your shit's together so you don't mess it up."

"…Yeah."

"I get it."

"Do you?"

"I do."

"Okay."

"So, kiss me one more time, then say good night."

"Good night?" I asked.

She obviously read my expression. "Yes, just good night. I'll see you tomorrow."

I kissed her.

"Good night," I said.

"Good night," she said. Then she reached into her purse, pulled out her car keys, and headed back down the hall. I watched her go.

About halfway down the hall, she stopped as Bear stuck his head out, glanced first at Monica, then down the hall to me. "Holy shit, Hedges, took you long enough."

Then we heard Grace yell, "Robert!" and Bear was yanked violently back into his room and the door slammed.

I looked at Monica, she looked at me, and in perfect synchronicity, we both shrugged at each other. She said, "For the record, Ms. Hedges, *if* you had asked, I *would* have said yes. But I like what you're doing here. This is better. Means you're planning on staying in town a little longer." Then she laughed.

Her laugh was music.

She gave me a small wave, and then she walked to the end, made the turn, and was gone.

It was only then that I thought to close my mouth.

Chapter Six

THE MORNING BEGAN with a very loud, very insistent knocking at my hotel room door.

"The hell?" I said as I struggled to both untangle myself from the bed sheets and to sit upright. I wasn't entirely successful with either endeavour, but I did manage some progress. Accepting that this was going to be as good as it got today, I dragged myself and half my bedclothes over to the door and clawed ineffectually at the door handle.

Yes, folks, I thought, *the struggle is real.*

Finally, I somehow managed to unlock the arcane secrets of door management. When I did, I was expecting one of the guys, or possibly Monica. Maybe even Annie or Ambrose.

But a cop? Hindsight told me I should have expected it from the way the knock had been delivered with such authority. Only police knocked like that.

Still, the uniform brought me up short. "Oh," I said. "Hey!" Thank god I threw on pyjamas before bed.

"Good morning," the officer said. "Lex Hedges?"

"Yes, sir." *Sir?* I mentally facepalmed myself. What was it about law enforcement that made me act and talk stupid?

"Constable Gustafsen. May I come in?"

"Yeah," I said. "Yeah, yeah." I waved him in. Then it hit me. "Gustafsen? Norman?"

Gustafsen smiled. "The very one. How are you, Lex?"

"I'm good. Damn, Norm, you got *big*." I stopped. "Wait, shit, is it cool to call you Norm?"

"Normally no, but here?" He looked around as though to ensure there was no one else in the room. "Yes, of course."

"Okay." I pulled the chair out from under the desk, motioned to Gustafsen to sit. I pulled the curtains open to let in the morning light, then smoothed a section of the bed and sat.

"Listen, I just woke up. You wanna grab a coffee at the restaurant?"

"Maybe in a bit," he said. "I'd like to talk to you a bit first."

"Okay, not a problem." I dug my fingers into my eyes to scrape out the last of the sleep. "But give me a minute?" I hooked a thumb to the bathroom.

"Oh. Yeah. I woke you up." It wasn't a question. "Of course. Take your time."

I went in, closed the door, took one of my patented ten-minute-long, morning-after-a-long-night-of-drinking pees. Kelly used to say, "I swear to god, your bladder must be the size of a swimming pool." I flushed, washed my hands, then ran my wet hands through my hair, trying, and mostly succeeding, to wrangle it down.

As I came back out, I said, "Sorry about the wait," and positioned myself on the bed, my hands supporting me on the tangled sheets. "What's up?"

"Normally I'd call first." Gustafsen emitted a small sigh. "I came by with bad news. Your brother Ray was killed last night. Sorry for your loss, Lex."

That stopped me. My fingers remained on the sheets of the bed, but it wasn't until Gustafsen glanced down at them that I realized I'd dug into them, pulling the sheets into knots. I jerked at the realization and unclenched them slowly, squinted at Gustafsen. "Say what?"

"Raymond Hedges was killed last night."

"When you say…killed…?"

"He was murdered," he said. "Looks like it was by the same person or persons who killed your mother a few days ago."

"What?" I stuffed the heels of my palms into my eyes, rubbing. "Sonuvabitch." My mind was skidding around like a car on ice trying to get traction. There was a lot of effort going into getting things going, but ultimately, very little was actually happening. I dropped my hands. Gustafsen gave me the time I needed. "I'm sorry, I'm… Shit, I don't even know what to say."

"How about I ask you a few questions, give you a chance to process?"

I nodded, not really looking at anything. "Fine. Yeah."

He pulled a small pad and pen from one of his many pockets, flipped to a clean page, wrote something at the top, then said, "When was the last time you saw Ray?"

"Yesterday, at my mother's funeral. We all went out to the gravesite for the ceremony, then a bunch of us skipped from there. I think he was walking back to the church with my fath…with Marcus for the get-together afterward."

"You didn't attend that?"

"No."

"Mind if I ask why?"

"No," I said. "I don't think it's a secret that I really don't have a lot to do with my family. Hell, this is the first time I've seen my father or brother since I left town in 2001. The World Trade Center was still standing the last time I saw them."

"All right. Every family's got their issues, so I'm not going to pry," he said, but I sensed an unspoken "yet" in there. "Can you tell me where you went?"

"Right here. Came back to the restaurant, had a few beers."

"Anybody with you?"

I rhymed off the names. Gustafsen nodded as he noted them. "I assume they'll verify your presence?"

"Yes, they will," I said. "Hell, most of them are in rooms down the hall."

"Excellent. And what did you do after that?"

"Here. Bed."

"What time was that?"

"I'd say just after midnight? Maybe twelve-thirty?"

"And you were here until…"

"Until you knocked this morning."

"Nobody with you?" he said.

"No," I said. *Has he heard about Monica?* I wondered. *Randy likely would have filled him in.*

"Norman, I'm not gonna play dumb here. The big elephant in the room is you're asking me this because you consider me a suspect?"

"Did you threaten to kill your brother recently?"

"Oh for chrissakes," I said. "Is that what this is about?"

"Did you?"

"Tell him I'd kill him?" I couldn't help the smile that came to my face. "Show me two siblings who haven't threatened to kill each other over the years."

"But how many of them are still threatening it in their late twenties?"

I barked a sarcastic laugh. "Probably more than you'd think, but okay, point taken. Norman, you know Ray. My guess is you've been a cop here long enough, you've likely had a few run-ins with him yourself. He's not exactly the salt of the earth."

"Okay."

"Yes, he showed up here a couple of nights before I put my mother in the ground. He made a fool of himself, as per usual. I shut him down—*verbally*, I might add—and I told him if he came looking for me again, I'd kill him. I could have just as easily said I'd kick his ass. Poor choice of words."

"Yes." He made a couple more notes in his book. "You don't seem overly surprised or upset about his death."

"You gotta understand," I said, splaying my hands out in front of me. "I've basically been waiting for this news in some format for years. He does drugs, he steals, he fucks other guys' girlfriends, and he likes to start fights. His mouth writes cheques his ass can't cash. Any one of those things could get him killed. The fact that he regularly multitasks on them?" I raised a hand up, up, up. "Just ups the odds." I dropped my hand to my lap.

"You wonder why I'm not surprised? That's why. Why am I not upset? Well, that'll take a lot longer, but the short answer is, he's an asshole. Always was, always would have been. He's twenty-nine years old and still lives in the home he was born in, and doesn't have a job, aside from pissing people off. I got to the end of my rope with that bullshit a hell of a long time ago." I dropped my head, let out a slow breath. *Like Monica told me yesterday at the funeral…breathe, Lex. Just breathe.*

When I was a little calmer, I continued. "If you're telling me he died in a similar fashion to Mom, then yeah, I feel bad about that. I wouldn't wish that on my worst enemy, and believe me, Ray fits that bill fairly closely. But I still wouldn't wish that on him. So yeah, the *manner* in which he died bugs me, but the *fact* that he's dead? No, not so much. I don't really have a hell of a lot of sympathy for my family." I huffed out a breath. "To be blunt, Norm, I don't consider them family at all. The ones down the hall are more family to me than Ray, Marcus, or Sandra Hedges ever were."

Gustafsen sat back. "Huh. That's…quite a statement right there." He captured his pen under his thumb, used the other hand to rub a hand over his close-cropped scalp. "All right," he said. "Off the record, no, I really don't think you had anything to do with Ray's death. Or your mother's. Point of business, can you account for your whereabouts the night of your mother's death?"

"I covered a lot of this with Constable Roberts."

"I know, but I don't think he went there," he said. "Indulge me?" I nodded. I didn't really sense any agenda or any malice.

You're good, Gutty. Your fellow officer didn't quite cross all the t's and dot all the i's, and you've quietly got his back. My respect for Gustafsen rose.

"That was last Friday?" I said.

"Correct."

"Yeah, I was playing a gig down in Windsor."

The cop waggled a finger at me. "That's right. I heard something about that. You're in a cover band?"

"Tribute band, but yeah."

"Heart, right?"

"Right."

"What do you call yourself?"

"Well, it's a full band. I don't like the name, but the good ones were taken. We're called Dreamboat Annie."

"After the song on the first album?"

"You know your Heart."

"I do. My wife says Ann's screechy, and she hates them. Me? I love them." Gustafsen chuckled. "And you play who? Ann Wilson?"

"That's right. The screechy one." Most people, unless they were either music freaks or Heart freaks, couldn't keep the two sisters straight at gunpoint. I figured Gustafsen had done his homework before coming here.

"Again, you can get someone to corroborate your evening?"

I smirked. "About a hundred older folks who dress too young for their age," I said. "But yeah, my band'll back me up. We didn't even get back to Toronto until about six or seven Saturday morning. Got the call from Ray not long after I got home." *After Kelly came in two hours behind me.*

"If you provide some contact info, that should do it."

I pulled some stationery and a pen from the nightstand. I located my phone, pulled up the contacts, and transferred some info onto the paper. When I was done, I passed it to Gustafsen, who glanced at it, folded it, and put it in a pocket.

"Thanks," he said.

"No problem. Any more questions for me?"

"Just one," Gustafsen said. "Any idea who might do this?"

"Not really, as I told your colleague. Anyone. My brother pissed off a lot of people through the years."

"But there's also your mother."

"Yeah, she was mostly harmless." I considered for a moment. "Nothing's coming to mind, but if I remember something later, I'll definitely let you know."

Gustafsen reached into another pocket, pulled out a very nice business card case, pulled a card from it, and held it between two fingers. I took it, looked at it, then set it on the desk. "That's it," he said. "That's all my questions. Again, for what it's worth, sorry for your loss."

"Appreciate it," I said, mentally tossing that sentiment straight in the garbage. "I've got one for you."

"Shoot," he said.

"Marcus. Does he know?"

To his credit, he made no reaction to me calling him by his name instead of Dad. "Yes, another officer should be letting him know now."

"Damn," I said. "Who'd the officer piss off to get that task?"

Gustafsen decided — likely wisely — to let that one slide.

"Okay," I said, "I've got the same question for you. Do *you* have any ideas or suspects?"

"Not that I can really speak of."

"Okay," I said. "Then I just have one last question."

"Go ahead."

"Half of my family's been brought down in the past few days. Should I be worried?"

"I'm not going to say no, Lex. That would be pretty stupid." He folded his notebook and stowed it. "We're going to have a cruiser swing by the hotel on a frequent basis. We're doing the same at your father's place."

"Makes sense."

"I'll also tell you to take some extra precaution when you're out in the boonies in your car. That's where both Ray and your mother were taken. Keep the doors locked, let someone know when you're leaving and when you should be arriving. Actually," he said, then pulled his business card from the desk, pulled out his pen, and scribbled something on it.

"I normally wouldn't do this, but it's you. I've known you for years. That's my cell. You can text me if you want to let me know your whereabouts."

"You sure?"

"Wouldn't offer if I wasn't sure."

I nodded. "Anything else?"

"Keep your cell phone close at hand. If there's another car travelling in the same direction, stick with it as much as possible."

"I can do that."

"How much longer you in town for?"

"Well, to be honest, I was going to try and escape soon. But I'm guessing there's another funeral to attend now, though, to be honest, I may not make that one. And…well, there's other stuff."

"Would some of that other stuff be Monica Holt?"

"Constable Gustafsen, have you been checking up on me?"

"Hell yes, I have. Wouldn't be much of a cop if I didn't."

"And I hear you're a pretty damn good one."

He rolled his eyes and smiled. "That would be cousin Randy, my personal PR agent."

We shared a laugh, but the presence of a uniformed officer of the law tended to shorten any levity to a bare minimum.

"Well, Lex, it's been good to see you again. Sorry it's been under these circumstances." He slapped his palms on the sharp creases of his uniform trousers and stood. "I'll let you get dressed and grab that coffee now. Sorry to take have taken so much of your time."

"Don't worry about it. Good to see you as well. Say hi to Kayla for me, would you?"

"Of course." He put out a hand and we shook. With a nod, he moved to the door. "Be careful and call that number if you need anything," he said, nodding to the card on the desk.

"Will do."

♦ ♦ ♦

IT TURNED OUT that today was a busy day. I met with Gustafsen once more, as well as with one other man and three women.

♦ ♦ ♦

THE FIRST MEETING was Marcus.

After Gustafsen left, I grabbed a quick shower and headed to the restaurant for breakfast and coffee. None of the group was in the room. I figured I'd either missed them during the questioning, or they hadn't made it yet. Either way, I was on my own for breakfast, which wasn't necessarily a bad thing. Gave me time to kick around all the information and see what I could make of it.

I polished off two eggs, too much bacon to be healthy, hash browns, toast, and two tall glasses of orange juice. I was fixing my first coffee of the day when he entered the room and, without even the briefest of pauses, headed directly to my table.

He likely knew if he asked permission to sit, I'd never have granted it, so instead, he simply pulled the chair out, sat down, and leaned back, swiping his too-long hair back.

I watched all this dispassionately, stirring my coffee. Without looking up, I jutted my jaw toward the mug and said, "I'd offer you one, but I don't want you to stay that long." Only then did I look up. "Ray's dead. What do you want from me?"

He was fairly put together today. Maybe a holdover from the funeral yesterday.

"You know what I want from you, Alexandra." He reached a hand out to touch me, said, "The same thing I've always wanted." I jerked my arm violently away before he could make contact. It wasn't even a voluntary reaction. I'd recoiled without thought. Sheer reflex.

He dropped his hand to the table again.

"You're one sick bastard, Marcus," I said. "You know that, right?" I pulled the spoon out, laid it on the saucer, then lifted the cup to my mouth. I blew lightly across its surface.

"I am your father, Alexandra," he said. "I expect you to show me some respect."

"Fuck your respect, Mar-cus," I said, purposely drawing the name out. A verbal twist of the knife. "And fuck you, too."

"I don't understand what the prob—"

"No," I said, cutting him off. *Jesus Christ, will I never be rid of this shit?*

Staring at my cup, I said, "I'm not going to talk about that. I think I made myself quite clear just before I walked out of the house all those years ago. I've spent a lot of time and a lot of money on therapy learning to not think about what you put me through." I sipped at the coffee. "So, the better question is, why are you here?"

"I want you to come and stay with me."

"Aw, you miss me?"

"You're my daughter."

"I love how you dodge those questions."

"I would be happier if you were in the house with me."

"So the whack job who's killing the rest of the family can get a buy one, get one free deal?"

"How can you be this callous when you've lost both your mother and brother?"

I paused with the cup partway to my mouth, flicked my eyes to him. *Didn't I give you shit for your callousness just a few days ago?* "I learned from the best." I took another sip.

He paused then, then stood at the other side of my table and tented his fingers on its surface. "Alexandra," he said, and there was something different in his voice. Something unfamiliar. "I know Raymond mentioned this to you, but…"

"Chrissakes, spit it out," I said. I could literally feel him attempting to manipulate me. Sinking his emotional claws into me.

"Fair enough. I have been having…issues. Mentally. I feel like I'm blacking out, but Raymond told me that I slip into a delusional state."

If he was looking for me to respond, I wasn't going to give him the satisfaction. If he was going to slip those claws into me, he was going to do it all on his own.

"Anyway, these 'spells,' as your brother called them, can last from a few minutes to a few hours. When they do, I'm helpless."

"That's gotta suck," I said, infusing the three words with as much disdain and sarcasm as I could.

"Alexandra, I'm telling you, I need you."

"And I'm telling you no. I'm sure there's some sort of personal care workers you can hire. Mom had pretty good benefits."

"I'm asking for your help, Lex."

I'd been about to take a sip of my coffee, but when he said that I stopped, then slowly, carefully set my cup down. *Lex. He never calls me Lex.* He watched me as I picked up a napkin and wiped my mouth. Then, finally, I met his gaze.

"I'm going to say this only once, Marcus. You may have fathered me, but I am…in *no way*…your daughter. Not by any stretch of the imagination."

"Alexandra…" *Ah, "Lex" didn't work, so back to the full name again.*

"Do you understand what I'm saying?"

"Alexandra…"

"A simple nod or shake of the head will suffice, Marcus."

He remained quite still, staring down at me. I read neither hurt nor disappointment in his expression. It was more calculating observation than anything.

He'd expected this. Planned for it. He has something else up his sleeve.

"So, is that a no?"

"Coming to stay with you?" I smiled. "Yeah, that's a definite, hard no."

"Will you attend Raymond's funeral?"

"Is there a single good reason why I should?"

"He's your brother."

"You know what?" I set the cup down, leaned in, my forearms on the table. "Husbands and wives divorce each other every day for the simple reason that they've learned they despise the other one. Happens every goddamn day. I did that with the three of you. I divorced you and Ray ten years ago because seeing *you* made my skin crawl, and dealing with *him* made me want to puke. You got Mom in the deal because, if she wasn't smart enough to walk away from you, she deserved all the shit she got." I picked up my coffee again. "If that's the best you got, you got nothing."

"How about because I want you there?"

"You're sinking fast. I don't give a flying fuck where you want me. I know where you wanted me when I was a teenager and I didn't play then. I won't play now." I stood, pulled my wallet out, and dropped some bills on the table, likely far more than I should, but I just needed to get away from him. Again.

"I'm gonna tell you the same thing I told you the first time I walked away from you, *Marcus*." I picked up my coffee, used it to gesture toward him. "Fuck you."

Then I turned and left the room. I didn't look back.

And the hand holding my coffee shook only a little bit.

◆ ◆ ◆

I GOT BACK to my room, slid the key into the lock—faintly impressed that it was still an old-fashioned key—opened the door, and found my second visitor waiting for me. I hadn't expected either of the first two visits, but this one? Hell no. I walked in, started, and slopped my damn coffee all over the rug.

"Jesus Christ," I said.

She stood near the window facing the parking lot, dressed in jeans and a T-shirt. At my entrance, she turned to face me.

And I thought, *Wow.*

She filled out those jeans and T-shirt like very few could. But there was more than just a physicality to her. There was...what? I couldn't seem to nail it down. So, I took a moment to just try and figure it out.

She gave me the moment.

The shirt was striking. The image on it had some slim, androgynous guy, cocaine thin, with platinum blond hair and wearing a skinny tie. He stood in front of a slightly overexposed white background that had no other details. It looked vaguely eighties, and vaguely Thin White Duke Bowie, but there was something off about that detail that I couldn't put my finger on. The shirt said *Japan* in ragged red letters and *Quiet Life* in clean black ones.

Her hair was still pulled back in a high ponytail, but the angle she stood at revealed its full length. It ended somewhere south of the seat of her jeans. She had a hand dug into her pocket. There was a lumpy bulge in there that clicked as her fingers first found, then manipulated it. *What the hell's in there?*

It was the woman from the funeral. I supposed I should be shocked by her being in my room, but after a visit from both Gustafsen and Marcus, and the fact that Ray had been killed sometime in the past few hours, I'd just blown out most of my dwindling stores of shock when I slopped the coffee. Now those stores were fully depleted and needed time to recharge.

"You here to kill me, now?"

The woman betrayed no surprise at my accusation. Instead, she said, "No."

"I don't know how you got in here, but there's cops—"

"Everywhere," she said. "I understand. They're not my concern right now." She paused, cocked her head to the side slightly, and said, "You are."

"You're concerned about me. Interesting." I set what was left of my coffee down on some papers on the dresser to avoid the ring, leaned against it, indicated the desk chair much as I'd done an hour earlier with Gustafsen. She nodded and sat.

"You broke into my hotel room the morning I find out Ray's been murdered to tell me you're concerned about me. Wanna explain that one?"

"Of course." She smiled.

"Let's start with the things we both know, okay?"

I nodded. It seemed reasonable. I reached for my coffee.

"I'm Talia Davis. Ambrose McDonald filled you in a bit on my story. Of course, he didn't know most of the important details, but for the most part, he was surprisingly accurate."

"He said you were pushing your midforties." I looked at her frankly and openly, obviously taking in her details. "I've seen a lot of women over the years at my shows, and I think I have a pretty solid handle on guessing someone's age. I've seen young girls trying to look older, and far, *far*, too many older women trying to look younger. There's only so much you can do."

One last, frank stare at her. In the giveaway areas. The skin around her neck, which was firm and tight. Around her eyes, clear of all but the faintest of lines. Her upper arms, also firm. Jeans could disguise a fair amount, but there were no telltale middle-aged spread. And her breasts were…well, they were braless and stunning. There was absolutely no way those breasts were forty-odd years old, unless they were fake.

"If you're any more than twenty-seven, then I'm way off my game."

"October thirteenth," she said. "1967. Just missed the Summer of Love."

"There's no way."

"There is. I am. You're way off your game."

"Okay," I said, putting my hands up. "You win. I think we have bigger fish to fry than guessing your age."

"Yes." She smiled and it was right then that I realized *exactly* how beautiful she was. Deal-with-the-devil beautiful. Her lips were full. Her teeth not perfect, but perfectly white. She had that very small overbite that all the best models had. "The second point is, I didn't kill your mother or brother."

"And I'm just supposed to take your word for it?"

"Yes."

"Why is that?"

"Because I know who did."

Okay, that shut me up for a moment or two. To buy a couple of seconds to process, I took a slow sip, then set down my coffee. I kept my hand on the mug for a moment, then met her eyes. "You know who did this?"

"I do."

"How long have you known?"

"Since your mother died."

"And you didn't tell the police?"

"I did not."

"Why?"

"I have my reasons. But the short answer is, the police are simply not equipped to deal with this."

"What, this is Hannibal Lecter we're dealing with or something? Some kind of diabolically evil genius?"

"No," she said. "Nothing quite as…pedestrian as that."

"Hannibal's pedestrian?"

"We're getting off topic again."

"We are. So, how can this killer be caught? Assuming, of course, that I actually believe you."

"You will," she said, and smiled that perfect smile again. "And I think there's really only one way to catch this killer. But you need to do two things first."

"I do?"

"Yes."

"I don't think so."

"If you don't, you're putting yourself in danger."

"Really." I tried to infuse the word with all the sarcasm I could possibly muster. I put everything I had into it.

"Really," she said, apparently unimpressed with my effort. "I know you still don't believe me, but I will tell you that, should you not do these two things, you *will* be the next one to die. And while I can't promise it, I'm quite certain that, as horribly painful as your mother's and brother's deaths were, yours will be more so."

Okay, full disclosure, she was getting under my skin a bit. "And you say this because…?"

"Because I know who is doing the killing."

"So you say. But you can't tell me."

"I can," she said. "I choose not to."

"You're quite frustrating to have a conversation with."

"My mother used to tell me the same thing."

"Before she disappeared?"

"Yes."

"How did she disappear? Where did she go?"

Talia simply watched me.

"You did it," I said. "It was you."

She didn't answer.

"If you could do that shit when you were a kid, why can't you just use it to help me now?"

"I am using what I can to help you."

"So use your powers and do something, dammit."

"No," she said. She shifted her disconcerting gaze away from me for the first time since I'd come in. She scanned around the room as though she didn't know where to settle her attention. Her voice dropped to a dark, ominous whisper. "I…lost most of my…ability."

"Almost sounds like someone stole it from you."

"In a manner of speaking, yes," she said. "If I still possessed the…ability…" *Does she look uncomfortable?* I thought so. "If I still had it, I would have been able to deal with this on your behalf."

"And why are you so interested in helping me?"

"Because I was called here."

"Pardon me?"

"I made a promise a long time ago, and I'm here to try and fulfill it now."

"Ambrose says you haven't been seen since Monica's dad's bookstore was destroyed. The Last Word, it was called."

"Yes, I'm familiar with the store, and Dan and Stanley Holt."

"Did you destroy that place?"

"Not on purpose, but I had, unfortunately, a hand in it, yes."

"And Monica's father and grandfather?"

"I…" And then this strange woman hesitated. "Lex," she said, "I'm not ready to talk about that."

"So, I just have to take everything you say —"

She raised her voice just a small amount, but it shut me up. "I said, I am *not* ready to discuss that."

Just that barely noticeable rise in tone and volume? Yeah, she scared the shit out of me.

"Fine," I said. "Who called you?"

"It's enough that the one who called me will know." *Will know. Not knows. Will know. Okay.*

"And you're here because this person who *will* know…asked you to come."

"Close enough."

"No other reason?"

She crossed her arms and leaned back. "Because it benefits me as well." She brought her eyes back around to me. "Protecting you protects me as well."

"So, this isn't entirely altruistic. You're in this for you."

"I am."

"So why can't you just go steal this ability back and take care of business yourself?" I placed a small emphasis on *ability*, and she seemed to pick up on this. Obviously, this was code for something else, but I couldn't figure out what the hell it was.

"My old ability is now beyond my reach."

"Can't take it back?"

"No."

"Can't get help to get it back within reach?"

"No." Funny how a single word could shut down a line of conversation.

"Therefore, somehow, it's down to me."

"It is."

"And I'm to simply believe you when you say I need to do this."

"Somewhat," she said, rocking her hand. "I believe I can show you that I do still retain the ability to gain certain insights. Make certain connections."

"Okay," I said, leaning back and crossing my arms. "Show me."

She eased forward. "Would you like me to tell you about what your father did to make you leave New Hope?"

The reaction was as immediate and involuntary as when Marcus had tried to touch my hand fifteen minutes ago. My body tensed, prepping for either fight or flight. I felt the muscles in my jaw bunch as I ground my teeth together. She couldn't know what Marcus had done. She would be wrong, but just the thought of that...

"No."

"I see you can close off a conversation as easily as I can with that word." *Did I say that? No, I just thought it. Didn't I?*

"I'm not ready to talk about that," I said.

"As you say." She nodded once, eyes downcast. "Let's talk about something slightly safer." She leaned back, once again crossing her arms under those remarkable breasts, which, of course, only accentuated exactly how remarkable they were. "Let's talk about your brother, Ray."

Not much safer ground, that.

"You didn't really start hating him until he was seventeen." *She can't know.*

"You were fifteen when the whole issue with Kayla came up, and you were done." *How can she know?*

"But you only heard his version of the events. You don't know the truth. You don't know Kayla's truth."

♦ ♦ ♦

"I CAN *TELL* you these truths," she said, and stood up, "but I don't know if it would be enough to convince you. I think I need to *show* you. Will you indulge me?" She crossed the room toward me, a hand outstretched.

"Depends," I said. "What do you want me to do?"

"Just hold my hand," she said, turning her hand palm up.

She was seriously creeping me out. Against my better judgment, I ignored the feeling, pushed down the fight-or-flight response, and acquiesced. I brought my hand up to hers, my palm meeting hers. As soon as flesh met flesh, her cool fingers wrapped around mine in a firm, yet surprisingly light grip.

I looked up into her beautiful, flawless face and felt my mind wash away. I was no longer Lex. I was someone else.

Jesus Christ! I thought. *I'm Ray.*

◆ ◆ ◆

I CAN'T FUCKIN' get enough.

Sure, I bang other chicks on pretty regular basis. Don't hurt that I supply a lot of the drugs, which is good for making them either desperate or unconscious. Either way's fine by me. I'll take a desperate fuck. Or a dead one. Of course, with my regular thing too, I'm getting it two or three times a week, more if I get some gash to the stage area at school.

But even with all that, I gotta get more sex. Between my regular lay, my hand, and whatever poon I'm getting on the side, hell I'm blowing my load a couple of times a day. Shit, there's days I've gotta jerk off in the school washrooms just to take the edge off. That ain't cool. The school washrooms are *skank*.

Last couple of weeks though, this Kayla Young girl? *Damn.* The new chick, her parents just recently moved to the area. Noticed her in the halls, but our lockers ain't far apart and I'm diggin' what I see. Then again, duh, there ain't much out there that I don't like. I'm one'a them equal opportunity ballers. Don't matter if they're fat or ugly, just means they're easier and try harder. And deniability is *totally* easier with a fat or ugly chick. Any time I get accused of that shit, I'm all, "Hell no, dude, you gotta have a grudge against your dick to fuck that!"

But I still do. All the time.

The school hall near our lockers is quiet, only a couple of dweebs standing around, shooting the shit, so I'm finally able to get a better look this Kayla chick. And damn if she don't look right back, almost defiant-like. I feel the Beast getting hard right here and now.

Then I remember, fuck, that I already told Moms I'd be home right after school, which also means I've gotta give Lex the Lez a ride too, but I watch Kayla's sweet ass as she reaches for a book in her locker, and I have a plan. Damn right I do. My fucking hands are all sweaty at the thought of getting my hands on that ass.

I've gotta angle my books in front of my dick so she won't see how hungry the Beast is, then I mosey all cool-like on over to where she's just finishing up at her locker. She gives me a smile.

I work my Laser Ray magic and it doesn't take long to get her to agree to let me drive her home, even though she lives about a thousand miles away, in the Opie. She smiles again, though, and I know she fuckin' knows what I'm after.

I'm totally driving her home. Which means I'm totally stealing the truck and leaving Lezzie Lex high and dry and hoofing it home. Again. Fuck it. Who cares? Builds fuckin' character.

Lex is gonna get all bitchy about it, but holy fuck, she'd just have to jam another tampon up her cunt and stop her fucking menstruating.

Plan nailed down, I go and hit the can. I've got just enough time to rub one out before my next class.

♦ ♦ ♦

THE PRESSURE ON my hand lessened slightly and I was me—I was Lex—again.

"What? What just—"

I feel like my head was under water. I'd just come up for air…

"Shhh," she said, "we're just getting started."

…when I was pushed under again.

Then I was Ray again.

◆ ◆ ◆

DRIVING HER HOME after school, I play it cool and ask if she minds if I take a different route. She says she guesses that would be okay.

Yeah, you totally know what's gonna go down, I think. *Mostly, it's gonna be you going down. On my Beast.*

I steer the truck down a secluded and seldom-used logging road about ten miles outside of Opeongo. That way, it's a quick drop-off once we've done the deed and I wouldn't need to talk to her that much. Maybe just a little small talk. Teachers and homework and shit. Just enough to get the point across that this doesn't mean fuck all and to keep her damn mouth shut so no one finds out. Not that it's gonna be horrible to brag about fucking this bitch. Goddamn, she's smokin' hot.

I park in a small, shaded turnaround just off the logging road where we can't be seen.

Dumb bitch asks me what I'm doing.

"Getting comfortable," I say.

"I thought you were taking me home," she says.

I'm gonna drive *you home,* then *I'm gonna take you home,* I think. "Eventually," is what I say.

Then, smooth as baby shit, I put my hand on her thigh. She looks down at it, then back at me.

"What—"

"Oh, come on," I say, cutting her off. I'm a little irritated now, if I'm honest. Which I am. "We both know what we're here for, so come on, ante up."

I switch hands, my left now on her thigh, even higher up, where the heat and the honey is, and with my other hand I start tugging at the buttons of her blouse.

"No, Ray—"

Yeah, whatever. I ignore her, feeling the blood pumping in my hands, in my face, in the Beast. I'm gonna have to unleash him soon.

She clamps her hands down on my wrists, and she almost sounds like she's ready to cry. And she fuckin' says, "Stop!"

"What the hell?"

"Maybe I misjudged you," she says. "I thought you were a nice guy. Every time I saw you talking to people, they were always laughing with you. I thought it might be fun to hang out with you as well. Maybe you could make me laugh."

So that's the only reason she agreed to let me drive her home? She had some stupid idea that maybe I was going to charm and fucking romance her into being my girlfriend or something?

Okay, I think. *Stupid, but I can work with this.* I back off the hands a bit. I'm willing to work a bit for the meal.

"Well, yeah," I say. "Okay, yeah. I *am* a funny guy." I bust out a sad face, look down. "But it's kinda like that tears of a clown thing, y'know? Everyone sees this guy that's laughing and joking, but inside, there's a whole other guy. A lonely guy. A sad guy. I figured you could, you know, cheer me up?"

"Oh, Ray," she says. "I'm sorry. I didn't know."

"Yeah, no one knows, but I've been like this a long time." I keep looking down, trying really hard not to bust out laughing. "And I'm so lonely." *And the money shot…now*, I think, looking up and right into her eyes. "I just want to be held." I do my damnedest to work up a tear, but goddamn it, it won't come.

No biggie. That *I just want to be held* line is fuckin' gold. Chicks dig it.

And right on cue, she leans in and fuckin' holds me. And that's when I know I'm gonna have to work a bit slower than normal, but I also know I'm damn well getting what I came for.

♦ ♦ ♦

I DO. MOSTLY. It ain't enough, but it'll do, pig. It'll do.

It takes a while, but once I get her sticking her tongue in my mouth, guaranteed I'm home free. I start in on her blouse buttons again. Her hands move as though to stop me and I think, *fuck, here we go*, but then she lets me.

At some point, instead of wrestling with getting her pants off in the confines of the car, I coax her out and get her naked right there in the middle of nowhere. I take a second to make sure she knows I ain't forgetting about her needs and feel her up. Okay, she digs it, but it's totally to make sure she's wet and ready for the main event. But first, I gotta get my dick in her mouth, because once that happens, ain't no way I'm going near her mouth again, that shit's just gross. And fucking gay. Besides, some girls won't go down on the Beast once it's been up their cooter. No way I'm taking that chance here.

I spin us around so my ass is against the warm metal of the truck door and I pull my signature Laser Ray move: I'm kissing her, but I'm also bringing both hands up to her head and slowly pushing those lips down toward the Beast.

She resists a little at first. Fuck man, don't they all? But I keep the pressure on. She gives me a look and I give her a smile and nod of encouragement and then she's lowering herself, kissing my neck, my chest, my belly…

...and then she fucking stops? What the hell?

So fucking close. I keep all the swear words inside and look down. "I've never..." She stops, looks down at my monster. "I've never done...that."

Oh, well. Shit. That's a bit of a bummer.

"It's easy," I say. "Don't worry, I'll help you."

She's a little skittish, but she's a trooper. She grips me. Then, looking up, she takes a long time, but finally...finally...opens her mouth.

And it's that sight that does it. The sight of her naked, the sun dappling her shoulders and ass, the Beast in her hand, out in the great outdoors like this, that I just can't fucking stop myself. Wouldn't even try if I could.

I don't try.

Instead, I curl my fists tight into her hair and jam the Beast deep into her mouth. I dig this part, seeing her eyes first go wide, then water. She coughs and gags and that just fuckin' gets me going more, so I let go of one side of her head and slap her across the cheek—yeah, maybe a little harder than I should, but hey, I can't cage my passion—and I yell, "Suck it! Suck it, you whore!"

And in there somewhere—between her crying and choking, and me pumping and slapping and gripping her hair so tight I can feel my own fingernails in my palms—I fucking cum with a titanic roar, thrusting even harder, gripping her even harder, ignoring her choking until my balls are fucking drained.

That's when I let her go and, gagging and vomiting, she falls back on her ass on the dirt and gravel, her mouth looking like a glazed donut. I shake the hairs from my hands that I'd pulled from her head with my uncaged passion. When I look up, she's angled off to the side, with a wet glop of puke soaking into the dirt between her hands.

Gross.

I check the time and I see we've been out here damn near two hours, counting the travel time. "Holy crap!" I say. "I should'a been home a while ago!" I grab the clothes from the hood of the truck, sorting hers into a quick, jumbled pile. "Crap!" I say again. "Listen, I gotta get going. You okay to get home from here on your own?"

She just sits on the road, drool and spunk running from her reddened mouth. As I'm getting dressed, I notice her cheeks are pretty red too. Damn, I'd done a job on her. Looked like she had a sunburn. But the drool and the jizz and the red cheeks? Gotta say. Fuckin' hot. I could go again. But the time.

Fuck!

She doesn't look at me, only stares, drooling, at the dirt.

Yeah, okay, whatever. I'm taking her silence for a yes. "I'll get the rest of your clothes," I say helpfully, and reach into the passenger side for her bra and blouse and backpack and shit. Gathering all her shit together, I put them in a pile on the grass beside her.

"So," I say. "Thanks. That was great. You really did cheer me up." This is always the awkward part. I'm sure as hell not gonna kiss her on the mouth. So, I pat the top of her head. I mean, yeah, I shot my wad, but really, she wasn't all that good. Once is enough for her. Too bad. Rockin' ass, which I didn't even get to tap. "I'll see you around school, okay?"

I scoot around to the driver's side, get in, and, without a backward glance, pull out and drive away.

Lex is gonna totally rag on me.

♦ ♦ ♦

AND THEN I was out of Ray's head and breathing shallow to prevent myself from vomiting.

I'd known Ray had done something—something bad—to

Kayla. I'd heard the rumours. But, hearing stories that may or may not be true, and this…experiencing it. *Jesus fucking Christ,* I thought. *If he wasn't dead, I'd kill him.*

But Talia wasn't finished with me yet. "Two more," she said.

Before I could even try and prepare myself, I was in someone else's head.

♦ ♦ ♦

Good God! Will it ever stop? When is it enough?

I stare at my locker. *Damn it. Damn them.*

Damn Ray.

I don't understand this town's need to punish any and all who live here. It seems that everyone here is on a downward spiral, and it's apparently not enough to go down alone. No, as they spiral, they've got to reach out, grab as many others as they can so that long ride down isn't so damn lonely.

It's the only thing I can think of, the only way I can justify the hate and the cruelty.

I reach into my backpack and pull out a thick, chisel-point black marker, my new weapon against the spiralling ones. I pop the cap with my teeth and, with a quick glance to make sure there's no teachers around, I scribble thick black marks on my locker.

Soon, the message there disappears under the obliterating swipes of my weapon. *FREE BLOWJOBS BEHIND THE SCHOOL EVERDAY AFTER SCHOOL* became a big black rectangle.

Everday.

Not every day. *Everday.*

I know who spells that word with the one missing letter. I've seen him put it on the board at least twice.

Randy.

The guy who has his own reputation to manage, and he's pulling this crap on me?

He's just reaching out to grab hold of something as he spirals, Kay, she thinks.

Like I'd ever lower myself to have any sort of relations with him, sexual or otherwise. He's another Ray, nothing but a loud-mouthed dick.

Though, his cousin isn't so bad.

I drop the thought of Norman Gustafsen from my mind. *No more guys, Kay.*

But Randy? Yeah, he's getting this crap from that bastard, Ray. I didn't clue into their connection until I started listening for Ray Hedges's name to come up in conversations, and heard that Randy gets his drugs from Ray. Hell, everyone does, from the sounds of it. How had I not clued into this before? How could I have been so stupid? God, I can't even look at that fucking bastard after what he did to me. I should press charges. He should be arrested, thrown in jail.

Yeah right, Kay. With your reputation? Who's gonna believe you?

No one's going to believe me. I'm the slut. I've heard all the names. KY Kayla, Lay Ya Kayla…all the others. And why?

Because the one and only time I've had sex — and I sure as hell don't count what happened with Ray as sex — was not that long ago. Same old stupid story young girls tell all the time: go to a party with a friend, get into a damn game of caps, drink way too much, and don't sober up until I clue in way too late and find some guy on top of me. A guy who somehow had gotten most of my clothes opened, if not off, while I was passed out, and he's busy humping away at me.

I woke up so late, I feel him ejaculate in me. He leaves a part of himself in me that I did not want, nor agree to. He forced himself into me, takes something that can never be retrieved, and leaves profanity behind.

No matter that I'd thrown him off and got the hell out of there, friend or no friend. But the next day. Oh, the next day. I close my eyes and fight back the tears as the memory surges like vomit.

The next day, it's everywhere around the school about how easy Kayla is, how Kayla will happily put out for a couple of beers, how Kayla will spread for anything.

Three times more, I'm pushed into things beyond my control. My parents won't hear my begging to have the kid charged. Refuse to even consider it. Instead, after my hasty, quiet abortion, my parents decide it's likely better to move towns. "A fresh start," they call it. They move their veterinary business to New Hope, running from disgrace instead of trying to correct it.

So, really, it's my fault. I'm the one to blame. I should have been more careful with Ray. I should have checked him out more. I should have…

I shouldn't have been so fucking stupid. It's absolutely my fault, obviously my fault. I'm broken, somehow. Maybe I carry the stink of what that first guy left in me. Maybe I put something out there, some signal, that attracts these guys. These assholes who think with their dicks.

I'm broken.

I'm used goods. Worthless.

I'm to blame.

I'm spiralling with the rest of them now.

After that horrible day with Ray, I suddenly find I'm the popular girl. I get a lot of invitations for parties — all from guys, naturally — and I decline them all.

I've stopped. But the rumours? No, they never stop. Why would they when she's now in that same spiral, just as much fodder for the rumour mill as anyone? I'm the whore, Grace Martino is the virginal Catholic girl, Monica Holt is the fat lesbian, Lex Hedges is the freaky dyke, Gerry McGregor is the fag, Norman Gustafsen is the drunk. There's always a new label and a new victim to hang it on. And Bear? He's the big dumb jock. To me, Bear seems harmless. He's been with Grace forever and they are headed for the altar as soon as they graduate. And Grace always seemed nice, no matter if she was the virginal Catholic girl or not. Her and Lex. I don't ever get any judgmental vibe from either of them when we pass in the halls. Grace even seems to toss me an encouraging smile on occasion.

But with everyone else, I feel like they look at me like I'm damaged goods.

Maybe they're right.

It just seems safer to stay quiet and just be with myself for a while. After Ray, my second stupid mistake in a year, I swear to myself I'll avoid all parties. At least until I can get out of this damn town and away from all these rumours.

Again.

◆ ◆ ◆

TWO MONTHS AFTER Ray, I almost go back on my promise.

Norman Gustafsen, the town drunk in a town full of drunks, asks me to go with him to a party.

Yes, Gutty's a drunk. Everyone knows that. But I've been watching him a lot at school and what I see is, when he isn't drinking, he's actually a good guy. A seemingly decent guy.

My radar for that seems a little more finely tuned now, not that I can trust it. Two months after Ray, I'm still asked out fairly frequently and I say no because, in each and every case, when I look in their eyes, I can see the hope. I can damn near read their thoughts, feel that hope as it oozes out of their pores. That hope, yeah, that desperation I see? It speaks to me and it says, *if I can get her to say yes, then I'm gonna get laid.*

I see it in the way they smooth their hair, in the way they lick their lips or hold on to their belt buckles. There's a million telltale signs.

I'm not naïve enough to believe I'm right every time. But I can say I'm right a lot more than I'm wrong. So, I say no. Every time.

Evertime.

But then, after all those guys, after all those requests and come ons and invites, Gutty approaches me, and I feel the difference immediately. For one thing, he comes to my house and quietly knocks on my front door. Every other guy always seems to want the world see him ask me out, as though, if I did say yes, everyone would know he was going to get some. Like some badge of honour or something.

Gutty's much more low-key. He actually takes the time to introduce himself, even though he has to know I know exactly who he is. We both have those tags stitched to our chests. Slut. Drunk.

He tells me there's going to be a "multi-unit" birthday party and that he's one of the units. Norman throws off none of the tics, none of the signs I normally see. Instead, he simply stands at my door, elbows slightly bent, palms upraised. When he asks me, his head leans in slightly, as though there's only interest in my response, but no hope or need. No desperation.

I gaze into his soft brown eyes. And I come so close to saying yes. *So* close.

This is the first time I've even been tempted. The first time my radar remains quiet. Despite my history, despite my misgivings, I know I can trust what I'm feeling and I want so badly to say yes, to see his expression change from questioning to smiling. I want to see him smile. Even more, I want to be the reason for his smile.

I feel the goodness of him, the decency of him.

But other voices, voices from the spiral, remind me of the pain. *Remember the pain in your jaw,* they say. *In your throat.* Though healed now, I still feel the bruises. I still feel Ray's rough hands in my hair, in me. I still remember not being able to breathe. I still remember choking.

I tell Norman no.

I crush him. I can read the disappointment in his face and that is bad. Because I know it's disappointment at missing out on my company, not the opportunity for him to bag and brag.

I stammer out an "I'm sorry," and turn to shut the door.

I hear him make some noise about some other time, but I'm back in my spiral, past listening.

◆ ◆ ◆

AND THEN I was back out again.

"One more," Talia said.

"No," I said, throwing up a palm. "Please. Jesus, please. No more."

"One more," Talia said.

"No," I plead.

And, one more time, I wasn't me anymore.

◆ ◆ ◆

FUCK ME, I'M drunk. Stupid drunk, but not fall-down drunk. And I'm not so drunk that I can't understand what I've just heard.

Instead, now I'm drunk, and I there's a trembling in my gut, and my hands twitch, wanting to curl into fists. Wanting to hit something. Some*one.*

Why did I ever start drinking? I think as the dry heaves kick in yet again, in a spirited yet ultimately doomed attempt to get me to blow my lower intestines out my mouth. But there's nothing left to offload. Not even my guts, I don't think.

Why did I ever start drinking? I wonder again. Up until last year, I hadn't even touched alcohol. But, I guess I'm a stupid fuck, because on a dare from my dumbass cousin Randy, and his buddy Bear, I'd pounded back three beers in rapid succession. From there, Randy and Bear kept feeding me enough beers to wipe my memory clean of the entire night.

But, from what I heard, I'd been funny as hell. Which is kind of a different thing for me.

The next weekend, there I am, drunk and funny again. And then, this drunk and funny rep follows me throughout the week at school. Girls who have never even looked at me before now come up and talk to me like we're old friends. Guys too, for all of that.

Why did I ever start drinking? Randy and Bear. *But why do I keep drinking?* Because this drinking thing definitely had its upside. At least, it did at the beginning.

But fuck me. The mornings after are killer. The headaches. The dry mouth. The needles in my eyes. The sad, disappointed looks from my mom.

Worse than all that, though, is the loss of memory. I get a couple of beers into me and my brain simply stops making any memories. Whole hours of my life, gone.

But apparently, I'm the life of the party. So they tell me.

Over the past year, though, and more and more lately, as the hot girls and the popular guys keep talking to me, I'm starting to question whether they're laughing with me or at me. Gotta say, I'm kinda coming down pretty hard on that last option.

Tonight, though. Tonight, yeah, I'm sure I'm gonna remember.

Tonight had started a little different from most other weekends. This is my birthday weekend. My birthday's tomorrow, but that's never stopped anyone from celebrating their Sunday birthday on a Saturday night, did it?

There had been so much anticipation at school all this week, so much speculation on exactly how ripped ol' Gutty — drunk and funny bastard that I am — was gonna get at a party partially in my honour. To the point where, though I really didn't want to put myself through another memory-erasing debacle, I kinda felt I almost owed it to them all. All those hot girls and popular guys.

It didn't help that Kayla, a girl I like a lot, and not for the obvious reasons, turned me down. Girl has seen some shit, and despite all the crap everyone talks about her, she's got this…I don't know…I guess it's dignity. I don't know much about dignity, especially with the year I've had, but if I was going to recognize it at all, it's in Kayla Young. If she'd said yes, no way I would have drank as much as I have.

But she'd turned me down.

And so, I drank.

I drank a lot.

I vaguely remember stumbling around the kitchen of whoever the hell's house I'm in — jeez, I honestly can't even remember — and I'm working my way from one beer bottle to the next on the kitchen counter and then kitchen table, looking for a bottle with something in it to actually drink.

At that point, maybe ten minutes or two hours ago, if someone had asked me, I absolutely wouldn't have been able to say exactly why I was doing it, I just kind of remember it seeming the reasonable thing to do at the time. Maybe I'd lost my own beer. Maybe someone cut me off? Could have been something stupid like that.

There's flashes of memories: frustration that most bottles had only dribbles left in them, me tossing them aside, not giving a damn where they landed. Happiness at hitting pay dirt. Squinting at a bottle with a little more heft to it, and the sweet swish and tinkle of liquid inside.

Prize in hand, I don't remember stumbling out to the living

room, but I remember the couch, and the couple necking at the other end of it. I remember thinking I'll just be quiet and drink this beer, and the smoochers'd never know I was even there.

Be quiet as a mouse.

A mouse! That struck me funny and I giggled. Giggled like a quiet little mousie-mouse. A mousie-mouse eating cheesy-weezy.

Shit, I knew I was gonna disturb the smoochy-woochies at the other end of the couch with all this giggling, so I tried to drown it by tossing back a big mouthful of beer.

I swallow a lot of it, feel some of it pour down my chin to my Nirvana shirt, but what puzzles me are the chewy bits.

Does beer have chewy stuff? Chewy-brewy bits?

There's movement from the smoochies and I look over. The girl on the other end of the couch is staring at me like I'm scary or something. "Omigod! Ew! That's so gross!"

Smoochie guy looks at me, gets the same expression as smoochie girl. "Gutty, dude!" he says. "Why you eating cigarette butts?"

I'm really only catching the odd word, but it looks like the guy's looking for me to say something. Yeah, okay. I say the first thing that pops out of my mouth.

"Chewy-brewy. Chewy-wooey," I say. Then I hold a finger up to my lips. "Quiet as a mousie-mouse."

Apparently, that satisfies the couple, as they get up and leave. At least, I think so. It kinda feels like one second they're there and then, poofy-woofy, I'm alone.

I remember wishing Kayla was there.

But it doesn't matter, cuz I'm not alone anymore. Gerry and some of the guys come by. They're visiting me! Yay me! But then Gerry takes my fuckin' beer and it doesn't make me happy, but as Gerry takes it away, Bear tells me the bottle's empty now. Okay. Makes sense.

Then Bear holds his hand under my mouth and tells me to spit out the butts.

"I shit out my butt," I say, quite reasonably, I think. "Stupid. Can't spit out my butt."

Stupid Bear looks in my mouth, hooks a finger and sticks it in and his finger tastes bad, but he pulls it back out and then my mouth tastes a whole lot better. Then stupid Bear tells me to lie down on the couch and he'll get me another beer.

"No chewies," I tell him.

"Right," stupid Bear says. "No chewies."

"Quiet as a mouse."

Seconds or hours later, Gerry, Bear, and some of the guys come running back in the room. They're all shouting and I can't make out what the emergency is exactly. Something about midnight and birthday. Who's birthday? And why so frigging late?

Then there's something inside me and good Lordy, it wants out. It wants out desperately. A mousie-mouse?

I'm still on the couch, but it's so weird cuz I feel myself bucking, my head lifting and falling on the pillow as the chewy mouse — though it really feels a whole lot more like a rabbit, or maybe even a raccoon — does its best to run up from my belly to my throat.

I want to laugh when someone says, "Dude, he looks like that guy in the *Alien* movie!" but I can't because of the raccoon rabbit, and then someone else yells, "Get him outside!" and then I kinda don't hear nothing much else.

The chewy mouse — which I really don't think is a mouse at all, *or* a rabbit, *or* a raccoon — finally flies free and it's absolutely fascinating to watch the brown liquid jet shoot up from my mouth and nose and climb climb climb up the wall and grab the picture hanging above it with its splashy tentacles before it all falls again, unable to grip, only to fall and fall and then I can't see as everything goes brown and black and then there's yelling and arms pulling me and the chewy mouse that isn't a mouse is trying to jump back out of my mouth and nose again and more yelling and then I'm outside hanging over a porch fence and the mouse is finally running away.

God, do I puke.

I puke until there's nothing left to puke.

Then I puke some more.

Then, when there's no more puke, my intestines try and crawl up my throat.

I manage to keep them down.

Once I'm all puked out and no longer a threat, Gerry, Bear and the boys reluctantly plod back into the house, I'm guessing to clean up my mess. By now, with all my ballast tanks blown, I'm feeling a little more sober. The cool night air helps, so I stick right where I am, taking big lungfuls and holding them as long as I can, exhaling only when I have to.

Bear comes out with a mug of coffee. Gerry brings me a clean shirt and a damp towel. I'm still wobbly, so he helps me peel off my shirt, gets me to wipe myself down, and helps me get the new shirt on. The shirt's too small and it stretches taut across my chest and belly. I pick up the coffee again. I hate coffee, but figure I need it right now. I take a swig. It's awful, but it's better than puke and cigarette butts.

There's a couple of lawn chairs farther down the deck, by the corner of the house, so I move over there, silent in my sock feet, and I ease myself into the Muskoka chair. As I sip at the awful coffee, I hear faint voices from around the corner of the house, and the unmistakable odour of pot. I ignore everything, breathe the night air, and take slow, careful sips of the coffee.

I'm not listening to the talkers around the corner. I'm really not. At least, I'm not trying to. I just want a quiet place to sober up and forget about mice. But they're not being quiet.

And I don't want to hear what they say.

But I hear it, just the same.

"…blew you?"

"Yeah, well, I had to kinda convince her, but she was into it."

"Convince her?"

"Well, you know, I gave her the whole 'I'm so lonely and confused an' I just need to be held' shit."

"No shit? And it worked?"

"Like it wouldn't. C'mon, man, you know she's a goddamn skank anyway. She'll do anything with a dick."

"Really? You think?"

"Man, I know."

"She good?"

"Took the entire Beast, man."

That's Ray. He always calls his dick that.

"Buried to the hilt?"

"Balls deep, my man. You know it."

At that, I hear the clap of a high-five.

"Then what? You bang her?"

"I fingered her and shit, but I hadda get the truck back before Lex's vagina exploded…"

"So you dropped her off with your spunk in her gut at her parents? Balls, dude!"

"Nah, I just left her there. She could walk home. Hell, she's good, but she wasn't *that* good, y'know?"

"You just left her out in the middle of nowhere?" Laughing.

"Nowhere, my ass. It's only a ten-mile walk." More laughing.

After the laughing, the talking stops for a bit. Guessing they're getting down to the end of the roach and have to do it or lose it. I'm about to get up and head back into the house when one of them speaks up again.

"You think she'd do me?"

"Man, you gotta dick? I told ya, KY's a skank."

KY. Kayla Young.

The girl I'd asked to be my date tonight. The girl I'd hoped would help prevent me from getting so drunk again. From doing exactly what I just did.

The look on her face had made me sure she was going to say yes. Instead, that look changed into something unreadable and she had said no. It was polite, but she'd still declined me. But when she did, I noticed the way she put a protective hand to her chest. I noticed the sadness creep into her eyes, haunt her face.

It was a sadness…no, it was a hurt…that no one should have to wear. Yet, she wore it.

Now I knew why.

I feel sick to my stomach. A completely different feeling from the burning of the vomit that I'd blown out a while ago. This was deeper, more painful.

I set the mug down quietly on the porch floor before my shaking hands slopped the coffee. Once free of the mug, I can't stop my hands from balling into fists. I want to go around the corner of the house and beat the shit out of both Ray and whoever else is back there with him.

But I know that's never going to happen.

I pick up the mug again, not trying to be quiet anymore. Something has finally crystallized for me. For the first time in a long time, things are clear.

I'm done. Enough is enough.

Tomorrow, I'm eighteen. I'm leaving this town. Maybe forever.

And I'm taking Kayla Young with me.

◆ ◆ ◆

IT TAKES ANOTHER month for Norman to come back to my door again, but this time, I see something else in him. The slightly cowed nervousness is gone. In its place, I see a fire that hadn't been there the last time. A slow-burning rage.

But while I'm sure that rage could be terrifying, I also know it's not pointed in my direction.

Strangely, that makes me feel safe.

He said, "Can I talk to you?" Then he said, "I need to tell you a few things."

I come out and sit on the concrete steps leading to my door. Norman keeps a respectful distance, and paces as he talks.

Over the next ninety minutes, he tells me about himself. About the mistakes that he's made. About how he thought making his friends laugh was the most important thing. About how he's now figured out that that isn't the important thing at all. He tells me about his last drunk, at that birthday party he'd mentioned a month back. Tells me about what he'd done, and how ashamed he was, despite his friends' laughter.

Then he tells me how he feels about me and he doesn't once feed me a line of crap. Norman tells me he knows very little about me, disbelieves all of what he's heard, and he tells me he'd like to start out as friends.

He tells me about the sadness that he sees in me, that he understands my reluctance to allow anyone inside my walls. But he also says something that surprises me. He tells me about a dignity that he also sees inside me. A strength. He says—and he's right—that he figures I feel weak and small and broken, but then he tells me that, to take all the shit this town's thrown at me, and to keep going? Yeah, he says, that takes strength. That takes dignity.

He tells me he needs a friend and that I'd be the one doing him the favour. And in return, he says, he promises to chip away at that wall of rumour and hate and jealousy and hypocrisy that surrounds me. He says he wants to earn the chance—he says *chance* and not *right*—to eventually be let inside the wall.

He tells me of his plans.

He tells me of his future. How it doesn't have to be just his. How he doesn't want it to be just his. Instead, he tells me, it could be ours.

And then, after ninety minutes of pacing and talking, he finally stops both and holds my gaze with his own. I see a young man, honest and clear-eyed, and I read absolutely no hint of malice in him. He has come to me raw and naked and vulnerable.

Something no one else has ever done.

He holds out his hand to me. "What do you say?" he says.

It's not lost on me how crazy and ridiculous this is. This guy that I've talked to for less than two hours. He's asking me to trust him like I've never, ever trusted anyone before, and that, with my history, I have no right to trust.

But then I look hard at him again, and I think about how raw and naked and vulnerable I am as well. As raw and naked and vulnerable as he is. We're both in the spiral, but we're not reaching out to drag anyone else down.

For the first time, I'd be coming to a friendship with complete honesty. And fuck whatever came before.

I look at his outstretched hand. I hesitate only briefly. Instead of answering him, I put my hand in his. It was all the answer he needed.

And then he smiles at me and my world changes. Because I'm the reason for that smile.

◆ ◆ ◆

THE NEXT DAY, there's a new rumour.

Everyone's talking about the anonymous someone who'd beaten the shit out of Ray. The same anonymous someone who also trashed the shit out of his pickup truck. Rumours that say whoever did it damn near put Ray in the hospital.

Ray comes up with a serious stream of bullshit, because it's Ray and there's no fucking way he's ever telling the truth.

The official story is that Ray lost control of the truck on a curve and slid into a rock cut. And one look at Ray, or at his truck, is enough for anyone to buy that shit. Easily. Though anyone who's ever seen Ray drive that truck knows damn well he's a better driver than that. I won't give the asshole much credit, but I'll give him that. He knows how to drive.

And it's probably those who know better that are slinging around the rumour.

But Ray's not talking and no one's owned up to it.

Norman has never said anything to me and I'll never ask.

In fact, we never mention his name. Ever.

Whatever had happened, it had been enough.

◆ ◆ ◆

I SAT ON the floor where I'd slid down to at some point during the vision. My back was against the chest of drawers, a handle digging into my spine, but I ignored it.

Talia had released my hand and now retreated back to the chair. While she looked a little rattled, and there was a sheen of sweat across her forehead, she still seemed a lot more composed than I felt. *Then again, she's been living with these memories for years*, I realized.

After a time, I got my breathing under control, wiped the sweat from my forehead, my cheeks, my neck. I tried to talk, but I felt my throat lock up. I stood, sipped at the cold coffee, swallowed hard.

Goddamn you, Ray. There better be a particularly terrible place in hell for you. A special little corner where only the worst of the worst go.

One more sip of cold coffee, and then I turn to Talia. "You said there were two things I needed to do."

"Yes."

"What's the first?"

"I'll tell you the second one first."

"Okay." I was in no position, mentally, to argue with her.

"You need to enlist the aid of some people more prepared than you are to deal with this threat against you." A touch insulting, but I kept quiet. I was too damned exhausted to respond, so I gave her the time she needed, responding only with a nod to let her know I understood.

"They will not assist you willingly." Nod. "So, you have to coerce them to do so. They rarely interact with our world anymore. So, you will need to bribe them with a possession they want but have been unable to attain."

Wait. What?

"If they—whomever this mysterious group of more-prepared people are—haven't been able to get this possession, how can I, the less-prepared lady, manage it?"

"You have the motivation and the mobility to do so."

"I'm not sure I even understand what the hell you just said."

"Right now, you don't need to," she said. "You will if you agree to carry it out."

"So I have to agree to do something without knowing what it is I'll be doing?"

"You're stealing an artifact from where It's being held, and bringing It to a group as leverage to bargain for their assistance."

"I'm going to rob something from people who are powerful enough to defeat the ones who you say can help defeat my enemy?"

She took a moment to run that through her head, looked out the window to the lake, blinked, then said, "Mostly."

"Fucksake, Talia, you're really not big on anything more than vague responses, huh?"

"For the most part."

"So, riddle me this, Riddler: what's to stop this mysterious group of prepared people from simply taking this wonderful possession off my hands and killing me. Am I not kind of just asking for that?"

"Not if you secure the possession."

I nodded again. "Oh, well, fine then." I threw up my hands. "No problem." *I'm stealing something and holding it hostage. Got it.*

"Once that is done, I will broker a meeting with you and them. They will do as you ask and the possession will switch ownership."

"And they won't kill me when I hand over their shit?"

"No," she said. "Not if you extract a promise from them ahead of time not to. Their word is trustworthy."

"Okay." I really didn't understand, but for now, I could roll with it. It's all hypothetical at this point anyway. "That works, I guess. That's the second thing. What's the first?"

"This task will be much easier for you."

"Good. What do I have to do?"

"I have not lived a normal life, Lex. I think you now see that I am…different…from other people. Most of them shun me."

"You want me to throw you a party? A debutante ball?"

She ignored my sarcasm. "I've been shunned my entire life." She stood, and motioned for me to stand as well. I pushed off from the wall as she moved closer to me.

Very close.

"I've been inside your head now, Lex. I know you find me attractive. More attractive than Monica."

"What are you saying?" I didn't trust my voice with much more than those few words.

"I've never lain with anyone, Lex. Man or woman."

And then I was having some trouble breathing again.

"I want you to lay with me."

"You want me to—"

"Yes," she said. "I want you to make love to me."

◆ ◆ ◆

TALIA SAID A few more things, then, perhaps sensing how uncomfortable she'd made me, promised to contact me the next day for my answer. I slid back down the wall and remained on the floor for a long time after she left.

My brain swirled and spun like a merry-go-round, images spiralling around in a confused jumble. Talia, Ray, Norman, Ray, Kayla…

Ray.

Ray and Kayla.

"You stupid fuck," I said, but was unsure if I was directing it at myself or at Ray. I dropped my head into my hands and tried to forget everything that had been pushed into my head in the past half-hour.

Turns out, that was flat-out impossible.

Eventually, I stood and somehow got myself to the bathroom to splash my face, but somewhere along the way, I saw clearly—way too clearly—Kayla on her knees in front of me, my cock—Ray's cock, but I felt it, felt the tightness of the muscle, the weight of it—slick with her spit, inches from her face, her eyes red and puffy from crying. And the emotion that was inextricably tied to that image—Ray's memory of that sight—was one of satisfaction.

Satisfaction.

That did it. That emotion, coupled with that image, was enough to make my belly roll over and push my breakfast back up my throat. I just made the toilet in time to feel the rough, chunky velocity of the food as it pushed over my tongue, slid along my teeth and the roof of my mouth, before ejecting in a violent splash into the bowl, the brown lumps a violation of the white porcelain.

And I was Norman, vomiting beer and cigarette butts. I was Ray, watching Kayla vomiting beside the truck. And felt

Ray's utter detachment, more concerned with getting home than anything she'd just gone through.

Goddamn you, Ray.

I waited a few moments to see if more would come, but, aside from some horrible-tasting burps, I was done. I flushed the mess after wiping the edges with a wad of toilet paper and dropping it in, watching it spiral down with the last gurgling of the water. Then I moved to the sink, ran the water until it was icy cold, and splashed my face until my hair dripped and the counter was awash.

I filled my mouth straight from the tap, spitting the mouthfuls back out.

When I finally felt somewhat human again, I brushed my teeth, reapplying toothpaste three times before I was satisfied, then rinsed with mouthwash until my tongue burned.

My shirt was soaked, so I peeled it off, meaning to simply change it, but instead stripped naked and had another shower. I ran the water as hot as I could stand it, exiting a few minutes later, my skin pink and tingling.

And I saw Kayla's cheeks from Ray's eyes, an angry pink where he'd slapped her. The tightness of my scalp where he'd wrapped his fists in my hair. I felt the burning of Kayla's abused flesh, felt the violation.

I brushed my teeth again.

And still, after all that, I didn't feel clean. Didn't think I'd feel clean ever again. Those memories were ingrained now. Like they were mine, evil thoughts and all. Mine. Not like I'd heard them from someone. Like I'd made them myself. Like I'd been Norman. Like I'd been Kayla.

Like I'd been Ray, with all his twisted compulsions.

Goddamn you, Ray.

Finally, I dressed. I pulled my phone from my discarded jeans and tried to call Monica. My thumb hovered over the screen. Somehow, I couldn't make the call. I held the phone in my hand, bouncing it lightly, as though gauging its weight. But I didn't make the call.

I know you find me attractive. More attractive than Monica.

Was that true?

I pushed the thought from my mind, texted Monica a message, telling her I'd catch up with her later, that I had a few things to do.

I didn't mention Ray, but I figured, in a town the size of New Hope, it wouldn't take long for her to get word. I hoped she'd read into the text and give me the time I needed.

Then I called Randy and got an address.

◆ ◆ ◆

THE GUSTAFSENS LIVED in a modest, well-kept house with a small lake, more of a pond, serving as their front yard. Large spruce trees cupped the back of the house and ran around the lake, opening only at the gravel driveway that led into the property. The home had once belonged to a prominent real estate agent in the area, who lost his son in the high school tragedy back in '81.

I drove by the place three times, each time wondering if I was doing the right thing. I remembered Norman's warning about not being alone in the car, but I was at a cop's house, and somehow I got the distinct impression that Talia was watching over me. With that in mind, I stopped the car on the road and thought long and hard about whether or not to pull in. This wasn't a big deal as I'd only passed one battered pickup on the winding path in the past five miles. I wasn't worried about blocking traffic any time soon.

I questioned whether or not I wanted to open this door. But really, there was no choice. I had to.

Abruptly, before I could change my mind again, I tapped

the gas, swung the wheel, and pulled in.

Kayla stood under a large umbrella that shaded two comfortable Muskoka chairs facing the pond. She had a cell phone in one hand and the other held a bandanna, which she used to swipe at the sweat on her neck.

I stopped the car, killed the engine, and stepped out, waving at her. She waved back, but I could tell she didn't recognize me. Why would she? We'd barely known each other at school.

The phone was still in her hand.

"Kayla," I said. "It's been a long time. Lex. Lex Hedges."

She smiled, but I caught a bit of a frown first. Maybe she was just searching her memory, but, with the last name Hedges and what I knew of what she went through, I doubted she needed to think too hard.

"Lex," she said, "it's good to see you." Then she set the phone down on the arm of the chair and headed over to me.

"I was wondering who was out there," she said. "I was cutting the grass and noticed the car go by a couple of times, then stop. Being married to a cop, that's usually not a good sign." Then I understood why she'd held the phone until she'd identified me. She'd likely dialled 911 and had only to press the Send button to complete the call.

"Shit," I said, "I didn't even realize what it would look like. I'm so sorry." *Yeah, way to go, Lex. Scare the shit out of her.*

"Don't worry about it," she said, brushing back a particularly unruly lock of hair. "No harm done."

"Truth to tell, I was kind of waffling on coming in. I didn't really plan to drop in on you like this, Kayla," I said. "Let me know if it's better if I come back later." I rubbed the back of my head. "Or if I just shouldn't come back at all."

"Of course not. Wouldn't be very neighbourly of me to send you away, would it?" Then she let the smile fade. "Sorry about your mother and your...I'm sorry for your loss."

I caught the pause. "Thanks," I said.

"You want a drink?" She pointed to the house. "I've got some Cokes, some lemonade, ice water?"

"Lemonade would go down great," I said.

She motioned to the chairs. "Great. You make yourself comfortable and I'll be back in a minute."

It took not much more than a couple of minutes, but she came back wearing a different T-shirt and her hair pulled into a loose ponytail. She held two sweating tall glasses of lemonade. "I didn't mean to put you out," I said.

"You're not putting me out, Lex," she said, "but after cutting a half-acre of grass, the smell of me might have put you out. Or put you down." She laughed, and it was an easy, throaty laugh. An infectious laugh. In my mind, I was trying to square a decade-old memory that I'd been given a half-hour ago, of a brutalized, beaten girl, with the confident, happy woman in front of me. My head was firing up a doozy of a headache in compensation for the confusion.

I sipped at the lemonade, then took a bigger mouthful. It was fantastic and I told her so.

"Mom taught me," she said.

"She taught you well."

She leaned back in the other chair and I watched her relax a bit, staring out at the pond. "It's a good view. Looks like you and Norman have done all right."

She nodded slightly, but her words were incongruent to the action. "Why are you here, Lex?"

She turned to face me and I took my first genuine look at her. Kayla had a strong face, a strong nose and deep green eyes. Her hair had been long in high school, but now was just long enough for the rudimentary ponytail. Most of the lines on her face were from smiling.

I didn't want to be the one to say anything to stop that smile.

I got another flash of her face, much younger, her eyes shut and tearing, her mouth —

Jesus. I pushed it away. *This was a mistake. I shouldn't have come.* It was too late now. I was here. *I feel like it was me who raped you, Kayla. It's in my head now.*

"You okay, Lex?"

"Sorry," I said. "I'm very aware of how awkward it is, you having to deal with anyone with the name Hedges."

I took another long drink of the lemonade to give myself time to get my composure back. I set the glass down carefully, then faced her. I felt it was important to meet her eyes.

"Why am I here? I'm not really sure, Kayla," I said, and that was as honest as I could get. "I guess part of it is to talk to you about something that I'm sure you've likely not wanted to ever talk about. And, though I, of all people, am not in a position to ask you anything, I'm also here to ask you a question that I need an honest answer to." I pushed the glass of lemonade in a tight circle to swirl the contents. "But I guess I'm mostly here to apologize for Ray."

She didn't evade the comment and she didn't play dumb. She didn't hesitate and she didn't get mad. Instead, she just said, "That's not your place, Lex, and you don't need to."

"I know." Tears slipped down my face. "But I…just feel I need to."

She lowered her head slightly, a small nod of acceptance. "Okay. Thank you."

"You're not surprised I know."

She raised her head again. "I am, but you obviously know." She turned back to the lake. "All families have their secrets. Perhaps this was yours."

"It isn't," I said, also turning to the water. "I just found out a few hours ago."

"Ah," she said. I wondered why she didn't ask how I'd found out. "And now you want to talk about it?"

"Is that okay?"

"No, Lex," she said, and though she said it politely, I heard the iron in that voice. "It's not okay."

"Okay." I nodded. "I understand. Sorry."

"You said you had a question."

"Yes, and please forgive me for asking this, but I kinda have to."

"All right."

"Norman," I said. Then I stopped. I didn't know how to ask what I needed to ask. Especially of the man's wife. The guy that had believed in her when no one else did.

"Yes," she prompted.

"Do you think…" I sighed, started again. "Is it possible…"

"Just ask the question, Lex," she said, her voice soft, but insistent.

"Do you think Norman could have killed Ray?"

"Is that the question you really want to ask?"

"I think so," I said.

"Because the answer is yes, he definitely could have. We have never spoken of it, but I know he beat the shit out of him back then, and I don't know how he stopped himself from killing him then."

I don't know, either. "You never spoke of it?"

"No." Kayla paused, considered, turned toward me. "Never said a word about it. But the next time I saw him, his knuckles…" She lifted a hand, made it into a fist. Considered it for a moment, then opened her hand again, reached down, and lifted her glass. "But if you're asking me if he *did* do it, that's a whole different question."

"Did he?"

"Well, Lex, you'll have to ask him that question, but, knowing him as long as I have, I can tell you that he absolutely did not."

"How can you be so sure?"

"Two reasons," she said, holding up her hand in a peace sign. "Because" — she lowered one finger — "if he was going to do it, he would have done it back then. And…" After a pause, she lowered the second. "And because we moved back here for a reason." I canted my head to the side in wonder, but let her finish. "We moved back here, of course, for the opportunity, as well as for Norman to be back in his hometown." It was only then that it sunk in for me that it wasn't Kayla's hometown. She'd moved to town not long before the incident with Ray. "But, we discussed the hell out of this before we made the final decision. And you know what we decided?"

"What's that?"

"That with Norman here, as a cop, your brother knew he'd be watching him every day. Norman would make sure that he knew. Ray would know that the threat was on him, not me."

"How about you?"

"How about me?"

"How did you feel about being back here?"

"To be honest, for me, it was reclaiming myself. I ran away for a while. I blamed myself for what happened…for all of it…that I was deserving of it. Believed I was somehow broken. We both did. But we both came back. We reclaimed our lives in this town. And, no offence, Lex, but it was kind of satisfying to watch your brother's life go down the tubes."

I nodded. I knew the feeling.

"And I take back what I said to you earlier."

"What's that?"

"I'm sorry for your mom, but I'm not sorry about your brother dying, Lex. I'm really not."

I let go of the glass, reached over and put my hand on hers, and looked her in the eye. "Neither am I, Kayla. He was garbage."

I held her hand and her gaze for a few moments so she would know I was sincere, then released both and picked up my glass.

It occurred to me that Kayla had not said Ray's name. Not once. And that was fine. Someone who'd done what he'd done didn't deserve the dignity of a name. However he'd died, he got what he deserved.

We both leaned back in our chairs and looked out at the pond.

We stayed like that for a long time. Both of us at peace, if just for now.

♦ ♦ ♦

I HADN'T REALLY gotten what I'd needed from Kayla, though I was glad for the opportunity to at least clear the air with her. But now, I needed to see if I could get the information from somewhere else.

As I drove away from Kayla Gustafsen's home, I pulled my phone out, as well as the card Gustafsen had given me. Then I called his cell.

We had a short conversation, then Gustafsen told me he wouldn't talk on the phone about this and gave me a location, partway between where we both were. By the time he hung up, he didn't sound happy.

Twenty minutes later, I drove down a gravel road that struck me as familiar. I was pretty sure it used to be an old logging road, but it was obviously getting more traffic now. There were stop signs dotting its length and a gas station right at the corner where it started, just outside of New Hope. Several houses, separated from each other by swaths of forest, sat at the back of massive green lawns.

A few miles down the road, I saw Norman's cruiser parked in an old turnaround and pulled in beside him. He leaned against the rear of his cruiser and gave me a nod as I approached.

"Norm," I said.

"Lex."

"Thanks for meeting me." Then I paused, took a breath. If Norman had a temper, I was going to find out, so I figured I might as well get this first part out early. "Gotta tell you right up front, I, uh…"

"You went and visited my wife."

I let out a breath. "Yeah." I squinted up at him. "You knew?"

"Kay and I don't have many secrets between us, Lex. I knew. She called me after you left."

"Okay."

"And I'll admit to being pretty goddamned angry at first, but Kay told me why you were there. What you said." He paused, fixed me with that cop stare. "Apologized for Ray."

"Yeah."

"Yeah," he said.

Norman lowered his head, looking at the dust on his boots, then raised his head again slightly to peer at me from guarded eyes. "When did you know about Kayla and your brother?"

"I knew something had happened back in high school only because he bragged about her for a while, then one day he came home beat to shit and never mentioned her name again. Didn't know who beat him up, didn't know why, and he would never mention it."

"I did."

"I know," I said. "Well, I know now. And I'm glad you did."

"So, when did you find out about it?"

"Earlier today."

"From who?" He breathed slowly, deliberately, and it appeared to me as though he was doing everything he could to maintain a calm demeanour.

"I'll tell you," I said, holding up a hand. "I will, I swear. But I need to ask you something first."

"Then ask."

"Between you and me, Norm," I said, "I need to know. Did you kill Ray?"

"No."

"I want to be very clear here, Norm." I paused, took a half step forward. "I wouldn't blame you if you did, I probably would if he did something like that to me, to someone I love. And if you say you did, it'll never leave here. Search me for recording devices if you need to. But I need to know."

He shook his head. "I did not kill Ray."

"Okay," I said, believing him. "Because I may be able to find the killer." At this, Norman's head jerked up. Before he could say anything, I plunged on. "And when I do, I don't think it will go good for whomever it is. I don't want it to be you. Do you understand?"

"I do…well…no, I don't," he said. "I didn't do it. Thought about it more than once, but never did it." Then he lifted from the car, faced me straight on. "But if you know who did kill Ray…Ray and your mother, you gotta let me know."

"I don't know who it is."

"Then how…?"

"Let me back up," I said. "What do you know about Talia Davis?"

Norman took a step back and kind of collapsed against the car again. He crossed his arms, and a smile came to his face. It looked like a smile, though there was no humour in it. It could just as easily have been a snarl. "Talia Davis," he said, shaking his head, staring at nothing. "Spooky fucking Talia. Should've known."

"Should have known what?" Hasn't she been AWOL for decades? Like, since 1984 or something like that?"

"Yeah, since Monica's dad's—"

"Yeah, The Last Word bookshop. I know. So how do you figure—"

"That if you were going to find out, it was going to come from that freak?" He huffed a laugh as he scuffed the ground with a boot. "Because she has a habit of turning up."

"What do you mean?"

"Kayla didn't tell you?"

"Tell me what?" Now it was just getting confusing.

"Talia. She was there," he said. "Just after your brother left."

"I'm sorry, I'm lost. She was there?"

"Your asshole brother…did what he did…and then left Kayla standing there when he fucked off." Then Norman did something surprising.

He spit into the dust at his feet. His finger stabbed down, pointing to the dirt. Then he said, "Left her right…fucking…here."

The surroundings suddenly snapped into focus for me. I looked around, through Ray's eyes, through Kayla's eyes, and I saw it. The trees were taller, there were hydro lines now, but this was it. We stood right where they'd stood all those years earlier. Where Ray leaned against the car sort of like Norman was doing right now.

I felt the heat from the car metal against my—*No! Ray's! Ray's!*—naked ass in a memory that wasn't mine, but somehow was.

"Jesus Christ," I whispered.

"Yeah," he said. "You just clued in, didn't you?" I nodded. "Yeah, this is where that fucker—" Norman abruptly cut himself off and glanced at me.

"It's okay," I said. "Calling him a fucker is a hell of a lot more charitable than I've been to him over the years. Don't worry about it. Call him whatever you want to call him. It won't bother me. He's earned every name thrown at him."

Norman nodded. Nothing more needed to be said. We both understood where the other stood now. "Anyway, it's about a

ten-mile walk back to Kay's old place. After she got herself" —
he paused, took a deep, shuddering breath—"after she got
herself together, she headed back home." He pointed vaguely
down the road. His hand was steady. "And about three miles
in, she said she noticed someone walking just behind her. She
said she kind of freaked out."

"I'm sure she did," I said. I flashed to a story told to me by
a friend I used to work with a few years back. She'd been
attacked in a parking lot and dragged into an alley. She'd
managed to escape her attacker before he did anything to her
and never told a soul. Three months later, she'd been working
in a darkroom when one of her co-workers played a joke on
her. He snuck into the darkroom and just clapped his hands on
her shoulders to scare her.

Less than a minute later, my friend had told me, she was
standing outside the darkroom, shaking and crying. Inside, her
co-worker remained on the floor where she'd left him with a
broken nose, two cracked ribs, a broken ankle, and two
seriously violent kicks to his balls. And that had occurred three
months after the attack. What would Kayla, mere minutes after
her own attack, have going through her mind?

"Yeah," Norman said. "So, the way Kay tells it, she didn't
look back, just took off running as hard and fast as she could.
And she could book it when she wanted to." I said nothing,
just took up position beside the him, both of us leaning against
the car. "So, she runs her ass off for god knows how long and
finally has to stop. Now she's at the side of the road, hands on
her knees, sure she's gonna puke from the running and
the...the other...you know."

I wondered briefly at how this man, this experienced police
officer, who had seen likely far more than I could or would want
to imagine, still couldn't say certain things about his own wife.

Hell, I thought, *could I?* I knew I wouldn't. I had my own
things I couldn't talk about.

Father.

"Anyway, she's standing there, and she told me she looked up and Talia Davis was right in front of her. Kay had run balls out, but Talia was *right there*." He stabbed at the air in front of him.

I wanted to ask how, but I knew Norman wouldn't be able to explain it. Hell, I couldn't explain much about Talia myself. Instead, I asked, "Then what happened?"

"Kay told me what she thought Talia said. She said Talia said something like, 'I'm sorry. I'm sorry for what happened to you, and I'm sorry I can't make him go away.'"

"'Make him go away'?"

"Yeah," Norman said. "Make him go away. Kay was pretty clear on that one. But then she said Talia said something else, but she figures she must have misheard her."

"What was that?"

"She said Talia's face kind of screwed up, sort of angry, but sort of...well, to tell the truth, Kay said it almost looked like she was having an orgasm or something." I stared at him, opened my mouth, but didn't say anything. Norman held up both hands, palms out. "That's what Kay said. Anyway, when she did this, Kay thought she heard her say, 'I'd have his teeth.'"

"What the hell is that supposed to mean?"

Norman's face was unreadable as he said, "No clue."

"'I'm sorry I can't make him go away'? Like, make him disappear? Like all those guys did back in the seventies?"

"Maybe," Norman said. "You think she did that?"

I did it, she had said. "Do *you*?" I said.

"You have a better explanation?" Norman said. "My department investigated the shit out of that. Two officers in a cruiser and a prisoner in a jail cell, among others. No clues." He held his hands up, fingers together, then shot them wide. "Poof."

"Are we sure we're talking about the same Talia? The woman I saw this morning doesn't even look like she could have been born in in the seventies, let alone ten years before that."

"Kay said when she saw her on this road—and this would have been back in 2000—she said she looked Kayla's age, maybe a bit older. No more than twenty."

"And she would have been, what…?" I did a quick calculation in my head. Math was never my strongest subject. "Thirty-three?"

"Thereabouts."

"So…" I gave Norman a look.

"No idea." The cop tried the look on himself. "All I can tell you is, she's Spooky Talia. And she can do shit. Weird shit."

"If she can do weird shit, then maybe she can do what she's promising to do for me."

"You've seen her?"

"Yeah. About two hours ago."

"Not long after I left."

"No."

"She hasn't been seen by anyone except Kay in thirty-six years," he said, staring at the dirt. He flicked his eyes to me. "And she said…?"

"Like I said, she's promising…well…to help me."

"How, exactly?"

"The details are a bit vague," I said. I filled Norman in on the meeting, what she did, clasping my hand. What I saw. Norman grunted a couple of times, nodded frequently, and got very quiet, his mouth a tight, thin line, through the part with Ray and Kayla. The only thing I left out was Talia's request at the end.

"Well, Lex," Norman said. "I gotta tell you, she's accurate as all hell on my part. Hell, she remembered stuff I'd forgotten. So I have to assume she's bang on with all the other stuff, too." He shifted position, the leather in his holster creaking. "I'd talk to Talia myself, but like I said. Thirty-six years. I don't know what it is with her. Spooky."

"Yeah. Spooky Talia."

"And now she's back."

"She is."

Norman breathed in, then out through his nose. Shook his head. "Maybe she *can* deliver the killer."

"Maybe."

"So, what are you going to do?"

"Sounds like I'll need to leave town for a few days."

"Sounds like it."

"Which means I have to talk to Monica first."

"You two…?"

"A little, yeah."

"Good," Norman said. "She's a good woman. Shame about her dad. Hell, and her mom."

"Yeah," I said. "She is a good woman. Don't know why I didn't see that back in the day."

"Because we were all a helluva lot dumber back then. Present company included." He clapped me on the back. "Keep me posted."

"I will."

We shook hands.

I headed back to my car. I heard, "Lex?" and turned. Norman was standing at his car, the door open, looking at me over the roof.

"Yeah?"

"Thanks for asking. You're a good person. Not like…" And I thought, *Not like my brother.* "You're a good person, Lex."

I thanked him and went to my car and we drove away from the turnaround in opposite directions. I hadn't realized how tense I'd been while standing there until I was moving away from it. It was only then that I felt the tension bleed out from my neck and shoulders.

After what Ray did here, I thought, someone should bomb it. Leave nothing but a smoking crater.

♦ ♦ ♦

MY LAST VISIT was with Monica. I dialled her cell and when she answered, I suggested the How You Bean? coffee shop in New Hope.

"Can we talk?" was all I said.

PART TWO
LEAVING HOME

"We live on a placid island of ignorance
in the midst of black seas of infinity,
and it was not meant that we should voyage far."

THE CALL OF CTHULHU
H. P. LOVECRAFT

Second Interlude

1981

THE BEAST BECOMES aware that there is more than just Mother. Soon, Father becomes known.

It had fed well for several weeks. It had become the dominant entity within the forested area it currently thinks of as home, as was its initial instinct. Always be the most dominant.

Though the other living things have learned to fear and avoid it, still it feeds well. It is a killer by nature, though, through the implanted knowledge of its Father—knowledge that it still considers mostly as noise, not much different from the initial noises of the surrounding forest—random scraps and bits of knowledge collide, coalesce, and soon become more structured, more distinct, more insistent, more urgent.

Father's noises were too complicated when first it became aware of them, but within days, it begins to comprehend. At first, it is simply a name, but a powerful one. It realizes that immediately. A Name, not a name, the distinctiveness singular and obvious.

That Name is *all'Gueroth*.

all'Gueroth, son of Nyarlathotep, son of Azathoth.

Father is a demon. Mother was not.

The beast is a demon, from a proud, powerful line of Outer Gods. And it has a name.

Tokq.

Tokq understands there are different ones, other demons that also exist, that share the area in which it lives. Bloodsuckers and shifters. Those others also seem aware of Tokq, but neither bloodsucker nor shifter believe this demon worth their time, so they coexist through mutual ignorance.

Instead, the demon focuses on its Father's words.

Over the days and weeks that follow, as Tokq feeds, it turns its mind inward, understanding that all'Gueroth had given it all it needed to not only survive, but possibly to one day rule this vile ball of filth. This world of small, fearful things.

A world populated by weak bags of meat and the weakest of demons.

It knows the form it must take. That of a human. A male, like Father. But one that appears human. One that is considered attractive.

Tokq takes a full turn of the planet around the too-bright sun. A full turn in which the temperature steadily drops, but eventually returns to heat.

In that time, *it* becomes *he*. He learns to walk straight and tall. His dermis loses its lustrous black and becomes soft, pink. Horns retreat, and hair grows. And he learns more and more about the world he had been born into. He listens to Father and learns and considers and plans.

And finally, Tokq is ready for what comes next.

Chapter Seven

I HAD A few minutes before I had to head out to meet Monica, so I called my editor at the web journal site and told him about Ray's murder.

Likely a good thing I was doing this by phone and didn't have to hide my expression as the surprise that I'd had a brother sank in for my editor. I'd never mentioned family, so the mother and brother things were both shocks, I knew.

Hey, guess what? I had a mother and a brother. Hey, guess what? Now that you know they exist? Yeah, they're dead. Oops.

Communicating all this by phone also meant that, while I had to toss some sorrow into my voice, there was no need to carry off the full look, which was good. There's no way I could have pulled it off for Ray. In the end, my editor granted me as much time as I needed. Pretty hard to argue with two murdered family members in a single week.

Of course, the bastard likely had someone else prepping an article on me and my murdered family, too. Then again, why not? It would be good reading.

Next, I called Kevin—my drummer and the guy currently throwing a hump into Kelly—and explained, quite civilly, I might add, the same thing I'd just told my editor. Gotta admit, I did feel like a bit of a shit as I took perverse enjoyment out of listening to Kevin squirm, struggling for that exact right tone of concern, empathy, and a small amount of I'm-hot-enough-to-have-brought-her-back-to-the-hetero-side-and-now-I'm-fucking-your-girlfriend-and-I-know-you-know-but-don't-want-to-bring-it-up-right-now superiority.

He did okay, and I only let him swing in the breeze for a little while.

Seriously, though…why did guys get all excited when they fucked a woman who'd also fucked a woman? Straight guys had no concept of bisexuality. Sad.

When I disconnected, I started wondering, *What is Kelly to me right now? Girlfriend? Ex-girlfriend? Girlfriend-on-hold until we work it out?*

Kelly.

Monica.

Fuck this.

I called Kevin back.

"Hello?" he said, obviously not knowing who it was. Guy never looked at his call display. *Drummers*, I thought.

"Hey, Kev," I said. "Me again."

"Oh. Hey." Instant change of tone. Sorrow and irritation. They didn't mix well.

"Listen, I would have called Kelly's phone, but she never has the damn thing on, and when she does, she never answers it anyway. And she's especially not going to answer any calls from me right now."

"Yeah?" Like I was just chatting with him, like Kevin didn't know what the fuck I was talking about. About as noncommittal as someone could get, I figured.

"Yeah. So, Kev, do me a favour and pass her the phone, okay?"

"Well, uh, she's, uh…"

"I know she's there. Just give her the damn phone, Kevin."

I listened to the charged silence and pictured Kelly standing away from Kevin, hands up, mouthing *I'm not here!* She'd be shaking her head, and her beautiful eyes would be wide.

The silence went on too long.

Kevin would be standing there, tall, bulging, bearded, all flowing hair and handsomeness, without the smallest hint of backbone in his body, struggling for some balance between his bandleader and his illicit girlfriend. I knew this could paralyze Kevin, so put I on my best bandleader voice and yelled, loud enough for them both to hear.

"Kelly, take the goddamn phone!"

A small rustling as the phone changed hands.

"What?" Her voice was cold.

"Nice, Kel," I said. "You know I just lost my mother *and* my brother and you're going to throw me attitude like that?"

A long, frustrated sigh. A whispered, "Jesus." Then she pulled herself together and her voice was, if not normal, at least approaching normal. "I'm sorry about your family, Lex."

"Yeah, thanks." I wanted to add more to that. More words, more sarcasm, but I swallowed it, forced myself not to. It would only ignite a fight neither of us wanted or needed right now. "Kelly, be honest with me, okay?"

"About what?"

"Kevin. You love him?"

"No." No hesitation. *Huh.*

"You care for him?"

Some hesitation here, as she weighed the question. "Yeah. I do."

"Would you rather be with him than me?"

"Lex..."

"I swear I'm not trying to start a fight here, Kel. And I know the phone's not the best way to do this, but I..." I softened my voice, all the edges gone. I wasn't doing it to manipulate her. I just wanted to connect with her, on some small level. "Ah hell, babe, I just need to know, okay?"

"Lex," she said again, and this time, I heard the tears. I knew exactly what they meant.

"It's okay, Kel," I said. "We had a good run, didn't we? We were okay together." I walked in a small circle, looking at the floor, seeing nothing, picturing her tear-stained face. "But if it's not working for you, then you need to find what will work for you. If Kevin's it, then…well…"

Sniffing noises. I gave her the time she needed. I continued to walk circles, scuffing at the thin carpet with my foot.

"I don't know if that's the case, Lex," she said and I knew Kevin was still nearby. "Probably not."

"Okay," I said.

"But you and I?" she said. "I just don't think it's going to work."

"Well, it takes two, Kel, and if you're not in it for the long haul, then, no, it won't work." Running that last sentence over, I realized it sounded harsh. "And I don't mean that in a nasty way, Kelly. Honestly. It's just kinda the math of the thing, right?"

More sniffing and deep breaths. "I'm sorry, Lex. Honest to god, it wasn't—"

"Shhh," I said. "Don't worry about that. Look, I just needed to know, okay?"

"I know," she said. "You're going through a lot. Your mom, your brother. You don't need this shit."

"That's the other reason I'm calling you." I stopped pacing, sat on the bed. "I know we've got some rehearsals set up for this week, but I've gone some crap to deal with. I may be a few days."

Kelly let out a breath, getting herself back under control. "Okay," she said. "Don't worry about it. There's a really good singer in one of the other tributes who was asking for more work. She'd work as a surrogate Ann, I think."

"Is it that one from Super Trouper? One of the ABBA women?"

"That's her."

"Yeah, you're right. She'd be good." Just like that, we were talking like two normal, intelligent human beings. Neither looking to tear out each other's guts. I found myself smiling a bit as I asked, "How's everything else? How's the day job going?"

"Ah," she said, her voice lighter. The voice I used to love. "Work's busy as hell right now. Summer tourism in Toronto." That last was said in a musical tone with all the sarcasm at her command.

"Do your ears ever get used to that?" I said.

Kelly worked at the CN Tower, a place that, for thirty-four years, held the title of the tallest structure in the world. It was still a huge tourist attraction, especially since they'd started up the EdgeWalk, a goddamn white-knuckle walk around the outside edge of the structure over a thousand feet up. Yeah, there were safety tethers, but still…

Kelly led the EdgeWalk, taking thrill-seeking morons with more money than brains for a walk. Of course, to get there, she rode the elevators up and down a couple of times a day, ears popping constantly.

"You don't really get used to it, but you learn to ignore it after a while," she said, then laughed. "Though I admit to taking perverse pleasure watching the newbies ride for the first time."

"Nice," I said. "Real mature." I laughed as well and, for just a moment, it was good between us. Still not completely normal, but for a few precious seconds there was no awkwardness, and, at least for me, I remembered why I'd wanted to spend time with her. It felt good. A small oasis in the desert.

"Thanks," she said. Then, switching topics, "So really, Lex, you doing okay?"

"Yeah." And just like that, I was back up and walking circles. "There's a few of my friends from high school here, they've helped."

"Good," she said. Then, with a little playfulness, "Any old crushes?"

It was stupid. I wanted to avoid the topic of Monica for a bit. I wanted to just figure out where we stood first, me and Kelly. Then again, I wanted to figure out where I stood with Monica as well. Not that it was any real secret where Monica's feelings were headed. I just needed to figure out my side of this new equation.

So, when Kelly lobbed that question out there, it caught me unprepared. I stopped walking circles. Stared up at the ceiling. Winced when I realized I'd taken far too long to answer, which further locked up any possibility of dropping a reasonable line of dialogue. I stood-stock still in my room, the goddamn deer in the headlights, too frozen with indecision to even move.

I was still hanging fire, still staring at the ceiling as I heard the sharp intake of breath. The exhale that could have been a sardonic laugh. Then a bit of a rattling, whooshing noise and I found I could once again picture Kelly easily. I'd seen this move with others, and knew it well. She'd dropped the phone from her ear and mouthed some foul language as her eyes bugged, unbelieving.

Then the phone was back in place, because she said, "You bitch." She wasn't loud about it. In fact, she said it quietly, almost intimately, which made it all the more terrible. "You fucking..." She searched for exactly the right word. "...you fucking *duplicitous* bitch."

"Hey," I said stupidly. "Hey."

"Hey what?" she said. "You met someone up there, didn't you?" She gave me time to deny it, but all I could do was emit a tortured creaking noise.

"And here I was, thinking how sweet you were," she said. "How you were being the bigger person. How I felt bad that I wasn't being that bigger person myself." More creaking on my part. "Just to fucking find out the only reason you're doing this, telling me to go off with Kevin was so you could get your lady-rocks off guilt-free."

Finally, *finally*, I found my voice. "Kelly, no. It's not like that."

"Yeah, it is," she said. Her words came out sharp, clipped. "Yeah, it is."

"Kelly."

"Don't, Lex. Don't give me any excuses. We're done," she said. There was a sound like a muffled sob. "We're just…done."

Then the line went dead.

I knew better than to call back a third time.

Instead, I stood in the middle of my hotel room, the phone warm in my hand, showing me the disconnected call and the duration, and all I could think was, *Wasn't she the one who had the affair?*

So, why the hell was I the one feeling like the asshole right now?

◆ ◆ ◆

LESS THAN TWO hours later, with my hotel room reserved for my eventual return, still feeling like an asshole, I met Monica at the coffee shop.

She was already there, two steaming mugs and a couple of pastries in front of her. "Didn't know if you preferred fruit or chocolate, so you can choose. I'm good with either."

I sat down, scanned the two of them, and said, with far more lightness than I actually felt, "Hey, if there's chocolate to be had, it always wins." I reached out for the chocolate pastry.

Monica slapped at my hand. "Oh hell no, Miss Grabby McGraberson. I was being polite. Step away from the chocolate and no one gets hurt."

And as we both laughed, I felt my heart lighten. A little, but enough.

We settled on tearing both the pastries in half and taking one each.

Monica brushed the crumbs from her hands. "You wanted to talk."

"Yeah."

I guess the look on my face was pained because she said, "Is this gonna be bad?"

"Well," I said, doing my best Howard Cosell, "it could still go either way."

She reached out and put a hand over mine. "Enough clowning around. What's going on?"

"Ray's dead."

"Pardon?" *Okay, so she hasn't heard.*

"Yeah, you heard me right." I moved my hand so our fingers touched. "He's dead. Murdered. Just like my mother was."

"Oh jeez," she said. She was quiet for a spell, staring at our entwined fingers. "I know how you felt about him, so I kinda don't know what to say."

I huffed out a sardonic breath. "S'okay, I don't either. I think the first thing to come to mind is, 'oh well.'"

She met my eyes, her lips tight, her brows furrowed with concentration and concern.

"Sorry, does that make me sound like a bitch?" *You duplicitous bitch.*

She squinted, raised a hand, held two fingers close together. "Little bit."

"Oh well," I said again, and that earned me another light slap.

"You truly are terrible, Alexandra Hedges."

"Stick with me, baby. It'll all end in blood and tears."

We both allowed smiles, but it did seem a bit crass to be cracking jokes when someone had been murdered.

We both went back to our food for a couple of minutes, then she said, "Regardless, Lex, I *am* sorry."

"Thank you," I said. "I appreciate that." I picked at my pastry. "So, I did bring you here for more than just good food, great company, and lousy tidings."

"Okay," she said, and once again, I noticed the magic of her eyes.

"I mentioned yesterday that I saw someone acting strangely at the funeral."

"Right," she said. "There was the whole Spooky Talia speculation."

"Yea-ah," I said, drawing the word out. "About that. Turns out, it *was* her."

"Plot twist!" Monica dropped both hands flat to the table. "How do you know?"

"It's a long story—and a rather weird one that I'm still processing, to be frank—but the upshot of it is…she's asked me to do something for her, and if I do, she'll let me know who's murdering my family."

Monica's mouth fell open, then her magical eyes scrunched up in confusion. "What…?" she said. "How…?" She stared at the table, seeing nothing. "But isn't she…? Like, when Dad's…?"

"Yeah, there's a veritable pant-load to unpack in that last sentence," I said. "I'm still doing a lot of unpacking myself."

Monica opened her mouth to speak, said nothing, closed her mouth. She shook her head. Opened her mouth again. Closed it again.

I smiled. "Exactly," I said. "Okay, so, we'll talk about all of this, I promise you, but I need to tell you something, then ask you something."

Monica nodded.

I took a breath. "I've been in a relationship for the past two years with a woman named Kelly," I said. Monica's eyes flashed something, and her mouth tightened down a bit. "It's over," I said, holding my hands up. "But it's just recently over. I knew it was done before I came to New Hope, but I just got the confirmation before I called you."

"Just got confirmation?" she said. "What does that mean, exactly?"

"She's with someone else, and…you came up."

"Oh." She rubbed a thumb over the handle of her mug. "How'd that go?"

"About as well as can be expected. I got the FOAD." I pronounced it foe-add.

"What's a FOAD?"

"Fuck Off And Die."

"Oh…kay."

"I'm telling you this to give you some context," I said. "We can discuss it in more detail whenever you want."

She was silent for long enough that the silence became part of the conversation. Everything in me told me to jump in with more words, but the more intelligent part of me kept my mouth shut.

"It's over?" she said. "You and Kelly?"

"Has been for a while, yes."

"And that's not just a line?"

"No."

"Lex, look me in the eye and tell me it's not just a line."

I reached out and held both her hands in mine, met her eyes with no hesitation, and said, "It's not just a line. Kelly and I are done."

She searched my face. I felt her hands hold mine a little tighter. "Okay," she said. "Okay. Damn, you're throwing a lot at me. Wow. So, what did you need to ask me?"

"I have to go someplace. To get something. And I'd like you to come with me."

Once again, I seemed to have gobsmacked her. She nodded one more time, just to let me know she'd received the message.

She stared down at her food. One hand released mine and she reached for her cup and brought it to her lips.

She held the coffee in her mouth as she set the cup back down again. Then she seemed to come to some conclusion. She swallowed, looked back to me, and said, "Where do you have to go?"

That's when I blew out a breath and thought, *Here goes nothing.* Then I gave her the answer I'd been dreading. "I don't know."

Again, her eyes scrunched and she shook her head. "Okay, what do you need to get?"

"I don't know that either."

"When will you know?"

"It will come to me as I go."

"Lex," she said, "are you unwell?"

"No."

"No recent head injuries?"

I laughed. "No, why?"

"Because you have basically just told me you're going on a quest to parts unknown for an unknown item, yet all will be revealed in the fullness of time."

I considered that. Yeah, she was right.

"It sounds like something some faithful disciple from the Bible would do on the Word of God."

"Well, shit," I said, "it sounds a lot more crazy when you put it like that."

"So…"

"Why am I doing it?"

"Yeah."

"I'm going to ask you to just take this on faith" — I held up my hands to ward off any protestations — "and I know how Word of God-ish that sounds, believe me. But what I can tell you right now is, Talia…how do I say this without sounding nuts? Talia demonstrated that she has powers that are…unbelievable.

But she proved to me, beyond a shadow of a doubt, that they're real."

"Hold on. You *met* her?"

"I did."

"In person?"

"In person."

"Huh. Okay." She shook her head, eyes wide. Shot her eyes back to me. She mumbled something under her breath. It could have been "Mom was right" or "out of sight" or "bombs are light" or something else altogether. There was an expression on her face that I flat-out couldn't read. She narrowed her eyes. "And you said something about powers?"

I tapped at my temple. "Monica, she's experienced a lot of things. Shocking, terrible things. And they've changed her. But she can basically download memories into your brain."

Monica stared at me.

"You're likely thinking I need some pharmaceutical assistance, but I'll just say I know exactly why Kayla and Norman left this town."

"She told you?"

"No, Monica," I tapped at my temple once again, "she made me *know*."

"And you believe it?"

"I do," I said. Then I told her very briefly about talking to Norman and, without giving her the gory details, told her that he had confirmed everything.

"And now you have to go on a quest somewhere…you don't know where…"

"It's west of here."

"Okay, lovely," she said. "You have to go west, to look for something…you don't know what…"

"Not yet."

"Right," she said. "Not yet. But, in the fullness of time, you will. And you want me to go with you."

I put my hand over hers. "I do."

"This is the craziest pile of bs I've ever been fed, Lex Hedges."

"Yeah, I know." My heart was sinking.

"And it's definitely the weirdest first date I'll likely ever go on."

Wait, did she just…?

Something in my expression must have changed, because she burst out laughing and said, "Yes, stupid as it sounds, yes, Lex, I'll go with you. If only to keep you out of trouble." Then the laughter faded, and she said, "And because, I…uh…I might be somewhat responsible."

I scrunched my eyes and cocked my head at her.

She held up a hand. "Miss Hedges, you and I? We've got a lot to talk about, and a road — who's length will be" — she made air quotes with her fingers — "disclosed with the fullness of time — to talk about it. So, can we just hold that thought for now?"

"If you're going with me? Yes, I can."

"Cool beans."

"I'd like to head out as soon as possible, and I think Bear and Grace and Gerry and Ruthless are heading out tonight."

"Not hanging around for Ray's funeral?"

I smirked. "Would you?"

"Point taken."

We made some quick plans to get together for the goodbyes, then we left How You Bean? and went our separate ways for now.

Well, damn, I thought. *That went better than planned.*

Then, on the heels of that, *I just hope Talia keeps her end of the bargain.*

◆ ◆ ◆

THE GOODBYES WERE quick and mostly painless, with a mixture of awkwardness on what to say about Ray. Mostly, we settled on ignoring him, as we'd done most of our lives.

Instead, it was the usual promises to stay in touch, to keep them updated on any news around the deaths, and admonishments to stay safe.

Of course, there were also the sly smirks around how Monica and I were standing so close together.

Seriously, I thought. *It's like fucking high school.*

Once the final goodbye was said, and the final hug given — even the begrudging one to Ruthless — Monica and I stood in the parking lot of the motel for a few moments more, just enjoying the silence.

And I was delaying my next meeting.

Talia.

♦ ♦ ♦

THE NEXT MORNING, I got up early and picked up some supplies, swung by Monica's modest apartment. Her bags were loaded into the car — along with some grumbling about not knowing what or how much to pack, because we didn't know where we were going or how long we'd be away — and she got in the car.

"Before we go, one last check," I said. "You're *sure* you're okay to go?"

"'To boldly go where no one has gone before'?" She pulled her seatbelt across and buckled it. "Yeah. It's all I could think about last night, but yeah. Got the three S's out of the way. I'm sure." She pulled a pair of mirrored sunglasses from where they'd hung on her shirt front, and put them on. "Let's go."

We were on our way.

At least, so we thought.

CHAPTER EIGHT

I T WAS HARD not to just keep looking over at the passenger seat. I had a beautiful woman sitting there, but more than that, just the fact that I had a woman who wanted to spend the next few days cooped up in a car with me at all…well, it felt a bit strange.

Then again, for the past few years, I'd had another beautiful woman who'd wanted to spend time with me…until Kelly didn't anymore.

Then again, Lex, maybe this is just the rough first step to getting your shit together. Maybe you always knew this first step was gonna be a bitch, and that's why you avoided it up to now.

I could only hope so. But still, that last conversation with Kelly kept replaying in my head.

And also my meeting with Talia last night, after I'd met with Monica to discuss this trip.

"No problems with getting more time off work?" Monica said.

"No, not really." I told her about the conversation with my editor yesterday.

"And what about the band? Dreamboat Annie? No problems there?"

Well, now isn't the time to start lying to her, I thought. *I can't do that.* I'd known it would come up sooner or later, but I'd wanted to just get a bit of time under our belts first, then I'd talk to her about Kelly in more detail.

And Talia.

And possibly even Ray and Kayla and Norman.

Yeah, I've got a lot of shit to unload.

But for now, back to her question. "We've got a couple of weeks before the next gig," I said. "I told them I didn't know if I'd make it back for that one, and they're looking for a replacement Ann. So, long story short, we're taking a break from each other." It wasn't a lie, but it wasn't the whole truth.

"And Kelly's in the band too, right?"

"Yes," I said. "She is."

"Hmm," was all she said. I looked over but saw only an unreadable expression partially hidden under big, mirrored sunglasses and a small smile lifting the corners of her mouth. Her beautiful mouth.

"How about you?" I said.

"Oh, well, they're not happy about it."

"They?"

Her smile spread a bit wider. "You know about the bookstore."

I did. Monica's grandfather, Stanley Holt, had owned a bookstore in New Hope. He'd called the shop The Last Word. His son, Monica's father, Dan Holt was pretty much ready to take the baton from his father when something bad happened.

One day The Last Word was there, the next day it was simply gone. Building and all. Nothing but a hole in the ground.

Monica was born a few months later, having never got to meet her father or grandfather. Nine years later, Monica buried her mother, Lila, and then Monica was an orphan.

I'd heard she'd reopened the store some time ago, and I'd been glad to hear it.

"You called it something close to the original, right?"

"It's kind of dumb, but I don't care. I called it The Second-Last Word."

"That works, too," I said. "So, 'they're not happy.' Who's these mysterious 'they'?"

"I hired my foster parents, Gabriel and Valentina Murack. Gabe and Val. Wonderful couple, been married almost forty-five years. Fantastic parents to me, fantastic employees. And," Monica said, and I thought I caught a note of darkness creep into her voice, just for a moment, "they saved my life."

She paused then, just for a moment. Anyone else may not have noticed it, but I was becoming tuned to her. I noticed.

"Anyway," she said with a shake of her tawny hair. She gave me a wide smile. "They know the store and customers better than I do, probably because they were regulars when the original was open."

"So, fantastic all around. I sense a 'but' coming."

"But," she said, drawing the word out over three notes, "they're also very old-school and traditional."

"Ah," I said. "Got it. Likely not the type I'd see at one of my shows." We both laughed at that.

"Anyway, after we talked at the coffee shop, I scooted over to the store and asked the Murack's if they'd be okay running things for a while."

"Let me guess, they'll do it, but they're concerned for you?"

"Got it in one," she said, shooting a finger gun at me. "Going off on an unscheduled and unchaperoned trip? With another woman of the lesbian persuasion?" She shook her hands, jazz-hands style. "Scandalous!"

"They're pretty religious, huh?"

"More like they're pretty 1950," she said. "They're very protective of me, but in a good way."

"So, then...?" I let the question hang.

"I pointed out everything they already know: I'm over the age of consent, I live on my own, I make my own decisions, and that I, too, am of the gay persuasion." She adjusted her sunglasses. "Oh, and, I own the place. They might be my parents, but I'm their boss."

"Ouch." I laughed. "True. But...ouch."

"Yeah," she said, laughing, "but what are they going to do? The only other employee I have is a seventeen-year-old kid named Colum who's just discovered the wonders of his penis. He's a whore."

"Aren't we all at seventeen?"

"Well, I mean, maybe? But Colum? He's special."

"How so?"

"Claims he has irritable bowel syndrome, or some such shit—"

"Pardon the pun."

"I think not! How dare you?" Monica said, quite indignantly. "Pun fully intended. Anyway, so, the kid with the IBS is constantly disappearing off to the bathroom. He claims he's shitting, so I've actually started calling him 'Poodini.'"

"Okay, that's not bad," I said.

She spreads her hands. "Right?"

"What's this got to do with—"

"But the staff washroom, despite walls and a door, offers little in the way of sonic privacy, so…"

"Oh," I said.

"So yeah, I hear him pullin' the python, and I know Gabe and Val have too."

"Right. Say no more."

"Right. So, with a walking ejaculation like him around, I can get away with a lot because I'm almost always the lesser of two evils. With the possible exception of the gay thing."

"Well, that's a plus, right?"

"I look at it as a challenge for them. They now have a limited number of days to turn Colum away from the sins of masturbation and extramarital sex, should he ever engage in any. God knows they seem awfully worried about that last one with me, too."

I laughed. "Listen, I don't want to be the one who leads you down the road of sin."

"You'd better," she said. "Otherwise, why am I along for the ride?"

And just like that, my mouth dried up. No spit.

Monica's throaty laugh filled the car and she placed both hands on the dash as she bent forward, her mane of hair falling forward. "What?" I said, trying to sound indignant, but smiling all the while. "I didn't say anything!" This only made her laugh harder, the throaty sound spiralling sweetly to a higher giggle. There was nothing to do but laugh along with her.

It took her a few minutes to get back under control. She leaned back in the chair, throwing her hair back over her shoulders, then pulled the sunglasses from her face and swiped at the tears there.

It looked a little weird until I realized I'd never really seen Kelly — or any other woman I'd been with — brazenly swipe at their eyes for fear of messing up their makeup. Kelly had always dabbed delicately, preserving the mascara. Hell, I did too, when the occasion arose. Monica wore none, and didn't need it.

"Okay," I said. "At the risk of setting you off again..." She giggled a bit but held it together. "...what so was so funny?"

"When I called you on leading me down the road of sin," she said and couldn't keep the shuddering laugh away as she finished her sentence, "the look...on your...face. It was...hilarious." Then she popped her face into a slack-jawed, wide-eyed blankness and I, recognizing myself in that expression, couldn't help but laugh in response.

"I so did not look like that," I lied.

"You so did."

"Goddamn," I said. "It's so hard to maintain that rock grrrl cool around you."

"Yeah," she agreed. "Especially when it looks like it's gonna be *me* that leads *you* down that road of sin."

This time, I made the face on purpose. And it got the laugh I was going for.

We drove on for a few minutes in companionable silence before she said, "You haven't really told me much about what we're doing or where we're going. I know now it's the road of sin, but you're still really not sure exactly where that's going to lead?"

I tilted my head toward her. "Gabe and Val might tell you it leads to hell."

"Gabe and Val believe damn near everything leads to hell. Everything from attending high school dances to eating McDonalds."

"That…" I said, but found I didn't even know where to go with it. The perceived list of offences bordered between those two goal posts was overwhelming. "That…covers a lot of ground," I said, shaking my head. "It does, however, explain one thing, though," I said.

"What's that?"

"With all the stuff that leads to damnation, it's easy to see why there's a highway to hell and only a stairway to heaven."

She was silent for a moment.

"What?" I said.

"I'm desperately trying not to groan at the dad joke. You killed any rock grrrl cool you ever had with that one."

"Sorry."

"You should be," she said, slapping my thigh. "Seriously, Hedges, you better commit to stepping up your humour." She hooked a thumb at the side window. "Or you can just let me out here and I'll thumb til I can find someone who will."

"Hedges?" I said.

"Hedges."

"That's a thing now?" I said. "That's a tag for me? Hedges?"

"Hedges." She considered. "Yeah."

I sighed loudly. "Fine, Holt. I will endeavour to please you to my fullest capabilities."

"That's better. You better have some damn rockin' capabilities, too." She smirked at me.

This really wasn't the girl from high school anymore. She really had obviously done some work to break away from that restrictive upbringing.

Guess we both had a fucked-up childhood, I thought. I didn't want to verbalize that, however, because I wanted to avoid those questions as well. Instead, I went back to her original request. "As to what we're doing and where we're going, I think I'll need to give you a bit more backstory so you can really understand, and I really don't want to do that in the car. Can we hold off until we're off the road for the evening?"

"I suppose I can allow that," she said.

"What I can tell you is that you called it right yesterday. We, fair maiden, are on a quest."

"A quest?" she asked. "For the Holy Grail?"

"No."

"So, we won't be fighting off killer rabbits?"

"No."

"And riding coconuts?"

"Again, no."

"No witches with carrots for noses?"

"Are you about done?"

She smiled sweetly. "Mostly."

"*Anyway*," I said, laying the mock exasperation on thick, "we're essentially heading to a small town. Just past it, there's a particular spot that's been chosen as a hiding place."

"For?"

"For..." I paused. *How much can I give her now without her demanding I turn the car around and check myself into a psychiatric facility?* "For something that's very important to someone. Important enough that they'll do a big favour for it."

"And that favour?"

"Will be explained to you somewhere after this road —"

"I would hope so. We haven't even passed Vilni, yet."

"Details."

"Okay," she said. "Somewhere after this road…but before the road of sin?"

I faced her, grinning broadly. "Something like that, yeah."

And that's when my phone rang.

◆ ◆ ◆

"LEX?"

"Yes, that's me."

"Constable Gustafsen. Norman," he said. "You have a couple of minutes to talk?"

"I'm just heading out of town, Norm," I said.

"Can I suggest you pull over, if possible? It's about your father. It's a matter of some urgency."

My phone was on hands-free and running through the car's speakers, so Monica was hearing this as well. At the mention of Marcus, she turned to me. She'd removed the sunglasses, and the expression on her face told me she was thinking the same as me.

He's been murdered, too.

"Gimme a sec," I said. I signalled and pulled off to the gravel, dropped into Park. "Okay," I said. "I'm not driving. Go ahead."

"Thanks," he said. "I'd rather do this face-to-face, Lex, but like I said, it's a bit more urgent than that. Your father is not in the best state right now."

Monica gave me another expression that was a little bit relief and mostly confusion.

"Meaning?"

"I think, due to the stress of his recent losses, his mental faculties have taken a hit."

"Okay, so…he should likely be in the hospital then."

"Yeah," Gustafsen said, and we both heard the exasperated breath. "We did. That's the problem. And the reason for the urgency."

◆ ◆ ◆

AFTER TALKING TO Gustafsen for a minute or two more, I hung up and Monica said, "Lex, we have to."

I didn't agree, but I did a U-turn and drove the five miles back toward New Hope and the hospital.

The hospital sat at the base of what we'd always called a mountain but really was just a large, rocky hill. There was a deep groove in the mountain, and the hospital sat snugly in its protective, stony embrace. I'd been here a few times as a kid. It hadn't changed a hell of a lot since the last time I'd seen it.

I pulled up to the Emergency entrance, where Gustafsen told me he'd meet me. And he was there.

With Marcus.

Unlike the building around him, Marcus had changed remarkably since the last time I'd seen him, yesterday morning. He sat huddled in a wheelchair, somehow smaller, as though he was collapsing in on himself like a star on its way to becoming a black hole.

As Monica and I approached, however, it was the look in his eyes that alarmed me the most. His eyes had sharpened to a feral brightness.

"The *fuck* do *you* want?" he said.

Marcus rarely swore. He'd always told me it was evidence of low breeding. He likely wasn't wrong. Then I realized he was zip-tied to the wheelchair.

Yeah, something's wrong. Seriously wrong.

"Sorry to drag you back, Lex," Gustafsen said. "Monica," he said, nodding.

"Tell me what's going on," I said.

"They're fucking with me," Marcus screeched. His hands fought the restraints, plastic biting into flesh. "They think I'm fucking crazy, but I'm not crazy, I'm not. I'll burn this world to the fucking ground."

"No one thinks you're crazy, Mr. Hedges," Gustafsen said, his voice calm and even.

"You do! You do! You're gonna burn too, Gutty."

Gustafsen canted his head off to the side, and I understood. We walked a few paces out of earshot of Marcus. Monica, to her credit, squatted down beside Marcus and put a hand on his and began talking calmly to him. It didn't seem to make a difference, Marcus still screeched accusations and profanities in equal numbers, but she didn't stop.

Gustafsen and I both watched it play out for a few seconds, then we turned to face each other. He didn't waste time. "The officer who delivered the news about Ray to your father yesterday said he took it well. Stoically, from what I understand."

"Sounds like his standard MO," I said. "He showed up at the motel about a half-hour after you'd left yesterday, and he was his usual Spock self."

"Yeah, you mentioned that. No signs of…" He angled his head toward him.

"No. None."

"You mind if I ask what you talked about?"

"It was pretty short," I said. "He wanted me to come live with him, I told him that was a hard pass, he told me he wanted me at Ray's funeral, and that was a hard pass as well, then I told him, as far as I was concerned, I had no family, then I left."

He nodded, lips pursed. "Well, somewhere between his meeting with you and when we got called in, he suffered a mental break."

"You sure?"

He angled his head and gave me a questioning squint.

"It's just that, during my little chat with him yesterday, I got the distinct sense that he had a Plan B if I didn't bend to his will."

"I wouldn't rule anything out, Lex," he said, "but from where I stand, this is a pretty excessive way to get your attention." He pulled out his notebook, and removed the elastic band that marked his last notations, securing it around his wrist. "The hospital's refusing to keep him anymore because—"

"Hold on, what?"

"They're refusing—"

"No, no," I said, waving a hand. "I understand what you said, but why? I mean, if he's being disruptive, can't they sedate him?"

"Maybe I should start at the beginning," Gustafsen said. "I'll make it quick."

♦ ♦ ♦

MARCUS HEDGES WAS found, naked and babbling nonsense, when he'd stumbled out of the forested area that surrounded the lake his house was situated on.

The problem was, it was well after midnight, and he was several miles from his home. He'd wandered onto someone's property, and their two dogs made a fuss.

"Owner, Kenneth Robeson, was a little confused, to be honest," Gustafsen said. "Normally they growl and, if that doesn't rouse the owner, they'll take to barking lightly.

They've been trained to alert him, not the intruders, unless he commands them to do it."

"What were they doing, then?"

"Whining," he said. "Apparently, one even pissed on the floor."

Frightened? I wondered.

Once he took a look and found out it was a man, and especially with no clothes, he didn't know what to think, but naturally, assumed the worst.

"He kept the dogs in the house and tried to talk to Marcus, but he said he was making no sense. He couldn't even make out if he was speaking English." Gustafsen looked up from his notes. "Does he know any other language?"

"Not to my knowledge," I said. "Unless he's learned one in the past twenty years."

"You never know," Gustafsen said. "Stranger things…"

He was going to drive Marcus to the hospital, but he was acting so weird, and he said he'd have these angry outbursts.

"Well, you caught a small one when you came up."

"Yeah."

Instead, Robeson called 911, and got fire and ambulance. He thought twice about bringing him in the house, on account of the outbursts, and he was scared to leave a naked and upset man alone in case he wandered off, so he gave him the robe he was wearing.

There was some confusion, because Marcus didn't know his name—or at least wasn't giving it away—and Mr. Robeson described him as a "young man" to the 911 operator.

"By the way, Lex," Gustafsen said, "how old is your father?"

"Funny you should ask," I said. "He's never really given up his exact age, and I don't think he even let my mother know his birthday."

"It's got to be on some documents somewhere."

"You'd think so, wouldn't you?"

"Okay, best guess?"

"I know my parents married in 1983. Assuming he was around the same age as Mom, maybe a touch older, and she was twenty-four when they were married, that'd put him around...what? Twenty-five to twenty-seven at the time?"

"Which would put him somewhere in his early-to-mid-fifties now."

"Sounds about right."

"Okay, well from what I saw of your father in the past few hours, I wouldn't put him much past our age. To tell the truth, Lex, he could pass for your younger brother."

"Yeah, our family's got some good genetics that way. I still get hit up for ID once in a while."

"Anyway, my point is, Mr. Robeson thought he was dealing with someone much younger, and so did we, with no identification to go on. So, we were a little slow to get hold of you until he finally gave us his name earlier this morning. I called you right after."

"Okay, so, he went for a wander, ended up at the hospital, and now he's being all high maintenance," I said. "Tell me why I'm here?"

"Two reasons," Gustafsen said. "First, like it or not, you're the only next of kin."

"Lucky me," I said with dripping sarcasm.

"And second, we have no one else to turn him over to."

I stared at him disbelievingly. There was absolutely no way I'd heard what I'd just heard. The moment drew on and got more awkward with each second that passed.

"Okay, I see I caught you a little off guard—"

"You think?"

"—but let me lay it out for you." He lifted his eyebrows in an unverbalized question. *May I proceed?* it said.

I rolled my hands. "Get on with it."

Gustafsen told me that Marcus—still a John Doe at this point—was loaded into the ambulance. By the time they arrived, the back of the vehicle appeared to have suffered a tornado, with virtually every machine destroyed, every container spilled of its contents, much of the stretcher twisted out of shape, and the two attendants in need of medical attention themselves.

"He went crazy."

"Why didn't they drug him?" I said. "Or, at the very least, restrain him?"

"They got one wrist into restraints, but he broke it."

"Slipped out of it?"

"No, Lex. He *broke* it."

"Okay," I said, drawing the word out in a manner that hopefully indicated I thought this was as equally far-fetched as if he'd told me he'd been anally probed by aliens.

"They also attempted to sedate him, but it didn't work." Gustafsen let that sink in. *It didn't work.* "He didn't give them a second chance to try."

"You think he maybe got into some of Ray's leftover drugs? Maybe bath salts or something?"

"Not sure. They haven't been able to actually do any blood tests. Because what he did in the ambulance? Yeah, times ten once they got him into the hospital. Seriously, Lex, it's a damn war zone in there."

"It can't be that bad."

"I can tell you that, in all my time as a police officer, never have I ever seen any one person cause so much destruction. Between the ambulance and the examination room? Tens of thousands of dollars, minimum."

"That sucks. But I still don't know where I come in."

"You are here because the attending physician also attempted to sedate him, and it was equally ineffective. All he got was a broken jaw, a few less teeth, and a wrecked examination room."

"To be clear, they're not actually getting the drug into him, right?"

"No, they are. It's just not working."

"Shit."

"Yeah," he agreed. "So now, they want nothing to do with him. You might have a lawsuit on your hands for refusal of treatment, but honestly, I can't blame them. And now, no other facility that has the room will take him, and no ambulance driver who'd agree to take him if they had."

"So, I'm supposed to deal with this somehow?"

"For the past several hours, he's been screaming for his baby girl."

"What?"

"Yeah, messed us up as well, until he finally gave up his name. When we got Marcus Hedges out of him, one of the officers clued in and called me, because he knows I'm working the Hedges' cases."

"And, long story short, you called me."

I'm asking for your help, Lex, he had said.

"I called you," he said. "Right."

"And now I'm just supposed to look after someone who's trashed both an ambulance and a hospital?"

Alexandra, I'm telling you, I need you, he had said.

"I wish there was another option, Lex," he said, and I could tell he truly meant it. "But we're literally hours away from any sort of proper facility for him and, as it stands, I don't know how we'd even transport him there because, my guess is, he'd have the back window of a cruiser kicked out before we were on the highway."

"And what the hell am I supposed to do with him?"

"The doctor's hoping that being with a family member might keep him calm, bring him back around."

"He's...hoping? Jesus Christ," I said. "We don't know

what's wrong with him, so let's roll the dice on a non-existent family connection?"

"Like I said, you probably have a good chance at—"

"Slapping all and sundry with a lawsuit, yeah, I heard." I ran my hands through my hair. "Doesn't exactly help me right now though, does it?"

"No, Lex, it doesn't."

"And you can't just put him in a jail cell? Destruction of property or something like that?"

"There's been a few higher-profile cases in the past few years that make those above my pay grade a touch reticent to lock up someone with obvious mental conditions."

"So then, what do they suggest?"

"Those facilities that are hours away."

And then we just stopped talking. I looked over at Marcus. Monica was still squatting beside him. But they appeared to be conversing.

Quietly.

Maybe the doc is right, I thought, but I wasn't going to admit that.

"Maybe the doc is right?" Gustafsen said.

"Sincerely doubt it," I lied. "All right, obviously I'm backed into a fucking corner here—"

"I apologize."

"Not your fault."

"I appreciate your understanding."

"Think I can get some help loading him into the car?"

"If he'll let me, sure."

"I suppose dropping him in the trunk is likely breaking some rule, huh?"

He smirked. "Yeah, pretty sure that's a no-no."

As we approached the two of them, Monica stood up. "What's going on, Lex?"

Gustafsen jumped in, likely thinking she might take the

news better from him than me. "We've asked—on behalf of both the police and the hospital—that Mr. Hedges be remanded to Lex's custody. She's agreed."

"Under protest," I added.

"Under protest," he said, nodding.

"He's coming with us?" Monica said.

"Yeah," I said. "Sorry. You don't have to—"

Monica held up a hand to silence me. "We'll deal." She looked down at the cuffs. "Norman, you wanna…?"

Gustafsen pulled a small knife from somewhere, bent, and cut the flexi-cuffs off the wheelchair. I think all three of us let out a breath when Marcus didn't immediately turn into the Tasmanian Devil and go on a winding path of terror and destruction.

He stood, smoothed his robe, walked to my car, and calmly opened the door and got in the back seat.

Gustafsen scratched the back of his head. "Huh," he said.

"What about the wheelchair?" Monica said.

"You might need it," Gustafsen said.

"It's the hospital's," I said.

He shrugged. "Oops." And in his face I read, *They're making you take him, I consider this a fair trade.*

I folded the wheelchair and muscled it into the trunk. Lucky Monica packed as light as I did. I slammed the trunk lid down. Gustafsen and Monica both stood at the back of the car with me.

"I really am sorry about this, Lex."

"I am too," I said. "But, not your fault."

Monica gave him a hug. "Good to see you again, Norman. Say hi to Kayla for me."

"I'll do that," he said, smiling. Turning to me, he shook my hand. "Take care of this one. She's a keeper."

"Damn right I am," Monica said and headed around to her door.

We all laughed, and I looked down at the hand that Gustafsen had just shook. There were a bundle of zip ties there.

I looked at him.

"You might need them. I can't let you take him without some sort of way to keep him in line."

I held up the ties. "You're a good man, Charlie Brown."

He gave me a smirk, wished me good luck, and angled off to his cruiser.

♦ ♦ ♦

IT TOOK ANOTHER hour, but after three stops we were on our way. The last stop had been to pick up some coffee because, quite frankly, I needed it.

I handed Monica her coffee and put mine in the cup holder. Marcus said he didn't want anything, so I ordered a donut and bottled water for him in case he needed something later. He was sitting quietly—weirdly quiet, actually—in the back seat. But he was behaving. As I pulled away from the drive-thru and got back on the highway, I let out a long breath.

"Okay, I'm just gonna say it," I said. "This past hour was weird."

Monica fiddled with the tab on her coffee. "You can say that again."

"This past—"

"Changed my mind. You can't say it again."

"Fine," I said. "Be that way."

She reached over and held my hand, and that was enough. It told me that, despite the banter, she agreed. It had been weird.

After the hospital, Monica had suggested we head back to Marcus's house to pack him some clothes. And to get him into some, as he seemed quite oblivious to all the flashing he was doing. And I couldn't handle that, not at all.

No child, regardless of age, should need to see their parent's private parts.

I fully expected to be picking up some of his less-filthy clothing from the floor and making do until we could find a laundromat.

We pulled into the driveway that was so familiar to me, and I drove down that same winding path to the house. The front door had been left hanging open, and it swung back and forth lazily in the morning breeze.

But it was the large mountain of ruins that smouldered in the middle of the large gravel turnaround that surprised us more.

"What the hell?" I said.

"Is that…furniture?" Monica said, leaning forward to see better.

Marcus chuckled quietly from the back seat.

I parked the car well away from the pile and got out. As I approached it, I still felt the residual heat. The flames had burned out, but glowing coals remained, slowly disintegrating the remains of the living room furniture, the dining room table and chairs, two beds, and god knows what else.

Monica opened the door for Marcus and he got out, all sounds overly loud in the morning stillness.

I turned on him, pointing to the smoking mound. "What the fuck?"

"Language, Alexandra," he said automatically. "Changes are needed." He looked to the smoking pile in admiration. "The old must be burned away to allow for the new."

"The fuck does that mean?"

But Marcus, uncharacteristically, refused to elaborate.

I shook my head, and the three of us went into the house, which held its own surprises.

Stepping into the foyer, the first thing I noticed was that the place seemed more echoey. I realized it was because all the furniture had been removed for the campfire outside. But it was more than that.

"You pulled up the carpets, too?"

Marcus just nodded with a small "mm" noise.

"Burned them too?"

Nod. "Mm."

Turns out there was a relatively nice hardwood under them. Who knew? And they had been swept clean. A glance around told me that the kitchen was also clean. Spotless, actually. Windows too.

I checked the fridge. It was completely empty, and gleamed like it was sitting on some showroom floor. I opened the cupboards. Empty.

Clean and empty. Everywhere I looked, clean and empty.

I glanced at Monica, who stood behind Marcus, staring at the empty house, her lips parted.

She's blown away by the sight of the place, but she didn't see the junkyard version before. She doesn't even understand the full scale of this yet.

Marcus, for his part, stood quietly, hands clasped in front of him, staring at the floor. He was making a soft "uh uh uh" noise.

"I don't think we're gonna find any clothes here for him," I said. "Guessing they were tossed on the pyre with everything else." Monica nodded. "Give me a sec," I said, and went down the hall, glancing quickly into each room as I passed.

Bathroom. Empty and clean.

My old room. Empty and clean.

Ray's room. Empty and clean.

Marcus's room. Empty and clean.

He did all this after he left me, and still had time to wander in the wilderness for several miles? Something fluttered unpleasantly in my chest, like a bird caught in a building, desperately hammering at the windows to escape. Was it fear? Confusion?

Was it sympathy? *Surely not*, I swore to myself.

All I knew was, suddenly, I couldn't fucking breathe anymore. The walls seemed too close, too confining, and there was no air, and my mind was spinning off in a million different directions at once. I couldn't handle this. This house. The pyre. Kelly. Monica. Marcus. Talia. Kayla. Norman. The trip. Ray. Mom.

I couldn't handle it.

Any of it.

I can't fucking deal with this, I screamed at myself. *I can't. I fucking can't. I can't.*

And then there were arms around me. I was on my knees — *When did I fall to my knees?* — in the doorway to my parents' room and Monica was there, and she was holding me, her hair brushing my face, her breath soft in my ear, her words quiet and comforting. "Shhh," she whispered and hugged me and rocked my gently. "It's okay, it's okay, it's gonna be okay, it's just an anxiety attack, shhh, it's okay, just breathe, deep breaths, it's gonna pass, you're okay, I'm here…"

It took only another minute or two, or another hour or two, but I felt my thoughts slow and the walls settle back and the air began to slide back in and out of my lungs.

She held me for a while after it passed, until I sniffed and swiped at my eyes. "I'm okay," I said, and my voice only trembled a little. "I'm okay. Thank you."

Monica let me go and we both stood. Then she hugged me again.

"The hell was that?" I said.

"Panic attack," she said. "I used to get them a lot. Back when Mom… Back when I was a kid, and then again when my husband left me."

"Umm…" I said, leaning back from her. "Your husband?"

"Yes," she said slowly. "Duane. I…I'm sorry, I thought you knew. It…was a long time ago. I thought you knew." She held up her hand. A ring on her left hand.

"I…did not," I said. I looked around at this strange, alien house that I'd grown up in. "We can talk about it later. Just one question for now: It's over?"

She smiled at the echo from our meeting in the coffee shop. *God, was that just yesterday?* "It's over," she said.

"Okay," I said. "Good."

We walked back down the hall and, while Monica got Marcus back in the car, I took a hose to the smoking mountain, making sure it was well-soaked. I put the hose away, went to lock up the house, realized there was nothing in the house anymore, so that likely meant keys as well.

Then a memory flashed through my mind and I went to where the eavestrough drain ran down on the far side of the garage. I reached up to a spot where it angled out from the wall a bit, and felt around.

There it is.

We'd always kept a spare housekey in a little magnetic box, mostly for Ray, who was forever losing his keys. I pulled out the box, opened it, and pulled out the key. *Now the next question…does it fit the lock?*

It did.

I locked the door, not that there was much to steal, but more to prevent squatters or teens looking for a place to party. Ray *did* teach me some things. I added the key to my key ring.

I got in the car and took what I considered to be my last look at my childhood home.

I was wrong about that.

◆ ◆ ◆

The Second Stop was in Opeongo, where Monica scooted into a couple of stores and picked up some stuff for Marcus. Three changes of clothes, a jacket, and some toiletries.

Gotta say, she blew my expectations, getting back to the car less than fifteen minutes after leaving it with several bags, indicating she was done.

Damn, I thought. *Power shopper.*

Our last stop was for the coffees and finally…finally, we were on our way.

◆ ◆ ◆

FINALLY…FINALLY THE three of them were on their way. The male, his bitch spawn, and the other.

He only cared about the bitch spawn. They told him that the spawn was the only one who mattered.

The other two were expendable.

But really, only one of them was.

He followed at a very discreet distance.

And the thoughts boiled in the terrible, dark valley of his mind.

Only one of those other two is expendable.

◆ ◆ ◆

SOMEWHERE BETWEEN ORDERING the coffees and indicating how weird the past hour had been, Marcus ended up laying down in the back seat, a bag of clothes for a pillow.

I cocked a thumb over my shoulder, and Monica looked to the back seat. "It must've been a long night for him," she said, her voice warm and low.

"Maybe the drugs are kicking in." Whatever the reason, I'd take the quiet. I didn't expect it to last.

We both settled back in our seats, enjoyed the thrum of the wheels on the road, the trees and rocky outcroppings of the Canadian Shield sliding by the windows, the low sounds of the radio and Marcus's faint snoring as background.

For me, despite all that had happened in the past week, despite the reason for this trip, despite the snoring Marcus three feet behind me, I could at least be present in this one perfect moment, this bubble in time that held me and Monica together, and keep it close.

I turned to her again, and she to me. "Honestly, though, Monica. I'm glad you're coming with me. Especially with our unexpected passenger. It means a lot."

"I'm glad too," she said and laid a hand on my thigh. I covered it with my own and smiled.

Will she still say that after I tell her everything? I wondered. *Marcus wasn't the only one busy burning the past last night.*

We drove on.

♦ ♦ ♦

THE FIRST DAY, we got as far as Sault Ste. Marie, a city within spitting distance of three of the five Great Lakes. Nobody I knew referred to the city by its name, and it's a place I'd always known as "the Soo."

We had been on the road only a couple of hours when Monica had asked, "How do you know where to go? You never seem to hesitate or need to look for signposts or directions."

I honestly hadn't noticed it until she mentioned it. I'd just kind of…gotten into the car and drove. It was like I had a GPS built into my head.

It was these damn memories. My false memories. Talia had implanted these like she'd pushed the ones from Kayla, Ray, and Norman into my brain. Inserted them. I knew this fact as well as I knew my own name.

But I didn't want to get into that with Monica just yet. The Talia Talk. That would lead to…

Well, it led to an area I wasn't quite ready for yet.

"It's a long story," I said, then immediately realized that was no excuse because, still at the beginning of this trip, we had hours and hours and hours to kill. A long story would be just the thing.

"It's a long story," I repeated, "but it's not one I'm quite sure how to tell just yet."

Monica set her eyes in a way that told me she didn't understand. And I got it. *She's gotta be wondering. How is it I'm not sure how to tell a story of how I know where to go?*

"There's some lead up to it," I said, and gripped the steering wheel tighter, realized it, pulled a hand off and ran it through my hair. "I need to fill in some stuff before I get to that." I tapped at my temple. "I gotta understand it better before I can explain it to you, if that makes any sense."

"Okay," she said.

"I just need to bit of time to get it all straight, okay?"

"Okay," she said. It came out noncommittal.

"Seriously, I'd tell you but—"

"Lex," she said. "It's cool. I get it. Tell me when you're ready."

"You sure? You're not mad?"

"Do I look mad?" There was a big smile plastered across her face.

"Gonna have to say no to that one."

"We made a deal. We'd be honest. Say what's on our minds. No secrets, no hidden agendas. Right?"

"Right," I said, feeling uneasy. *Kelly's voice. Duplicitous bitch.*

"Then you'll tell me when you're ready." She settled more comfortably into her seat, kicked off her shoes, and put her bare feet up on the dash. "Not like I'm going anywhere. I can wait."

"You sure?"

"I'm sure if you ask me that one more time, I'll kick your ass," she said. Thankfully, she was still smiling. She put on her oversized sunglasses that somehow just made her more pretty.

We fell silent then, but I watched her out of the corner of my eye. Her big sunglasses catching the sun, her tawny mane blowing in the breeze from the open window, her toes moving in time to the song on the radio.

And I wondered, *How in the hell had I been so…what? Naïve? Stupid?…back then?*

I'm a stupid bitch now, and I was a stupid, insecure bitch then.

I shook my head in wonder at my own stupidity and drove on, trying to figure out how, now that I was slowly getting my shit together, I'd manage to keep it that way.

◆ ◆ ◆

MARCUS WAS STILL asleep when we pulled into the parking lot of a faceless conglomerate hotel chain and I shut off the engine. Monica made to get out, but when I didn't move, she settled back into the seat.

"Something wrong?"

"No," I said. Then sighed. "Yes." *I'm overthinking it again.* I did that a lot. "I'm not…"

"One room with two beds will be fine, Lex." She smiled. "One for him, one for us." Then she leaned my way, putting that hand on my thigh again. "But make them king-size."

I glanced at her questioningly.

"If you're good, then we'll need the extra real estate."

"Oh, we're going to…um…get busy, with him not three feet away?" I said, drawing a disbelieving look out.

"If the opportunity arises, we'll take it," she said.

"You presume much, dear lady. And if I'm not good?"

"Then I can put some distance between us. Also, the extra distance comes in handy if you snore."

"I don't snore."

"Then that's a point in your favour, Hedges."

"Okay, but seriously, what about..." I thumbed over my shoulder.

"We'll work it out," she said, patting my leg.

I shook my head, smiling as we exited the car. I'd already made sure the child locks were active in the back seat, and locked up the car while we booked the room.

I had to slow myself to match Monica's more languid steps. She reached for my hand and, as our fingers touched, I wondered if she felt the electric thrumming through her body like I did.

◆ ◆ ◆

WE GOT THE room, parked the car closer to the nearest entrance, and Monica got Marcus moving as I dragged our bags up two flights of stairs.

I plunked my bag down on one of the fold-out support racks, unzipped it, and pulled out a smaller bag with my bathroom stuff, walked it to the bathroom counter, and tucked it off to one side.

Then I sat on one bed and Marcus glared from the other for the next twenty minutes while Monica carefully and meticulously de-tagged all of Marcus's stuff, packed it away, then unpacked her own stuff. I found it difficult to not lob out sarcastic comments, but remembered her comments about the bed I currently sat on and shut my mouth.

When she was finally finished, she plopped down beside me on the bed. I noticed that Marcus had fallen asleep sometime in the past twenty minutes. I was starting to think maybe the trouble had been somewhat exaggerated. I brought a finger to my lips and pointed at Marcus. Monica nodded.

"You finished?" I said, keeping my voice low.

"I think so."

"You *think* so?" I said, drawing back in disbelief. "You sure you don't want to empty your purse and pack that stuff away, too?"

"Listen, Hedges. *Some* of us take pride in our work."

"Pride in your work. Unpacking a suitcase?"

"As a matter of fact," she said, "yes. My suitcase. *And* your fath…Marcus's stuff, too."

I raised my hands, palm out. "Oh, well then. Far be it from me to—"

She reached up and intertwined her fingers with mine and I forgot what I was going to say.

She gazed directly into my eyes. "Carry on," she said. *My god, her eyes are beautiful.*

"Never mind," I said. Never taking her eyes from mine, she tightened her grip on my hands a little and eased back on the bed, pulling me along. Then I was over her, her hair fanned out in waves. I leaned in and kissed her, softly at first, our lips barely touching. I pulled back as her eyes slowly opened.

"Don't stop," she whispered. We kissed more then. Her lips parted and her tongue teased along my lips. She released my hand and I felt a gentle pressure on the back of my neck as she pulled me down.

I shouldn't be doing this, I thought.

I pulled away, breathing hard.

God DAMN it.

"Can we…" I paused. *Damn it damn it damn it!* "Jesus, I never expected it to be me saying this, but can we wait?"

I tried to read her eyes, but I couldn't decide if I saw confusion or hurt there. Probably both.

"Yes," she said, moving me aside as she sat up. "Yes, of course. I'm sorry…I…"

I placed a hand on her arm. "Monica," I said.

"It's okay," she said.

"Monica," I said again. She turned to look at me over her shoulder.

"There's a couple of things I need to tell you." I paused, then went on. "And, like I told you a few days ago, I don't want anything hidden between us. I don't want to start that way."

"There's some things you need to tell me?" Now I was sure I saw both confusion and hurt. "So, it wasn't that you weren't sure how to say it, were you? You were waiting. Am I right?"

"Yeah, you are."

"So, you kind of already have had some stuff hidden between us, haven't you?"

She's absolutely right, Hedges. "Monica…" I tried to keep the pleading out of my voice.

"No, I'm just making a point, Lex. Have we not been sitting in a car for several hours? You don't think you could have found a time…and maybe a way…in the past few hours that we could have found a quiet, private place to talk? Like, say, a *car?*"

"You said you were fine to wait until I was ready."

"Back when I thought you needed to figure it out. I think you had it figured out all along."

I didn't have anything to say to that.

"It just feels like you wanted to make sure we were well on our way before you dropped a bomb on me or something."

Shit, I thought. *She's not far off.*

She wasn't angry. Yet. From the look on her face, she was close, but I guessed—hell, I hoped—she was still more in the territory of hurt.

Yet all that kept running through my mind was, *I'm fucking this up.*

I sat up, stood, walked to the desk, and pulled open the drawer. I found what I was looking for and pulled out my phone. "What do you like on your pizza?" I said.

Her eyes narrowed, then squinted in confusion. "What?" She turned more to face me. "What?" she said again.

Once again, I held out a placating hand. "I'm going to talk to you—I'm going to tell you everything—and I don't want waiters and food to interrupt us, so I'm going to order a pizza and we'll talk. The only interruption will be the delivery." I spread my hands. "It's not what I wanted our first real dinner to go like, but that's my fault, so hopefully you'll forgive me."

Still looking confused, she threw out some toppings, none of which I found objectionable—not that I would have said so, considering the current climate. I dialled and ordered.

"It'll be about forty-five," I said.

"Oka then," she said, "you've got forty-five minutes. Start talking."

I took a deep breath, then dove in.

♦ ♦ ♦

HE HAD POSITIONED himself near the window. He was in the same motel, but at the other end, where the buildings angled back toward the highway in an L shape. It wasn't the best vantage point, but he wouldn't be spotted, and he could see if they came or left the room.

After an hour of no movement, he turned the phone on, waited for it to find the signal, then dialled a number from memory. As it rang, he swiped a sweating hand against his thigh.

He heard something pick up on the other end. There was no greeting. There never was.

"They've stopped for the night," he said.

"And?" The voice was deep. Deep as an abyss.

"And I remain vigilant. I will make you aware of any update."

"Do so." The phone's speaker crackled with the inadequacy of transmitting the depth of the speaker's voice.

The connection broke.

He erased the call log, powered the phone down again, and put it back in his small travelling bag, sitting on the table right by the window. He would not leave his station until they were heading back on the road.

He swiped his hands over his sweating face, wiped them on his pants again.

It was going to be a long night.

CHAPTER NINE

THE FIRST PART didn't take as long as I'd expected.

I told her about Talia's first visit to my hotel room. I told her everything. Okay, *almost* everything. How surprisingly young she looked, about being swept inside Kayla's and Ray's heads, the entire rape and, though it was hard for me, and I tripped and stumbled many times over the words, I told her about Talia's final offer. I kept only one thing back. The one thing that Monica didn't need to know.

I've been inside your head now, Lex. I know you find me attractive. More attractive than Monica.

What good would it do for Monica to know that? Especially considering what happened afterward between Talia and me?

Yeah. God. When I met up with Talia that last time.

"Wait a minute," Monica said. She stared at the floor, but her hands were up, palm out. "Hold on." She stayed silent for a moment, as though processing what I'd said one last time. "She actually said, 'I've never lain with anyone'?"

"Yeah," I said. "She did."

"And she actually made some…bargain…with you? That you had to…to…well, pardon my French, but you had to fuck her?"

"Yeah."

"And?"

And so, I told her the rest.

♦ ♦ ♦

"When she left, I visited Kayla"—and here Monica's eyes shot up in surprise, but she said nothing—"because I needed to…" I trailed off. This was harder than I'd expected. "I guess I needed to know if it had really happened the way Talia showed it to me and—"

"And you needed to know if Norman killed your brother and mother."

"Yeah," I said, pleased that she got it immediately.

"Because if he did, and she can somehow deliver the killer…"

"I don't want it to be Norman."

"Right."

"Right."

"And what did she say?"

I recounted their conversation, summing up that, while Norman could have done it, Kayla said he didn't.

"And that's good enough for you?"

"No," I said. "That's why I visited Norman next."

"You got around."

"I did."

"And?"

"And I found out that Talia had actually shown up there, right after Ray left Kayla in the middle of the road."

"Asshole."

"Asshole doesn't begin to cover it, Monica."

"True." She lifted her eyes to me. She'd been steadily staring at the ugly hotel room rug. "Talia was there?"

"She was." I shifted uncomfortably on the bed. Talking about Talia made me uncomfortable. Like she'd know I was talking about her, or she'd show up here, at our door. Something like that. "She apologized for not being able to make him 'go away.'" I made air quotes with crabbed fingers.

"Go away?"

"I don't know." Then I made the air quotes again. "She said if she could, she'd 'have his teeth.'"

"What's that supposed to mean?"

"I don't think I'd want to know."

"So, Norman told you all this?"

"Yeah," I said. "And he also denied killing Ray."

"You believe him?"

"I guess I have to. He knows the stakes." *Does he though? Does he really? Do I?*

"Then what happened?"

"Then I met you for coffee."

She watched me silently, obviously waiting for me to continue.

"And, when you agreed to ride on this ridiculous quest with me," I said, "I was ready to visit Talia again."

Monica still said nothing. She sat almost primly, her palms flat on her thighs, knees together. Her clear eyes watched me unblinkingly, her face open, eyebrows slightly arched. Silent.

Okay, this is uncomfortable.

◆ ◆ ◆

"WELL, TO BE technical about it, I was *ready* to talk to Talia. But I had no idea how to reach out to her. To be honest, the first time we talked, it was such a goddamn mindfuck, I didn't even think to ask her about how to meet again."

"So…" Monica said, rolling her hands for me to just get on with it. *Yeah,* I thought, *she doesn't give a shit about how we met. She wants to know about when we met.*

"So, not knowing what else to do, I went back to the hotel, figuring I'd ask Annie or Ambrose if they knew where she could be reached." I stopped, looked at the cheap rug, then back to Monica. I still couldn't read her eyes. *I shouldn't be drawing this story out, but dammit, I want to make sure she understands.*

"And when I got there—"

"She was already there. In your room."

I nodded. "She was."

Now we're getting down to it.

"And?"

"And…well…" I ran my hands through my hair. *Honesty.* "Monica, she was naked and in my bed."

Monica, to her credit, said nothing, but her mouth was the thinnest of grim lines.

"I might have expected a lot of things, Monica, but I hadn't expected that."

"And then what happened, Lex?"

◆ ◆ ◆

I SWUNG THE door open and tossed my hotel and car keys on the desk just inside the room. They jangled as they hit, and the car keys slid across and off the far side. I whispered "shit" as I bent to retrieve them.

When I put them back on the desk, that's when I realized I wasn't alone.

I turned and faced the bed.

"Talia," I said, the name escaping in a rush. "Jesus Christ. You scared the shit outta me."

"Lex," was all she said. She was in my bed, the pillows piled behind her. She sat, leaning against them, the covers up to about her hips. Above it, her absolutely perfect breasts were exposed, gently rising and falling as she took her slow, calm breaths.

"Talia, what…?"

"Oh, Lex," she said, as a small, delicate, and unbelievably enticing smile bent her lips. "Are we really going to do this? Go through this whole 'what are you doing in my room' game?"

"Talia…"

She leaned forward slightly, the muscles of her smooth belly tightening, and I took an involuntary step back, trying to maintain some sort of distance between myself and those breasts.

Those perfect, stunning breasts.

"You really need to increase your vocabulary, Lex," she said. "I believe we've established you know my name and covet my breasts."

You're inside my head again, aren't you? I thought.

"I am."

"Then you know my answer."

"You know my bargain. You do for me, then I will do for you." She crossed her arms. "That was my deal."

"Your deal. Not mine."

"Regardless."

"Regardless, shit. I can't do this."

"You can. You want to. I can feel it in your mind. I can feel it…" And she looked pointedly at my traitorous crotch. I don't know how she knew, but she knew. We both did. I was wet.

"I'm not going to deny that you are the most stunningly beautiful woman I've ever seen. I can't. You'd know I was lying."

"I would."

"And I can't even deny that the desire's there. I wish I could, but it's kind of obvious." I could literally feel the blood heating my face, my nipples two sharp, sensitive points, aching to be touched, pushing against my bra.

"It is."

"But, Talia, if you can get inside my mind, you also know something else." I looked down, away from her. I couldn't meet her eyes. "You know that I've recently found someone. Someone nice."

"Monica Holt."

"Yes," I said, swallowing hard. Fear? Was it fear I felt? *No, Lex, this is way past that. You're fucking terrified right now.* "Right. Monica." I swallowed again. Took my time. *You're getting your life — and your shit — together, so just push through this.* "Talia, if you're inside my head, then you damn well know that I'm really liking this woman. Really caring for her. Caring for someone for the first time in a long time."

Talia said nothing. Just stared at me.

"And you'll understand that I don't want to fuck this up." I scrubbed a hand through my hair again. "You gotta understand. If you had shown up like this even a week ago, Talia, there would have been no hesitation. I wouldn't be standing here with a goddamn lady boner and trying to talk myself out of it."

She smirked, but it didn't feel mocking.

"So, what I'm saying is that I'm not going to 'lay' with you. I'm not going to give you something because it's some part of an arbitrary bargain that you dictated the terms of. I'm not going to do something that's going to fuck up the first good thing I've had in a long time."

"You could be in danger."

"I could. I get that." I blew a long breath out. "I get it. But if that's what it takes, then fuck it, I'll take the chance. Because if I do this, if I end up going to bed with you, then I'll lose Monica. And that's as it should be. I *should* lose her for something like that. That's why Kelly lost me."

I didn't feel the need to tell her who Kelly was. *If she can get inside my head, then fuck it, she can do the mental Google and figure it out herself.*

"There's something else, isn't there?"

"No."

"Yes, there is."

"No, really, there —"

"Your father doesn't enter into the equation in any way?"

Jesus Christ, I thought. *You know about that, too?*

"Enough to know you —"

No, I'm not going to talk about this. Not now. Not with you. Cutting her off, I responded with, "Enough to know I have daddy issues. Yeah."

"And."

"And that..." Could I even get the words out? "That...I don't like...well, it's mostly uncomfortable when..."

"Aggressive older sexual partners aren't your fantasy," she finished.

"Whatever."

"And yet, here I am. And here you are. And you are tempted."

I waved my hands as though to erase her words. "Aroused? Yes. Tempted? No. *Big* difference," I said. "So, you get it? I won't do it."

"Even though those are the terms of the agreement we entered?"

"No, it was the terms you dictated. I was to give you my answer, and..." Another breath, another long, slow release of breath. "And I just did."

Talia was quiet for a long while. I waited her out. I finally brought my gaze up and met her eyes. She stared back into mine.

Neither of us said anything, but I could feel her inside my head. It was a strange feeling, like she was moving the furniture around slightly, pushing her fingers down behind tight cushions, looking under beds. *Rooting around in my head.* It wasn't pleasant in the least, but there wasn't a whole hell of a lot I could do about it.

I didn't know what she was looking for exactly, but I felt the exact moment when she exited. My head felt lighter, cleaner.

Though one word seemed to resonate around my brain. Just one word: *teeth.*

Then she nodded. A short tip of the head.

"Would you mind turning around, please, Lex?"

"Would I...? What?"

"I'm going to get out of your bed now, and I'd like to get dressed without you looking at me, if that is okay with you?"

I didn't know how to answer, so I didn't. I simply turned around and faced the wall.

I listened to the sounds of the bedclothes, then clothing slipping over skin. I did my damnedest to not think of that skin, or anything to do with Talia or her body.

Of course, I completely failed, simply because telling myself not to think of something only made me think of it more.

Still, a few moments later, I heard her voice, soft. "Okay," she said. "You can turn back around now."

I did.

"Thank you," she said.

"So, now what?"

"Now I give you more instructions and, when you've located the Staff, I'll set up the meeting."

"I'm confused," I said. "You're going to go ahead with the plan?"

"I am."

"But...okay, I know I'm totally looking a gift horse in the mouth, but I've got to ask: Why?"

She stepped along the side of the bed, then came to me. She came up close to me. Very close. Uncomfortably close.

"Because I asked you to do something unreasonable, Lex." Her eyes were soft. "I demanded something of you that was not mine to demand." Then I watched her eyes unfocus and soften. "Something that someone close to me demanded of their own as well. Something that also was not theirs to demand, yet still, they demanded it."

"I'm not sure I understand."

Her gaze came back to me. "There's really no need for you to understand, Lex." She put her hands on my arms and lightly kissed my cheek. "All you need to know is that you did exactly the right thing. The thing you were supposed to do. The thing I wanted you to do."

She stepped away from me then, and it was like I saw her for the first time. She was just as beautiful, just as ridiculously young looking, but she was somehow less alluring. Smaller.

Sadder.

And somehow, much more human.

Talia walked to the door.

"Wait," I said. "This thing that you were going to give to me. The next set of instructions or whatever. When…"

"I already did," she said, a sad smile crossing her mouth. "Think of where you need to go to find the Staff."

"Find the Staff?" I said, not knowing what she was talking about. Then I did. In the span of a heartbeat, I had the full memory of the Staff. I knew what it was, what it was capable of, what it meant.

Not only that, I knew exactly where it was, knew how to get there, knew how to get it.

"Holy shit," I said.

"Holy shit, indeed," she said.

She turned and opened the door to the hallway. "How will I get in touch with you again, Talia?"

"You don't have to worry about that," she said. "I'll find you."

"Are you following me?"

"Not necessarily following you, Lex. But I am looking out for you at times."

And somehow, even after all I'd learned about Spooky Talia, I felt comforted by the thought of this strange, strangely sad woman looking out for me.

"Okay," I said.

She turned, walked over the threshold, then turned back to me one last time. "Thank you, Lex," she said. "You're a good person. You *are* getting your shit together. You just need to learn that for yourself."

"Thank you, Talia," I said, meaning it.

With that, she turned and walked down the hall. When I walked to the door to close it, I looked out in the hallway.

She was gone.

Like she'd never been there.

◆ ◆ ◆

"And that's what happened," I said.

Monica sat across from me, tears standing in her eyes.

"That could be the biggest line of bullshit anyone ever told me," she said, swiping at her eyes. "But somehow, Lex Hedges, I believe every damn word of it."

"You do?"

"Is there a reason I shouldn't?"

"Well, yeah, I can actually think of a few..."

"Listen, Hedges," she said. "Didn't we make a bit of a bargain ourselves? A promise to cut the bullshit and just be honest with each other? And to simply take what the other says at face value?"

"Yeah," I said. "I seem to remember something along those lines."

"So, I'm taking you at your word."

"Okay."

"And besides," she said. "If I find out you're lying, you know you're dead."

"The thought did cross my mind."

"When?"

"When I talked to Talia," I said. "Seriously, Monica, I meant every single word of what I said. About you. About us."

"And it was some of the nicest things anyone's ever said about me."

"It's all true. You really are the best thing that's happened to me in a long damn time. Probably ever."

"And you're the one thing I always wanted to happen to me, Lex."

"I'm sorry about looking at Talia's tits," I said and, as childish as it sounded, I meant it.

"You can stare at tits all day if you want. Just don't touch any of them."

"So, we're cool?"

"Lex, I'll tell you one time, and let me be clear: I'm not the jealous type, so if you follow this one rule, we'll be fine..." She stood up.

"And that is...?"

She moved close to me. "You can look at all the menus you want." Then she poked her finger in my chest to accentuate each of the next words. "Just. Don't. Eat."

"Not even—"

"Oh, Alexandra, shush," Marcus said from the other bed.

Before either of us could react, there was a knock at the door. Our pizza had arrived.

◆ ◆ ◆

I PAID THE kid and put the pizza on the bed. Marcus had sat up on the bed and, as Monica raised the box lid, he made a face.

"Pizza, Alexandra?" he said. "You couldn't have ordered something more nourishing?"

Ah, so we're back to lucid Marcus mode, I thought. I handed napkins all around, pulled out a slice for Monica, another for

Marcus—who's puckered-up mouth reminded me shockingly of Gerry's wife Ruthless—and made a point of holding up one of the little cups. "Dipping sauce, Marcus?"

"No," he said. "Thank you." He looked at the slice cradled in his hand like it was roadkill. "Are there no plates? A fork? A knife?"

"My mother used to say, 'Pick it up with your fingers, it tastes better,'" Monica said. I could have kissed her. I probably should have.

"I sincerely doubt that," Marcus said. He lifted the slice and took a small, tentative bite, as though it may have been poisonous. The bite was so small, I doubt he even needed to chew before he swallowed it.

Before snipping off a second morsel, Marcus stared pointedly at me and said, "Alexandra, are you not going to introduce me to your little friend?"

Little friend? What are we…five years old?

"Monica," I said, "this is Marcus Hedges, my sperm donor. He was married to my mother, Sandra. Marcus, this is Monica Holt, and she is *very* important to me. So, none of your crap."

"Mrs. Holt," he said. "I am Alexandra's father."

"Mr. Hedges," Monica said, extending a hand. "We met earlier, but I think you may have been a bit preoccupied."

"Really?" Marcus seemed genuinely surprised. "I don't recall." Then he went back to whittling his pizza slice down, nibble by nibble. His brows were furrowed, and he stared at nothing. *Yes, he's actually bewildered.*

It felt a little too quiet, so I flipped on the TV as a distraction. I found some ancient *Three's Company* rerun, turned down the sound, and we all ignored it. With Marcus preoccupied by thoughts and pizza, I ignored him and turned all attention to Monica.

I found myself absorbed in how Monica handled herself. How she pulled a slice out and, curling it to stop anything sliding off, took small, careful bites, one hand just below her chin to catch any strays. When she pulled back and the cheese formed a span between her delicate mouth and the slice, I loved how she tilted her head and put her chin forward to try and stop it. When that failed, two long, manicured fingers broke the string and piled it back on the slice.

Then she noticed me watching her. "What?" she said.

"You," I said.

She smiled, but there was still a question there. But with the buzzkill sitting right beside her, it wisely went unasked for now. We ate without talking, with only the sounds of Jack Tripper, Janet Wood, and Chrissy Snow's farcical escapades to fill the quiet.

Marcus finally gave up after winnowing the slice down by half. He stood and announced he was going to take a bath. I thought that was a fine idea. Monica gathered some new clothing for him and set them in the bathroom. Marcus went in and closed the door behind him. Monica did an exaggerated swipe of her hand across her brow and said mouthed "whew" all very dramatically.

But now, at least for a bit, we were alone again.

♦ ♦ ♦

MONICA WENT STRAIGHT from the bathroom door to the little bar fridge and pulled out a bottle of wine. "You wanna?" she said.

Well, hot damn. I hadn't even seen her put it in the fridge. Must have done it during the Great Unpack. I nodded. I motioned to the pizza, and she nodded. I pulled out another slice for each of us.

Monica poured some wine into the hotel mugs, then handed one off to me and raised her own. "To interesting times," she said.

"Isn't that some sort of Chinese curse?" I said. "Ah well." I clinked my mug to hers. "To interesting times. May we survive them relatively unscathed."

"Hear, hear," she said, and we both drank.

I moved over to the bed she was sitting on. "Look," I said as I put down my mug on the nightstand. Then I grasped her hands in my own. "This is coming years too late, and likely at the wrong time, because it likely will sound like a line to let me get into your pants, but I'm sorry."

"Sorry for what?"

"For high school. For not…I don't know…acknowledging your feelings toward me? For not acknowledging your existence? For not acknowledging who I really was? For being an asshole?"

"You weren't an asshole."

"A stupid bitch, then?"

She smirked. "Not that, either."

"Yeah, I was. Still am, most of the time."

"I don't know that I believe that."

"You'd be one of the few then," I said. "You should have a chat with my last girlfriend." I winced inwardly and immediately kicked myself for bringing her up as any forward momentum with the conversation died. I handed off her pizza and took my own. We ate in a strange silence for a time.

Finished, we cleaned up the leftovers and set the box off to the side. I noticed a spot of sauce on Monica's face and moved to thumb it off. She watched my eyes as I did it. Her skin was so soft. I left my hand there, and hers came up to meet mine.

"Thank you," she said, and I didn't know if that was for the spot or for the apology, but either way, I took it with just a nod.

We stayed like that for a while, each of us, I think, trying to learn how to move forward in this strange new world we were entering. Then she leaned forward, smirked, and kissed me on the nose. She broke the contact and grabbed some napkins and wiped her hands off.

♦ ♦ ♦

AS I WATCHED her back while she cleaned her hands, the irony of the situation didn't escape me. This was a woman I really didn't pay enough attention to in high school, and now I was praying like hell she'll give me the attention I was hoping for now. I thought, *God, I'm such an asshole.* I figured the best way to conquer that problem was to admit it and move on.

I moved on.

♦ ♦ ♦

I REFILLED OUR mugs with more wine. When I turned back around, Monica was back on the bed, pillows piled up — briefly reminding me of Talia in my bed before I forcefully pushed that thought aside — and instead took in Monica and her legs — *oh, those long, long legs* — stretched out. She was looking at the TV, but she wasn't really watching it.

I piled my pillows the same way and stretched out beside her.

"So," she said.

"So," I said and smiled. I held out her mug. "More wine?"

"Sure," she said. Then, "Is this a little weird?"

"Hmm," I said, putting my thumb and forefinger to my chin in consideration. "We're on a quest because a witch told me to. I'm with a beautiful woman who I stupidly ignored for far too long, and who now I'm a little awkward around." I paused for a moment. "Oh, and there's a crazy old man in our bathroom who claims to be my father."

"He is your father," Monica said, a small laugh escaping with the words. Then she quietly but clearly mumbled, "Even if he could pass for your brother…not jealous, not even a little bit."

"So…weird? A little," I said. "But I like weird." Then I reconsidered.

My mother.

Talia.

Marcus.

Ray.

Kayla.

Norman.

I realized maybe I didn't necessarily like weird that much.

But Monica had already said, "Okay." I reached over for the wine bottle and topped us both off. In the small silence, I listened, heard Marcus's small bath sounds still going on.

I made myself comfortable again. "Tell me if you don't want to talk about this," I said. "Seeing as how significant others end up being such a buzzkill, as we've seen in an earlier segment of our show." She smiled, nodded, and I moved on. "But somewhere along the line, I heard you were married?"

She laughed, loud and unselfconsciously. "Oh, you *heard* that, did you?"

"I did," I said. "Think it was a really hot lady who told me."

"Hot lady, huh? Interesting." She took a sip of wine. "Well, for your information, Hedges, it's not 'was married.' I believe the correct term is '*is* married.'" She obviously saw my eyes widen and laughed again. "Technically, I am. On paper I am."

"Huh," I said with no humour. "Am I allowed to ask what happened?"

"To us?"

"Yeah."

"I don't know." Her eyebrows furrowed and she closed her eyes. "No, that's a lie. I do know." She changed position, shifting to her side and drawing a leg up. She took another sip of wine. "We were together for almost two years. Met him on a blind date, would you believe?"

"God, I hate those."

"Me too. But this one was good. Duane basically swept me off my feet. My Prince Charming. We were married two months later."

"Wow."

"In my defence, I was young. Barely out of school. I was nineteen."

"So, what? Around…"

"We met just after Halloween, 2002," she said. "Married Christmas Eve."

"Damn, that is fast."

"Yes. The first year was good. But, over the next, we just seemed to slowly go our own ways. It wasn't even as though we were growing apart, it was more like we weren't ever really together. He had his job, I was working a job I didn't like. By the end, we were more roommates than husband and wife."

"Sounds familiar. Well, not the *husband* part, but…you know."

"You too? We still slept together, we didn't really fight. We didn't really have much to fight about because our lives were so separate."

"Friends with benefits."

"Live-in booty call."

"Yeah."

"Yeah."

"And then?"

"And then, he did a country-song exit on me."

"Pardon?"

"He told me he was going out for a pack of cigarettes and I never saw him again."

"Did he smoke?"

Monica laughed. "Yes, he did. It would have been a little obvious otherwise, wouldn't it?"

"It would at that."

"But hey," she said. "I'm a survivor."

"You are," I said. "You've had to overcome a lot of loss, huh? Your dad, your mom, then your husband."

"We've all got some scars, Lex."

"We do. But you came back...*fought* back...from a lot."

"If I learned one thing from losing Mom," she said. "I can't speak to losing my dad as much because he was gone before I was born. But Mom? I did a lot of thinking after she was gone, and I basically settled on one thought that made me feel a bit better."

"What's that?" I said.

"That we're all more than just a life, going through its paces. It's easy to lose track of that, to get up, grab a coffee, go to work, come home, eat, scroll through Facebook, watch some TV, go to bed, do it all again." She grabbed my hand then. "We're more than that, Lex. We're more than our tasks. We're *possibility*."

I smiled, encouraging her to continue.

"I never got to meet Dad, or got to know him. But Mom did her best to make him real for me, to bring my father into my life as much as she could, you know?"

I nodded.

"So when I left her, I had to do the same thing with her. Keep her real. Keep her in my life. Same with Dad. And," she said, squeezing my hand, "in doing that, I realized that I was only here because they found each other. Out of all the possible outcomes for their lives, they found each other, Dan and Lila. And because of that one possibility, I was another."

"Okay," I said. "I see that."

"Right," she said. "My long, rambling point here is, we're born with a blank canvas in front of us. No map. No pre-defined route. Sometimes one is imposed on us, but often, we choose the path. And I think, of all the possibilities out there, most of us just choose the easiest, straightest path."

"You're not wrong." I remembered what I'd said at my

mother's service. *Our lives are a journey to become not what we could be, but what we should be.*

"I was kind of on that path myself. I worked. I had a husband. A house."

"And then it got shaken up," I said. "Country-song exit."

"Right. And considering all the possibilities that opened up for me, maybe Duane did me a favour." Then she looked at me. "Maybe Kelly did you one, too."

"Because we're each other's possibility now," I said.

She squeezed my hand again. Then we kissed, long and slow.

When we stopped some time later, I said, "You're a smart lady, Monica Holt."

She didn't deny it. I'd thought a couple of days ago that she'd grown a spine. I was beginning to realize that spine had some steel to it. Some spikes. She didn't just endure her hardships, she overcame them. And on top of that steely, spiky spine, there was a wonderful mind.

Good for you, Monica.

We both sat, sipping our wine, staring at the TV. From what I could see, *Three's Company* had given way to *Gilligan's Island*. Gilligan was obviously up to shenanigans again, because the skipper had pulled off his skipper's hat and was beating him good naturedly.

"And what about you, Hedges?" Another sip. "Where is the fair, could-have-been Hedges's significant other these days?"

I realized I'd only given Monica the bare bones story of Kelly. Yeah, it was probably time to fill in some details.

"Would you believe me if I said my drummer stole my showbiz sister — the Nancy to my Ann — and ran off with her?"

"Shockingly, yes I would."

"You're just saying that because Nancy was always the cuter sister. Blonde and all that."

"Well," she said, "I'm not going to argue that point, but Ann got a raw deal."

I agreed, but asked why anyway.

"Because she can sing like nobody's business, but everyone just sees the weight gain. She's still a beautiful woman, and talented as hell. Let's forget for a moment all the amazing songs and songwriting she did for Heart. Have you *heard* her belt out Zeppelin songs? Man, she can stand toe to toe with Plant, any day of the week."

"Wow."

"What?" she said. "You know what a music freak I was back in the day. Still am."

"Point taken." I turned to her, sitting up and crossing my legs. Then I continued. "Anyway, Kelly," I said. "We had a good run, but, in the end, I guess she decided she wanted to run with someone else instead."

Monica sang a couple of lines from "Who Will You Run To." Scored some points right there. "Nicely played, Holt," I said. "Anyway. So..."

"So, Kelly went out for a pack of cigarettes?"

I smiled. "Something like that. Ended up with a drummer."

She sat up and crossed her own legs. Those long legs. "And what about you, City Girl?"

I laughed and it came out as more of a surprised yelp. "What *about* me, Ms. Small Town Girl?" God, I'd forgotten how much she loved that band. I squinted my eyes, gave her the hard examination look. "You still a big Journey freak, Monica?"

"Yes, I am, and stop changing the subject."

"I apologize," I said. "Please, do go on."

"Kelly's obviously...moving on. What about you?"

"No, I've been kinda stuck in neutral. I don't wanna sing, I avoid work, I avoid writing, though I do tend to attend the odd — and I do mean odd — family funeral. This whole thing" — I waved an arm to encompass all the universe — "Marcus, Ray,

Mom…all of it. It's all made me take a step back and try and figure out who the hell I am. I think I've mentioned this, but, I'm basically trying to pull my shit together. But other than that, there's not much to me."

"I sincerely doubt that," she said, her mouth a small moue. "You used to tell me that back in high school. You were always trying to make it seem as though you weren't anything special, that you weren't that interesting." She put out a hand and touched my knee. "I didn't believe it then, and I don't believe it now."

We were now facing each other, not two feet apart. *All possibilities.*

She cocked her head to the side. "Lex, would you do something for me?"

"Yes, of course." Anything. But I hoped it was going to be a kiss.

She stood and I moved back slightly and watched her ass as she moved to her purse. She pulled her iPod out. "You mind if we play some music?"

"Sure," I said, wondering what she was up to.

"Remember back in high school, after Mom was gone, how strict the Muracks were?"

"Hell yes."

"How they wouldn't really let me go to any school functions?"

"Sort of."

"Including the dances?"

"Yeah," I said. "That I remember." We used to bug her about it. All the time.

"Back in high school, whenever there was a dance, I'd be at home, in my room." Her hand had stopped dancing on the screen. "You know what I'd do?"

"Is it dirty?"

"Stop it," she said. "Freak. No, I had a CD that I'd play.

There was a bunch of old songs on it that I loved. The benefits of a mother who tried to keep my father alive for me through his favourite music." She thumbed the click wheel and I heard an old REO Speedwagon song, "Keep On Loving You," come on. "I'd pretend I was dancing. With you."

"Fashion. Music. Hairstyles. What was it with New Hope that we were always twenty years behind?"

She stood and came over to me. "Shut up." Her voice was soft. Serious.

I said, "Okay."

"Will you dance with me now?"

I stood. "Yes," I said. "I'd love to."

♦ ♦ ♦

WE WENT THROUGH the songs and talked quietly for a time as the memories flooded back. Then we went quiet, just holding each other, moving with each old song that came up. Meat Loaf's "Two Out Of Three Ain't Bad." Journey's "Who's Crying Now" and "Faithfully." Frampton's "Baby I Love Your Way." The songs went on and on.

And then we were kissing. Soft at first, tentative. I tasted the wine on her lips. I felt her body under my hands, under her sundress. I felt her breasts against my own. I felt her breath on my neck, in my ear.

We kissed again, harder, but still restraining the hunger. Somewhere in the back of my mind, I still held back. I brought my hands up to Monica's face, touching her hair, her ears, her smooth cheeks. She also brought a hand up, her slim fingers sliding over mine, and I saw the wedding band on her hand.

It was shocking, because it was literally the first time I'd actually ever noticed it. The only thing I could think of was that I simply had not *wanted* to see it before now.

But now I did.

Possibilities.

I must have stopped, though I wasn't aware of it. Monica said, a little breathlessly, "What? What is it?"

I asked myself the same thing. *What is it?* I thought. She'd told me he was gone. Duane's gone.

We stayed like that, Monica looking at me, me looking at the ring on her left hand.

"It's nothing," I said.

"It's not nothing," she said. She seemed to make a decision. "I have to do something." She turned from me. "Something I should have done a long time ago. Months ago." She finished and turned back. "Okay?"

"You sure?"

"I'm sure," she said. "More sure than I've been in a long time." I moved in closer, put my hands around her waist, pulled her close, then pulled her down to the bed.

I was vaguely aware of Styx singing "Babe" and Prism singing "Night to Remember." But I completely ignored the fact that her ring now sat in the top drawer of the nightstand.

We were both, however, aware that her marriage was over. That Duane was gone. That Kelly was in my rear-view mirror and diminishing quickly.

What exactly that means, I thought, *we'll deal with those possibilities later.*

◆ ◆ ◆

AFTER IT GOT dark — long after the delivery man had come to their room with the pizza and left — his clothes became too confining, the room too confining, his world too confining. He had to get out.

He needed to get out into the night.

Ensuring he had his pass card, he eased out of the room and over to the small copse of trees, more decorative than anything, but a small oasis of nature in all this brick and concrete.

He pulled off his shoes and socks and let his feet sink into the soil. It smelled of piss and dog shit and garbage, but it was still of the earth.

It was small comfort, but it was something.

He watched the room from this new vantage point. The lights were still on.

He wanted to close his eyes, but he didn't dare. They'd commanded vigilance, and he would comply. Instead, he consoled himself with deep breaths of the night air, fetid with the smells of car exhaust and frying fast-food meat and cigarettes and marijuana.

But still, the air was cool in his lungs.

Around him, he heard the sounds of passing cars, of televisions and music. An argument was going on in one of the rooms. In another, the snores of someone already asleep for the night.

From the one he watched, there were other sounds.

Primal.

No.

He moved silently from the trees, back to the blacktop of the parking lot, to the concrete walks outside the room. He stepped past 116, his room, and drifted up the stairs to 305, their room.

Well aware of how obvious he was, he paused just outside the door, as though he'd just stepped out of it for a breath of fresh air.

From inside, louder now, the sounds of gasped breaths, of flesh on flesh.

The sound of rutting.

No.

Only then did he allow himself the small comfort of closing his eyes.

Only one is expendable, he reminded himself.

But he wondered if, perhaps, another could be expendable as well.

He glided back to 116, swiped the pass card, and re-entered his room, swallowed into the darkness and closeness of his prison for the next few hours.

He took up his position by the window once again.

It would indeed be a long night.

And he couldn't get the sounds he'd heard out of his mind.

◆ ◆ ◆

IT WASN'T UNTIL Monica rolled her flushed, sweating body off mine and collapsed beside me that Marcus said, "Are you two finished fornicating yet?"

Monica clapped a hand to her mouth and giggled.

"Honest to god," I whispered, "I totally forgot he was in there."

"Me too."

"Is it safe to come out now?"

That's when we couldn't hold it back anymore, and both broke out laughing. We got under the covers and gave him the okay. Marcus came out and climbed into the other bed without a word.

It took a long time for those giggles to subside.

◆ ◆ ◆

"NO!"

Monica's arms were immediately around me, her voice soft and calming in my ear, telling it was just a dream, just a dream.

The same dream. Every night.

The dream I'd had every night since I'd returned to New Hope.

When I'd calmed down, she said, "Wanna talk about it?"

No. Yes.

She kissed my shoulder. "I used to have this nightmare," I said. "Almost every night when I was a kid, still living at home."

She slid a languorous hand down my arm. "Tell me."

"I'm in my bedroom at the old house. It's very late. Like well after midnight." I took a shuddering breath. "I'm in my bed. Everyone's asleep. And..."

"And?" Her breath was warm on my cheek.

"And then there's something in my room?"

"Something?" Her hand slid down my arm, her arm sliding over my breasts.

"A monster. But I can't see it. It's black, and hunched over, and I can only see it when it moves. But it doesn't move. I know it's there. It knows I know. And it doesn't move."

"How do you know it's there?" Her hand moved to my belly.

"I can feel it."

"What does it want?"

"It wants me."

"Why?" Her hand slipped lower.

"I don't know."

"What happens then?"

"We just stay like that, neither of us moving."

"What happens if you move?" Her fingers glided up and down over my clit.

"If I move, it will move too." And then I whispered, "Oh god."

"How does it end?" Her fingers more insistent, pushed lower, slipping inside me.

"I…I don't remember…I wake up…"

"You don't know how it ends?" She moved her hand, her slick fingers gently easing my legs apart.

"No…I…god, that's good."

"You know how this ends?" She moved her head down, pulling a nipple into her mouth.

"Yesssss…"

And then, at the insistence of fingers and tongue and teeth, Monica vanquished the nightmare back to the shadows as light and heat exploded behind my eyes.

Chapter Ten

THE NEXT DAY, it took some effort on both our parts to get Marcus moving. He was basically catatonic once he woke up. His mouth hung open, and he could only make a disconcerting "uh uh uh" noise.

"You think he's had a stroke or something?" Monica asked.

"I honestly don't know." It could be a stroke, or some other physical ailment. It could be creeping dementia. Or it could be him just fucking with us to get us back for last night.

Monica, not knowing Marcus, or the full history between the two of us, had a lot more empathy for him than I did. I'm sure I came across as a stone-cold bitch, but honestly, it was going to take a hell of a lot more than dementia or catatonia to thaw the sub-zero disdain of his plight.

I felt guilty about leaving him to her, but she'd made it clear she didn't mind. And I couldn't fathom the idea of even touching him any more than I needed to. And I was going to need to shortly.

So, while she got him up and dressed, I got all Marcus's and my shit packed. Monica had such a system going, I didn't dare touch her stuff. Instead, once I finished, I hit up a local fast-food place for breakfast while she repacked, then put our bags in the trunk once I was back. Next came Marcus.

The dreaded moment was here. My stomach roiled at the very thought of having to touch him, and Monica picked up on that because she got Marcus to his feet and said, "You just manage all the doors, I'll get him to the car."

I held the door to the room while Monica led him through. As he crossed the threshold, Marcus looked down and, in between his "uh uh uhs," he mumbled something I didn't catch.

When Monica got Marcus down the stairs and installed in the back seat, I asked her what he'd said. Monica led me back up to the threshold and pointed down to some muddy footprints. It looked like someone had stood there in their bare feet. Could have been fresh, could have been there for days.

"He saw these prints and said something like, 'Oh hell, that's not good.'"

I pointed to the ice machine just down from our room. "Probably someone just grabbing a bucket of ice."

Monica nodded.

I'm not sure if either of us fully bought that explanation, but seriously, what else could it be?

Someone who wants to drag me off and torture me and flay my lady parts, maybe?

Someone getting a bucket of ice was the more likely answer. Surely.

Regardless, we were out of here.

Next stop, Thunder Bay. And damned if that ain't one of the coolest names for a city ever.

♦ ♦ ♦

The ride was depressingly quiet for the first few miles. We'd grabbed more coffee for the road, and were serenaded by the ever-present "uh uh uhs" coming from the back seat.

This will not do, I thought. "Whaddya wanna talk about?"

"Well, at the risk of beating a dead horse," Monica said, then paused.

"Go ahead," I prompted.

"This whole thing is freaking me out, just a little."

"What whole thing?"

"The whole thing about not needing a map, no directions, basically nothing but your noggin to get us where we're going."

"Yeah, I get—"

"Tell me again," she said, tapping her temple. "The meat GPS. One last time."

"You've heard it before," I protested. "Hell, didn't I roll it past you again last night?"

She smirked—"You rolled a few things by me last night"—and put an arm on my leg.

"You started it."

"You didn't stop me."

"Oh my god, we're like horny teenagers." I flashed to a memory, my mouth between her legs, looking up to her face, flushed with a rising orgasm. It was like we were doing something illicit and knew that, at least for now, we were getting away with it.

She laughed, not disagreeing with me. Then her expression turned serious. "Honestly, though. I'm still trying to wrap my head around it. Humour me."

So I did.

I told her again of how I'd seen Talia that first day, saw her making her strange, non-stop hand movements, felt something happening in my head, not knowing what it was.

Then I told her again of that last meeting, of how I'd asked her what she meant by telling me she would give me the instructions. And how she'd told me she'd already done it.

"But..." Monica said. "I still don't get it. Was it like, I don't know, a download into your head?"

I nodded slowly, still watching the road. "Yeah, I guess that's one way of seeing it." I reached for my stupendously large cup of road coffee, trying to finish it before it crossed that border between *not quite hot enough but still drinkable* to *too cold to consider*. "But it's more than that." I replaced the cup into the slot in the console, then waved in frustration. "I don't know how else to explain it. It's not just about the knowledge coming into my head…it's like she also downloaded all the pathways to make it feel like I've *always* had the knowledge, you know?"

Monica shook her head.

"I know. It's messed up. And I'm the one who it was done to. I'm the one who knows what the hell happened." I grabbed the coffee, took another swig. Then I had a thought. "Okay, think of something that happened to you a long time ago."

"Like what?"

"Don't care. Anything. First day of school. When you got your driver's licence. Whatever."

"Got it. First time riding my new bike," she said. "Okay."

"So, when you think about that, you have the sense of time, right? You can tell that it happened to you a long time ago, right?"

"Of course."

"I want to make this point clear," I said. "When you pull up that memory, you can hold it up, examine it, understand when in your life it happened, what came before, what came after. Right?"

"Yes," she said. "I remember Mom backing over my old bike, bending the frame. Telling me we just didn't have the money for a new one. Then getting one three weeks later for my birthday. The excitement, the love from my mother. Flying down that big hill in Opie, the wind in my hair. Yeah, all of it. It's a normal memory."

"Okay, well," I stabbed a finger at the road ahead. "As I'm driving this road, as I make every turn, come over every hill, see each sign, pass through each town, I feel the same thing."

Monica stared at me, her eyebrows knitted, trying to understand.

"I have that same sense of time. That this knowledge has been in my head for years. Decades. Like I'd driven these roads, turned these corners, passed through each of these towns when I was much younger." I sighed as I examined the memory of this road in my mind. "I can slot it into a specific time and place. I know what came before and after I experienced it."

"But you didn't." Her voice was exasperated. "You didn't experience it previously, right? It's not a true memory, right?"

"Hell no." I laughed. "Remember the fucked-up family I had? We never really went anywhere. I think we had a trip to Toronto once for Mom's work. That's about it. Vacations were spent in our happy family home."

"So then, how…?"

"Right. How." I tried my coffee one more time. Made a face. *Nope. It's crossed that line*, I thought. "I think, somehow, however Talia got this knowledge in *her* brain—and I get the distinct impression that it was downloaded into her brain much the same way as she downloaded it into mine—it came the same way for her, with all the sense of passing time and the integration and mixing of that knowledge into the vat of information that's in her head."

Monica shifted in her seat, getting more comfortable. "So…what? You're telling me that not only is there a sense of history, but that it's mixed in with your other memories? Like…I don't know…like you remember talking to someone about this trip that you never took?"

I actually turned and stared at her. "Okay, damn, girl. That's an excellent observation. I didn't clue into that one, but yeah…and…no. I get the sense that I *have* talked to others about this…but when I try to call up a name or a face…I can't."

"Because that's a memory she couldn't download."

"I guess." Then I considered, searched my own head for a second. "But what's even weirder?"

"Yes?"

"I can remember the time in my life when I drove these roads previously—without really having done that—but those memories are also squished up and jostling beside my real memories that I actually did experience."

"What's the real memory?"

"I'm maybe four? Five? And Mom's giving me shit because I decided my doll needed a new hairstyle. So I cut off all her hair."

"Nice."

"I figured I could glue it back on."

"You were wrong."

"I was."

"And that's mashed up beside driving this road?"

"Yeah."

"Weird."

"Right," I said. "Or schizophrenic. You make the call."

We drove in silence for several minutes, digesting the information. Then I turned to Monica. "I'm gonna hit the next turn off. I need more coffee if I'm going to be able to process all this shit."

♦ ♦ ♦

HE HAD WATCHED the direction they'd turned—still west—when they left the motel. He'd give them a ten-minute start because, this far north, there was only one highway out, so the danger of losing them was low.

Instead, with his gear ready to go, he watched the time, and watched out the window. And he watched as housekeeping came by and opened up 305.

He couldn't resist.

He took his bag to the car, then went straight to 305 as though he knew what he was doing. When he got to the opened door, he knocked and said, "Excuse me?"

A short, plump woman popped her head out of the bathroom. "Yes?"

"Sorry," he said. "I was in here last night, and I think I dropped my cufflinks" — *Jesus, man. Cufflinks?* — "you mind if I do a quick search?"

She gave him a sympathetic smile. "Oh sure, sure. Hope you find them." Then she ducked back into the bathroom.

He truly didn't know what he was looking for, but he had to be quick. It was probably a wasted effort, he knew. He opened all the drawers. Empty, save for a pad of paper with the motel logo, a pen, a phone book, and a Bible.

They still do that?

He closed the drawers. He scanned the rest of the room, checking the chairs, the table, and the beds.

Nothing.

He glanced around the base of the beds, running his fingers under them.

Nothing. Nothing. Nothing. Noth —

His fingers passed over something. He scrabbled them back to the spot. Found it again. Pulled it out, examined it.

"You find them?"

He looked up, startled, at the maid. Then he plastered a big smile on his face. He raised his fist, the object clasped within. "I did!" he said. "Thank you."

He couldn't get out of the room fast enough.

His hand remained tightly clenched all the way back to the car. Only when he was safely inside, away from the rest of the world, did he dare raise his hand again and slowly open his fist to see what he'd found.

A ring.

A wedding ring.

Monica's.

◆ ◆ ◆

A QUICK STOP to empty our bladders and me to empty my mind, to refill the snacks and drinks, and we were back on the road.

Somewhere along the way, the "uh uh uhs" had stopped and Marcus had grown quiet in the back seat. I'd stupidly assumed he was either back into Catatonic Land, or sleeping.

He was neither.

"Alexandra," he said, and I saw Monica jolt slightly in surprise.

Then I felt my entire body tighten up into one tense knot. *He's back.*

"Marcus," I said, and shot a glance over to Monica. Her eyes betrayed nothing. She simply watched me. Another glance in the rear-view. Marcus sat directly behind Monica, back straight, fully alert. "What?"

"It's 'Father,' Alexandra."

"We've been through that. No 'Father,' no 'Dad,' not even 'Dads.' Asked and answered, so we can table that. What do you want?"

"Where are we? What's going on?"

"We're in my car. And, what's going on is I'm talking to an asshole," I said.

Monica shot me a sharp look. I couldn't tell if she was disgusted with me, or just not approving the argument I was obviously starting.

"Alexandra, I'm your father."

"You donated some fluids. You've never been my father."

Evidently he chose to ignore that. That's how he operated, as though certain words and phrases hadn't been spoken, so he didn't dignify them with a response.

"Your brother will be buried soon," he said. "We need to be there for that."

"Why?"

"Because he's your—"

"He's my brother," I said, slicing through his shit. "Yeah, yeah. Blah blah blah. Except he's not. We were both expelled from the same hole. Sometimes I secretly pray we don't even share the same DNA." Monica's eyebrows furrowed as she looked at me. She knew my father and I didn't get along, but we hadn't gotten around to plumbing the precise depths of hate as yet. "Seriously"—I leaned heavily and sarcastically on the word while I shot another glance at him in the rear-view—"who gives a flying fuck?"

"He would."

"He didn't give a shit about anything or anyone."

His voice got hard and flinty. "He. Was. Your. Brother."

"He. Was. An. Asshole."

"Where are we going?"

One of those sudden topic changes that came with me shredding my brother's good name. *Fair enough*, I thought. *I'll play along.*

"None of your fucking business."

"And why is *she* here? The one from your mother's funeral?"

Does he even remember the fornicating incident?

"Because, unlike your company, Marcus, I *wanted* Monica to come."

"She's a slut, Alexandra," he said. "You need to make better choices for sexual partners. You could do much better."

"You…" I couldn't find the words. Rage consumed me. "You *evil* fucking *piece* of *shit*."

Monica put a hand on my shoulder.

"Hey," she said.

I couldn't speak. I gripped the wheel tightly, hearing the plastic flex under my white-knuckled hands.

"Hey," she said again, her voice soft. "Pull off, babe. Just pull off to the side for a minute."

I couldn't look at her, I couldn't talk right now. The world was squeezing in again, and I couldn't breathe right.

"Shhh, babe. Shhh."

It took another minute of her hand on my shoulder and her soothing voice for me to calm to the point where I became aware of more than what was just in my head. My hands ached from gripping the wheel so tightly. My legs felt cramped, my heart thudded dully in my chest, and my head throbbed.

I looked down at the speedometer.

I was doing 180. One-hundred and eighty kilometres per hour in an eighty kilometre zone.

I let my foot off the gas with some effort. The muscles in my thigh felt seized up. When the car slowed to a reasonable speed, I braked and pulled off to the soft shoulder.

The car had barely stopped rolling as I slammed it into Park, undid my seatbelt, and bolted from the car. I ran away from Marcus, up the shoulder away from the car, as though it was on fire.

It was my brain that was on fire.

How can anyone be like that? I thought. *How can anyone talk to their own daughter like that?* Of course, if I was honest, I'd also ask how anyone could talk to their own father like that too, but that all came back to…

To that thing that I never allowed myself to think about.

My running slowed to a walk, and then I just stopped. There was a sign indicating how far the next town was. I didn't care. I just leaned up against it, then, with no strength left in me, I slid to the gravel and sat, knees up, arms crossed over them, my head buried.

God, my shit's so fucked-up.

I heard Monica's slow footsteps approaching, but I couldn't summon the willpower to even raise my head just then.

The sound grew louder as she got closer, then stopped. I knew I should say something, but what? What could I say?

We stayed like that for a time, neither of us moving. Then I heard her move to my side, and then settle on the gravel, leaning on the other post of the road sign.

Still, silence.

"I'm sorry," I finally said. I still couldn't find it in me to raise my head and face her. Not after what that demon in the back seat had said about her.

"What?" Monica said. "I figure we just shaved a half-hour off our trip with you driving at supersonic speeds."

Okay, that was so unexpected, I actually guffawed. Then I looked at her.

She was doing everything to keep it light, to comfort me, but the worry was evident on her face. I'd scared the shit out of her. The speed and the vehemence directed at Marcus, which was something I usually kept hidden in my very own Pandora's Box.

I wanted to say something to her. Tell her he couldn't talk to her like that. Tell her...something. Something to make it right, to erase my father's hateful words, but I had nothing.

Instead, I could only stare at her, let her reach out to me.

Then the tears came. First mine, hot and hated, sliding down my cheeks as I tried to tell her I was sorry, then hers as she pulled me to her, holding me, making soft noises as she held me, my head against her breasts, my arms around her.

"It's okay, baby," she said. "Let it out. And when you're ready to talk about it, we'll talk about it, okay?"

I could only nod.

We stayed like that, by the side of the road, for a long time, until I was cried out.

♦ ♦ ♦

HE HADN'T WANTED to do anything after he found the ring, but he had to keep tracking them. Reluctantly, he'd started the car and headed off in the same direction he'd seen them go.

He knew, from following them up to now, that the chick—Hedges—had a bit of a lead foot, and usually did more than the posted limit. He goosed the car up to a solid twenty over.

He'd deal with any cops if he had to.

Twenty minutes in, he figured he'd be seeing the familiar black Chrysler 300 he'd been following any time now, when he topped a hill and had to arrest his automatic response to stomp on the brakes.

The car was pulled off the highway, with both front doors hanging open. Then he saw the Hedges woman and Monica down the road a bit, leaning up against a road sign.

What the actual fuck?

He couldn't stop.

Instead, he kept the pedal down and drove past them, keeping a watchful eye for a gas station or somewhere else to pull off. It only took a few minutes to spot a small cul-de-sac off to the side, probably used by police for catching speeders.

He backed in, killed the engine, and waited.

◆ ◆ ◆

MARCUS NEVER LEFT the car. Part of me hoped he had, and wandered off so I wouldn't have to deal with him again. But, when Monica and I eventually got back to the car, he was still there, still in the back seat, but no longer sitting up righteously straight and alert. He'd caved back in on himself, and a silver line of saliva ran from his lower lip, through his whiskers, to a widening dark spot on his T-shirt. He was asleep, like he had not a single care in the world.

I suppressed the urge to call him something foul. Instead, heart hammering, I got back into the car, we buckled in, and I signalled and merged back on to the highway again.

There wasn't much to say for the first little while. We'd said it all at the base of that road sign back along the highway. Instead, we stayed silent for a time, my hand holding Monica's.

Eventually, she sighed, then said, "Sing me something."

"You're kidding, right?"

"Isn't it how you make your living? Singing?"

"Yeah," I said. "Singing in the style of Ann Wilson of Heart."

"Then sing me some Heart."

I could have. God knows I've got their entire greatest hits package burned into my brain. I sang her "Dreamboat Annie," but it's imagery of riding on diamond waves didn't sit right just now. Instead, dredging around in my head, I pulled up some different songs. Elton John's "Someone Saved My Life Tonight." Then a couple of Beatles songs, "Yesterday" and "Eleanor Rigby." Monica surprised me by joining in on the chorus of the last one, her voice sailing sweetly over mine, naturally taking the background harmonies.

When we finished, I said, "Whoa, your voice is even better than I remember, and I remember it being great."

"I've been known to crush a karaoke competition or two," she said, huffing on her nails and buffing them on her blouse.

"Well, look at you," I said. "To hell with me. *You* sing *me* something."

So she sang me a stunning version of the Boomtown Rats' "I Don't Like Mondays," then America's "Sister Golden Hair."

When she finished, I clapped, then said, "Know any ABBA?"

"Do I know any ABBA? Are you serious?" She threw out the choruses of four or five hits. "Hell yes, I know ABBA."

"I could get you a job in an ABBA cover band," I said, snapping my fingers, "like that."

"Oh really? And how do you know this?"

"Because I happen to know they're going to have an opening, due to my absence in my band. And, that's actually where I got my start. I was the rhythm guitarist for Super Trouper, an ABBA cover band. Then their Björn Ulvaeus—"

"Whoa."

"What?"

"That just slid off your tongue like butter."

"It does now. *Ool-VEE-us.*" I put the extra effort into it and got the Swedish spin just perfectly on the first and third syllables. "Anyway, their Björn ended up running off with their Anni-Frid Lyngstad…"

"Another quality handle," Monica said.

"It is," I agreed. "Anyway, long story short, I was female, I could sing, I knew the words, and they didn't even need a wig for me. So, they handed me the mic and I was Anna-Frid for the next couple of years."

"You were ABBA before you were Heart?"

"Yeah. Never really liked ABBA, except, for some strange reason, "Knowing Me, Knowing You." It has a great guitar lick in it. Anyway, after a couple of years, it got pretty goddamn hard to put a smile on and act like I was totally digging the music. I was looking for a change."

"So, what happened?"

"I made some motions toward getting a band together of my own. A band where I could be Lex Hedges, instead of—"

"Beeyorn Yul-Vay-Us!"

"Close enough."

"No, wait, that's the dude. Anna-Fridge Ling-Stab."

"Okay, now you're not even trying."

"So, that band…?"

"I got a couple of guys. A drummer, a great lead guitarist. We started jamming, looking for a couple of others who would gel with us. But then the guy who managed a bunch of these tribute bands — Neil Diamond, Tom Jones, a bunch of others — and he asked if I could belt like Ann Wilson."

Monica laughed. "Could you?"

"Damn right," I said.

"And you became Ann Wilson."

I nodded slowly, my lips pursed. "I did indeed."

"And that other band? The one you were putting together?"

"The lead guitarist ended up joining the Gee Bees, a—"

"Oh, let me guess…Bee Gees tribute band?"

"Good for you!" I said. "Anyway, he joined them about two weeks later and the drummer went to Super Trouper. And…well…damn."

"What?"

"Well, I think I just realized the moment I sold my soul for thirty pieces of silver."

"I don't know if I'd necessarily categorize you making a living as selling your soul."

"Maybe. Maybe not." I tapped my thumbs on the steering wheel. "I think it's all still too fucking soon. I haven't got any perspective on a lot of stuff. The fucking band. The fucking writing. Hell, even Kelly and Kevin."

I continued to drum for a while. Then stopped when Monica looked at me wearing a smirk. "What?" I said.

"You swear a lot."

"Do I?"

"No one's ever told you that before?"

"Not really," I said. "Then again, I hang out with a band full of potty mouths, and I can't swear in my journalism duties that much, so I have to get it out some way."

"Think I'm gonna need to set up a swear jar for you, Hedges."

"Oh, fuck you," I said, but I was laughing

"You may have to pay for that."

"Pay for fucking you?"

"Lex?"

"Yeah?"

"Shut up and drive."

I pulled a voice out of my repertoire and sang, "'Just drive,' she said."

"What's that?"

"Stan Ridgway. His first hit after Wall of Voodoo."

"I have no idea what you're talking about."

"Wall of Voodoo? 'Mexican Radio'?"

"Lex?"

"Yeah?"

"Just drive."

I drove. Smiling.

My mom was dead, my brother was likely in some giant freezer bag awaiting someone to give enough of a shit to throw some dirt over him, the thing that fathered me was drooling in my back seat, and an hour ago, I'd been sitting at the side of a highway in the middle of nowhere, freaking out and wanting to run away from everything.

And yet…right now, I was happy. I had no real right to be, but for now, in this car, with this woman, at this time, I was happy.

I'd take it.

◆ ◆ ◆

IT TOOK ALMOST a half-hour—long enough that he was entertaining the thought of turning around for another pass— when the car streaked by.

He gave them a few minutes, then pulled back out to follow.

What the fuck was that all about?

◆ ◆ ◆

IT TOOK TWO more days for Marcus to find a path out of his mumbling dementia or outright catatonia, but he resurfaced again. As soon as I heard more movement from the back seat and checked the rear-view and noticed the brightness in his eyes, I felt my shoulders tense, my heart rate jump, and my breathing become so shallow I felt like I was drowning.

Despite Monica getting a taste of the real thing, we still hadn't broached the topic yet. Probably wouldn't until we had some privacy. But I had done some thinking about Marcus and me.

No, not about that *one* thing.

But about him and me, and the shambles of this relationship we had. And, even if it was only to myself, I had to admit that I likely spoke far worse to him on a regular basis than he did to me.

Even though I had reason to.

That being said, there was no reality that existed where I wouldn't give him shit for the way he talked about Monica.

Still, for whatever reason, much as I likely should have right now, as I geared up for him to start talking again, I couldn't bring myself to even pretend to be polite.

"Alexandra," he said. At the sound of his voice, Monica turned from looking out the window to me, and placed a hand on my thigh. She gave me a small smile.

"What?" I said.

"Must you be so rude?" he said.

"You should feel special because I wouldn't do this for anyone else," I lied. Actually I would. If Kevin called, I'd likely be equally as rude to him. "Consider it my special, loving response handcrafted just for you. A tonic for all the toxic positivity in the world."

I saw Monica cant her head to the side, lower her sunglasses, and mouth *toxic positivity?* at me. Followed by *what the fuck?*

Marcus remained blissfully unaware of the hilarity ensuing in the front seat. Instead, his voice dropped. Not angry, but definitely not happy. Not that I could remember the last time I saw him happy. "You don't have to treat me like this."

"Yeah, I do."

"Is this because of—"

I cut him off. "If you say one word...*one word*...against Monica, I swear to god I'll stop the car right now and drag your sorry ass out and leave you on the side of the road."

"You wouldn't dare."

"Go ahead," I said, my face a stone. "*Test* me."

He changed gears. Which showed an old dog could, in fact, learn new tricks. "Your brother's funeral."

One of the things I remembered that really dug under my skin was his very deliberate choice of words. It was never something like *Ray's funeral*, or even *my son's funeral*, it would always be *your brother's funeral*. He always went for the way it made it personal to me. He had always done that, had always pushed him on me with subtle reminders that this oversexed, over-opiated, underachieving asshole was my brother. The only one I had.

"What about it?" I said. "Pretty sure we dealt with that a few days ago."

"We never did."

Monica and I looked at each other. We both shot the same message to each other. *Does he really not remember?*

"Everything's on hold until we get back."

"What makes you think I'm coming back?" I said. "I might just stick you on a train or bus or mail you home in a FedEx box."

"You're going to just drive off into the sunset with this..." He raised his hand to indicate Monica.

"Choose your words carefully, Marcus."

"With this girl?" Not *this woman*. Not *Monica*. Not *your girlfriend*.

I took my eyes off the road for a moment and gave Monica a smile. She gave my leg a squeeze, leaned over and, angling her head back to address Marcus, she said, "We just might do that."

The silence was long and enjoyable. At least up in the front seats.

"I didn't realize you were allowing her to speak for you now," he finally said.

"Now you know."

Another silence, but this one, unfortunately, wasn't as long.

"Regardless. The funeral. I would like your brother to have family there."

"Then *you* go."

"I mean, Alexandra, more family than just me."

"Good luck with that. He hasn't been family to me in years. You either, for all of that."

Without looking in the mirror, I heard the exasperation in his voice. "Will you attend your brother's funeral or will you not?"

My immediate reaction was a clean, simple "no." Instead, I had a thought. Catching Monica's eyes, I waggled my index finger between her and I, then said, "You wanna go with me?"

At first she looked confused, then she glanced at Marcus, back to me, realized I was just fucking with him, and smiled that big, beautiful smile that lit up her entire face. She scrunched her eyes down and said, "yeah," back to me.

In the ensuing silence, Marcus was obviously pondering what had happened. He said, "Excuse me?"

"Yeah," I said. "Sorry, I thought it over. Monica's my family, so if I go, she goes."

He made a noise then, like a clearing of his throat. Could have been a growl, for all I know.

"Your brother's funeral? You're saying you will attend?"

"On two conditions."

He waited.

"The first is, Monica comes with me. No arguments."

He was silent for a long time. He pursed his lips much like Ruthless did, down to a tight, puckered sphincter shape. Like an asshole.

"If you must," he said. "And the second?"

"Once we walk out of that funeral, we're quits."

I'm sure his mouth tightened even more at that one.

"Fine," he said.

"Okay," I lied. "Oh, sorry, one last condition."

His tone was as dry and as dead as a desert as he said, "And that is?"

"You don't fucking talk to me from now until the funeral, except for requests for food or washroom breaks." I didn't think he'd actually honour either of the last two, but hope springs eternal, right?

"With all these conditions, why are you even agreeing?"

God, I was hoping you'd ask that, I thought. I laughed out loud, then said, "Because it will give me some small satisfaction to actually witness someone finally bury that garbage."

I imagined his puckered lips went to full vapour lock at that point.

It made me smile.

◆ ◆ ◆

AT A MCDONALD'S in Regina, she said, "We're going to Golden Verdure?"

Marcus declined any of the McDelicacies on offer with a guttural, "Can't eat that shit." Just the fact that he dropped a profanity told me he was in one of his altered states of consciousness. If there was any doubt of that, the follow-up comment—"Burn it to the fucking ground"—removed all doubt.

Regardless, the two of us chose to ignore him. Instead, I just responded to Monica. "Yes, ma'am. Golden Verdure, Saskatchewan." I grabbed the items from the bag, splitting them into mine and hers. Iced tea, fries, and a McChicken for her, Coke, fries, and a Big Mac for me. I would rather have had a break and sat down in the restaurant, but that wasn't realistic with Dadzilla in the back seat.

"Never heard of it."

"I haven't either. And yet"—I goggled at her while waggling my fingers at my temple—"somehow I have." I piled napkins and ketchup packets on the console. Not that I'd use the ketchup. Nasty stuff, made from tomatoes, which were evil, unless cooked within an inch of their lives.

"Right," she said, pointing a finger at her head, poking it in and out. "Downloading. Meat computer."

"Yeah," I said. Monica opened my Big Mac and dumped my fries in the other half, then set the box carefully on my lap. "Still, I'd be surprised if you had."

"Small place?" She held up her fries between the seats. "Sure you don't want some, Mr. Hedges?"

Marcus made to bat them out of the way, and Monica pulled them back to safety. "A simple 'no' would have sufficed," she said, turning and giving me the wide eyes.

"Yeah, less than forty people, total population. It's more of an afterthought than a town."

"And you know your way around this town, right?"

"Right."

"And you've never been there before."

"Never. But in some way, yes."

"Weird."

With that, she said nothing for a bit. She took a delicate sip of her drink, opened and arranged the McChicken box just so, slid her fries into the other half, then picked up two ketchup packets, opened them, and emptied them over the fries. Then she did it with two more.

I shut up about it. If she was going to partake of the evil tomato spawn, that was her business. Instead, I took the opportunity to glance at her over bites from my food.

She had long, delicate fingers and she'd been careful to empty the ketchup in the middle of the pile of fries, leaving the ends clean. She picked each french fry up individually and took small bites.

I figured it had to be love if I could be entertained by watching her eat fries. Or pizza. Hell, anything.

We ate in silence for a few moments, letting the sounds of the world rushing under our wheels fill in the empty space.

When she'd eaten about half her fries, she picked up a napkin and wiped at her fingers. Then she said, "And this is where we're going? Golden Verdure is our final destination?"

"Well, no," I said. "Not exactly. It's our last stop at a populated area. Then we're on our own."

"What does that mean, exactly?"

"Well, what I'd *like* to do and what you'll *agree* to do are likely different things."

"What would you like to do?"

"I'd like to leave you — well, you and Marcus back there, unfortunately — in Golden Verdure and go do what I need to do, then come back, pick you up, and get back to New Hope as soon as possible."

"Oh no," she said. "You're not leaving me —"

"Which is why there's that whole *what you'll agree to do* clause in there."

"And what do you believe I'll agree to?"

I set down my mostly finished Big Mac and snagged a couple of fries. I used them to point at her as I said, "Knowing the very beautiful, very adult, very confident Monica Holt, I'm assuming she would settle for nothing less than accompanying me on the full mission."

"You assume correctly."

"Then we've got a problem," I said. "And I'm not sure how we're going to get around it, because it literally means we're absolutely out of contact with" — I hooked a thumb to the back seat — "*that* for an unknown period of time."

"You know," Monica said. "Mary lives here. In Regina."

"Mary of Mary's Camel fame?"

"The very one."

"It's a good thought, hon," I said, "but if a hospital isn't going to take Marcus, I'm not going to drop his sorry ass on Mary."

"True," she said. "I just thought —"

Monica was in the act of turning to look in the back seat when someone said, "It's okay. I can help you with that."

Monica's McChicken gained the power of flight before hitting the dash and exploding into separate components.

"Good lord!" she yelped. For my part, I immediately recognized the voice and, in my shock, joggled the wheel — likely causing the demise of the flying McChicken — before quickly signalling and pulling off to a small chorus of car horns.

When we came to a dusty, gravel-skidding stop, I spun around in my seat.

There were two people in my back seat.

Marcus, who said, "Who are you?"

And Talia.

◆ ◆ ◆

"HOLY SHIT, TALIA!" I said. "You *trying* to get us killed?"

Talia leaned forward, her hand extended. "Mrs. Holt. It's a pleasure to finally meet you. I'm Talia Davis."

I think Monica was so stunned by her appearance that she shook the proffered hand out of reflex.

"May I call you Monica?" she said.

"What?"

"Please call me Talia. May I call you Monica?"

Monica's eyes scrunched as she said it again. "What?"

Talia held up both palms in a conciliatory gesture. "I'm sorry." She sighed. "I'm really not used to being around people anymore, and I forget my place. Please accept my apologies."

It felt like a couple of minutes, but it was likely only a couple of seconds where each of us met each other's eyes in defiance, amusement, or confusion. In between there, somewhere, Talia turned to her seatmate and said with a nod, "Marcus."

He chose to sneer at her, then turn to stare out the window. He seemed completely unsurprised at her sudden, unannounced, unexpected appearance.

"Okay," I said. "Let's start with, how the fuck did you get here?"

Talia nodded. "Fair question." She glanced from me to Monica, back to me. "I can…move under the skin of this world. I used to be able to do a lot more, to push others back and forth through it, but now, it's only me."

"Move under the skin of the world," Monica said, serious disbelief in her tone.

Talia's brows furrowed. "That probably doesn't explain it well. Put it this way: I can transport myself from one place to another. I did that."

"Spooky Talia," Marcus said.

"You," she said. "Hush."

"My father—" Marcus started.

"Is dead and gone," Talia said. "You need to get past it."

"But—"

Talia levelled a stare at him that made my balls retreat.

"Hush," she said. Under her breath, lower than a whisper, she said something else. It sounded like, "No more talk." But she pronounced "talk" strangely.

Let it go, Lex, I thought. Whatever she'd said, it shut him up.

Talia turned back to us. "So, long story short, you needed me to come here, so I did."

"And what do you mean, you can help?"

"I can babysit…" She looked over at Marcus. "…this one while you two do what you need to do. Though, I have to ask, Mrs. Holt, are you sure you want to accompany Lex? It *will* be dangerous."

"I'm going."

"Excellent." Talia broke out in a wide grin. She turned to me. "I do like this one. You chose well."

"Yeah, about that…"

Talia met Monica's eyes, tilting her chin to motion her to continue.

"You made a demand of Lex."

Talia dropped her head slightly, but not her gaze. "I did. Just as you made a demand of me."

Wait, what?

"I need to know," Monica said. "Had she chosen to do it…? Would you…?"

"No, Mrs. Holt," she said. "I absolutely would not have gone through with it. But I also would not have honoured the rest of our agreement either. The one with her or the one with you. Because I would have been profoundly disappointed, and profoundly wrong about our Ms. Hedges."

"*My* Ms. Hedges." There was a razor-sharp edge to her tone.

Talia angled her head. "I stand corrected."

"And just how can I believe you on that?"

"Don't listen to her," Marcus yelled. "*Don't you listen to the witch!*"

"Hush, demon," Talia said as she flicked a finger toward

him. Marcus pushed back, looking like he would have crawled out the window if he could have. But he hushed.

"As for believing me, Mrs. Holt," Talia said. She held both hands up, and make a few ridiculously complicated movements with her wrists, hands, and fingers.

I felt Monica sag more than saw her, but when I looked over, I realized she had just relaxed back in the seat a bit. Her face grew calmer, and she was nodding.

Goddamn, I thought, *now she's downloading into Monica's head, too.*

"Okay," Monica said. She shared a strange look with Talia, then nodded. "Okay. I get it. Thank you."

Huh.

A deep silence descended.

"What happens now?" I said.

"Are you okay with me monitoring Marcus while you do what you need to do?"

I checked in with Monica. She nodded. I gave her a tight nod, then gave the same to Talia.

"Fine," she said. "Then, when you get to where you need to be, I will come back."

"Okay—"

She was gone. Only the slowly rising leather of the back seat showed she'd been there at all.

◆ ◆ ◆

"Sooooo…" I said. "*That* happened."

"Yeah."

"I don't like that bitch."

"Hush, Marcus, no one's talking to you."

"Your friends are shit, Alexandra. This one is shit. The one that just left is shit. You need—"

"You need to shut your mouth, Marcus," Monica said. "I've been nothing but nice to you since we picked you up, and all you do is crap on me."

"Slut."

"Swear to god, Marcus," I said. "One more word—"

He opened his mouth and I threw a finger in his face. "*One. More. Word.* And you're sitting on the side of the road. Shut. The fuck. Up." I held the finger in place. Marcus glared at me, desperate to say something, but apparently smart enough to not call my bluff. We locked eyes for several long seconds, a lot of unkind words flowing between the gazes, but not a word spoken.

I finally dropped my finger, turned, reached out, and took Monica's hand. "Sorry about that. Sorry about him," I said.

"S'okay."

"It's not," I said. "You okay?"

"I'm...yeah...I'm just...still processing."

"Wanna talk about it?"

"Can we just hold off on that for a bit, Lex?"

"Of course," I said. "I get it. Been there, done that, got the memories and the souvenir T-shirt."

She put a hand on my leg. "Thank you for understanding."

I gave her a smile.

I started the car as she pulled out the napkins to wipe up her exploded sandwich.

♦ ♦ ♦

AN HOUR OR so later...

"So you're gonna stand by your woman?"

"Pardon me?" she said. "What brought this Tammy Wynette paraphrasing moment on?"

"Earlier, when we were talking about the whole *should do*

versus *agree to do* thing. You said you were in, all the way. Standing by your woman."

"You're my woman?"

"Might I remind you of the '*my* Ms. Hedges' thing?"

She smiled at that.

I dropped one hand to cover hers. "Monica Holt, I think you need to know…I was yours as soon as you walked into that hotel last week. You had me." I flicked a glance in my rearview, but Marcus was either sleeping or feigning it. Didn't care. He was behaving.

"Good to know I've got that power over you," Monica said, and I brought my full attention back to her.

"You have no idea."

"Too bad I didn't have it back in high school."

"Nah," I said. I grabbed my Coke and took a swallow.

"Nah?" she said. "What's this 'nah' you speak of?"

"Think about it." I put the Coke back in the cupholder. "Back then, if you had been as confident as you are now, you likely would have intimidated the hell out of me."

Monica laughed, unbelieving.

"Wait," I said. "You don't believe me?"

"Absolutely not."

"Do you think confidence didn't scare me back then?"

"Why would it? You were the most confident person I knew back then."

"Oh my god." It was my turn to laugh. "Not even close. I was your stereotypical ball of insecurity back then. I might have talked a good game, but I was terrified of any show of confidence. Hell, I was trying to talk myself into liking boys. I was seriously fucked-up."

"Really?" she said. "You hid it well."

"Monica, come on. We were seventeen. Who's confident at that age? Or at least, confident without being an asshole? And what teen isn't a black belt in hiding most of their shit? It may be under a façade of happiness, or sullenness, or sarcasm, or shyness, or whatever, but we all had something to hide back then. For me, it was being gay, even though you obviously saw right through it."

"I never really thought about it, but yeah, you're probably right."

"I know I'm right," I said. "Hell, I was so screwed up mentally, it took me another three years to lose my virginity. I was twenty-one years old."

From the back seat. "Alexandra."

So he hadn't been sleeping. Sneaky bastard. "Hush, Marcus, or I'll get Talia back here."

He hushed.

Monica was watching me and, in her eyes, I saw the questions there, but I still wasn't ready for those yet. I had promised her I'd be honest in all things, but I wasn't ready to be honest about this stuff. Not yet. I delayed any questions by barrelling on. "And I know one other thing."

"What's that?"

"That, even if somehow we'd gotten together, we likely wouldn't have lasted."

"I don't know about that."

"It wouldn't have been from lack of trying on your part, Monica, but let's face it, I had a lot of shit going on. I had a lot of baggage, and to be honest, I ran away and left most of it back in that godforsaken town of No Hope. And it looks like that's the baggage I'm going to have to deal with shortly." I stabbed my thumb toward the back seat.

"You won't be alone," she said, giving my hand a squeeze. "You wouldn't have been alone back then, either."

"No, I likely wouldn't have," I said. "But I sure as hell wouldn't have been mature enough or smart enough to appreciate it back then. I wouldn't have appreciated what I had."

"And do you now?"

"I hope that's obvious."

"It is."

"Good."

"But I'm still coming with you," she said, squeezing my hand again. "I meant it. I won't leave you facing this...this whatever it is...alone."

There were so many responses to this, but instead, I chose simply, "Thank you."

♦ ♦ ♦

WE STOPPED A little earlier than usual that night. We had a good meal in the room and settled down early for bed.

And that night, I dreamt once again of the shiny dark shape hiding in my childhood bedroom.

I woke up, covered in sweat, my muscles aching and taut with fear.

Monica worked her magic once again.

And then I worked my magic on her.

And again, the darkness was kept at bay.

♦ ♦ ♦

THE NEXT MORNING, we were up extra early. Five hours later, just around lunch time, we drove into town.

"Well, here it is. Welcome to Golden Verdure."

"Okay, I've heard of the don't-blink-or-you'll-miss-it towns, and have joked about a few of them. I even live in one. But this..."

"This is the real deal."

"How many people live here? Forty, you said?"

"I was rounding up. Honestly, it's probably closer to thirty-five or so. It was more like fifty-odd at its height, but that was a solid sixty years ago."

I told her of how, in 1928, the Canadian Pacific Railway had laid the last rails to the Northeast in the town and then just stopped, sticking a black-and-yellow checkerboard sign there to signify the end of the line. I talked about the first settlers coming to the land, mostly of German extraction. I pointed out where, at the town's height, there had been four grain elevators, but now, only one stood.

Driving by, I pointed out the corner where the hotel used to be, before it burned to the ground and was never replaced. I'd never been to this town before, but I saw the grain elevators. I saw the hotel. I saw it all, clear as day.

"There's a lot of space here," she said.

"Well, yeah, we're in the prairies, hon, there's not much else other than space here."

"No, I mean in this village—there's no way this is a town, Lex. New Hope is small. Carry's Cove is small. Opeongo is small. Hell, Vilni is tiny. But this? This is infinitesimal. But it's not that. I meant, there's a lot of space in this town. A lot of empty lots." She wrapped her arms across her front, holding her elbows. We passed a forlorn and abandoned ball diamond standing off in a field of tall, uncut grass. A shiver ran through her. "It all looks friendly enough, in an unkempt way, but I don't like it."

"Well, like I said, this is the last populated—and I use that term relatively loosely—area before our actual last stop. So, once we stop at the store there for some water and snacks…and hell, maybe a library book or to mail a letter while we're at it, then you can wave this place goodbye. We'll be heading out."

"Good."

♦ ♦ ♦

He realized there was no way to follow them into that ridiculous afterthought of a town without being seen. There simply weren't enough cars or people around for him to blend in.

Instead, he allowed them to keep going until he couldn't see them anymore, then did a quick U-turn and headed ten miles back the way he had come. He parked the car behind an abandoned gas station, spared one more glance at the cast-off wedding ring, shed his clothes, locked them in the car, then hid the fob under some rocks.

From here on in, he'd be following them on foot.

Now the real chase began. He looked forward to it.

♦ ♦ ♦

Now the real journey began. I wasn't looking forward to it.

Chapter Eleven

W E DROVE ANOTHER twenty minutes or so, until my implanted knowledge told me to stop. I parked the car. The two of us got out, leaving Marcus drooling in the back seat.

Monica looked around at the endless golden fields. "We're here?"

"No."

"Then why'd you stop?" Monica said. "No more driving?"

"Nope," I said, ignoring Marcus's prone body as I grabbed a few of the supplies from the back seat. "The rest of the way is on foot."

We exited the car. I said, "Now, we wait for Talia."

"I'm here," she said, making Monica jerk in surprise again.

"Talia," she said. "Is there any way you can appear in *front* of us, going forward? If not, I'm likely going to die of heart failure shortly."

"Your heart is strong, Monica," Talia said. "There's no danger of that."

"I mean…" She sighed. "Never mind."

Talia seemed to lose interest in the conversation, and turned in a slow circle, her eyes squinted down as she scanned the fields. *Looking for scarecrows?*

"Anyway," I said. "There's drinks and snacks in the car if you or Marcus want something. Other than that, we'll be back when we can."

Talia continued to scan the fields.

"You okay?" I said.

She nodded.

"Then we're going to go."

She nodded.

"Fair enough," I said, eyeballing Talia. "Good talk."

I went around to the trunk, pulled out a battered backpack, and loaded the supplies into it. Water bottles and some granola bars. Jackets, in case it got colder.

Monica looked around her. Aside from the road bisecting the view, there was nothing but flat, unbroken land. Not even a crossroad to break the monotony.

"Where are we walking?"

I studied the landscape, turning in my own slow circle, taking it all in. Though it all seemingly looked the same, there was a certain way, a certain angle that, when I turned to it, things seemed to *lighten*. I don't mean that it brightened up like god's sunbeam from heaven. I mean I felt lighter, happier, inside. As though a weight had been pulled from my shoulders.

I pointed toward what I figured looked like a completely arbitrary direction to Monica, and said, "That way."

To her credit, she accepted it all on faith, which meant a lot to me. She simply said, "Okay," and helped me with the supplies.

♦ ♦ ♦

PAST THE TOWN, and in the middle of nowhere. He realized now—far too late with his phone still in his car a half-hour's strenuous run behind him—that he should have checked in first.

He'd catch hell for it, but hindsight's always twenty-twenty.

As soon as the car stopped, he swung into a wheat field and settled down to watch. It didn't take long for the Book whore to show up, but what was disconcerting was how she seemed to be looking out at him. She obviously sensed him…or sensed something, anyway.

But she just as obviously didn't see him. He was ready for the fight, but it never came. She just held her ground. Each knew the other was there, each felt the other's threat, but as long as there was no direct aggression, the state of détente would hold.

He stayed hunkered down, watching. There was something about this place that twigged his instincts. He'd never been here, didn't actually truly know where he was, but there was a thin, low-level thrum of race memory. Not human memory, no. But what he was now. Something here was important. He just didn't know what it was, or why it was important.

With nothing more than an itch between his shoulder blades to tell him the place had *weight*, he decided to hold. To observe. He wouldn't follow the Hedges bitch because she had to come back to her car.

Unless she died somewhere along the way.

Either way, it worked for him.

◆ ◆ ◆

IT TOOK US a little over three hours, the sun high and hot off to our left, before I stopped, pulling the backpack from my back and dropping it to the dry grass. "Time for a break," I said.

Monica dropped gratefully to the ground. She looked around and — obviously seeing absolutely no other living thing except bugs, wheat, and me — pulled her T-shirt over her head and wiped at her forehead, her neck, and between and under her breasts.

I stood, a bottle of water frozen midway to my lips, staring at her.

She stopped when she noticed me. "Oh jeez, seriously? We're in the middle of some unbroken field to nowhere, it's gotta be damn near desert-like temperatures, I'm hot and sweaty, and you're getting horny?"

"Not getting."

"I thought women were supposed to be the more intelligent gender."

"Breasts," I said.

She made a face and cupped each one in a hand, jiggling them sarcastically at me.

"You shouldn't oughta do that, Holt. I may have to make them stop jiggling around. With my mouth."

She giggled. "How much further is it?" she asked.

"Not far. Twenty minutes, half an hour."

She giggled again, then stood on tiptoes, shading her eyes with her hand. She did a full circle. "Nope," she said. "Nothing." Then she unbuckled her belt and undid the button of her jeans.

"Monica," I said, my mouth going dry. "What in the hell are you doing?"

"Well, I wasn't horny until I saw that look on your face and that rather pleasing offer of your mouth on my tits. Now, the thought of doing it right here, right out in the open with nothing around us but more nothing? Well, yeah, don't ask me why, but it's kind of doing it for me." Then she kicked off her shoes, pulled off her socks, tugged down her jeans and underwear, and slid first one leg, then the other out. Then she was naked in front of me.

The bottle of water remained frozen halfway to my lips.

She walked over to me and reached for the buckle of my jeans.

I didn't even put up a token resistance.

◆ ◆ ◆

AFTERWARD, SITTING NAKED on our jeans, sipping water and sweating a lot more than we had been an hour earlier, she ran a finger down the back of my arm. "Why are we out here?" she asked. "What exactly is it we're looking for?"

"It's a staff."

"Like out of *Lord of the Rings*? The one the old guy carries?"

"Gandalf?"

"How did I know you'd know his name?"

"Because you know how much of a damn nerd I was in high school. You know the books I carried around in high school. It hasn't really changed much. Pretty much lost my shit when the movies came out."

"Anyway," she said, rolling her eyes. "The Staff. It's like that?" She stood and, to my utter and lasting disappointment, began getting dressed.

"Sort of," I said. "Only not really."

"Why does everything related to this have two completely opposing answers?"

"I don't know. Well, I do." I smirked. It earned me a light punch to the arm. "Ow," I said, rubbing my arm. "Careful. I bruise."

"Whatever," she said. "The Staff."

"Right. Okay." I started tugging on my own clothes as I talked. The image — the memory? — of it clear in my mind, I described the Staff as carved from an ancient piece of wood, with the head of a cat on one end and sharpened to a point on the other. The rest of it was covered in runes or hieroglyphics.

"Hieroglyphics?" she said, pulling her T-shirt back over her head. "So this thing is old? Like, ancient-Egypt old?"

"Crazy old," I said. "In fact, legend says it's actually older than the planet itself."

"Well, we know that's bullshit, right?" she said. "How can that be possible?"

"No idea," I said. I sat down to pull on my shoes. "How can it be possible that a woman—a woman who's in her midforties, by the way, but who looks like she's in her early twenties—how could it be that she somehow gave me the first-person experiences for several people, most of whom she's never met? How is it possible that she drops memories in my head for directions to a Staff that I know all about when I've never been near either the Staff or the location?"

"Yeah, okay, but this is in a whole different league. A staff that's older than the planet?" She shook her head. "That's like...I don't know...like saying you were born before you were conceived."

"Which you may very well be able to do if you're a mystical being."

"Not buying it."

"Okay," I said, pointing to the small, delicate cross that hung from a thin gold chain around her neck. "Talk to me about your religious upbringing."

"Shut up," she said, laughing. "You know it was strict Catholic, and I see where you're going with this."

"Where am I going?"

"'How can I believe in God—essentially a mystical being—but can't buy into a staff that's older than the world?'"

"Could you possibly accept it if you considered this Staff may have been made by your God-with-a-capital-G?"

She was tying her shoes, but stopped, looked at me. "That what you're saying, Hedges? That this staff we're seeking was made by the divine hand of God?"

"No, because I don't know."

"Okay. Tell me more." She finished with her shoes and stood.

I pointed in the direction we wanted to go, and we set an easy pace. As we walked, I told her about how the cat head on the one end of the Staff was believed to be the second carving, that there had been a different one originally, but if anyone knew anything about it, it'd been lost to time. I told her that the hieroglyphics were added later, during the time it may have had the feline head carved. Possibly by the priests of Bast in Egypt.

"Apparently Moses took the Staff with him when he fled Egypt."

"Really?"

"It's what's in my head," I said, tapping at a sweaty temple. "Might also be the same staff that was the Scepter of Israel, mentioned in your Bible."

"Oh, it's my Bible now, is it?"

"Sorry, Holt, but it ain't mine."

"Infidel," she said, laughing. She rolled a hand. "Continue."

"Sure, where was I?"

"Scepter of Israel? My Bible?"

"Right," I said. "Yeah, It might even have been around and in use when Atlantis was still above water."

"At…lan…tis."

"Yup," I said. "The mystical, magical lost continent of Atlantis."

"That you believe in as well."

"Never said that. Just telling you what the voices in my head tell me."

That earned me a sidelong look. "I'm kidding," I said, and tried to decide if I was.

"So, this thing's all that and a bag of chips. It's been there, done that, got the concert T-shirt."

"In a manner of speaking, yeah. It's even" — I put a hand on the small of her back, more as an excuse to touch her than anything — "supposedly been used to battle ancient magicians, capture spirits, and kill vampires."

"And does this staff have a fascinating name?"

"Well, interestingly, it does."

"Why is that interesting?"

"Because everyone knows that only swords are supposed to be named, not staffs."

She cocked an eyebrow at me. "*Every*one knows this?"

"Sure they do." I leaned in conspiratorially. "Gandalf never named his staff."

Which apparently Monica found hilarious, because she actually stopped walking and fell forward in a paroxysm of laughter. I stopped and admired her as she did so. When she was finally under some control, I did ask, "What? What'd I say?"

It brought on more giggles, but she was finally able to say, "'Gandalf never named his staff'…is that a euphemism?"

"Oh my god, that's what you were giggling about? What are you…a twelve-year-old boy?"

"Perhaps," she said, her voice all sweetness and light. And looking at her blinking innocently back at me, I just had to lean over and kiss her.

That ate up some more time.

Eventually, we came up for air. "What were we talking about again?"

She mimed a penis, with her hand near her crotch. "Your unusually named staff."

"Ah," I said. "Right."

"Okay," she said, making her point. "So, what is the name of this roguishly titled staff we're after?"

"The Staff of Solomon."

"Why Solomon? I don't remember you mentioning a Solomon in that story."

"He might have been the one doing the vampire slaying and such."

"Might have been?"

"Might have been."

"Hedges, are you fucking with me?"

"No, I—"

"How *dare* you? Why not?" she said, and her voice was so hilariously indignant that it was my turn to laugh.

Once I regained control, promises were made, oaths sworn, and we were able to continue on our quest.

◆ ◆ ◆

IT WAS STILL light out when we finally made our way to the spot I had in my head. This area was covered in grass instead of wheat, but that was the only difference.

I stopped and dropped the backpack again.

"Another rest break?" she said.

"Nope," I answered. "This is it."

Monica looked around once again at the barren, flat landscape, golden-burned grass under cloud-scudded blue skies beginning to pinken at the western horizon. "Sorry, babe, but I don't see any difference from that last place where we got naked."

"Well, there's one vital difference," I said. "Well, aside from you being naked." That earned me a look. "Give me a sec," I said.

I walked slowly to my right, moving deliberately through the dry grass, squinting intently at a specific spot. I travelled far enough that I knew Monica realized it was an arc of a large circle. "The difference..." I said, stepping carefully, staring, "...is that this place is the entrance...to the hiding spot for the Staff of Solomon."

I knew she wanted to ask how we would get in, but she would have to be patient. It was nothing I could tell her, I needed to show her.

She came over to me, meeting me at my position of the arc. She kissed my cheek. "What can I do to help you?"

"Nothing right now, hon." I kept my eyes on the spot, carrying further along the circle. "Just stick close by. You're gonna want to see this." I knew what I saw in my head, and it was kind of mind-blowing. Yes, it was a memory, but it was a fake one, one recorded by different eyes, stored in a different mind. I had not seen it for myself, though I knew precisely what I was looking for.

Not taking my eyes off that spot that sat at the middle of the circle my path described, I held out my hand and she immediately took it.

We walked along like that for a time. Every once in a while, I would check my location against the setting sun, but I always brought my eyes back to that one spot.

"What are you looking at?" Monica said. "I know you're looking toward the centre of a really big circle, but what is it you're looking at, exactly?"

Still holding her hand, I stopped, and took my eyes from the spot. I could find it again easily, I knew. At this point, I could see anything. It was like my eyes were some sort of hybrid of the Hubble telescope and an electron microscope, and they were attached to a Deep Thought supercomputer running some kind of hopped-up Google on steroids.

I didn't just see things. I *saw* them. I *observed* them. I *correlated* them. I *concatenated* them.

When I looked through the fields as they bent to the errant breezes, my mind described them artistically, mathematically, philosophically. Each small movement became a letter, a vital space, a point of punctuation in the story of the world, a small part of a huge, complicated equation describing it.

All of it.

I looked at a drop of moisture on a leaf and saw worlds. I looked at the earth beneath my feet and understood universes.

I was aware like I'd never been before in my life. *This is how god sees the world*, I thought.

Then I turned to Monica. And I saw her, really saw her, for the first time.

She was…magnificent. Breathtaking.

From the thirty-seven shades of green in her eyes, flecked here and there with hazel, to the fine hairs on the curve of her ears, to the tiny beads of sweat on her upper lip, to the way her tongue touched her lips to moisten them, to the fine strand of hair caught in an eyelash, she was beautiful. The smell of the moisture on her skin, the shampoo in her hair, her breath, the smell of her sex — she was intoxicating. The rhythm of her heart beating in her chest, the flow of blood to her veins. The air sliding in and out of her. The way her muscles moved under her skin. The grace and economy of each movement. The harmony of tongue and teeth and lips as she spoke. The musical tones of her voice, and the inflections and accents of her words. The small arcs between the neurons in her brain, like lightning between clouds. The way she held herself, tall and proud. The touch of her hand, warm and trusting in my own. All of this, each and every aspect, was the same as every other human being on the planet.

But no one else was exactly like her.

No one else was Monica Audrey Marilyn Danielle Holt.

I found myself drunk on her.

"Kiss me, Monica."

She furrowed her eyebrows slightly, but leaned in and we kissed. Our lips met, and it was more intimate than anything I had ever felt with anyone before. I felt her. I knew her. I shared with her.

The kiss wasn't long and it was only broken because Monica put a hand between my breasts and pushed me away. Her face was flushed.

"What—"

She gasped, grabbed my arms to support herself. "Jesus, Lex," she said, breathless. "What was that? My knees gave out."

"It was good, right?"

"Lex, I think I actually came."

That's when I realized I was incredibly aroused. It felt like gusher down there. And yes, another couple of seconds and I might have come as well.

"Yeah," I said. "I'm not…sure."

"A kiss, Lex. You kissed me and I came."

"If it makes you feel better, I was damn close too."

"What *was* that?"

"I honestly don't know," I said truthfully. "It's like…I don't know, I'm firing on all cylinders for the first time in my life."

"I'm not sure—" She was still breathing heavy. Her cheeks were flushed.

"Okay, what about…" I struggled to verbalize it. "You know that stupid cliché about how we supposedly only use something like ten percent of our brain?"

"Yeah," she said, swiping at the sweat on her lip.

"Well, it feels like I got boosted."

"But how does that explain me?" she said. "How does that explain how I…?"

"I don't know. I feel like I'm radiating heat and light. I feel like a fucking *sun* right now."

"And I kind of…what? Got caught up in your angelic glow?"

I smiled. "Yeah, you got dosed by my sunbeams."

"Well, Jesus, there's a pickup line I've never heard before."

We fell silent for a bit, simply taking each other in. Then Monica said, "Kiss me again."

"You sure?"

"Damn right I am."

The fact that we were both expecting it didn't change the outcome. Monica moaned and held me tighter. And this time,

I shuddered as I released my own orgasm. We didn't so much hold each other, but clench each other to keep from falling to our knees.

I actually didn't want it to end, and it was Monica who broke the connection first.

"Holy Mother of God," she said. "I could get used to that."

"Don't expect it to happen all the time," I said. "I think it's kind of a 'just now' thing."

"Either way, I'll take it." She dug into the backpack for a bottle of water, and drained it.

We both had to take a few minutes to get our pulses and breathing back to normal. We didn't talk, but we kept looking over at one another and sharing stupid, blissed-out grins. We both wanted to—I knew I did, and I could tell Monica did too—kiss again, but we might never stop, or ever walk again.

As it was, I was humming down there like I'd never hummed before.

"Okay, Sun Queen," Monica said, after draining a second bottle of water. "Orgasmic kissing aside, what exactly are you doing? Besides walking us in a big circle?"

Ignoring the slightly uncomfortable, mostly erotic wetness in my pants, I started moving again, keeping my eye on that one spot. "Weird as it's gonna sound, there's a specific blade of grass that I'm watching."

"A blade of grass?"

"Just one."

"How do you know it's the right one?"

"I just know."

"But…how?"

I answered by tapping my forehead. "My dose of sunbeams."

I stopped again, and though Monica seemed to appear worried that she was slowing us down, I was careful to not show even a trace of impatience. We had all the time in the world. I pointed, sighting along my arm and finger. "That one," I said. "Right…there."

She looked for a long time. I felt her eyes scanning and squinting. I kept my arm out, straight and steady, and let her find it on her own.

And she saw it. I felt it. I felt her hand involuntarily tighten, felt her body stiffen, heard the sharp intake of breath.

"You see it?" I said unnecessarily.

"Yeah." The word came out as a breathless rush of air. A rush of wonder. I couldn't help breaking my gaze to look at her. The look of awe on her face. "But how can that *be*?"

I turned back to the blade of grass. The single blade, nestled in amongst the others, not especially tall or short, not broader of leaf or different of colour.

The only exceptional thing about this blade of grass was its utter stillness. While the other fronds swayed, gently hissing in the soft breeze, this one stood unmoving.

"Because that's where the Staff is."

"How in the *hell* could anyone find this?"

"Well, that's the point, isn't it? Looking for a single blade of grass in a province full of it? It's the ultimate needle in a haystack."

She released my hand and moved toward it.

I reached out and caught her shoulder, but lightly. "No, hon. You can't." I saw the question in her eyes. "The blade of grass is just the marker. If you get too close, it'll move places. And we'll never know where the hell it is. There's only one way to get the Staff, and that's to find the opening."

"Move places?" she said. "What do you mean by that?"

"I mean it will disappear altogether. Then it will reappear elsewhere. Could be ten feet from here, or in Australia for all I know. And the problem is, I won't have the memory of where it is then. So, we can't disturb it." I started moving again. "Besides, it's only a marker. A route marker," I said, "not the destination."

Her mouth opened, but no sounds came out. I guessed that I'd systematically fried some of her circuits.

"We have to walk in a circle." As though to illustrate, I started up once again, pulling her by her hand behind me, talking as I went. "The entrance to the space is visible from only one angle. A very narrow one."

"How narrow?"

"A second of arc."

She tried to stop, but I kept her moving. "I don't get it. Is that a measure of time?"

"No, of a circle. You know a circle has three hundred and sixty degrees, right?"

"Right."

"Okay, well, a minute of arc is exactly one-sixtieth of one degree."

"But you said…"

"Right, a second of arc. Which is one-sixtieth of a minute of arc."

"One-sixtieth of one-sixtieth of a degree?"

"Yeah," I said. "One-thirty-six-hundredth of a degree."

I'm getting the idea that this is a very small area."

"If we were standing about two-and-a-half clicks from that blade of grass?"

"Yeah…"

"It'd be about as wide as a dime."

"At two-and-a-half kilometres."

"Yeah."

"We're what?" she said, squinting back at the spot. I knew she'd lost the blade again. "How far away?"

"A hell of a lot closer."

"So you're looking for…"

I slowed. Stopped. Angled my body side to side, side to side, each time, a little less, like a metronome winding down.

I let out a slow breath. "We're looking for this," I said.

♦ ♦ ♦

She stood, watching me expectantly. I pulled her close, putting an arm around her shoulders, bringing my head in close to hers. "Look at that blade of grass again."

"I'm sorry, I lost it when we started moving again."

"Sorry, yes," I said, shaking my head irritably. "I knew that."

She stopped me and turned to face me, cupping my face in her hands. Looked me deep in the eyes. Her gaze held me fast. "Hey," she said. "Hey."

I matched her gaze, raised my eyebrows.

"She's done something to you. Talia." Her eyes continued to search mine. "I don't mean in a bad way. But...you're different."

"Different?"

"Well, not different, more *becoming* different." She stopped, looked down, back up to my eyes, and hers crinkled into a smile. "God, listen to me. I'm starting to sound like you."

"Oh noes," I said, feeling my own smile matching hers.

"Oh, you didn't say that."

"Isn't that how the cool kids talk?"

"Okay, you may be becoming different, but I'm damn sure you're not turning into a child."

"No?"

"No. And don't ever say that again." She leaned in and kissed me. It was soft, delicate, but I felt my head go light, though it wasn't the same explosions as before. "Deal?"

"Deal."

"Okay, now show me this damn thing, Sun Queen."

We turned to face the centre of the circle again. I guided Monica's sightline and she found the blade of grass.

"Got it?"

"Got it."

"Okay, keep your eye on it, but if you can, I don't know, sort of unfocus your eyes?"

"Sort of like those weird, computer-generated 3D pictures where you have to come in close then back up?"

"A little." I had my arm back around her shoulders and slowly eased her sideways. Slowly…slowly…slowly…

"I see it," she said, her voice not fully carrying the excitement she felt. "Oh, shit I lost—no, there it is. Oh my gosh, it's *tiny*."

"Yeah, it's paper thin." I couldn't see it with Monica blocking the view, but I imagined it, a thin line, maybe only atoms thick, a slender, delicate dark line that pulsed and shimmered with light, as though from under a door or through the break in a pair of curtains, but more fine, and much more bright. A shining knife edge.

"And that's the entrance?"

"Yep."

"How in the hell are we supposed to use that as an entrance?"

"Hold my hand." I reached with my own and felt her warm hand slide into mine. It gave me a thrill to feel her warm skin against my own. I hoped I'd never take that for granted.

"Okay, follow me," I said. "I might have to go quiet to concentrate as we do it." Instead of continuing along that same arc of a circle, I now stared directly at the blade of grass, and found the opening again. "I've got the entrance in my line of sight. Now, I can't lose it."

"What happens if you do?"

"Remember when you wanted to get closer to that blade of grass?" I stepped forward slowly, carefully, my eyes never leaving the thin, coruscating line in my vision.

"The same thing would happen?"

"It would."

"But we're moving so slowly. What if you blink?"

"It's like the town of Golden Verdure. Blink and I'll miss it."

"You can't blink."

"No."

And already I felt my all-too-human eyes demanding relief, demanding moisture.

Demanding me to close my eyes.

We had crossed half the distance. It had taken perhaps three minutes. Could I go another three minutes without blinking? Of course I could. I'd heard somewhere that someone had won a staring contest by not blinking for forty minutes or something like that.

Still, my eyes burned. I felt the involuntary tears working up, and I couldn't blink them away. Of course, all I could think of was, *Blink. Blink. Blink.*

"You okay?" Monica said.

"Fine," I lied. "I'm just going to need to be quiet until we get in there, okay, hon?"

"Okay." And I found some relief in her understanding tone. She really didn't seem to have a lot of ego around me, something I was grateful for.

But later. Right now, it was my eyes. I didn't just want to blink, didn't even just need to blink, it was a mandatory, carved-in-stone law demanding my eyes to close and close this very instant.

I let the tears well and fall. I could not blink them away, didn't dare swipe them with my hand for fear of losing sight of the line, couldn't shake them away.

Maybe this was part of the price of admission. It needed the tears of the few who could see. Who knew? *There are more things in heaven and earth, Horatio…*

So, I let them come. Then I willed them away from me, willed them down my cheeks.

Finally, mercifully, I was there, right there, right at the blade of grass. I saw the frond on either side of the line, saw it bisecting the plant, and my foot was lifting as though to push against that single stalk of grass, to crush it underfoot.

Instead, I was somewhere else altogether, pulling Monica in behind me, my eyes streaming tears, burning.

But then, we were inside.

We had made it.

◆ ◆ ◆

"WHERE THE HELL are we?"

It felt like a cave, but not natural. Constructed. Like a…

"Are we in an abandoned subway or something?" Monica said, her voice echoing in the empty structure.

"Sure as hell looks like it, doesn't it?"

"Hold on," she said. "Are you saying this isn't part of your download?"

It wasn't until she said it that I realized it. But it was true. This was uncharted territory. "Yeah. This wasn't part of the download," I said.

"Seriously?"

And then I realized. "Talia was able to get the memories of someone who had seen the entrance, but not passed through it."

"Or it goes to a different place each time." I hadn't thought of that, but it was a possibility as well. There were questions I likely would never have answers for. I eased forward a little more, then stopped. "Look through there."

Monica followed me forward, the sounds of our shoes, our breathing, the only sounds in the structure. We came to an alcove, the platform of a subway stop. What should have been in that alcove was more rigid concrete structure. Instead, we saw the concrete ceiling end and a deep night sky take over. But it was what was under that sky that was terrifying.

A road, littered with spray-painted graffiti, the pavement

cracked and heaved, issuing a foul-smelling smoke, as though Hell had somehow been paved over, but badly. We could smell it, almost taste the smoke, but there was no sound. A television show with the sound muted.

Further on, within a different platform, sunlight filtered into the tunnel. Walking to it, we saw a desert, stretching as far as the eye could see.

And off to one side, a rusted ship, abandoned on the sand.

"What in the hell *is* this place?"

"The ultimate hiding place," I answered.

We continued walking, seeing abandoned cities, caves with the mummified remains of humans, the inside of a rusted-out ship overrun with rats, a forest that Monica stated she couldn't even look at…

And then we turned a corner and, just like that, my memories were back. I nodded. "This is the one."

"You're sure?"

I scanned my memories. "Absolutely no question," I said.

We clambered up to the platform and, not allowing myself to hesitate, stepped forward…

…straight into a thick blanket of heat that sucked the breath from our bodies and replaced it with searing heat. Ahead of us, cutting deep into the earth, a massive, glowing crater.

"It looks like Hell."

I thought, *The other places we've seen looked like Hell, too. Just different areas of it.* But I didn't say anything about that. They were all hells of one sort or another, every one of them. Then it dawned on me what we were actually looking at.

"I think it's actually called something like that," I said. "I think we're in Turkmenistan. I think this is the Door to Hell."

"You're saying we're somewhere in Russia?"

"Close enough. The former Soviet Republic." There was sweltering heat, there was insane heat, then there was the heat we felt now. "The fires of Hell."

"So it used to be Russia?"

"Again," I said, "close enough."

"It's probably a stupid question, but how do you know? Meat computer download?"

"Not a stupid question," I said. I found we were both gasping for breath now. "In this case, I have the memory, but there's no other info. Just the visuals and the heat. But I have a feeling I'm right. I did an article on this for the web journal a year or so ago."

"But we were in middle of Nowhere, Saskatchewan fifteen minutes ago." She looked at the glowing crater. "And now you're saying we're halfway around the planet."

"Yeah."

"Goddamn."

"Yeah."

"And you believe the Staff is here?"

"I don't believe it," I said, taking a swipe at the sweat on my forehead. "I know it."

I strode over to the crater. Monica held out her hands. "Jesus, Lex, not so close. That ledge doesn't look secure at all."

"It's not," I said. "That's the idea."

I moved slightly slower, then I saw what I wanted. A faint image, shimmering in the light from the eternal fire of the pit. Something that hung suspended, the carved surfaces catching the lights.

It was the Staff. The Staff of Solomon.

It hung just over the edge of the pit. I'd have to reach for it. *This is some Indiana Jones shit, right here,* I thought.

Still, there was nothing for me to do but go for it. It was why I'd dragged Monica along and driven halfway across the country, and then found myself halfway across the world.

All for a Staff that I somehow knew held far too much power to be fucking with.

With one last look back at Monica to give her a smile of reassurance that I didn't really feel, I then turned and strode purposefully to the very edge of the pit. The heat seemed to suck all the moisture from my body, making my skin feel like it was being stretched across my face. I felt my eyebrows curling and singing away, the same with my hair.

My body wanted to sweat, but the heat stole the moisture as it came out of my pores.

The Staff floated just a couple of feet out from the edge of the pit, swaying gently in the buffeting gusts of hot wind blowing up from the fiery pit. All I had to do was reach out and grab it.

That was all. Just grab it.

I slid my foot toward the edge of the precipice, slowly adding weight to it, ready to jump back if the edge crumbled. For now, though, it held.

I leaned forward, my fingers wanting to pull back from the heat, my arm forcing them forward, out toward the Staff.

Did it pull away? Did it just move out a bit farther?

No, it was my imagination. It was the heat.

I leaned out more, my fingers inches from the carved surface of the Staff. An inch.

I watched the fine hairs of my arm curl and singe and blow away in the gusting heat.

My questing fingers closed on the surface. The wood was slick, smooth, cool beneath my fingers. I tightened my grip.

And the ledge crumbled, lurched, then fell away.

I was aware of Monica's scream behind me as I fell toward the pit.

♦ ♦ ♦

I saw Monica's terrified, tearful face appear over the edge of the precipice.

"*Lex!*" she screamed, her voice high and ragged over the snapping rumble of the flames.

"Monica," I said. "I'm okay. Step back to where it's safer. I'll be back up there in a minute."

Though, how I was going to do that exactly? I didn't really have a clue. After the drop, I'd found myself about twenty feet below the ledge, maybe a little over a third of the way to the bottom. I'd simply stopped falling, one hand still clutching the Staff.

I wasn't hanging from the Staff. I still held it upright, one hand wrapped tightly around Its body, about halfway up Its length. Maybe seven feet. Taller than me. We hung in this hot space, both vertical, side by side.

As for me, I wasn't falling, but I could feel the drag of gravity wanting to pull me down. Yet I was safe, at least for the moment.

I knew it was the Staff.

I knew this was part of the test. The Staff had pulled me in here. Now, I had to get myself out of this predicament. Somehow.

Instead, I found myself twigging on some lyrics from a song I hadn't heard in a little while. Something about lighting a cigar on the fires of hell. Or something like that.

Well, I thought as the heat threatened to melt my brain, *let's light the fucking cigar.*

I brought in my other hand from trying to maintain balance to grip the Staff. Then I did the only thing I could think of. I held the carved wood with both hands, focused only on the cool surfaces beneath my fingers, and pushed every thought out of my head except one.

Get us the fuck out of here.

◆ ◆ ◆

AND I WAS back in the concrete cave. The sudden change in temperature felt initially wonderful, then quickly chilled me. I ignored it and, carrying the Staff, ran back to alcove to get Monica.

But the alcove was gone.

"No." It wasn't a statement of disbelief. It was a negation of the current situation. Monica was still near that Door to Hell, therefore, the alcove needed to be there.

I brought the Staff up, holding It high above my head. "*NO!*" I said again.

Nothing happened.

"What are you doing here?"

I spun. There was someone behind me, far down the tunnel, yet her voice sounded like it was right in my ear. "I'm trying to get my girlfriend back." Panic tinged my voice.

"Where is she?"

"Near a flaming pit. It's burned for years. It's where this was," I said, and held up the Staff.

"Shit, It was hidden there?" Then, quietly, she said, "You fucker, you held that from me." I couldn't see her, only a dark outline of a shape.

"*I need to get her back.*"

"Yes," she said. "Right. Of course."

She spread her arms, and said something far too low for me to hear. Frustrated, I gripped the Staff tighter, willing It to open the entranceway again. It didn't.

"Okay," she said. "Focus on your girlfriend. Think of her face and her name. And pull with everything you've got."

I pictured her face. Those eyes, the strong nose, the full lips. And then, with everything I had in me, I clutched the Staff until my hands hurt, and I thought, *I need her back here with me. Bring Monica Holt back here to me.*

And then there was a sound behind me, a huffing of breath. I spun, the Staff forgotten and clattering to the floor.

"Oh, thank god," I said. I turned to look down the tunnel.

The person down there was gone.

Chapter Twelve

I RAN TO her, dropped to my knees, initially simply holding her, not knowing what else to do. She sobbed hot tears into my shoulder. Her body, still leaking heat from the Door to Hell, was almost uncomfortable to the touch, still, I held her. She turned to the side and vomited, and still, I held her. It took a while before we were both back under control.

I found I couldn't take my eyes from Monica, scared that she might disappear from me again. I would not have been able to handle it if she did.

"Oh Jesus, Lex," she said. "I thought you were dead. I saw you fall…"

"The Staff saved me. I guess I passed the test."

"And then you were gone."

"I came back here. I went back to look for you and"—I pointed to the blank expanse of wall—"the path was gone. I didn't know what else to do, so I commanded the Staff to bring you back here."

"That's what happened?" *With some help, yes.*

"I guess so."

"Because if felt like someone fish hooked my spine and guts and dragged me here."

I wonder if that someone was me, or the other one? "Sorry."

"Rather be here than Russia," she said.

We both considered that for a few moments, both lost in

our own private worlds. Or maybe, our own private hells. I don't know. I didn't ask her.

Then Monica shifted and I relaxed my hold on her. Her eyes met mine. "Lex?"

"Yeah?"

"Can we get the hell out of here?"

I smiled. "Let's find out."

We stood, holding hands. First, I angled us over to the Staff, still sitting where I had dropped it. I picked it up, held it out from me so we could both see it better. "Doesn't look like much, does it?"

"Actually," she said, "it does."

We turned as one and walked back the way we had originally come, neither of us speaking. We didn't turn to look at the various alcoves along the way. Neither of us wanted any more glimpses into those places. Our eyes stared straight ahead, fixed on our target.

Finally, we were back where we'd started. The subway tunnel continued on, seemingly for miles, but we stared out at the alcove that showed nothing but a straight horizon of grass and sky.

"You know what worries me?" Monica said.

"No, what?"

"That every one of those openings showed a hellish place. A place I'd never want to set foot in, ever."

"Yes, I agree."

"And then there's ours."

"I don't follow."

"Is that"—she gestured toward the golden fields—"someone else's version of Hell?"

"Maybe it is."

"Well, right now it looks like Heaven to me."

"Me too."

And we went through the alcove...

◆ ◆ ◆

…AND BACK TO the middle of nowhere in Saskatchewan.

It was night now. "We have a three-hour walk back to the car again, don't we?" she said.

"Well, unless I ask the Staff to bring the car to us. Or us to the car."

"You really want to do that?"

"No. Not really."

"I'd rather not get fish hooked again, either," she said, rubbing her belly.

"Makes sense," I said. "So, we walk."

I tried to find the solitary blade of grass, but it was impossible in the darkness. "Besides, I think we may need that time to just decompress and absorb all the shit we just saw."

"You're probably right."

"And I'm not sure I know how to do it yet." I admitted. "You still glad you came?"

"Fish hooks aside and, as stupid as this is going to sound," she said, "yes, actually I am."

"You are? Really?"

"Come on, Lex. I've seen more in the past few hours challenging all that I've ever believed than most human beings get in a full lifetime."

"I'm not going to ask if it's changed your beliefs. I think it's too early for that."

"So do I." She stood, regarding me under the stars. She cocked her head to the side. "Gotta say though, having two orgasms from two kisses? Kinda life-changing. I always knew you'd be a fascinating person to hang out with, Hedges. I just never guessed *how* fascinating. Like I said, hell of a first date."

"I aim to please."

She moved closer to me, placing her hands on my chest. "You know, if we could put an hour between us and this spot,

I might even be tempted to take my clothes off again."

"Might?"

"It would depend on who's asking, I guess." I knew she was trying to keep it light. Trying to ignore the fact that both of us could have died back there. That we nearly did. Still, there was something about escaping death that fuelled certain urges within me and, I guessed, within Monica as well.

I grabbed her hand and started a brisk pace.

♦ ♦ ♦

NIGHT HAD SETTLED. It was time to gamble.

Either Hedges was going to come out soon, or she was never coming out at all.

Which meant, what he was going to do now would either be a big surprise for Hedges, the Conquering Dyke Bitch, or else it was just going to be a whole lot of fun for him tonight.

Either way, he'd decided he'd better get on it.

He backed slowly and silently away from the watchful eyes of that Book whore until he was sure he was out of range of her eyes and ears.

Then he headed back toward Golden Verdure. He broke into a run, and growled with pleasure.

♦ ♦ ♦

NINETY MINUTES LATER, we were pulling our clothes back on in the decidedly chillier night air.

"You worried?" Monica said.

"About what?"

"Considering this is still, at least technically, our first date," she said, "what are you gonna do on our next date to top this?"

I sat down hard. "Oh, shit," I said. "The *pressure*."

"You have some time," she said. "Think about it."

"Well, one thing's obvious, right off the top," I said.

"What's that?"

"Next date?"

"Yeah…?"

"I won't bring Marcus."

She cocked a finger gun at me, squinted one eye. "Good plan."

"Gee, thanks."

♦ ♦ ♦

"WE'RE NOT GOING to head back home tonight, are we?"

"No. What do you say we head back to Golden Verdure tonight, even if we sleep in the car. We'll grab some food in the morning, see if we can even scam a shower somewhere, then get going when we're a little more fresh."

"Sounds good."

It was midnight before we got back to the car.

Talia was standing guard in the moonlight. We were still a fair distance away in the field. I raised my voice and said, "Any problems?"

"No," she said. It was weird. It came across as her normal speaking voice, but we heard her clearly, even this far away. "You got it?"

"We did," I said, and moved to raise my arm with the Staff.

"*No!*" she said. "I don't need to see it." I dropped the Staff back down, out of her sight.

Then she was gone.

"I'm never going to get used to that," Monica said.

The first problem was getting the Staff into the car. At better than seven feet long, it simply would not fit. Eventually, we settled on putting the pointed end in the footwell by

290

Monica's feet, then running It out the rear driver's side window and rolling the window up as high as we could to trap It there.

Marcus, despite being in some sort of angry mood, recoiled viciously at the sight of It. "GetItoutgetItoutgetItout!"

There was nothing we could do to settle him down, not even when Monica draped a blanket over It to hide It somewhat.

"GetItoutgetItoutgetItoutoutoutoutout!"

We had no choice. We listened to him screech all the way back to Golden Verdure. I drove with only one hand, keeping my other firmly clasped in Monica's. We rode it out together.

♦ ♦ ♦

NOT FIVE MINUTES later, Marcus abruptly shut up, and Monica announced she had a bad feeling about the town again. Moments later, we saw the brightness on the horizon.

It took another ten minutes to confirm it.

Golden Verdure was almost gone. It was burning to the ground.

We didn't even go into the village proper. We couldn't.

There was another sign that allowed us to go no further.

"Oh no," Marcus said. "That's not good." But he was laughing.

♦ ♦ ♦

I DIDN'T TAKE the time to count them all, but I guessed every single resident of the town — something like thirty-five bodies — was stacked like cordwood across the entrance to Main Street.

Then the naked man separated out from the pile of bodies, and I had the sudden realization that he'd been waiting for us.

He stood up and I saw he was a big man. Though it wasn't until he finished stretching, as though waking up from a nap, and began his walk toward us, that Monica gasped.

At first, I thought it was the shock of someone alive out there. Then I thought it was because this guy was naked. Then, one hand white-knuckle tight on the dashboard, the other squeezing my right, she said, "Duane. Oh my god."

"What?" I said, but it was far away and stupid. I knew I'd heard the name, but I couldn't nail it down. She turned to me, eyes wide and panicked. Her trembling came up through her grip on my hand.

"It's Duane," she said again. "My husband."

"Oh dear," Marcus said. He was still laughing, the bastard.

♦ ♦ ♦

EVEN WHEN SHE said the words, it still didn't quite process.

Duane.

Her husband.

No, that can't be right.

And yet…if anyone was going to recognize him, it would be Monica.

"Are you—"

"Yes, I'm goddamned sure, Lex. I know that walk. I know my own husband."

I turned from her to the front window again. He was still fifty feet out, about halfway between us and the bodies. He walked slowly, but with purpose, an easy roll in his gait, his shoulders and arms sliding back and forth, loose limbed, his cock swinging from side to side. Like he was an animal, stalking us.

I reached for the door handle.

"No," Monica said. Her voice was quiet, but full of fear.

I ignored her and opened the door anyway. As I moved to exit the car, she clutched at my hand, trying to hold me back. Her eyes were focused forward, and her voice was low and quivering as she said, "No no no no no no no no no..."

Marcus, in the back seat, echoed her. "No no no no no no no no no..."

As though their simple negations would cease everything that was happening.

I got out. Duane had halved the distance. Without thinking about it, still watching him approach, I reached for the back seat window and pulled the Staff from the car.

It felt good in my hands.

Monica got out and worked her way around the back of the car.

Duane stopped.

"Duane," I said. No sense in going through all the "who are you?" bullshit.

"Give it to me," he said. He held one hand out.

Again, there was no bullshit, no asking what he was talking about. It was obvious he wanted the Staff. He stared at it.

His cock shifted a bit. Lengthened. *Jesus,* I thought. *He's getting a woody over this.*

I tried to ignore it. "You've been following us."

"Yes," he said. "Give it to me."

"That was you, right?" I said. "Back at the hotel? And who Talia was looking for?"

"Give the Staff to me." He extended his hand, palm up. His cock seemed to imitate that motion, also pointing straight out. He seemed either completely unaware or completely uncaring about his state of tumescence.

We stood, only a few yards apart, watching each other. Monica, still some distance from me, said, "Duane..."

"You took off your ring."

The statement was so opposite to what I'd expected that it

took me a moment to understand what he meant. I almost said, "Monica?" but glancing over at her, I realized it could be no one else.

Monica said nothing. He said nothing. I noticed his dick was no longer pointing straight at us.

You took off your ring.

But then…that meant… "You still love her, don't you?"

He made no movement, said nothing, gave nothing away. "Give it to me," he said, an edge creeping into his voice.

"Duane, I'm not sure how we ended up here, staring each other down, but you have to understand that, right now, I have the Staff. I have the power. You have—"

He attacked.

♦ ♦ ♦

I'D SEEN A lot of weird, unexplainable shit in the past few days, right up to and including the husband of my girlfriend standing in front of a stack of bodies that were once the inhabitants of a small town. Inhabitants that he presumably killed. And he had an erection.

But when I saw him drop to all fours and, in the span of two very quick heartbeats, transform from a normal human being into the largest, most feral wolf I had ever seen…it wasn't as big as the Door to Hell, but it was just as terrifying.

Especially when that wolf was coming straight at me, teeth bared.

Running on instinct and gut reaction, I raised the Staff of Solomon, more to put an obstacle between us. Duane—the wolf—angled his jaws to capture the Staff, like a dog retrieving a stick for its master.

Its master.

The ones Talia was going to arrange the meeting with?

Had to be.

The wolf leapt, and, eyes flashing, opened its mouth to clamp down on the Staff.

"Duane," Monica screamed. "No!"

Somehow, she was right beside me, and it brought the wolf—Duane—up short. He skidded to a stop, his paws kicking up dust from the dry gravel road. It was in this second that I was able to observe him, to really see him.

What I saw in that quick, one-second flash was a wolf that likely weighed a solid two-fifty. Muscles rippling under a grey-black pelt of fur. Paws as big as hands, tipped with sharp black nails. Grey eyes, intelligent, under expressive brows. A tongue nestled in a cage of craggy teeth, four extending into sharp, gleaming fangs.

This was the wolf.

This was Duane.

This was Monica's husband.

I thought, *What the hell do I do now?*

◆ ◆ ◆

THE THREE OF us remained in a tight triangle for a few seconds, the moment feeling like a standoff. Then Monica took a step forward. Duane did not back up, but did emit a low growl. It was a warning.

"Monica," I said. "I don't wanna—"

"I don't want you to, either." She hadn't taken her eyes off the wolf, and then she addressed it directly. "Duane. I hope you can understand me. I don't fully understand what's going on here. I don't know how you ended up here, or ended up like…this…" And she faltered, tears springing to her eyes.

Duane wouldn't meet her eyes, would glance quickly then look away. But through it all, through all her words, the low growl had kept up. It was clearly a warning and it scared the shit out of me.

When Monica stopped talking, it was obvious the words were either not getting through, or not having the effect they were supposed to. I took one step closer to her. Duane's growling increased.

"Monica," I said, "please get behind me."

Maybe it was the movement. Maybe it was the sight of his wife standing behind her new lover, her hands on my shoulders. Maybe it was just the wolf in him. Whatever it was, I saw his muscles tense and, as he launched himself at me, I slid my right hand down the Staff, tight above my left, and swung the Staff like the world's most ornate baseball bat. I held nothing back, putting full force into the swing.

It could have torn the head off a normal guy. It would have torn my head off.

The Staff connected with Duane, catching him mid-leap, impacting him along the left side of his face and shoulders, and two things happened at the same time.

The first was the scream that tore from his mouth. I'd never heard anything like it. It was the wail of someone having their soul torn from their body. A shrieking scream of pain, of despair, of irrevocable, heart-rending loss.

The second thing was the physical connection of Staff and body. When I hit Duane with the Staff, the impact changed his direction as though he weighed nothing. He spun off to my left, his body arcing as his limbs flailed, jerking and scrabbling for balance, for purchase. He found neither until he landed in a cloud of limbs and road dust, two car lengths away.

I'm not sure which of us was more shocked.

"Duane," Monica said, "please...just...stop, okay? Just stop."

Duane took a few moments, and when he got back to his feet, he was unsteady. He looked at himself. Naked. Human.

"The hell did you do to me?" he said.

The Staff was warm, almost uncomfortably so, in my hands, when I said, "I have no idea. I think I might have knocked the wolf out of you."

He shook his head, as though to dispel the words like insects from his head.

"Duane…" Monica said, and took a step toward him.

"No," I said. "Stay back."

"He's my husband. He's not going to hurt me." Her words stung. But she was right, he *was* her husband.

What did that make me?

She took another step toward him and I fought my instinct to protect her. Yes, she was right. He wouldn't hurt her, would he?

He was her husband.

But he was a werewolf.

"Where did you go?" she said, and the tone in her voice was heartbreaking. "Why did you not tell me you were leaving?"

He stared at her, shooting his head forward and widening his eyes as though saying, "Are you serious?"

"What?" she said, obviously understanding him. One of those married couple signals that outsiders didn't get.

I was the outsider here.

"The hell was I supposed to say?" he said. He raised a shaking fist to his cheek, his baby finger and thumb out in the universal sign for a phone. "Hey honey, it's your husband who you can't stand anymore. I'm not coming home cuz I caught a bad case of the wolfs." He dropped his hand again. "Jesus Christ," he whispered.

"But you could have…"

"I could have what?" he said. "Lied to you? What, you didn't get enough of that when we were still together?"

"No, it's—"

"No, it's nothing." He padded back and forth, back and

forth, his bare feet making soft slapping noises on the blacktop. There was a massive dark line along his face and chest, like a burn, where the Staff had connected. It had to hurt like hell. He was still unsteady on his feet, but he seemed to be regaining some composure and I wondered if he was going to wolf out again.

Then I looked at the Staff and wondered *if* he even could wolf out again. And I didn't know the answer. For now, I kept my mouth shut.

Marcus had somehow managed to get out of the car, and had come up beside me. He said nothing, just watched the two of them like I was.

Monica stepped closer to Duane. He didn't approach her, not yet, but I could see he was very aware of where she was. He mostly stared at the ground as he paced, but he shot occasional sidelong glances at her and at me.

"Talk to me," she said, her voice low, soft, even. "What happened to you?"

He barked a laugh. "You don't really want to know."

"Yeah, Duane, I do." She moved closer, now maybe half the distance. "You just left, no explanation. I'd like to know why."

"No, you really wouldn't."

"Duane…"

"Trust me, you don't want to know."

"Duane…"

Then he stopped pacing and faced her. He seemed to cross some mental threshold. His eyes blazed and his body tensed. "Fine! Fuck it! You wanna know?" He threw his arms wide. "Then I'll fucking tell you."

"Dua—"

"Shut up," he said, and his voice was cruel.

"Hey," I said, and I hoped it held the right tone of warning.

"Yeah, you shut up too," he said. "You want me to tell this, then shut the fuck up and I'll tell you."

♦ ♦ ♦

Back when Duane and Monica were still living together, still married, at least on paper, if not in reality, he'd been spending a lot of nights at the Vilni watering hole. Monica knew of the place, and had heard rumblings that her increasingly distant husband had been there.

There was a night, back seven years ago, that he'd come home from work. Monica had made dinner. They ate. While Monica did the dishes, he flipped through the channels, but his mind wouldn't settle on anything. None of the shows made sense. The laugh tracks were grating.

He reached for his cigarettes and pulled one from the almost-full pack. He put it in his mouth and popped the lighter.

Then he knew Monica would start ragging on him about smoking in the house. How it got in the curtains and the sheets and the towels and stank up the whole place. And he didn't want to hear it. Didn't want to hear her fucking ragging voice.

He left the unlit cigarette in his mouth, stowed his lighter in his pocket. He stood, put on his shoes, grabbed his wallet and keys.

At the jangle of his keys, Monica came out from the kitchen, dish soap like snow on her hands. "Where you going, hon?" she said.

She still called him hon.

"Out of smokes," he said. Then he was through the door and gone. Straight down the highway to the Vilni Tavern.

On this particular night, a rough-looking group of bikers, four of them, entered the bar. Though they got a lot of stares, they stuck to themselves, ordering beers and huddling close, talking quietly amongst themselves. Duane went back to his own poison and ignored them.

He'd been telling himself that he was getting out of the house so he could figure out what to do to save his failing marriage. Taking some time to himself to understand what was going wrong. He was smart enough to understand that not talking to the other person in the relationship likely wasn't the smartest move, and adding a liberal dose of alcohol into his thinking box probably wasn't assisting him in achieving any answers.

Still, he didn't really know what else to do.

In theory, this is what he was doing when the ruckus started. In reality, he'd been focusing on some old Kevin Costner movie—one old enough that he was playing a college graduate on some sort of road trip with some buddies—and trying to puzzle out the story with no sound, when the volume level of the bar rose several decibels.

"I don' have a fuggin' problem, man." Duane knew the voice. Rob Popper, son of the weird dude who had taught at Clarington District High School when all that shit went down in the eighties. The old man wasn't right in the head, and the apple didn't fall far from the tree. Rob was on the fast track for the title of both Town Drunk and Village Idiot. And he was now standing by the table with the four bikers.

Duane turned on his stool. "Rob," he said, "the hell you doing? Leave those guys alone."

Rob swung his bleary gaze unsteadily to Duane, doing a bit of a wobble and course correction as he did. "Doo-wane," he said, "I'm jes tryin' to find out if these gennelmen are like that movie?"

Duane was going to ask which movie, but Rob said, "Y'know, the Harley Davison an' the guy named after the smokes one."

It took Duane a few seconds, but he got it.

"*Harley Davidson and the Marlboro Man?*"

Rob stabbed a finger at him. "Thassa one! Knew ya knew it!"

"It's a movie, Rob. It's not real. Now, step away, leave them alone and let me buy you a drink."

Normally, that would have worked. Popper had a habit of pissing people off, but would usually come to heel if offered a drink. And it looked like it was going to work here as well.

Then one of the bikers said, "Listen to your friend, there, buddy."

Popper turned back to the group, stumbled again. He shot a hand out to steady himself and cuffed the biker across the cheek.

It had been an accident, but it had been enough. All four of the group shot to their feet. Popper tried to stagger back, but the one who had been hit snatched Popper by the front of his T-shirt—a ragged Mellencamp concert shirt that had seen better days, much like Popper himself—and dragged him forward.

Marty "The Worm" Wormser, the barman, then pulled a bat from under the bar and, brandishing it, said, "Take it outside, boys."

The bikers abandoned the table and, dragging Popper behind them, made for the exit.

"Worm, for chrissakes," Duane said. "There's four of them and one of him. They'll kill him."

"Relax," The Worm said, lifting a cordless handset to his head. "Callin' the cops."

"Then tell them to bring a goddamn body bag." Duane dropped from the stool and followed the five men outside.

♦ ♦ ♦

"ROB FUCKING POPPER," Duane said.

Guy was a bit older than me, but I'd been aware of him growing up. Never liked him. From the expression on Monica's face, she didn't either.

Marcus's face was unreadable.

"When I got outside," Duane said…

♦ ♦ ♦

…HE REALIZED HE should have just stayed inside, let Popper take his lumps. Or, at the very least, ask the bikers to not beat him too bad, then head back inside and wait for the cops to arrive.

Instead, when he saw Popper on the ground, mewling and pleading with them, and one of the guys — already shirtless — shucking his boots and pulling down his pants, he knew this was going someplace worse than a few guys putting a hurting on a deserving asshole.

At the risk of drawing naked biker attention to himself, Duane said, "Come on, guys, let him up. He's had enough. Let me buy you all a beer."

The three clothed bikers stepped back. One of them addressed the naked one. "It's your show, Angus. He's all yours." Angus was the one Popper had cuffed upside the head.

The naked guy — Angus — turned to Duane. But as he did, he dropped to all fours. He seemed to darken in the inadequate glow of the parking lot lights. Then Duane realized, he wasn't darkening.

He was sprouting hair all over his body.

Frozen to the spot, Duane could only watch as what had been a man turned into a massive wolf.

The other three laughed. One said, "Buddy, you're either the bravest badass son of a bitch I've seen in a bit, or the dumbest. Most people run like fuck." Then he shifted his eyes to the wolf. "Whaddya think, Angus? Kill the badass? Or keep him? Ain't like we ain't already late for the Hole."

Angus stalked forward two more steps. He stopped and sniffed the air. Duane held his breath, too terrified to move, to speak. If he just stayed really still, and really quiet, maybe they'd decide he wasn't worth their trouble.

Then the wolf named Angus turned his head, and his mouth opened and his tongue lolled. A thin, silvery line of saliva slid from tongue to pavement. Then he turned back to Duane.

And leapt.

Duane attempted to bolt for the door, but he'd only got as far as a quarter turn in that direction when he felt a violent shock of movement on his right forearm. He spun and saw his arm in the mouth of the wolf, felt the heat through the thin material of his shirt, felt the bright stab of pain as teeth broke through cotton and skin and muscle.

The only thing he could remember to do was to swing his free hand back as hard as he could, then bring it forward in a punch on the animal's nose.

It seemed to work because Angus released him and he spun to run for the door.

Instead, misjudging the distance, he ran headfirst into it.

As he slid to the ground, he heard laughing, and one of them said, "See you in a couple of days, badass."

Then everything narrowed and went black.

◆ ◆ ◆

"JESUS CHRIST, DUANE," Monica said. "I'd heard about Popper disappearing, but I had no idea you'd been involved."

"That was on purpose," he said.

"Why didn't you tell me?"

"Because of the rat hole I ended up going down."

Monica and I looked at him questioningly. But Marcus? He was still smiling.

◆ ◆ ◆

DUANE CAME BACK to consciousness still lying on the pavement by the door that had knocked him out. Constable Roberts was squatting over him, as well as a paramedic.

"How you doing, Duane?" Roberts said.

"Head's killing me," he said.

"We're going to get you to the hospital to rule out a fracture or a concussion," the paramedic said.

"Is my arm okay?" Duane said. He lifted his right arm.

"Yeah," the paramedic said. "Your shirt's messed up, and we cleaned the blood off, but—"

Duane remembered the feeling of teeth biting through his flesh. But now, with the sleeve rolled back, there wasn't a mark on him.

Did I dream that while I was out?

He was sure he hadn't. He'd felt it. Could still feel it, the lingering pain of torn flesh and muscle.

"Can you tell us what happened?" Roberts said.

The paramedic cut in. "Maybe we could hold off until he's been examined?"

"If I can get an idea of where the Rob Popper's gone, it's worth talking now."

Duane said, "Popper's gone?"

♦ ♦ ♦

ROBERTS FILLED HIM in on the fact that the bikers were gone, and there was no sign of Popper either, aside from blood on the parking lot.

Duane told him what had happened. Everything. Even the wolf.

The cop shared a look with the paramedic. Roberts said, "Maybe you're right. Better get his head checked out."

◆ ◆ ◆

"YOU WERE IN the hospital, and you didn't call me?" Monica said, her tone sharp and her eyes flashing. "What the hell, Duane?"

"I was gonna, Monica. I was. But...anyway, let me tell you."

◆ ◆ ◆

HE DECLINED THE nurse's offer to call his wife. He wasn't sure why, just yet, but this arm thing had him nervous. He'd call her once he knew what was going on with his head.

Two hours in to his time at Emergency, he was fourth in line, sitting in a chair waiting for his head X-ray beside guy number five, who was apparently desperately trying to get some emails done on his Blackberry while fighting mightily to not give in to sleep from the painkillers.

Duane mostly ignored him, until he saw the hands stop typing and the guy's head droop forward. The phone would have slid right out of his hands to the floor if Duane hadn't reached out and snagged it.

Dude didn't even notice. *Good drugs,* Duane thought.

But now, holding the cell phone, he remembered two things.

Whaddya think, Angus? Kill the badass? Or keep him?

See you in a couple of days, badass.

He held up his arm. Flexed his hand. Considered the bite on his arm that he could still feel but no longer see.

He opened the browser, and started searching.

◆ ◆ ◆

"IN THE TIME it took for them to roll the first two guys in line in and out of X-ray, I'd filtered through some obvious bullshit crap about satanic biker gangs and cannibal cults, and began to read some disturbing stuff," Duane said. He looked down at the pavement under his bare feet. "Stuff that I also would have passed off as obvious, bullshit crap had I not seen it with my own eyes."

"Werewolf stuff?" I asked.

He nodded.

"By the time they took in the guy ahead of me, I knew I was in deep trouble." He paused then. Coughed. Then he raised his eyes to Monica's. "And I knew, by extension, so were you."

◆ ◆ ◆

A NURSE CAME and rolled the guy in line just ahead of him into the room for X-rays. Duane was next.

He shot a glance at the Blackberry's owner, still passed out beside him, and he made a decision.

He stood and followed the coloured lines on the floor back to his curtained-off area in Emergency where his street clothes were. He jigged the keys to keep away any timeouts while he quickly threw his clothes back on.

Checking to ensure the nurses were busy enough to not notice, he slipped out of the room and out of Emergency. There was a small cafeteria down the hall and he headed toward it, not looking back.

Choosing an out of the way corner, he gave himself another twenty minutes to dig up more information.

It only took him ten.

And he knew he had to disappear.

He shut the cell phone down, set it on the floor, and coughed loudly as he stomped on it.

Satisfied the Blackberry was dead, he dropped it in a trash container and left.

♦ ♦ ♦

"I DON'T UNDERSTAND," Monica said.

Duane took a deep breath, but after barking out a laugh, it was Marcus who starting talking first.

"Aw, isn't this heartwarming," he said. He turned to Monica, who stood, staring wide-eyed at him. "He was saving you. He didn't want to have to kill you."

Duane's eyes widened in surprise. "You know?"

"Of course I know," he said. "You found out you're a stupid little werewolf, a pathetic, common offshoot of much stronger, more intelligent demons. You found out about their silly little ritual to baptize you into the pack, didn't you?"

He nodded, flicked a glance at Monica, back to Marcus.

Me? I just stood there with my mouth hanging open. *What the hell is he talking about, and how does he even know anything about this?*

Marcus let out a sigh of boredom. We were in the middle of a highway, outside a town burning to the ground, with a litter of that town's population piled up as a barrier. And Marcus sounded bored.

"There's a rite of passage," Marcus said. "You get bit by a werewolf and, a few days later, you experience your first shift to your new wolf form. Usually someone from the pack will show up, guide you through it." He paused, as if to ensure Monica was catching it all. Monica said nothing, so he continued. "The big part is, once you become a wolf, you're expected to erase any connection with your past by killing your family. Mother, father, sisters, brothers, wife, husband, kids, whatever ticks the boxes."

He stopped then, waiting for that to sink in, obviously.

"So," I said, "that means…"

"I couldn't do it, Monica," Duane said. "You have to understand, I knew they were going to show up and expect me to kill you and I simply was not going to do that. We may not have had much of a marriage left, but I wasn't going to do that."

"So you ran?" Monica said.

"I ran."

Marcus raised his hand. "I have a question, Duane. How'd you escape the massacre?"

"What?" I said. "What are you —"

"There was an…event," Duane said. "Call it a massacre, that's probably the best term for it." He took a second to gather his thoughts. "Not long after I left the hospital, I was actually looking for a boat to steal to get away from New Hope, and I felt a weird burning in my chest. I ended up on the ground, incapacitated, and I figured maybe I did have a fracture or something, and I was dying."

"But, sadly, you did not," Marcus said.

"I found out later it's an involuntary reflex that wolves experience, called 'digging a hole,' when a member of their pack dies. Only, what I eventually found out was, it wasn't just my pack. Something happened that wiped out all the werewolves. All of them. Everywhere. Globally."

"A massacre," Marcus said.

"Yes," Duane said. "I don't know much about it, and the only thing I can figure was, I'd only been bitten hours before. Maybe I wasn't…I don't know…*wolf* enough to count?"

"Not man enough. Then not wolf enough." Marcus huffed out a sardonic laugh. "Loser."

Not quite sure who I was addressing, I said, "Okay, what happens now?"

Duane pointed to my Staff, said, "I need that."

And then a thought pushed itself into my head. It was one that should have occurred to me before now.

My mother and Ray were each pulled from a car, tortured, their genitals mutilated, and their heads removed.

I pushed the thought away. "You're not getting It," I said. "Next option."

"I'm not leaving without it," he said.

A follow-up to the thought: *Duane could easily have done those things to my mother. And to Ray.*

I pushed that thought away as well. "Not. Going. To happen," I said. "Asked and answered. Next option."

"He dies," Marcus said.

Everyone turned to stare at him.

"Take the Staff," he said, "and drive It through his heart. He's nothing but a filthy, lowborn animal."

"I am not killing him," I said.

"Then give it to me," he said, shooting a hand in the direction of the Staff. "I'll do it."

I pulled the Staff out of his reach.

Maybe he should die. Maybe he's the one who killed half my family.

"Stop, just stop," Monica said. "Okay, I'm still not sure I understand this whole massacre thing, Duane, or the wolf thing, or the Staff thing, but the biggest thing I don't understand is you ran because you didn't want to harm—"

"Kill, Mon," he said. "Not harm. I didn't want to kill you."

"Fine," she said. She was pacing now, back and forth in front of us, not looking at Marcus or I, all her attention on her husband.

Her husband. Fuck. Anyone else, I would have reached out to hold her hand. But that would be accelerant on a fire right now.

"You didn't want to kill me. And yet..."—she pointed down the road to the stack of bodies, and the town burning behind it—"...you can do that?"

"You don't understand—"

"You're right. I don't. You're my fucking *husband*, Duane, and you fuck off and leave me without a fucking word and you show up all this fucking time later with this…" — she waved her arms at the town — "…this fucking *carnage,* then give me some sob story and what? What are you looking for? Forgiveness?"

"No, I—"

"Have you done this before?"

He stared at her.

"Have you killed others?"

"You don't—"

"Have you killed others, Duane?"

"Yes." He dropped his head. "I've been this way for almost seven years."

"Dear god," she said.

He said nothing.

Monica straightened herself. "How many?"

"I don't know."

"Guess."

"I don't fucking *know,* Monica!"

"Ten? A hundred? A thousand?"

"I don't know…"

He doesn't want to tell her, I thought.

"Duane…"

Then two things happened simultaneously.

He looked up at Monica, said, "Please…"

And Monica stepped closer to me, grabbed the Staff, angled It, and drove it into his chest. It happened so quickly my hand was still on the Staff, moving with the unexpected thrust.

He fell back, pulling the Staff out of both of our hands as he rolled back to the pavement.

Just like that, Duane was dead.

One of his hands fell open, and something fell out of it.

Monica bent down beside him, her initial gasp devolving into hysterical sobs.

I couldn't speak. I spared a quick look at Marcus, who was smiling widely. I fired the hardest stink eye I could at him. Some of it must have got through because he kept the smile, but he also kept quiet.

I dropped to Monica's side, putting an arm around her. With no idea what to say, I could only mumble noises I hoped were soothing.

She turned and buried her face in my neck, and the sobs got louder and more hysterical before they eased. I held her. I rocked her. I rubbed at her back. I didn't know what else to do or say.

◆ ◆ ◆

I DON'T KNOW how long that went on. I could only say it went on for a long time.

From my vantage point, I could risk a glance at Marcus occasionally, but he only stood either staring at Duane or lifting his head slightly to watch the town burn.

He seemed perfectly okay with both. I could only assume he was in one of those altered states, but if I had to guess, I would have bet he was as clear-minded as he could possibly be.

That scared the ever-living shit out of me.

But I could do nothing about it just then, so I waited until Monica seemed a little more stable.

I leaned back, my hands on her upper arms, and looked at her. I wasn't going to ask if she was okay because it was a stupid question. Instead, I said, "Can you stand?"

She nodded. I got up and eased her from her knees to her feet.

She stood, not meeting my gaze, only staring down at her hands clasped in front of her.

I leaned over and pulled the Staff from Duane's chest—it made a horrible sound as it exited—and hooked my elbow around it. "What do you need from me?" I said.

It took her a few moments, and her speech was halting when she talked, but she said, "I think…I need…to turn myself…in."

"To the police?"

A nod.

"And tell them what?" I said. "That your husband was a werewolf, and he killed a town, then tried to steal a Staff, so you had to kill him?"

She didn't move.

"No," I said. "I don't think we can do that. And I see no scenario where you don't get blamed for a lot of things that weren't your fault."

"I killed him. I killed my husband."

"Monica," I said, "I never knew the man, but I can tell you this with absolute certainty: the person you put a stake through was not the man you were married to."

Another long silence, and I was beginning to feel awfully open and vulnerable here. She said, "Then what do we do?"

"We leave."

"I don't want to leave him here," she said. "I know how stupid it sounds, but I don't want him blamed for the town."

"I don't—"

Marcus said, "Fine." He walked over to Duane, bent, grabbed his arms and, in a single motion, heaved the body across his shoulders. He carried him over to the pile of bodies and dropped him onto it. Walking back, he said, "Now he's just another one of the victims. May we go?"

My stomach roiled, and I fought the urge to throw up.

But I got Monica to the car, got the Staff back in Its spot, got Marcus in the back seat, and got the engine started.

And we left the wreckage behind.

◆ ◆ ◆

I LASTED ANOTHER ten minutes before I pulled over, opened my door, leaned out, and puked all over the blacktop.

◆ ◆ ◆

THE ORIGINAL PLAN had been to take turns driving on the way back, letting one sleep while the other got us closer to home.

Having a partner who shoved a Staff into her husband's heart tends to demand a change in plans.

I kept my body liberally dosed with caffeine, and with only one short stop when my eyes refused to remain open to sleep, we pretty much drove straight through.

We made it to our next destination in a little over three days.

I kept thinking, *I only have room for one somewhat catatonic person in my life*, yet, weirdly Marcus was as bright and lucid as he'd been all the time I'd known him.

That facility that had been too far away to get Marcus there? Yeah, I made some calls and got the name, the hospital organized the very-delayed transfer, and I got him admitted with a surprising minimum of fuss.

And I dropped him there like I was taking out the trash.

He didn't say anything to me when they led him away. Just gave me one last look over his shoulder, an enigmatic smile playing across his lips.

◆ ◆ ◆

WITH THAT DONE, I drove us to the nearest decent hotel, checked us in, got our stuff to the room, and put the Do Not Disturb sign on the door. I went to clean Duane's blood from the Staff but found not a drop on It. As though it had been absorbed into the wood. I chose to not think about it and, instead, placed It across the headboard of the bed, within easy reach.

There was shit that we were going to need to deal with, but not until later.

The two of us slept for almost twenty-four straight hours.

Chapter Thirteen

IT TOOK US two full days to feel human again.

When I finally crawled from the bed, Monica was already in the shower.

Not sure it was the right move, I didn't stop to question myself. I went into the shower with her.

"Hey," I said.

She swiped water from her eyes. "Hey," she said. There was an ache in her voice that broke my heart.

I put my arms around her and she eased into them. Then she moved closer. Then she was holding me tight.

Once again, my first reaction was to ask if she was okay, and once again, that tiny part of my brain that was smarter than the rest held me back.

Her forehead against mine, she said, "What have I done, Lex?"

A few responses came to mind, but I wanted to be sure I didn't wound her more than she already was, so I chose my words carefully. "I know what Duane meant to you," I said, easing into it. "But he hadn't had a normal life for quite a while. He was alone in the world, with something inside him that would never let him be happy again. He was going to keep doing…bad things. So, the way I see it, Monica, is that you did him a kindness of sorts. You took away the suffering."

"Do you really believe that?"

I searched my soul and found that, yes, I truly did. I was obviously biased against the man, but yes, I did believe it.

Then I said, "The more important question is, do you?"

She obviously took the same time to search her soul. She said, "Not yet."

"Okay," I said. We kissed then, tentative at first, but then with more longing.

It took us a while to get out of the shower.

◆ ◆ ◆

WHEN WE FINISHED, I got out, wrapped a towel around myself, and ordered breakfast.

We were both dressed and feeling slightly more human by the time the food arrived. I tipped the man more than I could afford, but after that shower, I was feeling generous.

The sleep, talk, and shower had seemed to do Monica some good as well. There was still a deep sadness in her eyes, but she was making an effort.

As we ate, Monica said, "Why do you keep rubbing at your eyebrows?"

"It's going to sound stupid, but I felt them singe off my face when I got that Staff. Felt half my hair burn off." I rubbed at them again. "When I saw them looking fine in the mirror this morning, I couldn't quite believe it."

"After all we've been through…"

"Yeah, it's the fact that my eyebrows are back that I'm having a tough time accepting." I smiled, gave them a final rub, then reached for a piece of bacon. "Pretty stupid, huh?"

"No, I think it's just that your mind's been through so much lately, maybe it needs to focus on the small things that it can handle first. I'm kind of feeling the same way."

"Ah yes, life's essential elements…" I swept my hand

around to encompass the room. "Shelter." I pointed to my plate. "Food." I pointed to Monica. "Sex." I pointed to my own face. "Eyebrows."

"Yeah," she said, a ghost of a smile crossing her lips. I'd take it. "Something like that." Then her face took on a more serious cast. "What about Golden Verdure though? Do you think we should call somebody?"

"And tell them what?" I set down my fork, sipped at some orange juice, then, as I wiped my hands with my napkin, said, "Besides, it's been, what?" I counted back. Three days to drop Marcus off. A full day of sleep. "Almost five days. Even with it being in the middle of nowhere, my guess is it's already been discovered. Anything we could add would only be confusion. And they wouldn't believe a word of it."

"Well no, when you put it like that, obviously not, but surely we can tell them something."

"We could, but likely nothing that wouldn't either implicate us in the destruction of the town and the murder of its entire population, or have them looking at us like we desperately need a visit to a padded cell." I paused for a moment. "Think about it, Monica. We were hundreds of miles from home, we can't really tell them why we were there short of saying we're on vacation. They won't buy that with me having to admit I had Marcus with us, with all of his bullshit on file at the hospital, as well as me delaying my brother's funeral. And we just happen to stop in one of the world's smallest towns and it gets wiped out less than twenty-four hours after we first hit it?" I sighed. "No, I don't think we can."

"So, we say nothing?"

"I'd say yes. Unless we can add something meaningful to the conversation—and by meaningful, I mean something that sounds reasonable and logical—I'd say we'd be better keeping our mouths shut." I poured Monica a coffee, then another for myself. "Have you seen anything on the news? I saw you checking your phone."

"That's the thing. Nothing."

"Five days and nothing? The entire town's gone. That can't be right."

"I did a search by the town name. Nothing."

"That tells me we definitely want to keep our mouths shut. There's obviously more going on here than we know."

"And what about that," Monica said, hooking her thumb back to the rumpled bed. I knew she was talking about the Staff.

"We need to put It somewhere safe."

"Why?"

"Because that's what Talia told me to do. Put It someplace it can't be found, then we bargain with…whomever she's setting this meet up with. They do what we want, we'll trade off the Staff."

"Why's It so important to them?"

"I'm guessing it's the power in that thing. You saw what It did to Duane. He was a wolf. A fucking *were*wolf, for chrissakes, and It made him…*not* a werewolf."

"But It was hidden. No one was using It."

"Maybe that's it. Maybe the owner is terrified of It falling into the wrong hands." I glanced over to the Staff, then back to Monica. "Maybe It's a medieval version of a nuclear bomb."

"And we're going to blackmail this whoever-it-is into bringing down your mother's murderer, whoever the hell that is."

"And basically protect Marcus and I in the process."

"Once they do this, then the Staff is returned to the rightful owner?"

"Yes."

"But for now, you have to hide It," Monica said. "And where exactly does one hide an ancient, highly powerful Staff?"

"Well, I do know that whoever the owner is, they're primarily earthbound."

"What does that mean?"

"I think there was the whole reason it was hidden in roughly the centre of North America, as far away from oceans as possible, and also kind of underground. They don't like water and they don't like being away from the ground, so heights and water aren't their thing."

"I'm getting the impression you have an idea of exactly where you want to put this thing."

"I do," I said. "But I'm not sure you're gonna like it." Then, sipping my coffee, I said, "And I know damn well the other person isn't going to like it."

◆ ◆ ◆

"Hey."

"I'm busy, Lex," Kelly said. "What do you want?"

"First off, thank you for answering the phone. I wasn't sure you would."

"I'm starting to be sorry I did." An exasperated breath. "What do you *want*, Lex?"

"I know I'm in no position to do this, and I know you'll likely not want to, but Kelly, this is important. Not just to me, but important."

"Okay, last time, Lex. What do you want?"

"I need you to take something. Okay, It's a Staff…like a big walking stick."

"I know what a fucking staff is. God knows you forced me to watch all those goddamn *Lord of the Rings* movies. Like that old guy, the one from the *X-Men* movies, has?"

I almost reminded her it was Ian McKellen, but thought better of it. "Right. Anyway, I need you to take this Staff and find a decent hiding place for It. In the CN Tower."

The silence on the line stretched long enough that, had I not heard Kelly's breathing, I would have thought we'd been disconnected.

"Kelly?"

"No."

"Kelly."

"I said no, Lex."

"Look, I know you don't owe me anything—"

"We're done. I'm hanging up now."

"No, Kelly." Silence. "Kelly?" More silence. *Dammit.*

◆ ◆ ◆

"Didn't go well?"

"Not so much."

"What if I tried…?"

"I know you mean well, but I see that going a lot worse."

"Okay." She looked at the Staff, then back at me. "Now what?"

I set my phone down, stood, walked over to the bed, and pulled the Staff down. I held it at waist level, in both hands, hefting it slightly as though testing Its weight.

I stood like that for a long time. Then I said, "I guess I'm going to have to go see her. Face-to-face."

◆ ◆ ◆

"Kelly. You look good."

She grabbed me by the arm and dragged me—rather roughly, I might add—over to a more private area of the observation deck. "Jesus Christ, Lex. You had me paged?"

"After dropping damn near three hundred bucks to ride the damn elevator and get the EdgeWalk ticket. You're not a cheap date, Kel."

"I told you we were done."

"And I told you this was important."

"I don't care." She stared at me, hate burning in her eyes. "I'm walking away now."

I laid a hand on her arm, but not forcefully. "Kelly," I said. "All I'm asking for is literally one minute of your time. After all we went through, can you give me just sixty seconds? If you don't want to deal with me after that, I'm gone. I'll never bug you again. I swear." I held up my right hand, palm out.

The hate didn't diminish, but she didn't walk away.

"Sixty seconds, Kel."

"You've got one minute."

I didn't waste my time trying to say anything else. Instead, I walked back to the desk where I'd had her paged, picked up a long, gift-wrapped object, and came back to her.

"You brought me a gift?"

"No."

I held the Staff in my left hand, and, muttering, "God I hope this works," I reached out with my right and held her hand.

♦ ♦ ♦

I WAS IN Kelly's mind.

I didn't mess around, I simply pushed a series of memories to her, much as Talia had done with me, though with a lot less finesse and skill. All the time I did it, I prayed I wasn't going to leave her mind a smoking crater.

I pushed out the experiences at Golden Verdure, then in the hiding place, then at the Door to Hell, then the burning of the village.

Then I pushed some of the conversation with Talia. The plan, and how the Staff needed to be hidden.

It was hours of memories, but it took all of a second to accomplish.

I released her hand.

She stared at me, stupidly, blank-eyed, and my first thought was, *I've fried her brain.*

Then she blinked, and a full-body shudder ran through her. Then she sagged backward against the wall. I reached out as she did, slipping an arm around her. An arm that still felt comfortable there, that still held the muscle memory of exactly the right position to hold her at.

"Kelly?" I said.

It took a second for her eyes to track back to me. She blinked slowly.

"All that happened, didn't it?" she said.

"All of it."

"And this girl...this Talia."

"Yeah, she happened too."

"You really love this girl, don't you?"

I was confused. Love Talia? No. Then I tracked around to what she was saying. "Monica?"

Kelly nodded.

"Love her?" I'd never said it. But did I love her?

If I didn't, I was damn close.

"Monica's..." What could I say that wouldn't be insulting to Kelly? "I've never really met anyone like her, Kel. We just kind of *fit*, you know?"

"I do," she said. "I've seen it." She tapped at her temple with a finger. "And I saw what you did for her. The whole thing with Talia. Turning her down." It hung unspoken between us, but I knew she was thinking I wouldn't have necessarily made the same choice if it had been Kelly instead of Monica.

"And that town."

"Yeah."

I watched as she stared first at the wall, then down to the carpet. I gave her the time she needed to process.

Finally, she looked back up at me. "That's the Staff?"

"Yes."

"You need It hidden?"

"Yes."

"Where?"

"Can you get It to the outside of the Tower? Like during an EdgeWalk? Secure It out there somewhere?"

"Yes."

"Will you?"

"Yes." No hesitation.

"I owe you, Kelly."

"The only thing you owe me is to not fuck it up with Monica, okay?"

"I can try."

"Don't try," she said, poking me hard in the chest. "Do it."

"I will." I reached out, touched her hand. "What about you, Kel? You think you and Kevin…?"

"You and I…and Kevin…*all* know that isn't going to work. It's a short-term thing. And that's okay, Lex. You and I were a short-term thing, too."

"There was a time I didn't look at us as a short-term thing."

"I know. Me too." She sighed. "But don't worry about me. I'll be fine. And I'll take care of your Staff."

I looked over at It, the height of It. "How exactly are you going to do that? It's not like It's a subtle little thing."

"After all the EdgeWalks are done for the day, we have to go out and ensure all is set up for the next day. It won't be easy, but I'll delay, or lie, or if I have to, bribe someone. Don't worry. I'll get it done. Today."

"Thank you, Kel." I reached out and touched her hand again. "I'm sorry for how we ended it."

"Me too." Then she leaned in and kissed me, just to the side of my mouth, then leaned back and regarded me from an arm's length. "You've changed. You're different. Better." I watched as her eyes cut over to the Staff for a moment. "You were always a good person, Lex. Always a little messed up, but basically good." She squinted as though really examining me. "But now you're a better one. I like this Lex. Monica's a lucky woman."

"And you're a good woman too, Kelly." *Too good for Kevin, that's for damn sure.* But I kept that to myself.

"Thanks," she said. Then, more awkwardly, "I've…gotta…"

"Yeah, you get back to work. Don't let me hold you up."

She touched my hand one last time, reached for the Staff, hesitated only a moment, then grabbed It.

Then she turned and walked away.

◆ ◆ ◆

"What's next?"

"Now, we go back to New Hope and hopefully stop this killer, whoever the hell it is."

PART THREE
COMING HOME AGAIN

"Mankind was not absolutely alone among the conscious things of earth, for shapes came out of the dark to visit the faithful few."

THE CALL OF CTHULHU
H. P. LOVECRAFT

THIRD INTERLUDE

1983

TOKQ MAKES ITS way back into the world, into the areas of confinement and enclosures. It took planning to become like one of the bags of meat, and it was not always successful. But it is a quick study and can draw on its Mother for experience.

Mother.

The meatbag Marcia.

Tokq finds it difficult to look at its memories of Mother, most from inside her because, of course, birth had taken its Mother away. Still, all that had been in Marcia is in Tokq now.

Mother's instincts and behaviours are painful to review, with her soft, stupid sensibilities. While Tokq views them with contempt and animosity, it does accept the fact that, without those experiences and simpering words, it never would have been able to accomplish what it needs to do.

No, not *it* anymore. These meatbags were dual-gendered, male and female, so now that it had taken this particular form, it—*he*—needed to think of itself in terms of male. *It* was *he*.

What Tokq needs to do, looking as he did as a fully grown and attractive male—based mostly on the two his Mother thought of as attractive, a meatbag called Theo, and another named Benmont—is to find a mate.

After a few false starts, he eventually determines a target and, with surprisingly small effort on his part, easily seduces a weak-minded female, Sandra Smythe, and convinces her to go through the silly pagan ceremony of promising themselves to each other. The words are small, unimportant, and carry no weight, no depth, no binding. This god they speak them to carries no power, no essential force or meaning.

When he is called upon to speak them, he lets the empty words fall from his mouth as he had let the bones and fur of the animals he had thrived on fall from his mouth not two years earlier. When he forces his smile and utters the simpering "I do" words, it takes all of his strength and control to not laugh. The god he pledges his promises to is laughable in the face of the beings he is related to.

Having married this female, he ensures they copulate frequently, hoping their union will create more demons. Sandra seems to enjoy these unions, so he needs to put little effort into this task as well, distasteful as it is. It is all so…polite.

How often, as he acted out the throes of passion and pleasure, had he simply wished to show this sweating bag of meat what true procreation entailed? To perform the procreation act as his father, all'Gueroth, had. Yet, each time, he somehow holds back.

Instead of spawning the demons he seeks, he finds mating with a full human doesn't achieve what he needs. His offspring are weak and too human. The first more than the second.

More weak bags of meat. Fearful, soft and mewling.

It takes all his control to not kill and eat them.

Still, he is demon. Perhaps mating with a full human dilutes the line too much.

Lacking the resources to summon forth a demonic entity worth seeding him, he comes up with a new plan.

Chapter Fourteen

ARRIVING IN NEW Hope for the second time in three weeks, I couldn't help but reflect on how much things had changed.

The first time, it had been over a decade and I'd approached the town with more than a little trepidation. Okay, fuck it, let's be honest: it was dread, pure and simple. And, of course, I had been alone in the car, lost in my own shit, not really knowing where I was with Kelly, with the band…hell, with anything.

Now, Monica was at my side. Things seemed worked out with Kelly. A lot of the shit that I hadn't worked out was still in flux, but where it had been overwhelming before, now it seemed so much more manageable. Of course, having that co-pilot likely helped immeasurably.

Still, now I had lost both my mother and my brother, neither a great loss, but I'd still need to deal with their losses at some point.

I'd also have to deal with the shit Ray had done. The shit with Kayla.

Marcus was going to be an ongoing struggle, obviously.

And, of course, Monica had her own shit, and it hurt to watch her try and maintain. I could see she was sliding into a deep hole over Duane's death. I would do what I could to help her with that.

Before all of that, however, I'd need to talk to Talia, get this meeting, put this killer stuff behind me.

I had a feeling it was going to be a long week.

On the plus side, I figured I could get a couple of articles—the New Hope killer; Golden Verdure, the town that died unnoticed—that could bring in some money. God knew I could use some of that. My account, while it had been reasonably healthy before all of this, was now close to going on life support. Even with Monica kicking in funds as much as I would allow.

I didn't want to drain her when all of this was my shit.

I thought again, *I really need to get my shit together*. I thought I had been, but I obviously had a lot more work to do.

The difference was, now I could see a light at the end of the tunnel.

I took my eyes from the road for a moment just to take in this wonderful, beautiful woman in the car with me. She saw me looking and gave me a small smile.

Smiles that seemed to be coming a bit more forced as the days passed. She was still suffering. She had her own shit to deal with.

But we would deal with it. Together.

For the first time in a long time, I actually believed that, while there was still a lot to wade through, the light at the end was, if not within reach, at least a possibility.

♦ ♦ ♦

"You know you don't have to stay at that hotel," Monica said.

"Yeah, I do."

"We've essentially been living together for the past couple of weeks. Hell, Lex, we've seen and done things that few people would even dream of. Hell," she said, "you've seen me pee."

I smirked. "It doesn't get much closer than that, does it?"

"So why don't you just come to my place?"

"Three reasons, off the top of my head."

"Really," she said drily. "Please." She made a rolling motion with her hands. "Elucidate."

"First," I said, ticking off a finger, "there's the judgment of the Muracks. Yes, I know you're pushing thirty—"

"Easy on the age thing, Hedges."

"—but they're your surrogate parents. And parents—surrogate or otherwise—often can't draw the line. Trust me with this one, I know of which I speak." I stopped to give her a chance to comment, but she made the rolling motion again.

"Second." I ticked the second finger. "There's the whole Duane thing. I've told you I'm there for you while you deal with it, and I meant it. But I do think you may need some alone time to deal with it. And I want to give you that."

She nodded noncommittally, but said nothing.

"And finally"—ticking the last finger—"this town loves to talk. The tongues rarely stop wagging. I don't want to be the lesbian lover providing them fodder. You have to live here, I don't."

"My reputation is my concern, Lex." She looked angry.

No time for sarcasm, I thought. *No time for jokes.* "I understand that, and you're right. If I've learned one thing living in Toronto, reputation is a factor. You can hook up with anyone you want, but if you end up in the papers the next morning, it's the local person that catches hell. Step out of line for one minute, or do one thing wrong, and you're screwed. You're Winona Ryder shoplifting, or Michael Jackson, dangling a baby over a balcony."

"I think we could argue they're both much more extreme cases. I'm not stealing or dangling."

"The cases have to be more extreme to cut through the clutter of information overload in TO. But here, there's no clutter. Up here, a business owner is the famous one. The talked-about one." I took a breath. "Up here, your stature in the town is a commodity. It's a living thing, and honestly, Monica, it's a terrible thing to lose."

"Oh no, you didn't."

"What?"

"You didn't just quote the Electric Light Orchestra to me, did you?"

"I did?"

"You did."

"So much for my credibility." *Did I really?* I reviewed the words. *Oh hell yes. I did.* "Okay, doesn't matter. Even if I did, the sentiment's there. I don't want to do anything that may cause you any difficulty, okay?"

"Okay."

"So, I'm staying at the hotel."

"Then let me talk to Annie, see if I can get you a better rate." She popped the door open.

"You have some kind of in with Annie?"

She leaned back into the car. "You could say that. She's my aunt." Then she closed the door on my surprised expression.

◆ ◆ ◆

"ANNIE SAYS SHE'LL cut a third off the price," Monica said on her return to the car. "But she says she's only doing it because you're a good tenant, you don't make a mess, and you pay up front." I got a laugh out of that one. "Oh, and because you're sweet enough to be worried about my reputation."

"See?" I said. "Being nice has its advantages."

"Including a third off. Better than a senior's discount."

"I'll go in and get the key."

Monica handed it to me. "Same room."

"Okay, well, I've got to go give her my credit card number."

"Same one you used before?"

"Yeah."

"Taken care of."

"Okay, then I've got to go thank her."

"I did that too, but yeah, that likely wouldn't hurt."

I got out of the car, went into the lobby. Annie had just come out of the back office. When she saw me, she smiled. "You scoundrel. Sending your lady friend in to do your bidding, sweet-talking me, then threatening me with bodily harm if I didn't do something for you. Then you come in, looking all cute to sweeten the deal." She came around the counter and gave me a peck on the cheek. "Oh, you smell good, too."

"Hey, if my womanly wiles will work on you..."

"Then of course you must use them. It's understood."

I glanced back at Monica, who seemed to be enjoying the entire exchange immensely.

"Anyway, I just wanted to thank you, Annie. You didn't have to do that, and I appreciate it. But if it's an imposition..."

She held up a hand. "You've gone through a lot, Lex. Your mom and your brother. But from a sheer financial standpoint, I should be thanking you. Because of your situation, I filled up for the better part of a week when I would have been almost empty. And with all the beer you guys put away? Well, if I had kids, I could now afford to put them through college." She smiled warmly. "So don't thank me. Thank *you*."

I ducked my head.

"Now, enough lollygagging. Go get your stuff into the room."

◆ ◆ ◆

WE GOT BACK to the car and drove it down to the far side of the motel, closer to the room, and parked in the mostly empty lot.

It seemed weird, not seeing my friends' vehicles there, but they had their lives to get back to, and Ray wasn't worth taking time off for.

I popped the trunk and pulled out my luggage. Monica grabbed hers, too. When I gave her a questioning look, she said, "I'm likely spending some time here. I might as well leave at least my travel bag here."

I wasn't going to argue the point. Yes, I'm a hypocrite. Sue me.

With everything pulled from the car, I locked it, tossed the hotel keys to Monica, and picked up the bags. "Lead the way."

We came in through the side door, made the short walk down the hall, and stopped at my door. At least, the door that I considered mine for the time being.

"Home sweet home," I said.

Monica unlocked the door, pushed it open, then stood aside to let me in first. Before I even entered the room, I saw Talia sitting at the desk chair. She held something in her hand, but I couldn't make out what it was.

"Just once, Talia," I said as I dragged the bags in. "Just once, I'd like to come into my room and have you show up and knock like a normal person."

"I'm not a normal person."

"Point taken." I dropped the bags on the bed. "Still, it's a little disconcerting that I find you in my room now, and it doesn't surprise me much anymore."

Talia smiled. To me, it actually seemed like a warm, genuine smile. Then she stood, dropping the small something in her pocket. I could have sworn it was a tooth. She walked past me, her hand out. "Monica. I'm sorry about Duane."

"Thank you, Talia." Then Monica shocked me by pulling the other woman close and hugging her. "Thank you for coming," she said. From the look on Talia's face, it shocked her too. Shocked and pleased.

"You know…?" Talia said.

"I do," Monica said. "Wasn't sure it was going to work, but…"

"I have no idea what the two of you are talking about," I said.

"You do, Lex," Talia said. "You just don't know you do. It will come to you."

I said, "Fucksake."

Monica laughed lightly and grabbed Talia again, pulling her in a second time. "I'm a hugger," Monica said. "And I never said it earlier. I want to thank you for what you're doing. For me and for Lex."

"You're not holding a grudge about…"

"Not gonna lie: still not wild about it," she said, stepping from the shorter woman and slipping her hand easily around my waist. "Would have preferred something a lot less intimate and something where she didn't actually get to see your boobs, but she made the right choice."

I didn't think Monica was trying to be malicious, but I still caught a touch of ice in that last sentence.

"I apologize for that," Talia said. "To both of you. It wasn't fair, but I needed to test Lex's character."

"I understand," she said. "But it's not going to happen again, right? Naked boobs and stuff?"

Talia smiled. "It won't. I promise. She's all yours."

"I am still in the room, you know."

Both the women turned to me. "Ah, good. I'm not invisible. Thought that might be a side product of the Sta—"

"Hush," Talia said.

I turned to Monica. "Did she just shush me? Seriously?"

"You have to take this seriously, Lex." Talia, though shorter than either of us, still seemed to command the room. "You do not speak of It, you do not speak Its name. Names have power. That…" She seemed to choose the word carefully. "That *weapon* in your possession has power."

Chastened, I could only nod in agreement.

"What happens next, Talia?" Monica asked.

"I've already set up the meeting. It will be this evening, in Vilni. Down Koechlin Road from Church Hill. There's a natural theatre there, a bowl where the trees won't grow."

"I know it," I said. "We always used to say it would have made a great place to go parking, but somehow, no one ever did."

"Not if they wanted to get out of there alive, they didn't," Talia said.

"When's the meet?"

"Very late. When everyone's asleep, feeling safe in their beds. Meet me at the entrance to the bowl at quarter to two."

"In the morning?" I said.

"Yes," she said.

"Why'n the hell is—"

"We'll be there, Talia," Monica said, clamping her hand over my mouth.

Talia walked over to the door. "You've been told before, Lex, but it's worth repeating: this one's a keeper. You hold on to her."

"She will, don't you worry," Monica said. I could only snort derisively from behind her hand.

Talia laughed, a high, sweet tinkling sound that seemed to brighten the room. Then she was gone, the door closing behind her.

Monica turned to me. "How many times have you been told I'm a keeper?"

Chapter Fifteen

W E SET THE alarm and slept for several hours. Well, Monica slept, her breathing providing a soft, comforting rhythm to my turmoiled thoughts. I sprawled in our bed, staring at the ceiling, listening to the night sounds outside the opened window, my mind churning over so many things.

Who killed my mother? Who killed Ray? Why?

When I could get no further with those questions, and they fell to rattling noise in my head, I moved on to question other things.

Who are we meeting tonight? How do they know who the killer is? Why can't they just tell me? What's their connection to the Staff?

Then, *What's with the Staff?* That question alone occupied me for a long time as I ran down its myriad pathways.

The Staff. I had so many questions. But the weirdest of the bunch was, while I had no ideas of Its powers, or Its limits, I seemed to be able to work It. And I didn't know how or why. I know there was no downloaded instruction manual in my head for It.

Though one thing was obvious. After seeing what It did to Duane, I can understand why the owners both want It, and want It hidden. It was too powerful to fall into the wrong hands.

Who made It? How did It get so powerful? How old is the thing?

So many questions…

I hoped Kelly was able to hide It okay.

Then the alarm shattered the quiet and my contemplations, and we rose and got ready.

◆ ◆ ◆

I TURNED THE car off the gravel road to the entrance to the bowl. Talia waited, as promised. Despite the heat of the night, she wore an ankle-length overcoat. It wasn't new. For all I knew, it could have been her father's.

Then I remembered, her father was one of the ones that disappeared. *I made them disappear*, she'd said.

Her voice was low and grim, her gaze intense. "Turn your car around so it faces the road. Leave it unlocked, but take the keys with you," she said. "Do you have a spare key?" I told her I did. "Give it to Monica." She turned to Monica. "Put it in a pocket where you can't lose it, but you can get to it quickly."

I nodded and pulled the car around as instructed. "What's that about?" Monica said.

"I think it's our escape plan." I shut the car off and pulled the key. "Doesn't exactly give me the warm fuzzies." Monica nodded. I leaned in and kissed her quickly. "Let's get this shit over with."

She leaned back in and kissed me slower, better. When she pulled back from it, she said, "Don't ever kiss me quick again, Lex. Don't take your kisses, or mine, for granted."

She was right, of course. I promised her I wouldn't.

"Now," she said. "Let's get this shit over with."

◆ ◆ ◆

TALIA HAD MOVED deep into the middle of the bowl. We followed her down. When we were together, I said, "Now what?"

"Now, we wait."

"Who exactly are we waiting for?"

Talia lifted her head and looked around the bowl, the natural theatre of this clearing. "Have you ever heard the name for this clearing?"

"I don't think so," I said.

"I seem to remember something about it," Monica said, then, more hesitantly, "Vetty…? Vesty…? Something like that?"

"Something like that, yes," Talia said. "Vesky Valley. But it's not really *Vesky*. It comes from the word—"

"Vjesci." I had seen Talia's mouth open to say the word, but the voice that uttered the word, a word that sounded like *vyeskee* to me, came from a voice much darker and more guttural, the sound of stone moistened with lava, somehow given the power of speech. The sound of it made my sphincter tighten and my breath constrict in my throat.

I looked around for the person who'd spoken the word, but I realized I couldn't tell the direction the sound had come from.

Off from the far side of the clearing, maybe the length of a football field away—far too distant to have heard the softly spoken word clearly—a figure emerged.

I couldn't make out much in the darkness, except the glint of moonlight on blonde hair. The figure moved smoothly across the field. Weirdly smooth, as though there was no rise and fall in their step, no gradations or imperfections in the ground under their feet.

The figure glided across the clearing in no particular hurry. Confident we would wait, no matter how long it took.

When the figure was about halfway to us, three more figures appeared at different locations at the edge of the bowl and moved toward them. They moved with equal grace and silence.

The closer they got, the more seriously creeped I got. I felt Monica's hand in mine, squeezing mine painfully. She was equally creeped.

The blonde figure finally reached us, and I realized it was a woman. Then she met my gaze, and I realized she was more a girl than a woman. Maybe fifteen? Hard to say, as she exuded an aura of agelessness.

I opened my mouth to speak, and her eyes flashed. Before any sound could escape my throat, Talia held up a hand for silence.

We would wait for the other three.

Eventually the others reached us. Three males. Though I'd expected them to stand behind her, they stood four in a line, equals. The males were taller, but as boyishly young as the female. I re-evaluated but still came back to a rough age of fifteen.

Then again, I was way off with Talia.

Then the blonde looked directly at me again. I felt that same pants-shitting, asshole-clenching feeling. Her eyes didn't glow like some bullshit horror movie, but when they fastened on me, it was like they were all I could see, the only thing I was aware of.

She opened her small, sweet mouth and again, the sound that came out was shockingly grating, tectonic plates sliding against each other. "You are Alexandra," she said, as though she had bestowed the name on me for the first time. "You are the Defender of men, the protector."

Then she turned to Monica and I felt a horrible disappointment that her eyes had left mine, at the same time as a gut-wrenching relief that I was no longer in her sights. Monica's hand tightened on mine again as though she was in fear of falling.

Then the blonde said, "You are Monica. You are the Advisor." Then her horrible, beautiful gaze fell on Talia and her punishing grip on my hand loosened.

"And you. You are Talia. You are the dew from God. But you are many. You are the Collector."

And then she stopped talking. As terrible as her voice was, the silence was more so because it was the absence of her attention, a thing I suddenly craved as much as I feared it.

Knitting her fingers together, she waited. She tilted her head forward in a gesture for one of us to continue. I didn't have a clue what to do. Talia obviously did.

She first faced the male on the left. "You are Will. You desire to protect." He nodded slightly.

To his right, she said, "You are Kurt. You are the bold and trusted Advisor."

She then turned to the last male. "You are Rory. You are brother to she who is the Verdant Glory. You are the Red King." He also acknowledged her with a small inclination of his head.

"And you. You are Chloe. You are sister to the Red King. You are Verdant Glory. You are the summer incarnation of Demeter."

But Talia added something different. She raised her hands to indicate both Chloe and Rory. "You are the Green Goddess and the Red King. The green and the red. Life giver and life taker. You are the Alpha and the Omega."

Chloe nodded as well, acknowledging Talia's words. "Thank you, Collector. Names are power. We call upon them with care and never forget their hold upon us. We are well met." It was Talia's turn to nod. Not sure whether I should or not, I chose to do nothing. I simply marvelled that this shockingly bass tone, instead of grating, fell like a balm to my ears.

Will said, in a voice like thunder echoing off distant mountains, "You called this meeting, Collector. State your purpose."

"Thank you," she said, and knitted her hands together. That's when I realized she was actually scared of these four.

Talia. Was *frightened*.

Of *them*.

They looked like teenagers.

Then again, I thought, *how far off was I with Talia? She looks two full decades younger than she is. Could be the same with these three as well.*

I knew I was likely dealing with something that didn't appear as it was. *Kind of like you, Ms. Ann Wilson. From a distance, yeah, you can pass for a woman who's famous. But come up close and the whole façade crumbles.*

"I will be brief," Talia said. "But I ask that you allow me to explain fully before you—"

"State your reason, Collector," Rory said, his voice the booming echo of thunder off distant hills.

"Of course, Red King. Recently, two members of the Defender's family, her mother and older brother, were murdered." It took a moment before I clued in that she was speaking about me, about my family. I was Defender.

"Her request—our request—is for the Vjesci to locate and bring that murderer here so Defender may pass judgment upon them."

Chloe turned those eyes to me again. "She speaks the truth, Defender?"

I took a moment to work up a modicum of spit, then purposefully—as though preparing for my next song—chose my tone and pitch before speaking.

"She does," I said.

Chloe turned back to Talia. "You explained to Defender and Advisor the price that would be demanded for this ask?"

There was a long pause where the two women, both short, both radiating power, regarded each other, took the measure of one another. Then Talia stated flatly, "No."

Though none of the four so much as twitched or blinked an eye, I felt a shift in the atmosphere. Like the entire clearing had suddenly become dangerous. The desperate desire to flee became almost overpowering.

"You did not," Will stated.

"No, Protector."

"Explain this failing," Rory stated.

"Several days ago, Defender and Advisor captured the Staff of Solomon and—"

I almost ran right then. My legs tensed, the copper-tinged taste of adrenalin squirted into my mouth, the world became brighter, my breath huffed from my flared nostrils.

"Gather yourself, Defender," Chloe said, and I, though no less panicked, lost the will to run. It ran off and away from me like water down the drain. I truly had no idea what the fuck was going on.

"Continue," Chloe said.

"They took the Staff and placed It in hiding. Believe me when I tell you, you can threaten and torture them to find Its location, but you will never be able to reclaim It. Pains were taken to find the right location to shield It from you."

"As pains were taken to protect It from—"

"Red King," Chloe said, the softest whisper from her lips. The sound was as enticing as a lover's breath, but it stopped him. *What's that about?* I wondered.

He gathered himself. "Still, you found It and took It," Rory said, the rumbling voice now with a sharp, jagged edge.

"True enough," Talia said. "Still…"

"We have heard your story. State your formal request," Chloe said. Her voice had not changed in any way, nor had her expression, but I sensed the deep, smouldering anger in her. She was seething.

"We formally request that you four Vjesci—you, Rory, you, Kurt, you, Will, and you, Chloe—use all means and powers at your disposal to uncover any and all beings involved in the murder of Alexandra's mother, Sandra Hedges, and her brother, Raymond Hedges, and bring all those involved back to this clearing in no more than three days for Alexandra to pass judgment. At that time, if you are successful in this task, Alexandra will turn possession of the Staff of Solomon, with no conditions or limits, to the Vjesci. You will also agree to hold no animosity nor exact any revenge upon Alexandra Hedges, Monica Holt, or myself, Talia Davis, or any of those we hold dear in any way." She took a breath. "In essence, you will provide the killer or killers, we will provide the Staff, and we will never see each other again." Then she held up a finger. "But. No killer? No Staff."

"That is your full and complete request?" Will said.

"It is."

"Defender, you agree to this?"

"I do."

"Advisor?"

"I do."

Chloe looked to her companions. They took a long time to agree, but they all did.

"Return to this spot in three days with the Staff of Solomon," Chloe said. "You will have your murderer." She smiled then, a dreadful thing to see. Still, it was the shock of seeing the fangs that almost brought me to my knees.

Then they turned and left the clearing.

And it was only then that I realized there had been no night sounds. No crickets, no frogs, not even a breeze.

Chapter Sixteen

"Vampires, Talia?" I was incredulous, and I couldn't have named all the reasons why if I'd wanted to. "We entered into a fucking binding contract with fucking vampires?"

"If you want the killer found, you will need them," she said.

"Why?" I was up and pacing. Monica, her mind blown, had requested a drive home. I suspected she needed the familiarity of her place to settle her mind, to give her some normalcy. It had been a decidedly unnormal couple of weeks for her. "Maybe it's just better to take my chances with the assholes who killed Mom."

"Trust me, Lex," Talia said drily. "You don't want to enter death by either means."

"I thought you said they knew who killed my mother and Ray?"

"They do."

"Then what's all this bullshit about three days?"

"It's all part of the game."

"Game," I said, whirling on her. "Game, Talia? This is people getting tortured and killed. It's no fucking game."

"It is for them," she said simply. "And they need time to bring the killer to you."

"And, just for the record, *you* know who did it, too, right?"

"I do."

"How?"

"Like you, Lex," she said, "I, too, have many demons that whisper to me in the night."

I didn't know what to say to that. But the thought of what she just said chilled me to my core.

Instead, I said, "And you still refuse to tell me who did the killing?"

"I do."

"Why?"

"It will be clearer in three days."

"Fucksake."

Talia's eyes followed me as I walked the length of the hotel room, turned, stalked back, repeated my question. "Why does it need to be vampires?"

"You have a problem with vampires?"

I stopped, leaned in closer to her. "I didn't fucking think they existed until a couple of hours ago," I hissed, then, resuming my stalking, whispered, "Jesus Christ."

"You'll have to trust me, Lex."

"Lex. Lex," I said, stalking by her again. "You sure you don't mean *Defender*? Apparently that's my vampire name or some such shit."

"Not so," she said. "It may help you to understand that there are various races of vampires, of which the Vjesci and the Wupji" — which she pronounced as *woopyee* — "are only two. Each has their own culture, their own traits, their own beliefs."

I stopped pacing again. Stared at her. "The *woopyee*? That's a vampire name? That's supposed to fill me with dread? Fucking *woopyee*?"

Talia had become agitated. "Lex, enough."

"What?"

"Please don't throw these names around lightly. As the Verdant Glory said last night —"

"You mean Chl —"

Her voice became as hard and cold as steel. "I mean the Verdant Glory, Lex. Do not speak her name to me again. Or the names of the others." She sighed, softened her tone. "This is what I'm trying to tell you. We're deep into things I know a little about, but you and Monica know nothing. And of the demons, I must tell you, vampires are amongst the most terrifying. Many have a goal, a need, an itch that needs to be scratched, but the Vjesci and the Wupji? They are maliciously evil."

"I got that much."

"I know you did. I sensed you almost bolting before Verdant Glory calmed you."

"She did do that, didn't she?" I thought back to that moment. "She…somehow *commanded* calm into me?"

"Coercion. Yes." She smoothed out the imaginary wrinkles on the bedspread. "My point here is, don't take anything for granted with them. That entire introduction with the names…"

"Yeah."

"That was a test."

"I don't understand."

"One doesn't simply *request* a meeting with the Vjesci, those making the request must prove they are worthy of the relationship. They must prove they have some power."

"Prove their worthiness and their power through the knowledge of the names of the vampires they are meeting," I said.

"Exactly," she said, nodding.

"And had you failed that test?"

She waved her hand to me, back to her, to me again. "Had *we* failed that test, had we not known their names…" Her hand stopped its back-and-forth motion. "They would have obliterated us."

I simply stared at her, images of damn near every vampire movie flickering through my head.

"I see the imagery in your mind. Them sucking our blood, leaving the drained husks, but it would have been nowhere near that civilized. It would have been agony, it would have taken forever, we would have been alive through all of it, and, in the end, there would be no traces left of us."

A connection clicked in my mind.

"They were the ones that took your family," I said. "Your father, your sister, your mother…the others. All the people who disappeared that night. The vampires made them disappear."

She smiled thinly, her eyes tired as she rolled them up to me. "No," she said. "They weren't responsible."

"But the way you said…"

"I said the Vjesci are some of the most terrible of demons, but I did not say there were not others equally or more capable of such cruelty. Evil is legion in this land, Lex. Much closer than you think. A fact you will soon come to know."

"So, it wasn't the vampires?"

"No."

"But it did happen, didn't it? The disappearing?"

"Yes."

"You know who did it?"

"Yes."

"And you still won't tell me what or who it was, will you?"

Here she hesitated. Hesitated long enough that I thought she actually might. Then she said, "Let's just say that the evil that took my family was also very close to home."

Without another word, it was apparent to me that the topic was not only closed, but also nailed shut, never to be opened again.

♦ ♦ ♦

"Lex," Monica said, the following day. "I've been doing some research into these..." — she looked around, then lowered her voice — "...these vampires, these Vjesci and Wupji...what would you call them? Tribes? Races? Whatever they are, I've been doing some digging."

We were in a small, family owned restaurant in downtown New Hope, both needing to just get out in the sun and walk around a normal town on a normal day. Monica had put it best when she'd told me she "just needed to get grounded in the world I used to believe in."

"What did you find out?"

"A lot, actually. You know Vilni is one of the first Polish settlements in North America, and the first in this area, right?"

"Yeah. I remember wondering, as a kid, why in the hell someone would travel all the way to this rocky, godforsaken place, passing a lot much more fertile land, to sink their roots."

"You ever heard the original name of the town? Before it was changed to 'Vilni' in the '30s?" she said. "Because I'm wondering if it's a clue."

"Um...something weird. Started with a *U*?"

"Ujica."

"Right," I said, snapping my fingers. "I remember now."

"So, it got kind of bastardized over the years to Ujica. The original Polish is 'ucieczka'" — she pronounced it *oo-JYECH-ka* — "means 'to escape' or 'flight'...as in to run away."

"Well, maybe they were trying to outdistance something."

"The Vjesci, maybe?"

"Could be. Would also explain why the original settlers ended up in an area that's basically a thin sheet of grass over rocky Canadian Shield. What better place to end up when you're trying to escape the vampires?"

"Maybe," she said, chin in her palm, staring reflectively out the window of the restaurant. "But that's just conjecture on my part. It's not something I read anywhere."

"So what'd you find out?"

She lifted her chin from her hand, pulled a sheaf of papers from her purse. "The Vjesci and Wupji are the Polish vampires. The Vjesci in particular are similar to a German strain, known as the…" —she checked her papers—"…the Nachzeher, which is sort of part-vampire, part-scavenger. Anyway," she said, dropping papers on the table, which I spun and pulled toward me, but didn't pick up, "turns out you can identify these vampires pretty easily. A Vjesci is always born with a caul over its—"

"What's a caul?"

"A caul," she said, "also known as a cradle cap." She swirled a hand above her head. "Like a cap made of amniotic tissue. Sort of like an extension of the placenta. It can cover just the head, or the head and the face, sometimes right down the torso. It's pretty rare overall, but there's a few cultures that believe a caul is sign of some supernatural powers. In this case, if a child is born with a caul, then it will be a Vjesci."

"So, none of this *blah, blah, I vant to bite your neck* shit?"

"Yeah, none of that. The interesting thing is, there's a cure."

"Oh yeah? What's the cure?"

"The caul is saved after birth. It's dried, ground into powder, and fed to the child on their seventh birthday."

I drew the next word out. "Whaaaat?"

"I'm serious."

"That's gross."

"The alternative's worse."

A pause. "Okay," I said. "I'll give you that one." Still, I pushed my plate away. "But you also said there were the other ones. The whoopies or whatever."

"The Wupji," she said, making a face.

"Okay, easy for you to say. Anyway, are they preordained from birth to be vampires too?"

"As a matter of fact, yes."

"The caul thing again?"

"No. Teeth."

Teeth. Where has that word come up recently? "Like, vampire teeth?"

"No, just born with two teeth."

"And what's the cure for that one?"

She looked at me. "There is no cure."

"Damn," I said. "That's harsh."

"Lex, I know you're trying to deflect a bit here, but you can't be overly flippant with this stuff. I don't know how much of this is real, but obviously some of it is. We *met* them, for chrissakes."

"And we'll meet them once more, then they'll be out of our lives."

"But we'll still *know*."

"Yeah, but still…"

"You don't get it," she said. She stabbed a finger down on the folded pages. "The shit they do—I mean the humans here—to kill them or prevent them from turning. Feeding them some powdered cradle cap is the least of it."

"Like what?"

"Well, first, they bury the children. If they survive, they'll reawaken in the grave after midnight. Then they'll eat their clothes and even some of their own flesh. Then they'll dig their way out and destroy their family, taking their blood…"

"Kinda sounds like the werewolf thing," I said, obviously not thinking that line through.

Monica paused for a moment. "Yeah," she said quietly.

I put a hand out. "I'm so sorry, that was really stupid."

"It's okay, Lex," she said, and summoned a small smile. "I'm dealing with it."

"I'm still sorry." Because I wasn't quite sure she was dealing with it. She had a wan look, dark circles under her eyes. Small signs here and there that spoke volumes.

"Thank you," she said. "Anyway, they dig their way out and cause some mayhem. If that doesn't satiate them, they'll move on to the neighbours."

"So," I said, "what do the loved ones have to do to prevent it that's so bad?"

"Some of it isn't. Adding dirt to the coffin when they bury them, for one thing."

"Wait, isn't that the whole Dracula deal? He sleeps in a coffin with the soil of his native land?"

"Yeah, not these guys. The dirt confuses them. You can also bury them facing down. Apparently that causes them to dig down instead of up."

"Huh. Simple, yet effective."

"There's weirder. Apparently if you tossed a bag of sand in there, they'd need to count each grain of sand prior to escaping. Or a net, because they could only untie one knot a year."

"Sounds like they were kinda dumb, if you ask me."

"You met them. You think they're dumb?"

Quietly. Chastened. "No."

"Other things that can be done include stuffing a cross into the corpse's mouth for them to suck on. Or driving a nail into their forehead. Or cutting the head off the suspected vampire and placing it between their feet."

"Jesus."

"Apparently there are reports of families digging up their loved ones and, as the vampire is trying to escape the grave, they decapitate it."

"And yet, after seeing what we saw the other night, I'd likely do the same."

"I also read some reports from the area. There's a lot of strange stuff. Unexplained. But one really stuck out to me."

"Tell me."

"In 1953, apparently during her son's birthday party, a woman named Cheryl Koechlin—"

"Koechlin? Like the road leading to the bowl where we met the vamps?"

"Yeah," she said. "I'll get to that in a sec."

"Okay."

"So, Mrs. Koechlin and the kids at the party were all…" — she stopped, grabbed the papers, found the one she wanted — "…were all 'killed in an apparent attack by a wild animal, possibly a bear.'" She looked up from the paper.

"A bear," she said. "In the afternoon. In the middle of a small suburb of houses. What's the likelihood of that?"

"Pretty goddamn slim, if you ask me." Then I thought of something. "Wait. Afternoon? Thought these guys couldn't go out in the sun?"

"Thought of that," she said. "Checked the weather. Deeply overcast. Rain."

"No sun."

"No sun," she said. "Guess what birthday it was for the son?"

"Seventh."

"Yeah."

"Born with that cowl thing?"

"Caul?" she said. "Couldn't find records on that, but I'd be willing to lay money on it." She looked down at the paper again. "And guess whose body was never found?"

"The one who's birthday it was. The seven-year-old."

"Right," she said. "The one they named the road after, in memory of."

"Shit. And they suspected vampires back then?"

"Not even close." She tapped the papers with a splayed hand. "Says here they think he was the one the bear dragged from the home."

"Does it mention anything about drag marks?"

"Of course not."

"Paw prints? Scratches on the furniture? Anything like that?"

"You'd think, right? But no. Nothing."

"So the boy went missing. Never found?"

"No. Never." Another tap. "At least, not until the other night."

"By whom?"

"Us."

"What?"

"The boy was William Koechlin."

"The Protector."

I thought, *Jesus H.*

♦ ♦ ♦

SOMEHOW, IN THE middle of my days now filled with the thoughts of werewolves and vampires and magical staffs, the local funeral home contacted me.

I saw the caller ID on the phone and almost let it go to voicemail, but that would just delay the inevitable.

"Ms. Hedges?" the caller said. "Ms. Alexandra Hedges?"

"Yes, that's me."

The caller introduced himself—I immediately forgot the name—and went on to explain that Marcus had indicated that arrangements would be made this week for the service for Ray.

"Then why aren't you contacting Marcus Hedges?"

He explained that all calls to the number were going to voicemail. Of course they were. Because he's not there. *I should have let this one go to voicemail too, dammit.*

"So, you want me to make the arrangements, then, I'm assuming?"

"If you would be so kind," he said. "Could we set up an appointment whenever it's convenient for you?"

I flashed back to my Ray memory of him and Kayla.

"No," I said. "I'll tell you right now, it's never going to be convenient for me."

"Ms. Hedges—"

"I'm going to suggest you do whatever you'd do if someone with no relatives and no money ended up at your home. Leave it in a ditch. Burn it. Flush it. Toss it in a dumpster, I really don't care."

Ms. Hedges..."

"Have I made myself clear?"

"...yes."

"Thank you," I said. "I appreciate your assistance in this matter. Have a good day."

I stabbed the End button and stood, looking out my motel window.

Well, I thought, *one problem solved.*

◆ ◆ ◆

IT WAS THE night before the meet, about twenty-seven hours before we faced the vampires again. Twenty-seven hours before I would face the one—or ones—who murdered my mother and Ray.

I'd be tempted to shake that person's hand for that last act, before doing...

Then my mind locked up.

So that Defender can pass judgment.

What the hell did that mean, exactly? I was to pass judgment on the person who cut my family in half? Did that mean I would be responsible for taking this person's life? What would happen if I judged the guy guilty? Would the vampires provide the proof? Would I be able to know beyond a shadow of a doubt?

And what if I did?

What would I do then? Because, as far as I could see, I only had two choices: either let the guy go, or not.

And if I let them go, well then, I would likely die.

What if the vampires expected me to do it? I couldn't kill anyone. I thought of Monica. Saw the tip of the Staff enter Duane's chest. Saw the look on his face. Heard her howling grief.

Could I do the same? Even if they did kill my mother? Would the vampires do it? Would there be another price?

Then I thought, *Is it too late to back out of this?*

Maybe I needed to find out. Maybe I needed to talk to Talia.

First, I needed to talk to Kelly. I needed to get that Staff back.

I pulled out my phone and sent her a text.

Kelly. It's Lex. Need that item I dropped off a few days ago. Driving down early in the morning to get it. Should be there by 10.

IT TOOK A few minutes, but Kelly texted back.

No problem. I'm working late tonight. Will get it in the building. Text you in a few with arrangements to pick up.

Thanks.

A few then turned into a half-hour. Then an hour.

I checked my phone for the hundredth time. Monica blew out an exasperated breath and said, "Seriously, in the history of telephones, not once has someone successfully coerced someone to call them by staring at the phone, Lex."

"Then I guess I gotta be the first," I said.

She stood up, grabbed her purse, and said, "I'm going to go get us some dinner, because I can't sit and watch you watch a phone all night." She grabbed her keys and left. Not sure if she was going because of the incessant phone checking, or because who I was waiting for to text back, or if she just wanted to be alone.

Or maybe it was all three. Whatever the reason, I got the impression there was a bit of a valley between the two of us now. A Duane-shaped gulf that I couldn't seem to cross over.

We just had to get through this last meeting, then I'd put all my focus on Monica.

The door closed, I checked the phone twice more and had decided I was just going to call her when the display lit up with her image and the *Incoming Call* message. I answered.

"Kelly, holy crap, that took—"

"It's gone, Lex."

The silence spun out for a few seconds. "Kelly, please, this isn't the best time for joking."

"I wish to god I was, but I'm not."

"What happened? Did It blow off or something? We shouldn't have stashed It outside, dammit."

"It couldn't have blown off. I'll send you the picture I took after I stashed it. I wrapped It up in a couple of old blankets like a damn Christmas present, then stuffed It into an access panel that no one ever actually accesses. It's an old one, and all the switches in there have been rerouted. Then I locked It down with about a hundred bungees, then I actually closed the panel and put my own lock from my locker on it. Honestly, it was the biggest case of overkill I'd ever done."

"No one could have gotten in there? You're sure of it?"

"Absolutely sure. Besides, even if someone managed to pick my lock—which they didn't—and then steal the Staff—which they didn't—why the hell would they go to the trouble of leaving that gift wrapping back under all those bungee cords? Seriously. The blankets It was wrapped in were still there."

"They couldn't have slipped It out?"

"Ever been up on the roof the CN Tower? It's all slippery metal and weird angles. We send people out to walk the edge, but the place was never designed for that level of stupidity. There's no way. Someone wanted to steal this thing, they'd need to do it quickly, quietly, and with a minimum of effort. Which is why I set it up to be a reasonably lengthy, loud, exceptional effort."

"Huh."

"Still. It's gone. And I don't know how."

I was quiet. What was there to say?

"You're mad at me."

"Honestly, Kelly, no. The shit I've been going through, the shit I've seen, being mad at you isn't even on my radar. You did exactly what I asked of you. It's not your fault it went pear-shaped."

"I'm sorry, Lex."

"Me too." I gripped the phone a little tighter, knowing this would likely be the last time I talked to her. "I appreciate that you helped me. You didn't have to, so, it means a lot. Take care of yourself, Kel."

"You too, Lex."

It felt like I should be saying something like, "I love you," or, "Have a nice life," or something, but nothing was quite right, so we both just said goodbye.

♦ ♦ ♦

SETTING THE PHONE down, I realized, beyond a shadow of a doubt, that I was well and truly screwed.

♦ ♦ ♦

EVEN TALIA DIDN'T know what to do.

We gathered a few hours prior to the meeting in my hotel room. "Should we run?" Monica said.

"And go where?" Talia said. "I set them on a task to find and return a killer that could have travelled the globe, and I have no doubt they will deliver. So, tell me, where do you think you can hide from them?"

"So you're telling us we simply have to show up in a few hours and die in that same horrible way you described to Lex a couple of days ago?"

"You can face it in a few hours, or in a couple of days. The only difference is the duration of time you live in fear."

"Jesus, Talia," I said. "You really know how to raise morale, don't you?"

"It's never been a talent of mine, no."

If I wasn't so freaked out, I would have laughed. But right now, there was no laughter, no light in me.

And if I was ever going to get my shit together, it should be now. What else was I going to do with the last hours of my life? Talk to Marcus? Make peace with him? Not bloody likely.

I checked my watch.

"Talia," I said. "If you don't mind, could I ask you to leave?"

"Why?"

"We have about three hours before we have to leave."

"And?"

She wasn't getting it. "Talia," I said. I pointed to my head. "Look into my mind."

"Oh," she said. She slid a quick glance at Monica. She stood, walked to the door. "I'll see you in three hours."

"You will," I said.

The door closed softly, leaving us alone.

Monica smirked. As she came into my embrace, she said, "What have you got up your sleeve, Hedges?"

I put my arms around her, pulled her close. "Monica, you really don't have a lot of skin in this game. What if I gave you a three-hour head start to get out of here?"

"I wouldn't."

I hated that my tone was pleading as I said, "Why?"

"It's the fact that you want to save me so badly that I realize I have to stand beside you, no matter what." She kissed me. "Don't you realize I've never had anyone that would put themselves in harm's way for me? How can I walk away from the person who cares that much for me?"

"Okay," I said softly. She kissed me again.

"So, if that's off the table, then what?" she said.

"Look into my mind."

"Don't have to," she said.

This time, when she kissed me, we didn't stop for a long time.

♦ ♦ ♦

THREE HOURS LATER, we held hands as we walked out to my car. Talia leaned against the front bumper.

"You ready?" she asked.

"No," Monica said.

"No," I said.

"Good," she said. "Me neither." She raised herself and put an arm out. "Shall we?"

And then my phone rang.

Oh thank god, I thought. *She found it.*

But it wasn't her calling.

I told them to give me a minute and I angled away from the car, putting a bit of distance between us.

I figured it wasn't going to be a good call.

But I never figured on it being so fucking bad.

♦ ♦ ♦

I STUMBLED OVER to the car. Monica and Talia were waiting for me. "You okay?" Monica said. "That was a long call."

360

I looked at her.

Though I said nothing, Monica took a halting step forward. "Oh god, hon. What's wrong? What happened?"

It took three shuddering breaths, but I finally got it out.

"It's Kelly," I said. "She's dead."

CHAPTER SEVENTEEN

"TELL US WHAT'S going on," Monica said.

"From the beginning," Talia said. "And make it quick, we have fifteen minutes until we meet the Verdant Glory again."

♦ ♦ ♦

IT WASN'T KELLY calling. It was Kevin. *What the fuck?*

I answered the phone. "Kevin," I said, "What can I—"

"YOU FUCKING BASTARD," he howled.

Again…*what the fuck?* "Kev, sorr—"

"SHE'S DEAD," he said. "SHE'S FUCKING DEAD." He was sobbing the words out.

"Kev," I said. "Slow down. Who's dead?" Stupid question, because the sinking in my gut already told me who it was.

"KELLY," he said, and now he broke down into full-on, lung-sucking sobs. Tears sprang to my eyes as well. I'd ambled back toward the motel and sort of fell against the wall as the name hit me.

"I'm…oh god, Kevin…I'm so sorry…I…what happened?"

It took an agonizing minute or two for him to gather up the reins of his control again.

"They…found her…"

It took a lot of time for Kevin to get the facts stated because the words wouldn't come easily, and he broke down four more times.

What I made out from his disjointed rambling was, about a half-hour after Kelly had told me she couldn't find the Staff, another group of EdgeWalk customers went out to do their thing. And that's when they found Kelly.

She was everywhere.

She'd been eviscerated, and the entire area was covered in bits of her. Her intestines had been strung around the edge of the building like Christmas lights. Her organs, heart, lungs, stomach, all of them jammed onto sharp points or stuffed into recessed spaces.

But her head had been cut cleanly from her body and bungeed into place just outside the entrance to the staging area for the walk.

Whoever had done this had wanted to ensure she was easily identified.

Kevin made it clear he thought I was somehow responsible for her death.

And the goddamned thing about it was he wasn't wrong.

Fuck.

◆ ◆ ◆

"Oh god, Lex," Monica said. "That's...god, there's no words. That's terrible. I'm so sorry."

"I am sorry as well, Lex," Talia said. "It's the vampires."

"How sure are you?" I said.

"Reasonably so." She ran her hands through her hair. "It smells like them. Technically, the distance from the ground and the proximity to water should have stopped them, but there are precedents for vampires occasionally overcoming these obstacles."

"I thought you said—"

"Live as long as I have, Lex, see what I have seen, and you'll understand that certainties are rare in this life."

"Your lack of certainty got someone important to me killed."

"As I said, I'm sorry," Talia said. "But we have to focus on this meeting now, or we may not have much longer to live either."

◆ ◆ ◆

IT WAS, ONCE again, precisely two a.m. when three forms glided again into the clearing. Chloe opened her mouth and let the horrible sounds issue forth and the ritual of the names was repeated.

Only Kurt and Will with her. No Rory this time.

"We have completed your task, as requested," Chloe stated.

Talia inclined her head in thanks.

"You bring the Staff?" she said. Her eyes moved from Talia to Monica to me.

I saw Talia's troubled expression and knew she was going to say something that shouldn't be said. I jumped in before she could. "We've got the damn Staff, Glory. Give me the piece of shit who murdered my father."

Kurt didn't appear to move, yet he stood in front of me, his appearance so sudden and unexpected that I had to take a step back. *"You will not speak to the—"*

"Step back, Kurt." This from Monica.

"You dare," his voice was a detonation that promised worlds of pain.

Then Will was there as well, facing Monica. Kurt still in my face.

The situation was escalating far too quickly for my liking, but Monica then proceeded to throw gas on the fire. "What's the matter, *William*," she said, drawing the name out.

Then several things happened at once.

Will's hands moved to Monica's throat.

Kurt stepped forward, his face in mine, his eyes laying me open, his breath hot and fetid.

Will's mouth opened and all those sharp teeth were exposed as he darted his head in.

At the same time, I felt a weight in my hands.

♦ ♦ ♦

THE STAFF OF Solomon thrummed in my sweating hands, as though through divine intervention.

I did not think, I simply reacted.

I shot my hands out, feeling the crack and thud of the impact of ancient wood against ancient muscle and bone, the wood carrying the weight of Its years and power, heaving the vampire back several yards.

As the wood was still making its first impact on Kurt's chest, the might of Its power crackling through me, I raised my voice, awesome and terrible in its agency and fury, and said, ***"WILLIAM KOECHLIN YOU WILL STOP."***

Will simply stopped, frozen where he was, hands outstretched, head extended, tendons tight, his eyes rolling furiously in their sockets.

Through it all, Chloe and Talia stood to the side, both shocked into stillness.

♦ ♦ ♦

WHEN I GOT my breathing under control, my hands trembling as I gripped the Staff, I looked over at Will once again. Monica had stepped back and now stood at my side, openly staring at the Staff.

365

After giving him the once-over, content in the knowledge he wouldn't move again until I released him, and not quite sure how to do that, I turned to Monica. "You were right. Names do have power."

"So does that," she said, pointing her chin at the Staff. Then leaning in close, she whispered, "Where the hell did It come from?"

Not trusting my voice, I simply shrugged my shoulders.

Then I turned my attention to Chloe. She glared at me, her lip curling, her rage a palpable thing.

"Will you please bring out the person you brought to this trainwreck of a meeting?"

"I will kill you for this," she said. Her voice was small, a hint of breath past her lips. Her voice was a sonic boom in my head, coming from the valley floor, from the trees, from every blade of grass, from the sky.

I had never been so terrified of anything or anyone in my entire life as I was in that moment. I opened my mouth to speak, but no words came out. I was close to fainting. I couldn't do this.

Talia and Monica took positions to each side of me, each placing a hand on my shoulder. And, at the same time, the Staff thrummed in my hands, but differently this time. A wave went up both arms, seemed to coalesce at the spots where Talia's and Monica's hands made contact with me, then shot to my brain.

And for a moment, everything changed.

I felt the pulse of life in both the women supporting me. I felt the grass, bending but unbroken, under my feet, felt their roots in the soil. I felt the rock beneath that. I felt the expanse of the world beneath me, down to the core of the planet, and I felt the planet as it spun on its axis, and the slide of its path around the sun. I felt the caress of the light of the moon, the vibration of all that radiated heat and light around me.

I felt the profanity of the beings that stood before us — of this world, but not of nature.

Through the Staff, I felt all of this in a single moment.

I smiled.

It felt like ages, millennia, since Glory had promised to kill me. It had been less than two seconds.

I stepped up to Glory, fear now a distant dream, and said, **"Chloe Susannah Tyler, bring me those I seek or I swear I will beat the fucking vampire right out of your bones."**

A small widening of the eyes. A finger snap-quick look at the Staff, back to me. Then, with only a hint of hesitation, a slight movement of her head and Rory came out of the clearing, four forms behind him, supporting two more between them.

Monica said, "Two?"

Even Talia appeared surprised.

The four vampires stared at our little group of three with open disdain, but refused to look at the Staff, or Kurt and Will. With a quick nod from Chloe, Rory remained, but the others turned and left as quickly as they had come.

Leaving the murderers.

"Lex, you gotta believe me. Honest to god, I had no fucking choice."

"Shut up, Randy," I said. Randy immediately closed his mouth and stared at the ground.

The other person stared at me defiantly.

Marcus.

My father.

Dad.

"That can't be right," Monica said. She turned to me. "This isn't right, is it?"

"It's right," Talia said.

"Is it, *Father*?" I said, leaning into the term I'd avoided so hard lately. Marcus held his mouth in a grim line and stared at nothing.

"What do you—"

"ANSWER MY QUESTION."

"Yes, it's true." Even though he admitted the truth, he held his defiant gaze.

I turned to Talia. "You knew this." It wasn't a question.

"I did."

"You wouldn't tell me." Rage seethed in me. "All the time he was in the car with us. You watched over him while we…" I literally ran out of words. I gripped the Staff and took a breath. I stared at her. "You. *Didn't*. Tell me."

"What would you have done?"

That stopped me. What *would* I have done?

What could I have done?

"What's going on?" Monica said. "Talia, how did you know?"

"Because he's a demon. He's been hiding in plain sight for years, but he's a demon."

"A demon…" I said.

"Lex, deep down, you always knew this," Talia said. "You had nightmares about—"

"Let me in," I said. "Let me in his mind. Let me see inside his fucking head, Talia."

"I can't, Lex," Talia said. She pointed to the man, still on his knees. "I can do my talent with humans, but he's only half human…enough for me to inform myself, not enough to see inside him."

She walked closer to Marcus. "But you're his daughter." She turned to face me. "You *can* see inside him."

"What about her?" I indicated Chloe. "You aren't going to be a problem, are you? You and your three stooges?"

Then, a thought stabbed across my brain. Before I could think it through, my mouth engaged. "Kelly," I said. "Which one of you killed her?"

The four of them stared at me, quizzical expressions across all four faces.

I held the Staff up. "The woman in the tower who was guarding this." It was subtle, but I caught the dart of Chloe's eyes from me, to Rory, back to me again.

Without really knowing what I was doing, I kind of *flexed* my mind and Rory fell to the ground, but quickly picked himself back up. This being exuding timeless evil while in the body of a child.

"Tell me," I said.

Then Rory opened his mouth and, with the sound of a mountain landslide, he laughed. "Yes, girl. It was me. I did it." He fixed me with black, hate-filled eyes. "I made her screams pour forth and rain down upon the entire city. I consumed her and destroyed her and obliterated her."

He stepped closer.

"And I ensured that each of her last minutes on this stinking earth were wracked with the most pain I could deliver," he said. "I drank her blood, and pissed it out. But her wails of pain I drank, and they'll stay with me forever."

I wanted to puke. I wanted to cry. I wanted to scream. I wanted to run.

I felt Talia's hand on my shoulder again, but I shrugged it off. "You fucking—"

"Shut up, girl," Rory said. "You're nothing. I've pissed on better than you."

In a single, swift move, I twisted the Staff horizontal, then, with both hands, thrust It forward and up into the smirking vampire's chest. I held nothing back, using every ounce of strength and rage in me. I plunged It in just below his ribcage and drove It up, lifting him off the ground.

"You don't know what obliteration means," I said, my throat constricted, my voice tight. If Kelly's pain would live forever in him, I would erase him.

My mind didn't flex this time. It spasmed. I swear I felt something run from my head to neck to shoulder, down my arm, and through the Staff.

And then the Red King blew into atoms.

◆ ◆ ◆

"NO!" WILL THUNDERED. Somewhere in there, I'd released him. God knows how or when. No matter. I let him get one step closer. Then I stopped him. I stopped all of them.

Then, I simply stood for a moment, my mind whirling, my chest heaving. I wiped tears from my eyes.

Retribution felt good, but only briefly. It wouldn't bring Kelly back. It couldn't change or erase the hell she'd gone through in her last minutes.

Her last moments. I couldn't think about that. It would haunt me forever.

I looked down at the Staff. It eliminated the one that had caused her pain.

But It could never bring her back.

Then I thought, *Could It?*

I pushed that thought away. That was not a good road to go down.

"I'm beginning to understand why this thing was kept hidden. You've wanted this for a long time," I said, hefting the Staff. "There's a lot of power here. Especially against your kind. That's why the wolves kept it hidden from you. And when they were gone, you couldn't find it."

Chloe bared her teeth. Her voice was distant thunder as she said, "This is not over, meat. You *will* die for what you've done."

"No," Talia said, following it with a sigh. "It's very likely not over. But none of us will die for this." Back to me, "Send them away."

"I'm sorry?"

"Use the Staff. Send them away. Bar them from this clearing."

"*No*," Chloe said.

I smiled. "**Yes.**" I gripped the Staff and did as Talia told me.

The vampires disappeared, a small pop of rushing air to fill the space they had occupied.

"Despite my bluster, they will kill the three of us," Talia said. "You know this."

Monica gestured toward the Staff and said, "They can try."

♦ ♦ ♦

ENOUGH OF THAT. I'd dealt with the vampires. Marcus and Randy were still to go.

Marcus first.

I gripped the Staff, met my father's eyes, took a breath, then allowed myself to fall into his mind.

Chapter Eighteen

T HE BEAST COMES aware as it finishes chewing its way out from its mother's belly. It has no words yet, but sounds are in its hindbrain. Three distinct noises.

Mar. See. Ah.

Then, not a word, but a knowledge: *Mother.*

It's mostly blind, but it knows it's enclosed in an artificial structure and knows it shouldn't be. It needs the open, not the confined.

It escapes into a more natural area, full of mostly living things and strange upright structures with rough skins and outstretched arms with soft appendages that spread out and provide shelter.

There is knowledge buried inside the beast, but its brain needs to develop more fully before that knowledge can be processed, sorted, understood.

Utilized.

But it feeds well and its growth is exponential.

◆ ◆ ◆

FATHER'S NOISES WERE too complicated initially, but within days, it begins to comprehend. At first, it is simply a name, but a powerful one. all'Gueroth, son of Nyarlathotep, son of Azathoth.

Over the days and weeks that follow, as Tokq feeds, it turns its mind inward, understanding that all'Gueroth had given it all it needed to not only survive, but possibly one day rule this vile ball of filth.

It knows the form it must take. That of a human. A male, like Father. But one that appears human. One that is considered attractive.

Tokq takes a full turn of the planet around the too-bright sun. A full turn in which the temperature steadily drops, but eventually returns to heat.

And finally, Tokq is ready for what comes next.

◆ ◆ ◆

TOKQ MAKES HIS way back into the world, easily finding a weak-minded female and marrying her, copulating frequently, hoping their union would create more demons.

Instead of spawning the demons he seeks, he finds mating with a full human doesn't achieve what he needs. His offspring are weak and too human.

Still, he is demon. Perhaps mating with a full human dilutes the line too much.

He comes up with a new plan.

◆ ◆ ◆

IT'S AT THIS point that I felt the splitting of the images into those from his—Marcus/Tokq—point of view as well as my own.

I knew this part. Knew it too well.

◆ ◆ ◆

RAY IS OUT. Mother is at a church meeting, or curling or something. Anything to be away from the house.

It's just me and my father. Marcus.

We watch a horrible old movie on TV. All these years later, I still remember it. A cheesy low-budget thriller, the type the two of us used to watch just to laugh at the bad acting, bad special effects, and improbable storylines. This one is no different. *Killdozer!* starring a very skinny Robert Urich, still new enough to die quickly, and the man's man Clint Walker.

When it ends, my father, instead of laughing, has a strange, sad look on his face.

(It has to happen. It has to happen now.)

"What's the matter, Dad?"

(It has to happen. It has to happen now. How do I do this in human terms?)

He looks around the big, empty house. "Come and give me a hug," he says, letting a little whine creep in to his tone. "I need a hug, Lex."

I'm almost eighteen, too old to be cuddling with Dad. But he also never calls me Lex. It's always Alexandra. So, Dad needs a hug. The thought of it makes me feel awkward, but I move to his side. He's prone on the couch, and lifts his legs up to the back to give me room to sit. I lean in, put my arms around him and give him a hug. Very awkward, but still, I give a gentle squeeze.

(She doesn't respond like Sandra does. Then again, she's not Sandra, is she? She's half human, and half me. Appeal to the side that isn't Sandra.)

Then I feel him move under me and then his tongue is in my ear.

I'm so shocked, I can't move. His tongue roots around in my ear like a slug.

Then I feel his hand on my crotch, kneading and probing.

Instinct kicks in, pushing the shock down, and I back away violently, knocking the coffee table aside, spilling popcorn and Coke.

(No! What did I do wrong?)

"What..." *God, there's no words!* "What are you *doing*?"

(Should I explain? Tell her what I need from her? To bear my offspring? The look on her face says not yet.)

"I'm so lonely," he says, swinging his legs down to sit on the couch.

"What...?" It's the only word that I'm able to form. I feel the heat in my face, can still feel that tongue — my *father's* tongue! — in my ear.

He stands to face me. Before the movie, he'd put on his ankle-length bathrobe.

(She's a female, close to her sexual prime. Work with that!)

"It's been so long," he says. "It's been so long since I've had..." — his hands grasp at the air — "...anyone love me." His hands pull at the belt of his bathrobe and, with a shrug, it falls to the carpet.

He stands before me, naked, his erection obvious, a violation.

"I need — "

(Why is this not working? Why is the demon side of her not responding to this? Why is the human side not?)

"*JESUS FUCKING CHRIST, DAD!*" The tears spring to my eyes, mercifully blurring the sight before me. "*WHAT ARE YOU DOING?*"

I swipe at my eyes, averting them from my father. I desperately fight to bring my breathing under control. "You need to get dressed and get help. Right now."

I look up quickly to see if I'm getting through to him. What I see instead stops me cold.

(I'm in heat. I must arouse her as well. That's all it is. Simple animal arousal.)

He stands, face pleading. One arm out to me, beckoning.

And the other working at himself.

(Tell her. Tell her the truth.)

"I need this, Lex," he says. "I need another child."

I can't breathe. My chest works, hitching, but I can't breathe. I can't make my lungs work.

I barely mutter a soft "fuck you" as I run past him and out the front door.

♦ ♦ ♦

I RUN THE length of our driveway, ignoring the cruel jabs and barbs under my feet. When I reach the road at the end, I stop, hands on knees, sobbing uncontrollably.

Who can I talk to about this?

No one.

I can tell no one.

As far as I understand, my father is somehow in possession of a mind so broken it no longer knows wrong from right. It can't distinguish between child and lover.

And I see his hand again, working at himself.

I vomit.

I don't stop vomiting for a long time.

♦ ♦ ♦

I DON'T KNOW how much later it is when I finally find the strength to get up from my hands and knees, my arms splashed with my own sick, my mouth tasting foul and metallic.

I walk. I had been hollowed out, scraped raw. I'm completely empty, my mind blank.

I wander down roads and past homes where real people live real lives.

I walk fields and meadows in the dark. The stars shine sharp and cruel, each one an accusing voice.

You must have done this, they say.

You brought this on, they say.

This is your fault, they say.

I hear them all. All the accusations and pronouncements. I don't know how to respond.

What if they're right?

There's only one choice, I think. *Run. Run away.*

Never come back to this hell ever again.

I run.

♦ ♦ ♦

BUT I CAME back.

Part Four
Can't Go Home Again

"There are black zones of shadow close to our daily paths,
and now and then some evil soul breaks a passage through.
When that happens, the man who knows must strike before
reckoning the consequences."

The Thing on the Doorstep
H. P. Lovecraft

CHAPTER NINETEEN

AND THEN I'M back again. In my own head.

Beginning to feel a little crowded in here, I thought.

Then I turned my attention back to Marcus.

"It was you all along, wasn't it?" I said.

He cocked his head.

"My nightmares. Waking up thinking something…evil…was in the room with me. It was you."

He smiled.

◆ ◆ ◆

I DON'T KNOW what to do about him. I walk in a slow circle around Marcus and Randy. As I pass him, Randy opens his mouth to say something, and I twitch the Staff and shut his mouth.

I'll deal with him, but I need to deal with Marcus first.

I don't know what to do about him.

Somewhere in the back of my head, I know I'd been harbouring vague thoughts of what I'd do if I ever met the person who murdered my mother. Vague imagery of punching, of hitting, of making them feel some measure of the pain they had wrought themselves.

It felt very familiar because it was the same thoughts I'd had toward Ray, once I knew more about his secret past.

He got what he deserved. But my mother? My mother was

basically a blank space in the world. She had really done nothing to anyone. Did she deserve what she got?

No.

And Marcus.

What did he deserve?

I kept on walking my slow circle, the damp grass making soft sounds under my feet, the night air cool on my skin, the stars looking down, uncaring, on this scene of judgment. Monica and Talia remained where they were, understanding this was my issue now.

I finally stopped, facing Marcus, on his knees in the grass.

Using the Staff as support, I lowered myself to my haunches, facing the one who murdered his wife. Who murdered his son.

The demon who had attempted to seduce me.

My father.

"Tell me," I said. "Tell me what you expected to get out of all of this."

If I can give Marcus credit for anything, I'd give him credit for not shying away, not trying to beg, plead, or lie. He faced me, looked directly in my eyes, held his head high.

"I was born to breed, Alexandra," he said.

I stayed very still, very quiet. I would give him this one opportunity to explain himself. I didn't expect to understand, but I wanted to hear it. Needed to hear it.

"After the Book abandoned Talia, it found another whore, who summoned a demon from another plane—call it R'lyeh, call it Carcosa, call it one of a thousand, thousand names, it doesn't matter—and the demon came to the high school."

From the corner of my eye, I saw both Talia and Monica nodding.

"The demon that answered the call of that stupid boy was *all'G—*"

"You will not speak its name, demon," Talia said sharply.

Marcus smirked. "Just making sure you're all still attentive. Let's call the demon 'Swlabr' then, shall we?" I had no idea if that was copacetic or not, so I looked to Talia. She nodded, with a "don't ask" expression on her face.

"Fine," I said.

"Swlabr is one of the many progenies of Nyarl—"

"I'll not warn you a third time, demon."

"…one of the many progenies of the Crawling Chaos," he said, not skipping a beat. "It would be, to put it bluntly, a walking penis. Its only purpose is to procreate, to further the line of…the Crawling Chaos."

"Okay, so that was Swlabr. I'm asking about *you*, Marcus."

"Swlabr, unfortunately, was somehow defeated by yet another Book whore. Yet, before its demise, Swlabr did place one last seed in one of those who survived."

Talia said, "Marcia Mayer." There was a sadness in Talia's voice, but I'd have to ask about it later.

"Yes," he said.

"It was suspected at the time that her sometimes-boyfriend, Theo Clarke, had murdered her," Talia said. "But that's not the truth, is it, Marcus?"

"No," he said. "Marcia Mayer died so that I could be born. I ate my way out of her body, and escaped."

"I saw all this. You're a demon," I said. "How do you…" I waved a hand up and down in his direction.

"How do I look like a human male?" he said. "When we need to, we are adaptable. It's part of the survival instinct of the Outer Ones, I suppose. There are others living in this world."

Fan-fucking-tastic, I thought.

"We're getting sidelined," I said. "Get to your point. Quickly."

"Swlabr was able to implant me in the Mayer girl. I am a full-breed demon. Unfortunately, in adapting, I could only procreate with others. I somehow lacked the seed to create more full-breeds."

"So you found Mom, and…"

"And had Raymond, who was a disappointment," he said.

"No shit."

"And then you. You were…less so."

"Wow," Monica said. "Ringing endorsement, right there."

"Shut your mouth, slut."

I didn't think. My hand shot out of its own accord and slapped Marcus across the cheek. Hard.

He laughed.

"See?" he said. "Raymond was weak. He filled his mind with chemicals. He had the demon need to procreate often but, while he lacked any empathy for others, which was good, he also lacked the necessary tenacity for survival. To fight for what is yours." He poked a finger into my chest. "You, Alexandra," he said. "You've always had that."

I grabbed his wrist, pushed his hand away. "I think you're wrong."

"I'm not." He looked over to Monica and Talia, then up at the stars, closed his eyes. Remaining like that, face to the sky, he said, "You are demon. You are tenacious. And you would have given me the right offspring to unleash on this filthy ball."

You are demon, I thought. *Fuck me.*

Then, *Deal with it later, Lex.* I said, "So?"

He dropped his gaze back to me, his eyes open and flashing anger. "So, we could have woken the Dreaming One. We could have opened the door to the Old Ones." He spread his hands. "Don't you see? We could have made this world into a paradise."

I noticed that Randy was now staring at Marcus in open horror. He still couldn't say anything because I wouldn't let him.

"Not quite the bill of goods you were promised, I'm guessing?" I said to Randy.

The tears down his cheeks were all the answer I needed.

Angling back to Marcus. "I still don't understand why Mom and Ray had to die," I said.

"Your mother was useless," he said. "She barely gave me something useful in you. And, despite all my attempts to bring you home, you never would."

I thought of all those times Randy had organized let's-get-together-it's-been-too-long events. I'd refused every one.

"Then, taking this human form, I found I was also subject to its weaknesses and frailties. I don't think forcing myself to hold this ridiculous, soft, human form helps. It…splinters me. Divides me. My mind is going, Alexandra."

"It's seemed fine for a while now."

"Only because of that," he said, nodding to the Staff.

I saw the dawning realization on Monica's face as I figured it out as well. Marcus had had only moments of clarity on the way out west, but he had been clear as a bell all the way back.

Son of a bitch. I was going to need some time with this thing. I needed to understand Its limits.

If It even has any.

"So, what, your mind was going, so…"

"So, I enlisted Randall here in one last attempt to bring you home."

"You had him kill Mom?"

Randy was furiously shaking his head no. Marcus did so more calmly.

"No, he only got them out to where I needed them to be. I took care of the rest. For a few glorious moments, I was able to relax and take my true form." He smiled, and then, Marcus began to change.

♦ ♦ ♦

Marcus shuddered and sagged, as though his bones had turned to water. That lasted less than a second, and he warped, and Talia, Monica, and I stepped back. Randy couldn't make a noise, but his breath bellowed in and out as he fell to his side and scrabbled away.

And through it all, Marcus darkened. Twisted. Grew. And he laughed.

His eyes angled, subdivided from one pair, to two, to three, the pupils blackening. And then there was no he anymore. Only an unamenable it.

Its jaw shrunk into an elongating face, while another mouth began to split along the top of its skull.

Its torso shortened and thickened slightly, the clothes falling away. I heard breath heaving from somewhere other than its face. Then I saw the lengthening of a terrible appendage that could only be its penis.

It was a thing as much weapon and torture device as it was a tool of insemination.

Tokq's true form, not completely revealed, was horrible. The entire form was a black so deep in was hard to see, as though it profaned the light that illuminated it. A small blessing.

Randy pissed himself. If I'm honest, I wasn't far behind.

I raised my Staff, my hand trembling. I said, "**Tokq, son of all'Gueroth, you will take the form of Marcus. Now.**"

Tokq sighed. It sounded human.

But it changed back.

Then Tokq said, "I killed Sandra." It said, "And it brought my baby home."

◆ ◆ ◆

WE ALL STOOD silently for a few moments. Tokq simply smiled at us.

Then Talia said, "Keep going. Find out what you need to know."

I took a breath, tried to push the thought of that demon penis from my mind. "Ray," I said. "Why kill him?"

"I hadn't been able to get you to…do what I needed you to do" — and here it shot a cold look at Monica — "so I needed to delay you."

"And killing your first-born accomplished that."

"I need this, Alexandra." It put its palms together, as if in prayer. "You don't understand the need inside me. It burns. I need to procreate. It burns within me."

Tokq grabbed at its crotch. It was hard.

Facing me. Facing his daughter. Facing death.

And it was hard.

I'd seen enough. I'd heard enough. I knew what I had to do.

◆ ◆ ◆

TOKQ WAS STILL talking. "Enough," I said, with another twitch of the Staff. I stopped it as I had done with Randy.

"Randy?" I said. He turned his tear-soaked face to me. A twitch of the Staff. "Your turn. Explain yourself."

"Lex," he said, "you gotta — "

"**Randy**," I said, putting all the vampire command tone I could into my voice. "No begging, no pleading, no 'you gotta understand' horseshit. **You tell me the part you played in this.** You tell me why. No bullshit. Understand?"

He swallowed hard. Nodded.

"Take a moment to get your shit together, then start talking."

He nodded again. Looked at Tokq, then at the ground, then at me.

"I'm gay," he said.

Monica huffed slightly. "Well, no shit," she said. "Tell us something we don't know."

I shot a look at her. *You knew?*

She shot her own look back at me. *You didn't?*

Randy looked at Monica a little fearfully, then back to me. "And…um…Ray was always my hook-up for pot, and sometimes harder stuff."

No surprise. He was a lot of people's hook up. There's a large vacuum just waiting to be filled now that he's gone.

"But…" — he blew out a breath, swiped at his nose — "…this is hard, Lex." He stared at the grass. "I…um…"

"You had the hots for Ray," I said.

"Yeah," he said, barely meeting my eyes. He looked ashamed. Terrified. But also a little relieved. "But you know how Ray was."

"Yeah," I said. "Ray never really accepted anything other than guy on girl, in whatever forms that took."

"He tossed around the 'fag' term a lot," Randy said. "Anyway, your dad —"

"Marcus."

" — what?"

"After what I've gone through, after all it's done, that term will never apply to it again, Randy. Not in relation to me. It's Marcus."

"Oh…okay," he said. "I get it." He dropped his head again, whispering "Marcus" as though to fix it in his memory. "I was over at the house a lot, hanging with Ray, getting high, whatever. And your…Marcus, well, there was one time where Ray got really stoned and passed out. And he…uh…he tried to…"

"It offered to fuck you if you'd do something for it."

"…yeah."

"What did it want you to do?"

"Get you home," he said. "That's when I started trying to get the gang back together. Sending out the emails and social media invites and stuff."

"You did it?"

"What do you mean?"

"I mean, the father of your best friend offered to fuck you, and you did it?"

"Dude, I'll never turn down a blowjob."

"Oh, sweet lord," Monica said. "I did *not* need to hear that."

I stared at him. He stared at Tokq. I couldn't even imagine the thoughts in his head.

"I'm sorry," he said. "But he sweetened the pot later. To…you know…keep me on his side."

"What do you mean by that?"

"He could…oh shit, I shouldn't be telling you this…"

"But you will, Randy."

"He could make Ray forget things for a while, okay? I don't know how he did it, but he did. So I got to…to…"

I stared at him. He was going to say it. I wasn't going to bail him out this time.

"I got to have sex with Ray without him knowing."

"You raped him." Monica's voice was flat and cold.

"No, Monica, it wasn't like that…"

"It's exactly like that. You got Marcus to basically roofie him for you."

Randy sagged. Stared at the ground again. "Fuck," he said.

He had painted a good enough picture for this aspect. I didn't think my gorge could handle much more. "Tell me about the murders."

"I didn't know what was gonna happen with your mom, Lex. I swear I didn't."

"Tell me."

"Marcus made sure Ray wasn't around, and asked me to call the house and say I had car trouble, and could your mom come and give me a lift. That was all."

"That was all?"

"Hell, Lex, for all I knew, he was trying to throw her a surprise fucking birthday party or some such shit."

"Were you even there?" I said. "When it happened? When it dragged her from the car and mutilated and tortured her?"

Through most of my questions, he just shook his head, a guttural "no…no…no…" coming from deep in his chest.

I believed him.

"But when it came time for Ray," I said. "You had to know."

He grew very quiet then.

"You knew."

"*I BEGGED HIM NOT TO*," he wailed. "*I FUCKING BEGGED HIM!*" A sob wracked him, throwing him forward. "I fucking loved him," he whispered.

"And yet," Talia said, "still you did it."

His eyes were puffy and streaming tears, searching each of our faces for compassion, finding none.

Then, his voice quiet, lifeless, addressing the ground, he said, "I just had to make sure we were at a specific place at a specific time. I got him there, then told him I needed to piss and left the car." He gulped a couple of breaths. "I walked into the bush a ways, heard the screaming. It went on way too long. *Way* too long." Another heaving sigh. "I came back to the car, made sure I got anything of mine, and left. Marcus told me not to worry about fingerprints or anything because I'd been in the car a million times."

"And then?"

"And then," he said, crying hard now, "I walked home. And Ray…my Ray was gone."

I stood over the man, not sure what I should be feeling. I looked to Monica and Talia, but both just looked disgusted.

Then Randy said, "I was the only one there when they buried him. I know he was an asshole, Lex. I know that. But I fucking loved him."

I should have felt something, shouldn't I?

I feel nothing.

◆ ◆ ◆

AND NOW I had to figure out what to do with the both of them.

Chapter Twenty

RANDY WAS FIRST. We took him home.

As he got out of the car, I asked Talia and Monica to hold on a second. I got out of the car, pulling the Staff out with me. "Randy," I said. "A word."

He stopped. I approached him, leaned forward, spoke a few words. He nodded, hesitated, then stuck out his hand. I shook it.

Then he turned and walked into his house, and I turned and walked back to the car.

And that was it for Randy.

Well, almost.

♦ ♦ ♦

TOKQ WAS MORE complicated.

I had to drive quite a distance for the second time in two weeks, but once again, the Staff showed me Its power. Instead of a four-day trip, it took a shade under five hours. When I say the scenery flew by, I mean it.

When we got to where we were going, this time I didn't need someone to watch after Tokq.

This time, I was dragging the perverse thing along with me.

Knowing where that blade of grass was, having actually found it myself, made the process faster.

Finding the specific room in the tunnel also took less time.

The only struggle I had through this entire journey was Tokq fighting against me. It knew what was coming.

It just didn't know exactly what it would be.

♦ ♦ ♦

AND THEN WE stood near the Door to Hell in Turkmenistan.

"I guess should ask if you have any last things to say?" I said.

"Please don't do this, Alexandra."

"Make no mistake. It's going to happen."

"I'd rather you killed me."

"I know," I said. *That's part of the reason I'm doing this instead.*

"Go," I said.

It stared at me.

"Go."

"Alexandra…"

I raised the Staff, met Tokq's eyes for the very last time, and said, "Go."

It dragged forward, unseen forces pulling at it. Its human feet scrabbled on the dusty earth, digging furrows that got deeper as its form changed from the one I'd known my entire life back to the thing it really was once again.

Its skin blackened and flaked away in the ever-increasing heat. Tokq's body hunched, its hands stretched, grew two extra fingers, and each finger grew another joint. Its eyes angled, subdivided from one pair, to two, to three, the pupils dilating to black.

Its jaw appeared to get swallowed into its lengthening skull, its mouth squeezing tight, then disappearing, only to reappear, jagged and lipless, on the top of its head, the jaw shifting and lifting from the skull in an agonized scream, the sound shambling out through a forked, questing tongue and jagged teeth.

Its torso shortened and thickened, sprouting smaller, vestigial arms, and smaller, finger-like protrusions down its sides. Breath bellowed in and out of its heaving chest through wet, leaking holes sprouting over the front of its body.

More changes wreaked havoc on its form, but I lost sight of them as the demon slid and slipped and scrabbled over the edge and down into the eternal flame of the pit. The demon would be fated to fall forever, never landing, never touching anything solid again, suspended in a fury of heat and light forever.

It wasn't Hell, but it was very close. The flames wouldn't kill it, but the heat would burn with a never-ending pain.

Marcus…Tokq…had been spawned from evil, had done despicable things, and had broken lives.

This was a fitting fate.

And end that never ended.

◆ ◆ ◆

I TURNED AND made my way back out without a final glance.

The screams followed me all the way out.

Epilogue

RANDY'S FUNERAL WAS as tragic and sad as was to be expected.

The gang all showed back up at the motel the night before, the only difference was Bear and Grace left the brood at home. Gerry unfortunately decided to once again bring the human sphincter he called a wife.

The service was mercifully short. Bear, Grace, Gerry, Ruthless, Norman, Kayla, Monica, and I all hung out at the grave until everyone else slowly drifted away. We broke out a bottle, and, after pouring one out for Randy, we all took a swig.

Bear and Grace, and Gerry and Ruthless, were heading back to the motel and then straight back home, so we said our goodbyes as we headed back to our cars.

Norman looked like he wanted to say something, so Kayla and Monica headed off to give us some privacy.

"I need to ask, Lex," Norman said, looking uncomfortable, a look that didn't suit him. "Before you left, you said you were going to find out who killed your mom and…"

"Yeah," I said. Neither of us wanted to say his name.

"Did you?"

"I did, yes."

"And now," Norman said, "Randy's dead."

"Your cousin was not the murderer, Norman, if that's what you're asking."

He nodded. Heaved a sigh.

"Why do you think he did it?" Norman said. "There was no note, nothing."

"Norman, my turn to ask a question."

"Shoot."

"Did you know that Randy was gay?"

He smiled. "Did anybody *not* know he was gay?" he said. "Well, aside from my aunt?"

Yeah, I thought. *Apparently both Randy's mother and me.*

"And did you know he had feelings—a lot of feelings, if you know what I mean—for Ray?"

"Oh," he said. "No." He rubbed at his chin. "That, I did not know."

"Yeah."

"So, you think he was just overwrought at losing him?"

"Ten, fifteen years of unrequited affection can mess with you," I said. I felt bad, leaving out all the stuff around what I was telling Norman, and I'm sure he knew I wasn't giving him the full story, but I was giving him something he could move on with.

"And your killer?" he said. "You found him?"

"Yes," I said. "That issue…has been dealt with. I know it'll be an unresolved case for you, but I can assure you there is no danger from that…from them anymore."

"You choose your words carefully, Lex," Norman said. "I'd almost think you wrote for a living."

I smiled and nodded. Stuck out my hand. "Thanks for your help, Norman. And, more importantly, thanks for your understanding."

He shook my hand. "Take care of Monica."

"I will, but I think it's more a case of Monica who's taking care of me."

"As long as you're there for each other," he said, "and be honest with each other." He looked over to Kayla, who smiled and gave him a wave. "It's the secret of a long, happy marriage."

As he walked away, I realized that, at no point had the officer who had turned custody of my father over to me, ask me how my father was.

◆ ◆ ◆

NORMAN AND KAYLA drove away.

"What now?" Monica said.

"One more person I need to say a proper goodbye to," I said. She made to hang back, but I took hold of her hand and pulled her along with me.

We stopped in front of my mother's grave. I looked at Monica, and she nodded for me to go ahead.

"Hey, Mom," I said, not having a clue what I was going to say.

"Not sure what to say to you," I said. "I'm just coming to say goodbye." Then I remembered the impressions I got of her from that demon's mind. "He thought you were weak, Mom. He picked someone he thought was weak-willed. After what I've seen for the past few weeks, I can't say I truly know you, or ever really knew you, but I'm pretty sure you weren't weak."

I paused, and I felt Monica's hand slide into mine. She gave me a reassuring squeeze.

"You put up with all his shit. You put up with Ray's shit. Hell, you put up with my shit. You dealt with it, somehow. That's not weakness, that's perseverance. I didn't have that. I ran away from everything, including you."

I felt the first real tears for my mother come now.

"I abandoned you. But I had to, Mom. I had to. I hope you understand." I swiped at a tear. "And you should know something else. Good or bad, right or wrong, seeing what's come since you passed, it's pretty obvious you were the one who held it all down. I don't think you got much thanks for that. So, thank you, Mom."

I squeezed Monica's hand.

"It's my turn to finally persevere, instead of run. My time to hold it together. If I have any success with that at all, I owe it to you. Goodbye, Mom."

I glanced over to Monica again. *Okay?*

She met my eyes with her own, still haunted. *Okay,* hers said.

◆ ◆ ◆

I LOOKED UP and, just like the first time I stood at this grave, I saw a woman, standing well away from us. "One more thing," I said, and nodded my head. Across the graveyard, near the trees, Talia stood alone.

"Want me to come with you?"

"Would you mind if I talk to her on my own, Monica?"

"Of course not," she said, giving me a smile I could very much get used to seeing every day. "Just...if she offers you something in exchange for—"

"No boobs, no sex," I said, and laughed. "Just say no, Lex. Message received."

She leaned in then, and gave me a long, slow, wonderful kiss that I felt all the way to my thighs.

"I'll be back for more of that shortly," I said.

"You better."

I headed off across the graveyard, being careful to step around the graves. I had an image of some poor child vampire furiously digging downward, trying to escape, then pushed it from my mind.

I'd deal with the vampires when I needed to. Today wasn't that day.

"Hey, Talia," I said, approaching her.

"Lex," she said. "How are you?"

"I don't want to hear of any more funerals, if that's what you're asking, but other than that, I'm fine."

"You still have one more to attend? Kelly?"

"Kevin's convinced the family to uninvite me from that one," I said. Though I was considering doing a Talia and hanging off to the side. I owed her that much, at least. To thank her. To ask forgiveness. To say goodbye.

"And the Staff?"

"Is very safe," I said. No one else was going to get killed by a vampire trying to get their mitts on the Staff again.

"Okay," she said. "I wanted to check in on you. You've experienced a lot, and I understand—better than most—how overwhelming that can be."

"Monica's helping."

"I'm not surprised," Talia said. "Take care of her."

"You're the second person in ten minutes to tell me that," I said. "I promise I will."

She smiled at me. "Good."

"I have to ask," I said. "You did know about…"

"Marcus?"

"Yes, him," I said. "I still can't bring myself to utter that name."

"I understand."

"You knew he killed Mom and Ray, right?"

"I did."

"And, you had power enough to help me make him pay for what he'd done."

"A bit more than I let on, yes."

"So," I said, "why the damn quest?"

"Did you ever watch *The Wizard of Oz*, Lex?"

"Hasn't everyone?"

"Why didn't Glinda the Good Witch, if she was so good, just show Dorothy how to get home with the ruby slippers as soon as she saw she was wearing them?"

And that stopped me. I'd never thought of that before.

"Well, because…um…the movie would have been over in twenty minutes?"

"You're smarter than that," she said. "Why?"

"Because, I guess, Dorothy wasn't ready to go home yet. She had to learn the value of home. And she had to learn to trust in herself more. To stand up to the Wicked Witch of the West."

"There you go."

"So, you're Glinda?"

"Perhaps."

"Well, I'm not telling Monica this story," I said.

Talia looked confused. She cocked her head to the side. "Why not?"

"Because her first question will be, 'What, you're saying I'm Toto?'"

Talia let out a rare laugh. "I think she's more the brains of the outfit, Lex. She's the Scarecrow."

"Okay," I said. "I think she'll be okay with that."

And then it was time to go. I put out my arms, and Talia gave me a hug. "Thank you," I said in her ear. "You're a good person, Talia Davis."

"As are you, Alexandra Hedges."

One last squeeze and we separated. "So," I said, "I guess this is goodbye. I don't know that I'll see you again."

She gave me an unreadable little grin. "Don't be so sure of that, Lex." Then she turned and melted into the forest.

Don't be so sure of that.

What the hell was that *supposed to mean?*

♦ ♦ ♦

I WALKED BACK to the car. Monica leaned against the fender, looking at her phone.

"What now?" she said.

"Not sure," I said. "Whatever comes next."

"And what do you think that—"

My phone rang. I held it up, looked at the call display, made a face. "I guess this is what comes next," I said.

It was.

And it changed everything.

◆ ◆ ◆

I HELD MY breath as I drove down the familiar lane.

Then we rounded the last corner, and I put the car in Park and shut off the ignition.

"Okay," I said. "Hear me out."

◆ ◆ ◆

THE PHONE CALL had been from the family lawyer, probably glad to be shedding himself and his firm of the last duties of managing the Hedges estate.

Turns out there was a modest amount of money left to me, as the sole surviving family member. And there was the house.

My old house.

The one in which I'd had nightmares.

The one in which I'd lived a nightmare.

The one I'd run away from ten years and a lifetime ago.

I now owned the house that I swore long ago never to come back to.

"Okay," I said. "Hear me out."

I undid my seatbelt and got out. Monica followed my lead.

We both stood, staring at my family home.

"I think..." I said.

Monica rounded the car and came to me. She put her arms around me. She said, "It's okay, Hedges. Tell me."

"I think I want to keep it," I said. Monica drew back, shocked. I surprised myself, if I'm being honest.

"I was sure you were going to tell me you were selling it."

"I was too," I said. "But…this is something I think I need to do."

We both moved around to the front of the car, leaned against the hood, the metal ticking as it cooled.

"I told you about the nightmares I had as a kid," I said, and Monica nodded. "I never told anyone about them back then."

Monica reached out for my hand.

"And when I left for the last time, I ran. I ran all the way to Toronto. I never told anyone what had happened."

She nodded again, staying silent, letting me speak. Being there for me, just like Norman said.

"I started writing. Other people's stories. I joined Dreamboat Annie and became Ann Wilson on a nightly basis."

She gave my hand a little squeeze.

"And then I came back here and basically wiped my father and brother from my life, refusing to acknowledge their connection to me." I lifted our joined hands. "And now…"

"Now?"

"And now, I have you," I said. "And I have this house."

"Yes," she said. "You do." Said this last almost as a question. I could hear the unspoken, "Soooo…?"

"All my life, Monica, I've pretended to be something—some*one*—other than who I really am. And it all started here. And I think, if I can take this house, tear it down to its bones, and rebuild it into…I don't know…"

"Rebuild it into you?"

"Maybe," I said. "I think, if I can rebuild it, I can rebuild me, too."

"Lex, I think you've been rebuilding yourself for a while now."

"Maybe," I said. "Probably. But this feels like a necessary next step."

"This is what comes next?"

I breathed the next word out as a relieved sigh. "Yeah." Glad that she got it.

"Will you..." She held out a hand, holding an imaginary Staff, swung it around while she whistled.

"No," I said. "None of that. I've gotta do the work. I have to deal with every scar in there. I've gotta earn it."

"That's gonna take a while, Ms. Hedges," Monica said.

"It will. I may need your help renegotiating my motel rate."

"I'll do you one better," she said. "I'll give you an even better rate at Motel Monica."

I stared at her. "Really?"

"If you're okay with it, I am," she said. "And when this place is done—"

"We both move here."

"Rather presumptuous of you, isn't it?"

"You just invited me to live with you..."

"Yes, but what if I find out I don't *like* you anymore?" she teased. "What if this new, improved Alexandra Hedges isn't to my liking?"

"Guess I'll just have to deal with that when the time comes."

"Like I said, presumptuous." She dropped my hand in mock anger and walked up to the house. I saw her nod.

"You okay with all of this?" I asked.

She turned around, smiled, and said, "Ms. Hedges, I do believe you're getting your shit together."

And I thought, *Damn. Maybe I am.*

Author's Note

THIS IS A gonna be a weird one, folks. Grab a chair and sit a spell.

Before I get into the main story of how this one came to be, as usual, there's a few things pulled from life that I always like to point out because, sometimes, truth is more hilarious, or weirder, than fiction.

First, the vampire names of Chloe, Rory, and Will. I'll talk more about the Muskoka Novel Marathon below, but for now, all you need to know is, I was raising money for it, and one of the things I did was auction off naming rights. A good friend from my college days offered up a ridiculous amount of donation money and gave me her two kids' names, as well as her son's best friend's name. Susan, if you're reading this, I hope you don't mind what I did with them.

At the same marathon, I was casting around for the perfect suburban housewife. Sitting directly across from me was the lovely and wonderful author Cheryl Cooper (who writes fantastic historical fiction, and you should really check out her *Seasons of War* novels). She was perfect, exactly how I saw Will's mother. Cheryl's heard an early version of the prologue that opens this novel, and she's always been most gracious with the fact that I introduce her, then kill her off a few pages later.

There's a story that the friends talk about in this novel about Mary's Camel, and how she got tagged with it after someone watched the *M*A*S*H* episode with Klinger and his imaginary camel, Habibi. That story is ninety-five percent gospel truth. There was a Mary. And I was the idiot dragging an invisible camel around the high school, somehow managing to dump it on Mary in calculus class. Mary, if you're reading this…it's still funny, and I'm not sorry.

Finally, that painful scene where a stoned Ray butchers his mother's funeral service? I won't say whose funeral I attended, but that scene was pretty much a word-for-word, play-by-play transcription of what I witnessed. Absolutely awkward for everyone.

And now, on to my ridiculously convoluted story of how *Blood Relations* came about.

◆ ◆ ◆

MANY YEARS AGO, I felt I was getting into a bit of a rut, writing-wise. I was having a hard time getting inspired, and didn't really know what to do next. A very good friend of mine, who shares a name with a certain police officer in this series, suggested maybe I take a break from horror and try writing something else.

"Like what?"

"Why not a mystery novel?" she said.

I explained that I'd only read a few mysteries, but really didn't have a firm grasp on the genre, at least, not enough to spit out a short story, let alone a novel. She explained—quite rightly—that the goal was more to get me writing, and to get me *excited* about writing again, not to put out a perfect product.

"Besides," she said, "you know as well as I do that the first draft is always crap. You can fix it up in the rewrite/editing stage."

Which is true. She was smart enough to know that I believe two quotes to be absolute truth. The first is from Ernest

Hemingway (an author I've tried to like, but simply can't, but this quote is gold), and he says, "The first draft of anything is shit." Short, direct, to the point.

The second quote is something I saw originally attributed to Harlan Ellison (an author I love for his ideas, his writing, and his overall take-no-shit, give-no-fucks attitude). And, while the quote sounds like something he might have said, I've never been able to officially substantiate its source. Regardless, it's a great quote: "Writing a novel is like travelling a great distance to take an extremely small shit."

So, armed with some plotting suggestions for a mystery novel, I girded myself for a long trip and a small shit, and started writing.

♦ ♦ ♦

YOU'RE WONDERING WHAT the hell a mystery novel has to do with the novel you just read. Trust me, I'm getting there.

So, I wrote the novel of a guy named Josh Hedges coming back to his hometown because someone had killed his father. He had a bad relationship with his mother and brother, and had no desire to see them.

Starting to see where this is headed now?

Anyway—and, uh, spoiler alert, I guess, not that anyone will ever read that shit first draft—my really bad mystery novel ended up having one of his classmates, Monica Holt, doing all the killing.

When I presented the completed novel back to my friend, she read it and stated, bluntly, honestly, and correctly, that it was really predictable. It was. It sucked.

But, it *had* got me writing again.

Flash forward a few months to the Muskoka Novel Marathon (MNM).

♦ ♦ ♦

I MAY HAVE mentioned this before and, if so, indulge me for a moment. The MNM is a 72-hour novel-writing marathon that takes place every year in beautiful Huntsville, Ontario. It raises money for various adult literacy programs, and, for the five years I attended, it was mostly a hoot.

It was also a place to really get lost inside my writer's mind and get…shit…written.

The only problem was, though the mystery novel had got me writing again, and even excited about writing again, I didn't have an idea for that year's marathon.

There was also this really irritating other side of my head that simply wouldn't shut up about all the time I'd spent on that damn mystery novel, and what a shame it was just going to sit as a bunch of 1s and 0s on my computer, forgotten and unloved, like that wad of gum that you toss and it ends up on the bottom of someone else's shoe.

And, somewhere along the way, yet another voice in my head — don't believe any writer who tells you they don't have at least a couple of voices in their heads — started up with the damn what-ifs.

What if it wasn't Monica who did the killing?

What if I could tie it to Out for Blood *and* Blood Loss *somehow?*

What if…vampires?

Okay. That last one? Yeah, that got me.

I would throw out almost everything after the first few scenes, and get going.

At that year's MNM, I ended up writing about three-quarters of the novel, and jotted notes down about how I'd planned to finish it.

And while I was happy with it, for the most part, there was something missing.

I couldn't, for the life of me, figure out what it was.

◆ ◆ ◆

The novel sat on my computer, a bunch of 1s and 0s, half-forgotten and kind-of-liked, for quite a while. I moved on, wrote some other stuff, and kept rolling that one over in my head. Nothing was coming.

Then came the year 2019. I know it's a cliché to quote Dickens's "It was the best of times, it was the worst of times…" but sue me, I'm quoting him. Because it was. Mostly though, I'll go with that second, worst of times, part. To be fair, this may be TMI, but I promise it all goes toward the writing of this novel.

I was just about eighteen years into my time with my Big Corporate Company and, for a change, I'd taken on a temporary role for a year. It was a stressful job, made more so because I was expected to bring some change to the team, as well as introduce a whole new way of dealing with the customers being forced on us from upstairs that everyone knew wouldn't work but went along with anyway.

I'm not one to go along with stupid decisions, so…that caused some friction.

Adding to my stress was my mother.

Ah, good old mom.

My mother was ninety-two, had suffered several strokes, and was utterly, abusively nasty to me, her one and only caregiver. I have a brother who lives several provinces over, and did nothing but take money from my mother. So, to be clear, I wasn't a fan.

There came a point where my mother had a particularly bad spell when she didn't know who she was, didn't know who I was, couldn't name the year, couldn't decisively state much of anything. As I said earlier, I'm not one to go along with stupid decisions, and the doctor's decision was to pull a ninety-two-year-old, frail, prone-to-strokes woman off all pain meds, cold turkey. I watched my mother roll around on a stretcher for almost three days, in constant agony and withdrawal, while I fought with the staff to do something to help her.

It took three days, but I finally got her some relief. Throughout all of this, the nurses kept me updated on my brother's calls. He'd called the hospital several times, and always got an update. I know, because they told me. Me? I didn't have time to deal with his "it's all about me" bullshit, so I didn't call him.

Finally, Mom was released. I got her home, went out, got her some groceries and meds, got back, made her a meal, got her into bed and, once the PSWs were there to care for her, I left.

An hour later, she called me, pissed that I hadn't contacted my brother through the whole ordeal. I told her he was getting the updates, but she didn't care. And then she dropped a bomb on me.

Don't ever let anyone tell you words can't hurt you.

My mother told me something I'll never forget. She said, "I'm ashamed of you."

♦ ♦ ♦

I FELL INTO a pit of depression like I'd never experienced before. I was useless. Everything I touched died, failed, or fell apart. I was a shit parent, a crap husband, a lousy employee, a useless friend, a bad person.

I didn't write for almost two years. I could barely function.

My mother kept up the abuse then, for the rest of that year. Obviously, I couldn't hide it from work. I stumbled through the days. Luckily, I worked from home, so I could load up ASMR videos to keep the anxiety at the lower end.

I let my manager know what I was going through. She was empathetic, but offered no help. And then, though I wasn't supposed to finish that temp role until October, she told me in July she was going to hire someone else. I was moved back to my original team at the end of August (after she also pulled my long-planned week's vacation literally the Friday before, the bitch).

By December, I was out of the company I'd worked at for almost nineteen years.

◆ ◆ ◆

SOME STUFF HAPPENED between December 2019 and February 2021, but not enough to go into. I will only say that I got counselling for how to deal with my abusive mother, and my brain was somehow still chewing over that novel.

In February of 2021, my mother died. I literally have shed no tears, nor do I miss her. Cold? Maybe. But I've got a pair of my shoes you can borrow to walk a mile in, if you want. At the end of that mile—again, spoiler alert—you'll get to be called an asshole two days before the mother dies, pretty much her last words to the last child who talked to her.

So, yeah. Cold. But be my guest, walk that last mile, and keep the damn shoes. I'm done with them.

Less than a month later, we entered the fourth and longest lockdown of the whole COVID-19 debacle.

And there was Tobin, contemplating his still-somewhat-fresh release from the corporate world, his release from his mother's shenanigans, and an unspecified amount of time to shelter in place.

And wonder of wonders, while my body was in lockdown, it turns out my writer's mind began to soar.

♦ ♦ ♦

THE FIRST THING I figured out was that *Blood Relations* needed some conflict during the getting-together scenes of Monica and Josh. I amped up the brother Ray's scenes and nastiness (I'm sure you don't have to guess who's brother I modelled him on). And I also had to amp up the mother, Marcia's nastiness as well (no points for guessing who she was modelled on). And then I put her in the back seat of the car on Josh and Monica's travels.

Next, as Josh and Monica were getting acquainted, I was getting more acquainted with the two of them as well.

And that's when Josh told me that she wasn't actually a boy at all. She was a wonderful, surprising woman named Lex. What's the lines from Lou Reed? Something about eyebrows getting plucked, and legs getting shaved, and then he was a she?

Like Josh, though, she really had to get her shit together.

And here's where I'll say I liked Josh, but I absolutely love Lex. And I love Lex and Monica together so much more.

And, because Lex switched genders for me, basic biology also demanded that Marcia became Marcus.

And, while this book was about a demon's plans to procreate, and the introduction of vampires into my mythos, this book? Yeah, the title says it all.

It's about relationships. It's about parents and children. It's about siblings. It's about friendships, new and old, new loves, and recently-out-of-loves.

Relationships can be about beauty.

But, they can also—and especially when it comes to my relationship with my family members—be about horror. We can do a lot of terrible things to those we profess to love, to those who share our genetic material.

If I've learned nothing in this life, I've learned that family is what you make it, in a couple of different ways.

The first way is the importance of how you treat your family. I wasn't treated well in mine growing up, because mother, father, brother, and sister were all very damaged. Virtually everyone who once told me they loved me ultimately turned their back on me. So, when it came time for me to treat others as family, first my wife, then my daughter, and then my son (and that's since grown to their partners), I looked at what my family — my mother, my father, my stepfather, my brother, and my sister, all of them — had done, and did the opposite. It's worked out well, so far.

The second way is, family is literally what you make it. And for me, my family extends to my best friend, his wife, and their kids. It extends to friends as well. They're family. Those men are my brothers. Their wives and girlfriends are my sisters.

My point to all this?

Well, I guess the first is, if it hasn't been obvious in my notes of the other books up to now, a hell of a lot of me ends up in these things. When I'm asked why I write the stuff I write, my answer is because it's my way of controlling the demons, my way of rewriting the bad shit.

My second point is, whether you're a mother, a father, a son, a daughter, a friend, a boss, a co-worker, or anyone else who happens to come in contact with another human being, just remember…you've got all your shit going on, and so do they. Neither may know much about the other, and know nothing of the other's shit. But everybody's got their shit to bear…

So, just treat others like you'd want them to treat you.

My final point is, life's a mystery. Sometimes, it can be as shitty as a mystery novel written by a guy who writes horror. But maybe you can look at what's going on and find a different, better story in there somewhere to chase down.

That's all.

As always…thanks for reading.

ABOUT THE AUTHOR

TOBIN ELLIOTT HAS written for most of his life. After some unfortunate incidents with walls and permanent markers, he switched to safer things like pens and paper, and later, typewriters and then computers. Though science fiction was his first love, horror has always had a powerful hold on him, even back before he wore big-boy pants. He likes to have the shit scared out of him, and he likes scaring the shit out of others. Somehow, it always comes down to shit with Tobin.

Tobin spent his formative teenage years in a small town about four hours northeast of Toronto. Those experiences, and the magic and wonder of that place, never left him, though he left the town through no fault of his own. He currently lives within a three-hour drive of the place, and occasionally gets back to top up on his sense of wonder and nostalgia.

Based on that town and surrounding areas, Tobin has written several novels in his Aphotic World series.

Along with those writings, Tobin has been fortunate enough to have had three horror novellas published, as well as seven stories in various anthologies. He has been a board member of both the Writers' Community of Simcoe County (WCSC) and the Writers' Community of Durham Region (WCDR), and, for five years, was an annual participant in the Muskoka Novel Marathon, a 72-hour writing marathon to raise money for adult literacy programs.

Finally, he also taught creative writing for two different continuous learning programs. Tobin writes ugly stories about bad people doing horrible things, and it was his pleasure to show other people how to do the same thing for almost twenty years.

If you're interested in more ramblings by Tobin, well, he's not much into social media. He sees it as a blight on humanity of almost Bookian proportions. And yet, still, he's on there.

Facebook: The Horror Guy (/tobinelliott.horrorguy)

Twitter: @TheHorrorGuy91

Instagram: @tobinelliott.horrorguy

♦ ♦ ♦

I HOPE THAT this book captured your imagination, and I hope that this series will turn you into a loyal reader.

Because loyal readers are an author's secret weapon. They can influence other readers…how?

Through reviews.

If you loved this book, and yes, even if you hated it, please also consider leaving a review on the site where you purchased it, and/or Goodreads, or anywhere else. You can also drop me a line at TheHorrorGuy91@gmail.com.

As a reader, you have an immense power to influence others.

Please, use that power.